The Convictions of
John Delahunt

ALSO BY ANDREW HUGHES

Lives Less Ordinary:
Dublin's Fitzwilliam Square 1798–1922

The Convictions of
John Delahunt

Andrew Hughes

PEGASUS BOOKS
NEW YORK LONDON

THE CONVICTIONS OF JOHN DELAHUNT

Pegasus Books LLC
80 Broad Street, 5th Floor
New York, NY 10004

ISBN: 978-1-60598-794-1

10 9 8 7 8 6 5 4 3 2 1

Printed in the United States of America
Distributed by W. W. Norton & Company, Inc.

For my parents

DUBLIN

Published under the Superintendance of the Society for the
Diffusion of Useful Knowledge.

1

I won't be welcome in the Delahunt plot. I doubt they'll make the slightest effort to reclaim me. Perhaps I'm promised to the dissectionists on York Street, though these days they've the pick of the workhouses. Most likely I'll end up in some forsaken corner of Kilmainham's grounds. Pitched in with my peers. Lying at odd angles and uneven depths, depending on the diligence of the digger. Quicklime poured in to hasten the process. And unmarked, save a scrawled entry in a spineless ledger, to be shelved and forgotten, filthy with dust. The fate of my remains had not given me a moment's pause until today's visitor. Now I can think of little else. It's tiresome, that such morbid fancies should master me in my remaining hours.

Helen might make some petition for a decent burial. My wife has been disowned, disinherited; she is soon to be widowed. Her plaintive letters will be mired in bureaucracy. Still, it will do her good to keep busy.

At about noon I started at the rustle of keys and scraping of bolts as Dr Armstrong was shown into my cell. He was a spare man, a little below the average height, but with a dignity of carriage that made him appear taller. Clean-shaven, and obviously particular in his habits and dress. He was accompanied by an assistant, whom I took to be one of his medical students. As they entered, the doctor held a handkerchief to his nose – it's amazing how soon one stops noticing it – but immediately folded it into a pocket and regarded me with professional interest.

'Has Mr Turner told you the reason for my visit?'

I set aside my pen. 'Not in much detail.'

'Mr Delahunt, I'll begin by saying I care not about the nature of your crimes.'

I reminded him I had only been convicted of one.

He took the interruption in his stride. 'Quite.' It was his belief that the manifest failings in my character, which had led me to commit my admitted crime, resulted from grave deficiencies in certain faculties of my brain and the profusion of others. 'Your cranial bone will have conformed around these undulations, leaving a discernible map for the trained hand.' He flexed his fingers as if in demonstration. He said my co-operation would aid his research and further scientific understanding. 'Of course, you are free to refuse my interview, and if you wish me to leave I shall do so immediately.'

He fixed on a point above my shoulder as if my response either way was of no concern. My first impulse was to tell them both to get out. But how could I refuse the final courtesy extended to me in my short life?

I offered to vacate the only chair but he waved me to remain. His assistant inspected my stained mattress with some distaste; then he sat at the edge of the bunk without my leave. He placed a file on the frayed blanket beside him, opened a leather-bound notebook and took a pencil from his jacket pocket.

I must admit to an uneasy sensation when Armstrong walked behind me to take hold of my matted head. That feeling soon gave way. After several minutes I had to stifle a smirk at both his earnest kneading and tender caress. I couldn't see his face, but I'd hear the occasional guttural response to an interesting knoll. I pictured Dr Armstrong in his private moments, head in his hands, deeply contemplative, on a journey of self-discovery. Then again, if he was convinced of his calling perhaps he couldn't bring himself to touch his own head. Maybe he was loath to scratch an itch, or fix his hat, lest he happen upon an unsettling trait.

He spoke his observations aloud in a distracted voice. 'The head is well sized. The base regions very fully developed, and the coronal portions . . . by no means deficient.'

I was flattered. The pupil, a young man with round spectacles and a thin beard, carefully jotted down each comment. I knew his type well: the class pet plucked from the group to assist with the professor's own research and experiments. He no doubt considered it a great honour rather than an unpaid chore. Some characters can be discerned without the use of phrenology.

At one point he was called over for a practical lesson and he joined the doctor behind my chair. Armstrong took a step back. 'Our conjecture was correct. Feel Caution's Causeway.'

The young man's fingers were cold and his nails unclipped. He probed behind my left ear, fixed upon a certain spot and rotated the skin with a firm rub. It seemed to me he wasn't sure what he sought. His only expression was a vague murmur.

'Now mark the Carnal Cleft.'

He steadied my head before pressing his ring finger between the bridge of my nose and lower eye socket. This time his reaction was clearer. He was amused, enough to exhale sharply through his nostrils. I wasn't let in on the joke.

When the cranial reading was complete, Armstrong went to stand in the middle of the cell, using his handkerchief to wipe my residue from his fingers. The exact nature of his questions seems vague to me now. I recall he commended my learning and enquired into my habits of reading. He asked was I musical. My childhood stints singing in the choir were among my only happy memories, but I told him I couldn't hold a note, had no ear for harmony – there was little point being an open book.

More trying were questions that seemed pertinent to my conviction. He asked had I ever sworn falsely against another.

I scrutinized his face for a hint of mockery. 'It's a matter of public record that I have.'

'Have you ever been compelled to act because of religious fervour?'

I said I wasn't a believer.

The doctor smiled. 'Mr Delahunt, I fear you are betrayed by your make-up. The Organ of Marvellousness is particularly full. I have no doubt you are in awe of your creator.'

'Then why ask?'

The transcriber spoke for the first time. 'What about the note found on your victim?'

The doctor and I regarded him. I hoped the upstart would be berated but instead Armstrong retrieved the file and leafed through it. 'That's right. A passage from the Bible was clutched in his hand.' He found the relevant page. 'Identified as Philippians 1:21, "For me, to live is Christ and to die is gain."' He looked at me with the folder held open before him; the other sat with his pen poised.

I no longer found their presence diverting. 'It didn't matter what was written,' I said. 'I knew the child wouldn't be able to read.'

It had been my hope that after a brief examination the doctor would be able to reveal some underlying cause, fix me with a solemn gaze and say: 'Worry not, this was always on the cards.' Instead I grew weary of his petty enquiries and was relieved when he indicated he was about to go. Despite myself, I fished for a diagnosis as he gathered his coat.

'Have you come to any conclusions?'

He drew himself up, as if glad to be asked. 'All I would say is this. There is no doubt the capacity to commit your crime is strongly written in your development.' He narrowed his eyes. 'But so also was the power to resist it.'

Such insight. He lifted the lapel of his coat to cover his neck. 'But those are only preliminary observations. I shall require several more hours of study.'

'You mean you intend to return.'

'Why, no,' he said and looked away. 'I have made arrangements with the prison authorities.'

'Arrangements for what?'

'Well.' He patted his pockets as if he had mislaid something. 'It won't concern you.'

The student had been observing me all the while with the corners of his mouth upturned. 'We shall be using a plaster cast of your head,' he said. 'Taken after your punishment.'

Armstrong reproved his charge with a touch on the arm and a stern look. I merely nodded. No doubt it's odd that this was the first realization of what awaited me. After all, there had been ample time to consider the mechanics of my demise. But this thought chilled me – of my rough handling, of some anatomical stuccodore gouging my eyes, pressing his wet plaster into my nose and mouth and leaving my enclosed head to set. Throughout the afternoon I lay awake, opening and closing my fist, holding my breath, listening to my pulse in a cupped ear, trying to sense the source of their animation.

After some consideration I've come to look upon the notion of Armstrong's mould with less dread, though the thought of my face encased still causes a shiver. The cast of one's head is an interesting relic. The idea of being preserved for future study also appeals: to be labelled and catalogued, stored and retrieved, admired and pored over by scientists not yet born.

I recall when I was six or seven years old stealing into my father's study in Fitzwilliam Street, darkened in his absence to protect his books from the sun. I drew one shutter ajar, enough to allow a rectangle of light to fall upon the writing desk, and took down a volume of faunal studies. There I stood, fascinated by the exquisitely etched plates of various animal specimens in jars of embalming fluid: lizards, birds and even a tiger cub. Soon after, I came upon a fallen fledgling in our stable-lane: a specimen of my own. Believing the agent of preservation was simply a well-stoppered jar of water, I pilfered one from the kitchen. I gathered the tiny form and placed it into the receptacle, dunking it when it began to bob. I even labelled it: 'Baby sparrow, Lad Lane, March 1825'. Naturally, when I checked on it a week later I was distressed at the putrid soup that had resulted. The sense memory of that odour still causes a turn.

My cast should prove a neater artefact. Certainly better than an entry in a burial ledger; better even than a tombstone. I can't help but ponder its fate. Shall I sit as a curio on a high shelf in a dark oak study, a source of nightmare for Armstrong's grand-children? Perhaps the doctor possesses a whole collection of criminal crania that line the walls of a special room, and I'll remain in stony-faced congress with my fellows for decades – until a clumsy maid nudges the shelf and tips my replica into oblivion. The promise of this unusual preservation buoys me slightly. Still, I admit to hoping that Helen does make some effort at claiming me. She will need the support of the few remaining Delahunts to wrest my remnants from the government's possession, and that will be impossible. Her lonely petition will be in vain.

My warder is a man named Turner, an old Kilmainham guard with a grey moustache stained yellow and one eye turned inward. He treats me well enough because of my refined manners and clean habits. The details of my conviction don't seem to bother him. He told me once, 'You can never judge a man's character by the crimes he commits.'

He came in yesterday with a few sheets of cotton paper, an inkpot and some worn nibs. He said the condemned were permitted to write a final statement. 'It'll probably find its way into the press so make it good.'

I leafed through the thin blank sheaf. 'I'll need more paper.'

Where to begin? I wrote that, then crossed it out. For me, there's no need to dwell on the nature of providence, or trace back through decisions that led me here like a genealogist compiling a pedigree. It's clear when all this started. It was two years ago; during my second last term at Trinity. Walking through Front Square on an evening in early spring, I crossed paths with two others known to me. One was Helen's older brother, Arthur Stokes, a tall and amiable fellow with trimmed fair hair and a weak chin. We had been friends since childhood, though we'd drifted apart during the three years at college. He was a medical student and active member of college societies. I read natural philosophy and found those fraternal gatherings juvenile.

His companion was James O'Neill, a law student with a green ribbon attached to his lapel. It was O'Neill who said they were going for a drink in the Eagle and suggested I tag along. In College Green cab drivers clattered through the empty thoroughfares. We turned right into Eustace Street and soon heard the sounds of the tavern spill on to the road. Once inside it was much like any other night. Raucous laughter and howled conversations; smells of stale drink and sweet tobacco; blazing fires and body heat – I was forced to remove my coat immediately. We climbed the crooked stairs to a snug in a back garret favoured by students, where more than a dozen young men occupied tables surrounding the hearth. Illumination was provided by the embers as well as gnarled candles dotted on tabletops.

At around midnight we were joined by two others unknown to me, students of law from O'Neill's class. I tried to keep up with the conversation. I've always found it a struggle to discern individual voices in a loud pub, and besides, I was unmoved by the topic. O'Neill was defending a newly formed association committed to repealing the Act of Union. The others decried it. They argued its leader, O'Connell, could no longer survive without the roar of popular assemblies and he would drag the country into civil strife rather than retire gracefully. Arthur tried to arbitrate by saying there was no cause for alarm, as only a handful had attended the first repeal meeting.

O'Neill spoke into his glass. 'When the people see he is in earnest they will flock to his banner once more.' He looked at me with heavy eyelids and asked me what I thought.

I said I didn't care. Arthur began to speak again, but O'Neill cut him off. 'What did he say?' His brow had furrowed as if he'd been presented with a conundrum. 'You mean you don't care about Ireland?'

Nor about England, France or Japan, but before I could say so O'Neill dismissed me with a waved hand. 'A man so unconcerned with his own prospects could hardly care much for his country.'

We were pitched out at closing time. Rain had blackened the

uneven cobbles on Essex Street. O'Neill's debate with his two classmates descended into argument and he grappled with one. A policeman happened by. There was a scuffle during which the officer fell injured with a blow to the side of his head. He lay unconscious, but his fingers unfurled and a truncheon rolled on to the road. The bristles of his moustache dipped into an inky puddle. We scattered to the five wards.

A few days later I was skirting the rail of St Stephen's Green when another man matched my step, and struck up a conversation as if we were old acquaintances. I slowed in order to distinguish his features, but he touched my elbow in a way that impelled me forward.

'Have you ever seen a more odious day, John?' It was blustery and a little overcast. Not unusual for the time of year. I agreed it was very bad. The man leaned closer so our shoulders almost touched, and he asked after the health of my father, his voice tinged with concern.

I said his condition was much the same. They must have been old friends. His name would come to me in a minute.

'And Cecilia. Is she finding married life agreeable?' He referred to my younger sister, who lived miserably with her new husband in Coppinger Row.

'She's quite happy.'

'And how is your friend Arthur Stokes?' On the path before us a barefoot boy scampered on to the muddy roadway, causing a passing horse to shy. 'And James O'Neill. The three of you still frequent the Eagle, I believe.'

I stopped walking, as if I hoped the man would continue on and leave me be. He wheeled about to face me, unhurried, his hands deep in his coat pockets. He didn't look like a policeman, more like a banker or civil servant, but I was sure at any moment he would order me to Little Ship Street. In the same conversational tone he said the officer involved in the brawl the other night had suffered deafness in the stricken ear, so the Castle was taking a special interest. He looked about. We were standing across from the Winter Palace pub. 'Why don't we step in for a drink?'

'I can't. I have to attend a lecture in ten minutes.'

'But I insist.' His eye didn't waver.

'Very well.'

We went to a snug attached to the bar, where he sat with his back to the door. I faced him across a table upon which two glasses of port appeared. He took off his hat and smoothed back thick brown hair. His face was framed by neat mutton-chop whiskers and a prominent brow. He gently caressed the inside of his hat, feeling along the silk lining to pop out a small dent in the crown. 'My name is Thomas Sibthorpe.' He nodded at the table. 'Drink up.'

I was greatly relieved when he said I wasn't suspected of the offence, that he was merely speaking to me as a witness. They had a very good picture of what transpired that night, though they had to ensure all information was collected before warrants were issued. They knew that James O'Neill struck the blow.

A bead ran down the side of my glass. I used my thumb to smear it before it touched the table. 'Others saw O'Neill strike the blow?'

There was no need to concern myself with what others saw. All that mattered was what I saw, and was willing to swear to. This was such a serious incident: one of Her Majesty's officers maimed for life in the course of his duties. Stokes and I would be in cells at the moment, but for the fact that they knew it was O'Neill. All I had to do was swear to what I saw.

'Have you interviewed Arthur Stokes?'

He took a sip for the first time. This wasn't an interview. Witnesses to a crime make statements as they are obliged by civic duty. Stokes had already offered an account which was deplorably vague. For Arthur, yes there would have to be further questioning. He leaned in. 'It's always unpleasant when young men of learning are brought for interrogation into the bowels of the Castle, and such an embarrassment when police boots invade the family home.' And all so unnecessary, for they knew it was O'Neill.

And what of O'Neill himself?

'Delahunt, I will visit you at your home in two hours' time. You will be required to make a statement to me regarding the events of Tuesday night, and the extent to which you assist our efforts is entirely up to you. I would consider that point carefully.' There was no need to give him my address. He threw back his drink, fixed his hat and left me to pay.

I pondered my position in the Winter Palace for an hour. I knew O'Neill hadn't struck the telling blow, and I suspected Sibthorpe knew that as well. Still, it appeared that was the narrative the authorities had decided upon. They seemed loath to allow contradiction.

Stokes, I guessed, had adopted the tack of claiming not to have seen the pertinent punch, which had not gone down too well. What would be my reward if I did the same? A night in a dank cell; interrogated and physically cajoled into saying what I was at liberty to say already.

I drained the last drop from my glass. O'Neill and I had attended the same college and caroused in the same circle for nearly a year, during which time he never missed an opportunity to humble me in some fashion. My family's straitened finances, my poor grades, my weak physique; he deftly cut to my every insecurity like a surgeon. Nonetheless, if put in my situation I knew he would not swear against one of his fellows. I brought the empty glasses back to the bar. Maybe that's why the authorities had picked up on him.

I made my way home to Fitzwilliam Street and awaited Sibthorpe. At that point the house was almost empty. My father lay bedridden upstairs, subsisting in darkened, gouty squalor in a room from which he had not emerged for over a year. My mother was dead, my brother served abroad, my sister married off. A middle-aged servant lived adjacent to my father's chamber; his care was her sole responsibility and she and I had no other interaction.

I took a seat by the parlour window and saw Sibthorpe approach at the appointed hour. I opened the front door so he wouldn't have to ring and showed him into the front room. He carried a dark leather satchel which he laid upon a writing desk.

'Are you ready to make your statement?'

I told him I was as he walked towards the closed double doors that separated the parlour from the back dining room. He nodded towards them. 'Is there anyone in there?'

'No. But you can check yourself if you wish.'

'Oh I will,' and he folded back the doors to reveal the gloomy, disused room. Those doors were only opened on evenings my parents hosted dinner parties. I can remember the long dining table laden with sparkling crystalware and mother-of-pearl cutlery, the hinged leaves at both ends hitched up like trapdoors in a platform. Alex, Cecilia and I would be shooed upstairs where we listened to the arrival of carriages, the greeting of guests, and then the happy murmur as the evening progressed. My sister and I would steal down below. We peeked in at the gatherings: the gentlemen in tailored black jackets, the women in their finery, the soldiers in dress uniform. Our parents would sit at each end, basking in the conviviality and gentle light. Whenever we were discovered – by a maid carrying decanters of claret or the butler with a broad silver platter – we fled, giggling, to the top of the house and our nursery. Cecilia would find some paper and begin to draw the ladies in their jewelled dresses. I liked to draw the soldiers. For some reason I always imagined them captured and enchained.

The room Sibthorpe stepped into was shabby and decayed. The table had been pushed to one side and chairs were stacked beneath dust sheets. He locked the far dining-room door leading to the hallway, closed the double doors again and also locked the parlour door. He took a sheaf of paper from his satchel and found a nib and inkpot on the writing desk.

'If you dictate your statement I will transcribe.' He said I had to speak slowly anyway so I should consider my words. When I saw the top of his pen fall still I could continue. 'Begin at the point you left the Eagle tavern.'

For several pages my testimony came easily, for it was the truth. Stokes, O'Neill and I left the pub with two others that O'Neill had known. Stokes and I were not particularly inebriated, the other three very much so, and we meandered towards the river. There was a quarrel. O'Neill and one of the others began to exchange blows in Essex Street. I had seen nights end like this several times so simply continued on. After a minute the shout of an unfamiliar voice made me look back. A policeman had come upon the scene. Only Stokes seemed aware of his arrival. O'Neill landed a punch on his original opponent, who went down. The other friend took up the fight, and the policeman laid him low with a baton to the shoulder blade. He then grabbed O'Neill in a headlock to make the arrest. Stokes chose this moment to remonstrate with the officer to go easy. Fearing another attack, he caught Stokes with a backhand blow. All the while O'Neill flailed at the man who had him restrained.

It was at this point my story diverged from fact, but I continued seamlessly. I said O'Neill managed to free himself of the grip for an instant, enough to swing a wild punch at the constable's head. I warmed to the task and used words like 'gasped' and 'recoiled' and 'shuddered' to describe my reaction to the blow.

Sibthorpe met my eye. 'Let's not over-egg it.'

He was quite right. When the statement was complete I read it over. He had been editing what I said while transcribing, and it was an impressive piece of writing: so efficient, so plausible. Nonetheless, I was afraid to affix my signature.

But I knew my dilemma was nothing compared to that faced by Stokes. Of course he had been the guilty one. The backhanded blow dealt by the officer had not felled him. I can still see the change that came over Arthur's face, usually so genial. He approached the constable from behind, closed his fist by clumsily gripping his own thumb, and struck it against the man's ear. The two lads unfamiliar to me couldn't have seen; they were barely getting to their feet. O'Neill was so drunk and oblivious he continued to flail for a second after he was released from the policeman's grip. When he saw the officer slump to the ground he let out a triumphant yelp. Stokes bent over the injured man, then raised his head and saw me watching from the corner. The rolling truncheon clicked against the kerb. A whistle sounded some streets away, and each protagonist stumbled into the dark.

It was Arthur who had to worry. He could get O'Neill off the hook if he had a crumb of honour; my involvement was by the by. If Arthur confessed, he would contradict my statement, but then I could claim I took it upon myself to save the Stokes family's reputation for his and Helen's sake. I was surely in the clear, so took the proffered pen and wrote out my name with a flourish. Sibthorpe folded the statement carefully into his satchel and sized me up. 'I wasn't sure you'd do it.'

'It wasn't as difficult as I thought.'

Without saying anything more, he unlocked the parlour door and let himself out.

A few hours later, I grew uneasy as I considered the consequences of the affidavit. I took a handful of candles and an armful of books and ensconced myself in my chamber for three days. It was still cold during the night so I slept in my overcoat. I would hear my father's helper, old Miss Joyce, pass through the house, going from the bedrooms above to the kitchen in the basement, occasionally leaving the house on errands. Late one evening her footfall was accompanied by the light from a candle, which glowed against my doorjamb from without. She paused, and we both listened to each other stay perfectly still, until she continued on, and the door's outline dimmed once more.

On the second night I left my den to forage. Miss Joyce had brought in provisions, and I returned to my room well stocked with food, firewood and a bottle of wine. I set the fire, hunkered beside its glow with a book, and finished the bottle as rain drummed against the leaden return roof below my window. Such comfort. When I woke beside the cold ashes, shivering with cramp and a splitting head, my stomach knotted as I remembered my dilemma. I was tempted to go abroad in the city to discover what was happening. Had magistrates executed warrants against O'Neill and dispatched enforcers? Perhaps I was already identified as an informer, and my name was spat in the public houses around Trinity. Even if that was not yet the case, it would certainly be my fate when the testimony was read at trial, and I would be called upon to denounce my supposed friend, this time in public.

My agitation forced me from my room on the morning of the third day. I waited in the hall below for Miss Joyce to pass on her way to the kitchen. I must have looked frightful: unshaven, having slept two nights in my clothes. She stopped on the first-floor return when she saw me. Her thin hands were clasped together. From her vantage she couldn't help but appear superior. I was unsure how to broach the subject, but there was no need.

'Your friend has been arrested.'

'Which friend?'

She regarded me for a moment, as if surprised I had more than one. 'The O'Neill boy. The police came for him early yesterday morning.'

I asked if she had heard anything of Arthur Stokes. She said there was a rumour he was also arrested, but he had returned to his home last evening. She began to descend the stairs again. 'You picked a curious time to retreat into your studies. Who came to the door last Friday?'

I told her not to mind. 'Just see to my father.' As I pushed past her mid-flight she leaned to one side so our clothes wouldn't brush.

He had let O'Neill take the blame after all. I waited for evening to fall, intending to visit Arthur in the Stokes family home on Merrion Square. I imagined him there in abashed conference with his father and old legal advisers. But a few thoughts stopped me. For one, it would not do to appear as if Arthur and I were somehow in cahoots, meeting to get our stories straight while a friend languished. Also, I took some pleasure in knowing that he was surely fearful of me and what

I might reveal. I pictured again his face looking into mine as he stood over the prostrate policeman a week ago that night. I could let that uncertainty undermine him.

Late that night, someone knocked on the front door and I went to answer. A young man stood outside, with one thumb hooked in a waistcoat, and his head tilted so only half his face caught the street light. He had a cast of countenance that seemed Italianate, and a beard trimmed to resemble a chinstrap.

'John Delahunt?'

There was no use denying it.

'I've a message from Tom Sibthorpe,' he said. 'Better heard indoors.'

I brought him up to the study, placed a lamp on the green baize of the writing desk and sat behind it. The young man introduced himself as Devereaux, and went to look at some books on the shelves.

'You study anatomy?'

I told him they were my father's books. I was a student of natural and experimental philosophy. He gave a low whistle and my patience ended. 'You said you had a message for me.'

He pulled a volume down and opened it. 'That's right. You've made quite an impression on Tom.' He glanced up. 'And he's not exactly the impressionable type.'

He leafed through a few pages, paused, and held the book open towards me. It was a plate showing surgery performed on the abdomen of a woman. An incision below her breast revealed bone and muscle tissue. He shook his head and chuckled, then snapped the book closed and came to sit at the desk.

'Sibthorpe appreciates the statement you gave. It greatly assisted our efforts. He also likes that you went to ground for a few days while loose ends were tied up.'

Devereaux picked up a framed silhouette of my mother in her youth.

He said they were mindful of the delicate position I was in. When someone had demonstrated admirable willingness to assist the Castle authorities, it didn't seem fair to allow his reputation to be tarnished with any kind of stigma. 'The case against O'Neill will be strong enough without your testimony.'

I asked how so?

'Any number of the injured man's colleagues in the DMP are willing to swear against O'Neill. And their word is believed above any other in the kingdom.' All they had to guard against was contradiction. Stokes had already sworn that he had not seen the incident, and they were sure he would not backtrack in court.

'How can you be sure?'

'We're sure. Your position is easier, as on the night you had already walked away from the scuffle. But it's inevitable you'll be called as a witness.' I need simply say that I turned a corner and was wholly unaware of what transpired. 'Maintain that, no matter the jibes, or sarcasms or disbelief of defence counsel.' He waved a hand. 'It'll be child's play. You're a natural.'

I felt reprieved, enough to allow the snide compliment to go unanswered. Devereaux sensed the lifting of my mood and flashed an engaging smile. 'You should remember that you now have Tom's ear in the Castle, and can call in to the commissioners at any time with information.'

I doubted I would know anything else that would be of interest to the authorities.

He shook his head. 'You'd be surprised, if you just remain vigilant. Especially now O'Connell is agitating again. Students always have loose tongues after a few drinks.'

Such matters didn't interest me. Besides, what motive would

I have to inform on my fellows if there was no peril to myself?

He made a show of looking at my drab clothes, and around at the faded grandeur of the room.

'Lucre, of course.' The devil drips from the word.

James O'Neill got a few months' hard labour for his trouble. The authorities never cared about the officer with the shattered eardrum. O'Neill's father, a close associate of Daniel O'Connell, chaired the first meetings of the Repeal Association. The embarrassment of his son's arrest and conviction meant he had to resign that position, and it put the new association immediately on the back foot. Newspaper editors and pamphleteers had much sport with the idea that Repealers were already attacking policemen. It was intriguing to think that faceless men in a Dublin Castle office had played with O'Neill's life and reputation merely to create some unflattering headlines.

The main benefit of the whole episode was the power it gave me over Arthur Stokes. I was able to play up my silence on the affair as an act of loyalty, to save him from the cells, and though we never spoke of the matter directly, he considered our friendship very much strengthened. I'm also sure that was how he described my involvement to Helen, with whom he confided everything, and who subsequently looked upon me with great favour.

One thing I recall from the trial was the testimony of two policemen who swore that they came upon the scene in time to witness O'Neill throw the punch. The story they told was exactly the one I had recounted to Sibthorpe. Here were words I picked on the spur of the moment being related by officers of the Crown, taken down by clerks of the court, noted by judges on the bench, entering the public record as irrefutable fact.

History would show that James O'Neill struck officer D32 on the side of the head in a drunken melee, and the man suffered permanent deafness in his left ear. It seemed I had been telling the truth all along.

In the month following O'Neill's conviction there was a return to routine. After a few weeks of temperance, Arthur and I began to frequent the Eagle once more, where our reputations were much enhanced. Students everywhere like to brag of japes and the hazards of mild criminality, but ours was a different story. Not only had Stokes and I been involved in the skirmish, we had maintained honourable silence in the courtroom. Arthur could not meet my eye as he accepted these plaudits. No one doubted O'Neill's guilt, and his overbearing presence was not particularly missed. It was all rather agreeable. My usual aloofness, seen before as antisocial, was now taken as a mark of deeper character. My well-timed sardonic interjections were now met with appreciative mirth. I knew O'Neill's date of release weighed upon Arthur, and he made every effort to cement our friendship.

It happened that his sister Helen was first presented at court that month, at a levee hosted by the Lord Lieutenant in Dublin Castle. I've seen those carriages converging on Castle Street, backed up in congestion, allowing the lower orders to gather and gawk and mock the fluttering girls folded within. I would imagine the Viceroy and Vicereine graciously hosting their subjects in the Castle's resplendent rooms of state, while Sibthorpe and his agents scuttled in the shadows below. The Stokes family hosted a gathering in their home to celebrate Helen's coming-out. Arthur invited me along.

That night in Merrion Square, the folding doors between the front and back drawing rooms were open. Fires blazed beneath both marble chimney pieces, while the rooms were lit from above by glinting chandeliers. The floor was thick with revellers, who stood in groups or sat on couches that lined the walls. Many of the young men wore uniforms, the others wore finely pressed suits, and even the servants were better dressed than I. The women were like unwholesome confections: a blur of satin and gauze, lappets and ostrich feathers, lace trims and silk trains in an array of colours. Upon my arrival I spied Arthur speaking with one of his college tutors, so thought to find a glass of wine and rescue him. I stalked a servant who meandered with a tray of drinks.

Glass in hand, I was now opposite one of the fireplaces; Helen stood beside it in conversation with a young lieutenant of the Inniskilling Dragoons. Unlike the other girls, Helen was dressed quite simply in a pearl-white gown. Her thick brown hair was pinned up and she wore no headdress except for some topaz crystals. I had known her since she was little, and had been in and out of her house and company several times. But seeing her in this finery, as the strains of a quartet drifted over the gentle hubbub, and her gown reflected the roseate light, it struck me that she wasn't really beautiful. Her mouth has always been too wide, and her lower lip heavy-set. Still, she was tall like her brother and moved gracefully, she had vivacity and spontaneity, and her eyes shone with intelligence.

Helen saw me and I raised my glass in greeting, though a passer-by bumped my arm, which caused some of the wine to spill. When I looked again she had withdrawn from her companion. He bowed stiffly to her retreating back and flashed me a dark glance, which I found gratifying. She was then in front of me, all smiles and thanks for my coming. I told her she looked wonderful, and punctured any awkwardness by calling her Nelly, at which she laughed. She had been standing by the fire too long, so suggested we sit together in a corner beside one of the front drawing-room windows. Away from the hearth and in a slight draught it was more pleasant and we spoke of small things. She said it was a relief to chat normally. Every woman was speaking inanely of fashion and marriage, while every other young man wished to crow of his prospects and career. To be needled and bored at once. George May – she nodded at the lieutenant who had spoken with her – had talked for twenty minutes of his graduation from Woolwich, his commission in the dragoons and imminent deployment to the Far East to fight against the Chinese. 'He just went on and on. It was torture.'

'I've heard the Chinese have a peculiar genius for methods of torture.'

I hadn't meant it like that. I'm not sure what I meant by it, but I feared she would be aghast at the callousness of wishing harm to befall the young man. Instead there was a gleam in her eye as she glanced at me sideways, and then back across the room to May in his scarlet coat. 'Heaven forbid.'

I decided not to backtrack. I pointed out that May had found himself a new companion, whom I knew to be Miss Waring. We quietly derided her attire, commented on each gaudy feature: the pink gauze, blond lace, feathered headdress. I noted she stood perilously close to the fire and Helen craned her smooth neck to see. She wondered what if some rogue spark was to elude the guard and catch in the gauze. 'The poor girl would flare up like a moth in a candle,' she said. 'The night would end in tragedy.'

I agreed. All the work of that Grafton Street boutique gone for nought.

For a pleasant quarter-hour we picked out other attendees at random and for each imagined a bizarre demise. When others wandered near, Helen seamlessly shifted into chat about my studies, or Cecilia's marriage. Then when once more out of earshot she would picture Mr Goodshaw, who was speaking with her father, on a hunt, one eye peering down the barrel of his muzzleloader, wondering why the powder had failed to ignite.

Our furtive laughter was no doubt unbecoming, and it wasn't long before Mrs Stokes loomed above us. I rose to greet her. She didn't smile, but said how thoughtful it was of me to attend. She then turned to Helen. 'We didn't arrange this gathering so you could talk with old neighbours.' There was someone she wanted her to meet. Helen rose decorously and was led away.

Nothing appals and delights the general public so much as the trial of a murderous woman. Sarah Blackwood was a young wife who killed her husband so she could take up with a French medical student with whom she was having an affair. Her means of assassination was arsenic, which she slipped into the meals of her spouse in tiny but increasing quantities. Her trial kept Dublin enthralled for several weeks. The accused was found guilty and sentenced to hang at the start of April.

On the morning of her execution there was a knock on my front door. I ignored it at first until it sounded again. Despairing of Miss Joyce's idleness, I went to answer. Helen stood alone on my steps wearing a travelling cape and dark grey bonnet.

I greeted her with surprise, smoothed my hair and closed over the door behind. There was no sign of a chaperone. I dithered about inviting her in because the parlour was in such disarray, strewn with clothes, empty wine bottles and days-old remnants of dinner. But she was the first to speak. She had decided to go and view the hanging of Mrs Blackwood and wondered if I would like to accompany her. She looked at me steadily, as if challenging me to ask about the consent of her family, or general propriety.

I pulled the door on to its latch. 'I'd be delighted.'

I hailed a hansom and assisted her within, her fingertips resting on mine. I called up to the driver, 'Thomas Street,' but he said crowds had blocked the roads around St Catherine's Church. In that case, I said, as close as he could manage.

Safely hidden in the cabriolet's enclosure, we could relax. Helen had followed Blackwood's trial since it had commenced and was eager to discuss its intrigues and protagonists, but I had to plead ignorance of many details. She wondered how I was unaware of so many of its particulars since the papers had reported little else.

I looked out of the window. 'Not the papers I read.' A drift of citizens moved in the same direction. On Dame Street, people spilled from the pavements on to the rutted roadway, hindering traffic.

Helen was happy to describe the pertinent elements of the trial. Mrs Blackwood had administered tiny doses of poison to her husband for some time. He had begun showing symptoms of illness, and his death would have been attributed to that mysterious ailment but for a nauseating accident. One day, after his evening meal, the husband was tending to his animals, when the effects of the poison took hold and he emptied his stomach. One of his brothers went to clean up the mess in the yard, but he found a pig was already at work, slurping up the spillings with apparent relish. When the poor animal keeled over a few minutes later, poison was suspected and the investigation began. My nose wrinkled at some of these details. Sarah's solution of arsenic was discovered in a drawer. Most presumed her lover had provided it but that was never proved. The husband was beyond help and died a few days later.

I told Helen if she was ever minded to murder her husband she must think of a better hiding place for the poison than her linen drawer.

She looked across to me. 'I'll try to remember.'

She said Blackwood's defence claimed her husband had been abusive. Neighbours testified that they could often hear her cries at night. But all that was forgotten when the letters she wrote to her lover were produced, their contents drawled out in a thronged courtroom by an ancient prosecuting counsel. Blackwood could only sit and listen to the galleries snigger at her exposed heart. Helen's eyes had lost some focus. 'But the letters were beautiful.'

The congestion on the road, both vehicles and footfall, meant we moved in fits. Those in the crowd were in good spirits, anticipating the spectacle. There was a larger proportion of women than would be usual because of the female felon. Street hawkers did a brisk trade, while some pubs had set up stalls outside their doors, selling bottles of liquor to the cheery passers-by.

The flap in the ceiling was pulled up and the jowly face of the driver peered down. He said traffic was blocked completely ahead. The low crenellated spire of Christ Church was within sight so I suggested we walk. Once we had alighted, the current of pedestrians pushed us forward and I told Helen to stay close. She hooked her hand in my elbow, leaned towards me with her other hand resting on my upper arm. Beyond Christ Church the crowd was thicker and our progress slowed. We rubbed against shoulders covered in every style of fabric, and in every state of cleanliness, but Helen seemed oblivious.

The stream of people widened in the expanse of Cornmarket

Square; then we were funnelled into Thomas Street and the
vista before us cleared: a multitude of hats and heads jostling
for a good vantage, the wide street almost completely filled for
two hundred yards. The scaffold came into view and there was
a murmur from those around us. Necks were craned to see the
temporary wooden structure in front of St Catherine's Church,
still quite a bit in the distance. A long line of policemen kept
one side of the road clear, awaiting the arrival of the leading
lady. Helen walked on tipped-toes to catch her first glimpse of
the twisting noose.

On the corner with Meath Street, a horseless cart was
propped up so it sat flat. A large sign on white canvas was
hoisted above, which read, 'Cease to do Evil, Learn to do Well'.
Two ladies dressed in what looked like mourning attire handed
out printed bills, while a man stood on the bed of the cart
haranguing the crowd. His clothing looked costly, but
dishevelled and stained. His white hair stood on end, and the
tip of his nose hung down as if tugged by a small weight. When
he lurched from one end of the cart to the other he dragged his
right foot, which scraped lamely along the slats. He scorned
those beneath him, said we must each be examples of Christian
perfection to revel in the sight of one hurried to ultimate
judgement, uncalled by her maker. For a moment I thought he
railed against the entire system of capital punishment, but I
underestimated him.

'Where is the noose for the adulterer, the idolater, the
violator of the Sabbath?' The zealot said we were each as guilty
as she who would swing, and he began to point into the crowd.
He pointed to a spectacled man, a clerk in a pinstriped suit.
'You are as guilty.' He pointed to a gypsy woman carrying a
liquor bottle, her face red and hardened. 'You are as guilty.' And
then he fixed me along the length of his crooked finger and

gnarled knuckle. He trained his extended arm on my move-
ments; his eyebrow arched and his fervent eye flashed. This
time he spoke in a hoarse whisper. 'And you are guilty.'

Helen looked up at me, delighted. I tore my gaze from the
evangelist, shrugged and said, 'I think he was pointing at you.'

Cheers and loud laughter made us both turn. A fat drunkard
had lowered his britches, bent double in proud display to those
in and around the cart. The preacher gazed down in revulsion
at the ample white flesh and its dark heart, all his opinions of
human baseness confirmed. Helen laughed through a hand
that covered her mouth. She looked rather more closely when
the man immodestly bent back up and struggled to fix the
front of his trousers. I tugged at her arm. 'Let's keep moving
forward.'

Helen was adept at spotting gaps in the crowd; she would
take my hand and bustle through the press. Eventually, we
reached a good vantage point about a hundred feet from the
gallows. A looped rope hung suspended from a simple frame
on a high wooden platform. A large drape concealed the space
beneath the stage and trapdoor. The backdrop was the front of
St Catherine's Church, with its classical entablature and squat
bell tower. The shopfronts on Thomas Street were shuttered,
but faces appeared in every one of the upper-storey windows.
The owners hired out the rooms to wealthy spectators on days
such as this. They looked down, with wine glasses and cigars,
as if from the boxes in a theatre.

Then a cheer rolled through the mob, heralding the arrival
of the prison convoy. Two horse-drawn carriages led the way.
The prisoner followed in a covered cart. We couldn't see the
woman being taken out, but a hush had fallen over the people
as the guards prepared to bring her up the steps. Jeers rang out
a moment later when the masked hangman emerged on to the

platform. Even Helen hissed as he walked over to examine the noose and the lever that operated the trapdoor. He was joined by a number of prison guards and a priest who intoned prayers while holding a bible before his chest.

The woman stepped up and the crowd fell silent once more. Her dark hair was tied back, and I wondered if the ponytail would interfere with the slipknot. Flyaway strands rose in the breeze as she gazed across the assembly, her gaunt face pale against the dark prison garb.

A gasp went up when her knees gave way and she fell forward in a faint. Her hands were tied so she would have suffered injury if a guard had not caught her in an awkward embrace. Perhaps it would have been more humane to take her senseless to the rope. Instead a medic was called for, and he tended to the doomed woman until she revived.

Once beneath the gibbet, her shoulders stooped and head bowed. The hangman bent down to tie a restraining belt around her shins for the sake of modesty. It caused the skirt to billow about her knees. He then withdrew a hood that had been folded in his pocket, daintily snapped it so it unfurled and pulled it over her face. Helen's hand squeezed mine and she stood closer. The rope was lassoed about Blackwood's head and tightened beneath her chin like a necktie. The slack drooped down beneath her shoulders.

Just as the hangman stepped back there was consternation as the woman fainted again. This time the noose checked her fall and she was in danger of strangling herself before they were ready. Two guards rushed forward to take her weight as the hangman tried to loosen the rope. There were groans from the crowd. Women blessed themselves. A man behind us called for them to just pull the bloody lever. When the woman once more stood unaided the executioners acted quickly. All guards stood back. The hangman looked to an official at the edge of the platform who gave a nod, and without further hesitation the lever was thrown.

I often try and imagine the events of that day from Blackwood's perspective. To ascend the stage and be the focus of every eye. The sea of faces framed by the gibbet and noose. The steadying hands of the prison guards. The hangman restraining my legs, his face covered like a coward. I just hope my knees don't weaken, though I fear the mob will not be kind. Not if the one at my trial was any indication.

Mrs Blackwood fell through the hole in the platform to the level of her navel before her jarring stop, like a conker dropped from a string. Her neck didn't break. Helen's hand came up on impulse to the skin around her throat. In the hush, the creak of the rope could be heard, as well as the far-off voice of the preacher drifting over the crowd. The woman continued to kick for about a minute. Several people around us began to look away, but not Helen. Her fingernails dug into my knuckles and her shoulders rose as she held her breath. Finally Blackwood's agonies ceased and she came to rest, though she rocked back and forth somewhat, like a pendulum.

Smatterings of applause broke out in the crowd, and some cheers; above all there was just a resumption of conversation. People began to drift away. I spoke Helen's name. When she continued to look towards the scaffold I touched her shoulder, just where the skin met the wide neckline of her dress.

2

My final-year examinations were imminent. A few days after Mrs Blackwood's hanging, I was studying in my room, skimming through a tattered edition of Lloyd's *Treatise on Light and Vision*. But my mind was elsewhere.

As a prospective suitor I had little to offer. If I attained my degree perhaps I could find work as a research assistant in the college, or at Hamilton's observatory, but my income would be paltry. Helen's father would not consider me an option.

Miss Joyce knocked on my chamber door and said, 'John, may I speak with you a moment?'

'Just a minute.'

I looked at the damp brown patch in the corner of the ceiling. It had seeped into the stucco work and over the cheek of a plaster cherub, like a birthmark, or a bloodstain. The mosaic tiles in the hearth were cracked and their colours faded. The wallpaper by the window box had begun to peel away, revealing an old pattern which had not been put up in my lifetime. Mr Stokes would not permit his daughter to live here.

Miss Joyce knocked again. 'I really must speak with you.'

I walked past the door to place Lloyd's volume on my shelf, then thought again, and clasped it beneath my elbow.

When I opened the door, Miss Joyce glanced down at the book. 'I'm sorry to disturb your studies.'

'Not at all.'

'I wanted to tell you that I have dispensed with the services of your father's physician.' When I said nothing she added, 'He isn't making him any better.'

Dr Moore had been a mainstay of our house for much of my life, attending when anyone in the family suffered from poor health or infection. He had nursed my mother through her final illness. I remembered overhearing a conversation he had held with my father on the landing outside their room, telling him there was no longer any hope. I was only ten, and sat perched on a step out of sight beyond the return. I recall holding my breath so as not to betray my presence.

I could have argued against Moore's dismissal, but I didn't wish to become embroiled in my father's care. 'Whatever you think best.'

Miss Joyce had already hired two new doctors – Blythe and Warren – who, she claimed, had managed to cure her sister's rheumatism after years of suffering. They were both homeopaths, and immediately put my father on a course of infinitesimal prescriptions. I occasionally bumped into them as they prepared tonics in the kitchen. Their meticulous measurements, with phials, tinctures and droppers, reminded me of the experimental workbenches in college.

Arthur Stokes was a medical student, and I spoke to him about the treatments one evening in the Eagle. He looked at me with concern. 'I fear if your father has stopped receiving care from allopathic doctors then it's inevitable he will suffer a decline.'

I wasn't sure what to make of that. That the current ministrations might hasten my father from the world wasn't all that troubling. Rather, I feared the new doctors would prove adept at keeping him alive until his money ran out.

Soon enough, every spare penny in the house was going towards the new medical bills. A meagre allowance that I received each month was halted, and for the first time in my life I was penniless. Of course I wasn't destitute – my college fees were paid up, I had several rooms in the house in which I lived undisturbed and could survive on the provisions brought in. However, I could no longer buy new books, or a bottle of wine, or a bouquet of flowers.

Seeing Helen again became a preoccupation. I skipped afternoon lectures to walk home by Merrion Square, aware that she took a stroll in the enclosed park each day with her elderly governess, Mrs Bruce. The red-brick terraces of the square hem in a large and rambling pleasure garden, with tall trees, manicured lawns and serpentine paths. I had no key, so could only skirt the iron rail, but occasionally I caught Helen's eye as she walked within.

One afternoon, a woman with an infant in a baby carriage approached the gate from the inside. She withdrew a key from her apron and attempted to back out, but the sprung hinges of the gate closed against her. I took hold of the railing and said, 'Allow me, madam.' She thanked me, called me a gentleman, and didn't mind that I walked past her into the garden.

I crunched along the gravel path, past green benches and flowering shrubs. That day Helen was wearing a pale yellow dress that complemented her sloping shoulders. Her light brown hair hung beneath a white bonnet in corkscrew curls. Mrs Bruce wore a shawl despite the warm weather, and carried a clasped parasol. She had been employed by the Stokes family since before Helen was born, and she knew me well enough because I was a friend of Arthur's. After greeting me, she asked how I had come to be in the garden.

'I was invited in by my tutor, Professor Lloyd,' I said, knowing he lived on the square. 'But he had to return to college. It was so pleasant I decided to walk on alone.'

I fell into step beside them, holding my wrist behind my back as my father used to, and enquired after the Stokes household.

Helen moved a low-hanging branch aside with the back of her hand, as if parting a curtain. 'What subject does Professor Lloyd teach?'

I looked to see if she made sport of my white lie, but she seemed genuinely interested. 'Well, he's the chair of experimental philosophy,' I said. 'But he only teaches me one class, which is optics.'

The governess asked if I meant the grinding of spectacles.

'Why no. It's the study of light and all its properties.'

'Imagine.' Mrs Bruce noticed another woman walking a little further ahead and said it was Mrs Saunders. She quickened her step. 'I wanted to have a word with her.'

Helen and I were able to drop back and we walked for a while in silence. With each stride, a slim shoe emerged from the bottom of her skirt, then disappeared once more.

I thought of a question. 'Was your absence noted when we went to Thomas Street last week?'

She said she managed to sneak back into the house unseen. 'They thought I was in my room the entire time. What about you?'

'I tend to come and go from the house as I please. I'm rarely missed.'

We were strolling through a circular arbour, sheltered by newly green branches of ash that wove together overhead. In front of us, Mrs Bruce and Mrs Saunders emerged on to the sunlit path. Helen moved closer and took my hand. Her neck craned as she put her lips against my cheek, and she exhaled through her nose, which I felt down my jaw and beneath my collar. The arm she clasped was pressed firmly between us, against the smooth fabric of her dress, along her side and the top of her leg. I could smell sweat beneath her perfume. After a moment she disengaged, and stepped quickly on to the main path behind her governess.

That April, an election took place among ratepayers to select a poor law guardian for the St Stephen's Ward. The new Repeal Association put forward a candidate, and on election day they left little to chance. To ensure a full turn-out at the hustings, they employed the canvassing abilities of a large number of coal-porters from the north quays, who were provided with cudgels and hackney cars to escort reluctant electors to the meeting. A menacing body of such men also stood at the back of the hall, to remind hesitant voters of the consequences should they display a want of patriotism. Several prosecutions were brought after the election, for threats and actual assault on voters.

There was one case in particular. Captain Craddock, a retired military gentleman of Leeson Street, declined to vote because of poor health. On the evening of the election, three canvassers gained entry to his house, dragged him from his sickbed, and beat him in his own chamber.

A few days later I left Trinity by the front gate, intending to go straight home, but stopped at the window of a curiosity shop on College Green. An item in the corner had caught my eye, and I checked to see if I had enough money to buy it as a gift for Helen, but I was a few pennies short. It was a Chinese finger-trap. A little further up the street, some men had gathered around a printed proclamation. The notice described the assault on Captain Craddock and offered twenty pounds for information that led to the discovery and conviction of his assailants. I examined each detail on the poster. My eyes lingered on the amount.

When I got home I went down to the kitchen. Miss Joyce was at work near the stove, attending to a pot of bubbling stock. She had already arranged a tray to bring up to my father, containing a glass of claret, an empty soup bowl and a folded newspaper.

The front-page article dealt with the Craddock case. I paused at the table and began to read.

Miss Joyce noticed me and said, 'I believe that poor man is at death's door.'

It didn't say so in the report. 'How do you know that?'

'His housekeeper is a friend of mine. Mrs Skerritt.'

'Did she see what happened?'

'I don't think so.'

'Does Captain Craddock have any family?'

She looked at me over her shoulder. This was the most I had spoken to her in several weeks. 'I believe he lives alone.' She used the sides of her apron to carry the pot over to the table, and ladled some soup into the bowl. 'Why do you ask?'

'I just feel sorry for the man.'

She picked up the tray. 'I must bring this to your father.'

If I discovered some small piece of information about the attack, I could bring it directly to Sibthorpe and perhaps claim the reward. I went up to the study and retrieved a Dublin almanac, only a few years old. Its binding was of red leather with a paper inlay of marbled ink. I flicked through the pages, then scanned the list of addresses under 'Nobility, gentry, merchants and traders'. The tip of my finger traced down the

Cs to: 'Craddock, Captain Nathaniel, 41 Leeson Street, lower'. There could be no harm in having a look. I found a hat, buttoned my coat and went to investigate.

It rained as I walked over, and water dripped from a pediment beneath the stained-glass fanlight of Craddock's home. Passing hansom cabs sprayed mud on the uneven pavement where I stood, impeding pedestrians. A moment after I knocked, the polished brass letter box opened and shut with a metallic click before the door was pulled slightly ajar.

'Mrs Skerritt?' The woman inside nodded, and opened the door further. Without pretence I told her I wished to enquire about the attack on her employer. The woman rubbed her hands nervously, as if she had been in distress before my arrival, and surprised me by asking directly if I had come from the Castle. I thought that an odd assumption to make, but I had arrived at an opportune moment.

Without hesitation I said, 'Yes.'

'For once your timing is good. I was about to send word.' She said the Captain had regained consciousness for the first time since the assault, though he was driven to distraction by the agony of his injuries. 'He groans and struggles to breathe. I fear he cannot survive long.'

'In that case I should ask him about his attackers at once.' I walked past her into the hallway. 'Is he alone?'

Her eyes darted to me, perhaps with suspicion.

'I mean is he attended by his physician?' She shook her head. 'Then the best thing you can do, Mrs Skerritt, is fetch the doctor and inform him of the change in condition. I will glean what information I can and make sure Captain Craddock is comfortable in your absence.'

She considered this for a moment. The concern for her employer was overriding, so she fetched a shawl and departed.

I was left in the gloom of the hallway with the echo of its closed door.

I climbed the stairs in search of Craddock. The first-floor drawing room had been converted into a bedroom, and there was a thick crack in the wood beside the keyhole. I gave the door a nudge and it swung inward loosely.

Familiar odours assailed me, reminding me of my father's chamber. Craddock's iron bed was positioned between a shuttered window and the hearth. Two duelling pistols were mounted above the fireplace, crossed at the barrel. A small bed-side table contained bloody rags and a stoppered bottle of red laudanum with brown sediment gathered at the bottom.

Craddock himself looked small beneath the covers. His head was cocked back and away from me; his breath short and ragged. One eye was closed over by a swelling so neat and round it was like a tumour. Gashes and welts distorted his features, gouged in silver mutton-chop whiskers. Most striking of all were the colours. Like some demented jester, his face was painted in the deepest crimson and violet, flushed in the firelight. His shoulders and chest were dressed in stained bandages, girding his broken frame.

When he failed to sense my presence I spoke his name. After a few seconds his head rolled towards me.

'Sir, can you speak? You must tell me anything you can of the people who did this to you.'

His dry tongue extruded and scraped along his lower lip. I looked around to see if there was a jug of water.

My doubts as to whether he could speak at all were dispelled when he said, at the edge of hearing, 'Is that you, Richard?'

His son, I presumed. I leaned over the bed and tried to meet his eye. I told him that men had come to his house. I described how they had broken through his door and beaten him for failing to cast a vote. 'They shall go unpunished unless you can tell me what they looked like, what they wore, how they spoke.'

But it was no use. His good eye swivelled unfocused, and the few things he uttered were muted and nonsensical.

Then an unsettling change came over him. Even in his mangled features I could recognize panic, but I couldn't fathom its source. I soon gleaned that he simply felt the approach of a coughing spasm, which was terrible to witness. He gasped to fill his lungs before great racking coughs were dragged from his chest and throat. Every heave caused him to lean forward, compressing his broken ribs. After each cough he attempted to suck in air that wouldn't come, resulting in terrifying inward groans.

I stood above him, unsettled by my inability to help. I took his hand to offer some kind of comfort, but then realized his arm was broken, and that I was adding to his torment. I was sure he was about to expire, and began to wonder how I could explain his death to Mrs Skerritt.

But the Captain's fit subsided and the room quietened. I took up the bottle of laudanum. The label had no indication of dosage, but I couldn't leave the man to this ordeal. Thinking back, I'm sure I believed an overdose was a lesser evil. I removed the tapered glass wand attached to the stopper, and watched the russet liquid form droplets at its tip.

'One of them had a cleft lip.' The Captain's eye fixed on me for the first time.

I put the bottle aside. 'How many were there?'

His eye began to waver, but he brought it back. 'There were three. I first heard them on the stairs shouting my name. I left my bed to lock the door and fetch my sabre.' I saw the sword propped in a corner. 'They put a hole in the door and one stuck through an arm to turn the key. I sliced him across the knuckles.'

I looked again at the door and spotted a smear of blood beneath the broken panel. That's what earned him his beating. The men had only come to drag him to the polls.

Craddock grew weaker as he described how they kicked in the door, wrested his sword away and began their assault.

'You said one had a harelip. Are you sure?'

He said he was. Also he thought the man he cut came from Belfast.

He was spent. A tear ran from his good eye. 'Let me drink the bottle,' he said. I told him his physician was on the way. His eye began to wander again. 'Let me drink the bottle.' And he lost consciousness.

Craddock's chin slumped forward on red-flecked sheets. I took a deep breath and detected a tang from his soiled bed-clothes. I went to the window and opened enough of one shutter to look outside. Mrs Skerritt was bustling from the corner with Pembroke Street; the doctor in tow was pulling at his lapels and hurrying to match her step. Skerritt's gaze swept up and across the front of her house and I stood back from the window. I considered maintaining the charade – that I had been sent from the Castle to enquire about the attack. But the Captain was again unconscious, so what could result except time for them to ask searching questions and memorize my face?

The front would be closed off by their approach. I slipped down the staircase and went back through the hall, then descended the stairwell leading to the basement. I heard the main door open. The gloomy passageway below went past sculleries and larders to the rear exit. I tried the handle and found it locked. Muffled voices reached me from the landing above. The keyhole was bare. I felt along the top of the lintel, scratched my thumb on an exposed nail, then brushed a key that fell with a clatter on the flagstones. I listened for a reaction. There was silence, so I scooped it up and turned the lock with a clunk.

Craddock's yard was long and unkempt, with heaps of rubbish and empty coal scuttles. A path ran down its centre, overgrown with weeds. I hastened through without looking behind, hoping that those inside were tending to the Captain in his front room. The perimeter wall was about ten feet high, but some intact masonry from a demolished outbuilding offered the means of scaling it. Standing atop the rubble, I leaped and grabbed the wall-cap with both hands.

Still suspended, I scraped my right leg up towards the ledge and managed to catch my heel on top. In that ridiculous pose I had to pause and rest before attempting the final heave. A cat seated further along the wall in the neighbouring garden regarded my unseemly scrabble with mild interest, in the same way that I would observe him attempt a doorknob. I vaulted my legs over, maintained a grip as I lowered myself down the other side, and then dropped the remaining five or six feet, which sent a shock through my heels up to the knees. I found a stone, pitched it at the cat – who turned his head sharply as it sailed by, but was otherwise unmoved – and lurched down the lane towards St Stephen's Green.

The coal-heavers worked on Arran Quay, where the fuel was taken from barges, brought into Smithfield Market and distributed throughout the city by horse and cart. A few dozen men unloaded the cargo. One stepped nimbly along a gangplank, seized a coal sack by both corners and lifted it on to his back as if he was throwing on a cloak. Those broad shoulders carried the load as if it had no weight, but when he tossed it into a waiting cart, the bed shook and the horse flinched. He lifted his cap to wipe his brow, adding another dark streak to his face, then turned to retrieve the next bag.

I've always been wary of coalmen, ever since I was very small. Our first maid used to threaten that if I misbehaved I would be carried away by the coalman in his empty sack. This was a real terror, and I dreaded the sound of that great grimy fellow clomping up the stairs to the wooden coal bin located just outside our nursery door. The thunder that came when he pitched in his heavy load, I can hear it now, and then the sound of his wheezing. He was just catching his breath, but I always thought he was weighing up my indiscretions, deciding if they warranted my abduction.

I looked more closely at the coal-porters on the quay. Some wore gloves, but none carried his hand as if it was injured. From my vantage point, I couldn't tell if any had a misshapen lip.

On the far side of Whitworth Bridge, an old stevedore stood alone near the quayside wall. He lifted both sides of his coat to rummage in a number of pockets that had been sewn into the lining; the stitches were visible on the outside as several haphazard scars. He seemed to satisfy himself that whatever he searched for wasn't there, for he withdrew his hands, leaned against the wall on his forearms, and gazed over the Liffey.

I went to stand beside him. When he looked towards me with a raised eyebrow I said, 'I wonder if you can help me. I'm trying to locate a particular man.'

The old docker turned his face and spat into the river. 'And does he wish to be found?'

I smiled and said undoubtedly so. I told him I was a scrivener in a solicitor's office, sent to find a man named in the will of a wealthy client recently deceased. 'We were told he worked on the docks of Arran Quay, and so here I am. His name is Arthur Stokes.'

'Never heard of him.'

'That's a pity. I've made numerous enquiries now and all of them fruitless. You'd have thought it easy enough to find a man with a cleft lip.'

He glanced at me, and I made a point of peering at the clock on the pepper-canister cupola of St Paul's Church.

'I do know of a man,' he said, still wary. 'Though not personally. I've seen him drinking several times in Nowlan's up in Stoneybatter.'

'Thank you. I might look there.'

He cocked his head twice as if to say I could do as I wished, then walked away. He sensed he had spoken loosely.

Smithfield Market was a maze of stallholders through which local children dashed barefoot. Vendors put lanterns over their booths as evening fell. On the pavement outside Nowlan's, an old street hawker cried at me. She held dozens of rosary beads looped over her outstretched palms and up the length of her arms. Our family had had a Catholic nanny once, who prayed nightly with beads made from jet and amber. She showed them to me one evening, and tried to explain what they meant. I was only interested in the larger beads that symbolized the mysteries. It fascinated me, that the events of a man's life could be remembered on a string of stones.

Nowlan's pub consisted of two large rooms connected by a single bar that ran the length of the wall. Labourers and dock workers sat on benches, where decades of grime had given every surface a polished black varnish. A group of well-dressed students occupied a table in one corner, most likely apprentice barristers from King's Inns.

The back room was darker. Pipe smoke hung in the air and yellow tobacco stains covered the walls. With the last of my money I ordered a drink, and sat on a stool just inside the partition. My attention was caught by a child's porcelain doll that sat incongruously among the bottles and glasses behind the bar, on a shelf backed by a large mirror. I observed the other customers in the reflection. For the most part they hunched in groups at tables. One old man sat alone and warmed his fingers over a shivering candle. The gloom made it hard to distinguish features as I looked from face to face.

As I surveyed the room in the mirror, I locked eyes with a man who stood close to me at the bar. He wore a wrinkled yellow cravat beneath a grey flannel shirt, unbuttoned at the neck. His hands rested on the counter, fingers laced protectively around a glass of stout.

He turned to me and said, 'I haven't seen you in here before.'

'No. I'm just passing through.' I rotated my whiskey so a chip in the rim pointed away.

'You sound as if you're not from around here all right.' His glass was a third full, but he finished the stout in one swallow. Then he wiped his mouth on his sleeve, and said, 'Mine's a Guinness, if you're buying.'

'I'm leaving after this one.'

'Who were you looking for just now?'

'Nobody.'

His lip curled up, and he was about to speak again, but then another man approached. The newcomer was tall and broadly built with cropped fair hair. Streaks of black grime covered his face and forearms. He nudged the man with the yellow cravat and spoke quietly to him in a Belfast accent. 'Would you leave that lad in peace, for Jesus' sake. I'll get you a drink.'

I kept my head forward. As the Ulsterman called for Nowlan, he placed his right hand on the counter. A blackened bandage covered his palm, wrapped over the webbing of his thumb like a fingerless glove. Spots of blood had seeped to the surface, marking the peaks of his knuckles.

He paid for the drinks, and I watched in the mirror as the two men went back to a table in the corner. Three others were already seated there. One was small and youthful, with brown hair unevenly cut. He took a pipe from a waistcoat pocket and placed it in his mouth at an odd angle, then struck a match and dipped it in the pipe's chamber. The flame illuminated his face for a few seconds, and I could see his upper lip was split by a cleft that disappeared into his left nostril. When he smiled at some comment made by a companion, the lip parted like a curtain in the theatre.

'Would you like another?' The barman Nowlan stood before me, pointing at my glass.

'No,' I said. 'I think that should be enough.'

I glanced again in the mirror. The young man shook the match until it went out. An orange dot gyrated in the gloom.

I went to the Castle the following morning, but before leaving the house, I checked the letter box as usual. A single envelope addressed to me contained something hard and heavy. Someone must have delivered it personally, for only my name was written on the front in a neat hand. I broke the seal and fished out a dull grey iron key. A note attached said, 'So you don't have to sneak into the garden.' I read the short line three times. Helen had squeezed the apostrophe into 'don't', as if she'd forgotten it at first, which I found endearing. I slipped the key into my front pocket.

On Little Ship Street, a soldier stood watch at a pedestrian entrance to the Castle beneath a raised portcullis. I walked up to him and said I had some information for Thomas Sibthorpe. He didn't move for a few seconds, and I began to wonder if the name meant anything to him, but then he called to another man inside the gate. A porter dressed in blue livery emerged from a shelter. After a word with the sentry, he beckoned and said, 'Come with me.'

The guard stood aside and I entered the Castle grounds. A long straight road lay before us, which cut through government buildings. We passed the Ship Street barracks and the Georgian state apartments. A white stallion was being led through a circular walled garden to the Viceroy's crenellated coach house. The porter told me the garden was the site of Dublin's medieval black pool, where the Vikings first docked, and from which the city took its name. The pathways were busy with court officials and office clerks, civil servants and army officers. Further on, a large Norman tower loomed above us on the left, formerly a prison fortress. The Gothic Chapel Royal was surrounded by scaffolding. My guide said the foundations had to be reinforced because the church was built on the site of the original moat, and had begun to subside.

I feared he planned to give me a tour of the entire grounds. 'Is Sibthorpe's office near?'

'Sibthorpe doesn't have an office.'

'Then where are you taking me?'

But he didn't say any more. We reached the police barracks, which consisted of a series of low, grey buildings. He brought me in a side entrance and up an oak staircase to a small room, which contained a desk and a few simple wooden chairs, all well lit by a sash window slightly ajar. The porter took my name and said someone would come to speak with me.

An elaborate Vienna wall clock sounded the interminable seconds as I watched an hour elapse. At one point I looked into the corridor, but there was no sign of life. I rehearsed my statement. Diversion for a time was provided by a bluebottle that flew through the window, only to alight on a flycatcher sheet and become ensnared. The pest's wings hummed vainly for a minute. In resignation it ceased, sucked at the sweet resin in which it was fixed, before another futile attempt at escape.

'John Delahunt. I knew it wouldn't be long before you showed up.'

Devereaux, the young man with the chinstrap beard who had called to my house some weeks before, had entered the room. He pushed the door closed, harder than was necessary. 'You have some information for us?'

'I only want to speak with Sibthorpe.'

With a grin he presumably thought disarming, he said that Sleeky Tom hadn't the time to grant an audience to every snitch that wandered in. 'Sibthorpe took a special interest in the O'Neill case, which was the only reason you met him before. From now on you'll have to make do with the likes of me.' Devereaux took the seat opposite. 'But I'll report whatever it is you have to say. As long as it's of interest.'

'What's to stop you passing the information off as your own?'

He shrugged. 'Not a thing. But believe me, I have bigger concerns. You can either talk to me, or the first drunk willing to listen to you in the Eagle.'

I remained silent, and after a moment his tone softened. Surely I could at least identify the case in question.

He wasn't to be trusted, but in truth I was eager to tell. 'I know who carried out the assault on Captain Craddock. I can describe them, tell you where they can be found, and wish to claim the twenty-pound reward as advertised.' I took a tattered copy of the proclamation from inside my coat, unfolded its yellowed edges and laid it on the desk between us.

He frowned slightly as he took up the sheet. 'Twenty

pounds; the assault on Craddock,' he said, as if reading directly from the notice. Then he looked up. 'I'll be right back.'

A shorter wait. Devereaux re-entered with an inkpot, pen and a sheaf of blank pages, each stamped with a Castle seal at the top. Behind him, Thomas Sibthorpe stepped into the doorway. I rose from my seat, but he made no allusion to our previous meeting. He simply wished to allay any mistrust I felt towards my questioner.

'Mr Delahunt, I cannot remain, but please furnish a statement to Mr Devereaux.' With that he reached in and pulled the door shut.

Devereaux was tapping the edge of his papers on the table-top to make them align. He laid them flat, dipped his nib in the inkpot and said, 'In your own time.'

I gave a good account of what I knew, embellished some details, and kept others back. Devereaux only interjected once or twice. He wondered why Mrs Skerritt was willing to leave me alone in the house with Captain Craddock.

I hesitated, then said, 'She thought I was a police agent.'

He nodded in approval, but said for me to have given that impression wasn't quite legal so we left it out. He was impressed by the level of detail in my description of the attackers. I said Craddock had only managed to describe two of the three, but Devereaux was unconcerned.

'There's a man here who's adept at extracting information from suspects once they're in custody.' He looked at me across the table. 'You might meet him someday.'

As I signed the statement, he commended my work, and I was affected by this rare praise enough that I found him less offensive. He said the particulars would be sent to the station in Bow Street, where the local constables could probably name the men simply by their description. The

affidavit in itself was strong enough to bring before a
magistrate to issue warrants for arrest, which could happen
within a day or two.

'And the reward?'

'What about it?'

'When will I get it?'

'These things take time, Delahunt.' He placed the statement
in a folder. 'But don't worry. Here in the Castle, each man gets
what he deserves.'

Two days later, I was leaving a lecture hall in Trinity when a
don came up to me and asked if I was Delahunt. I nodded and
he handed me a note. I thought perhaps my father had died.
When I was younger, I used to daydream that lessons in my
school might be interrupted by news of the death of one of
my parents. The master, usually so stern, would have to treat
me kindly, and the other boys would solemnly shake my hand
in an attempt to appear grown up. It actually happened one
year to a boy called Lennon. But he wept when he heard the
news, which rather spoiled it.

The message simply told me to go to a certain coffee shop in
Baggot Street at midday. It was signed 'Dx'.

When I entered, I saw Devereaux reading a newspaper at a
table near the far wall. As I joined him, he turned over a cup that
lay rim-down in a saucer, and poured some coffee from a pewter
pot.

He said, 'Arrests have been made.'

Devereaux reached into his coat to retrieve a brown
envelope, which he slid across the marble tabletop with the tip
of his index finger. 'Usually you'd have to wait for a conviction.
But Tom seems to think you deserve it.'

I opened the envelope enough to glance inside at two

pristine ten-pound notes. After weeks of scraping by with pennies, it was such a luxury to hold them.

Devereaux folded his newspaper open on a certain page. His easy smile had returned. 'Have you begun to see the attraction in this line of work?'

I had to admit my perceptions of it were changing.

He leaned forward with his fingers in a steeple. 'I know there's some stigma attached to the Castle's methods, but it's undeserved. As if we live to skulk in the shadows and pry into the business of honest men.' He picked up his cup and gestured with it. No one could find fault with my actions of the previous week. Through wit, and some daring, I had helped bring those thugs to justice.

He took a sip, then returned his cup to the saucer with a clink. 'There is something I have to tell you, though.' He passed me the newspaper. 'Did you see this?' he said, pointing to a column in the corner.

It was that morning's *Dublin Gazette*. The article announced the death of Captain Craddock from his injuries in the early hours two days ago. It said the case was now a murder investigation. The main thrust of the article was to denounce the despicable electoral tactics of the Repealers, but it ended by saying the police were on the cusp of making arrests.

Two mornings ago. I looked at Devereaux. 'You knew he was dead when I spoke to you.'

'If you'd only waited another day, the reward would have been increased to fifty pounds. You'd been too eager. You couldn't wait to tell, and it should be a lesson. The information you collect is precious.'

'Why didn't you let me know?'

It had been Sibthorpe's decision. That was why he had gone

to fetch him early in the interview. 'If it had been up to me, I'd have filled you in, arranged to split the extra thirty.' He took the newspaper back and wedged it beneath his saucer. 'But you don't cross Sibthorpe.'

A waiter came over and asked me if I wanted anything. I shook my head without looking at him.

'We'd been preparing to announce Craddock's murder on the morning you arrived.' He said the Castle had a printing press in the basement of the barracks for its own proclamations, confiscated from some underground newspaper back in the twenties. 'After you left I had to rush down and tell the operator. He had already cranked out a hundred bills announcing the new reward.' The printer was sorely disappointed because he had acquired a new typeface to spell out 'Murder' in huge Gothic capitals, and was looking forward to seeing the results posted in the city.

Devereaux seemed to think I'd find this amusing, and he chuckled into his cup, but the laugh died in the silence between us. After a moment, he began a slow thoughtful nod.

'Murder,' he said. 'That's where the money is.'

3

The key Helen gave me was poorly cut, and tended to jam in the wrought-iron gates of Merrion Park. Muttered oaths and whitened knuckles were of no avail. It required some finesse, gradually increasing pressure with a faint waggling until the bolt released with a satisfying thud. For some reason it was always much easier to relock. I would spot Helen walking alone and fall into step beside her, tipping my hat as if I had stumbled across an old acquaintance. The start of May was warm, as it always seems to be in the weeks before examinations, and the cut of Helen's dresses loosened and the necklines lowered. She no longer wore headgear, and her mousy hair shone lustrous or lank, depending on when she last bathed.

The enclosed paths were well trod, and not suitable for open conversation or displays of affection. When a path cleared, Helen was emboldened, closing the space between us to take my hand, which I would shake off at the sound of voices or footfall.

One afternoon she spotted a gap in the undergrowth, which barely concealed a disused trail. Without a word she disappeared along it, and I had little option but to follow. After a few yards it emerged into a grove, unkempt and overgrown.

The main paths of the garden skirted close by, but were hidden by trees and thickets. The small space was wreathed by the limbs of elms and willows, its floor covered in uncut grass, not too tall because of the shade, all dotted with wildflowers. An old bench with black iron legs and green wooden slats sat beneath the awning.

Helen was delighted at the discovery. She walked into its centre and playfully twirled once with her arms outstretched. She looked towards me with a smile so open that I knew: if ever there was a moment to march over, cup her face in my hands, lean in and let her lift her chin to seal the kiss, it was now.

'I don't think we're allowed in here.'

Her shoulders sank and she said I worried too much.

Over a number of weeks we would meet at that spot. Its seclusion meant we could arrive and depart separately, converse freely. Helen always spoke at length, and I wondered how she thought of so much to say. I believe what she valued in me most was my acceptance of ideas others thought eccentric or improper. She would describe to me her dread at the life that had been set out for her – the monotony of afternoons in the salons of respectable women, all creativity and spontaneity withering in restrictive dress and stifling air. She was adamant that she wouldn't be married off against her will, to some ageing rector with creeping fingers, or some preening soldier with thick fists. She admitted she had no intention of ever bearing children; she could not abide their clinging and mewling. Perhaps others tried to dissuade her from these notions, but to me they seemed perfectly reasonable. I think she mistook my indifference for approval, or at least understanding, and it seemed to give her comfort.

When she spoke, her thoughts would play on her face, and

I'd note each detail: the way her eyelids would widen or narrow or languidly blink, the small quaver in her throat, and the motion of her lips as the words were formed – they hardly required any movement at all. Once, I was so absorbed that I failed to notice she had stopped speaking, and was regarding me coolly.

She said, 'Don't you agree?'

'Yes,' I said. 'I do completely.'

I wasn't put off by her taste in literature, which tended towards the Gothic and fantastic; I even read some titles she recommended – though I didn't finish them. She in turn was intrigued by what I studied, so I lent her some volumes on natural philosophy. I remember she asked for them tentatively, as if scared I would refuse or scorn her request. It never occurred to me that she might not understand the contents, or that the knowledge would be wasted on her.

Whenever I spoke, it was about Cecilia's marriage, or my father's health, or my prospects after college. While caressing my hand, she noticed my little finger wouldn't bend at the middle knuckle, and I told her of the time it was injured, when I fell from the banister of our nursery in Fitzwilliam Street.

One afternoon, thick clouds darkened the grove, squalls shook drops loose from the canopy, which fell through the leaves in an arrhythmic patter, and Helen confessed that she loved me. I considered my response. I had never before had a companion like her, but still I remained reticent. During our next few meetings she repeated her declaration. The fact that I had not yet said I loved her in return didn't escape her notice, and she pointed it out.

I said I'd soon rectify that.

We had been leaning back on the bench, her head in the hollow of my shoulder. She sat up and turned to look at me.

'Say it now.'

I regarded her face: an anxious pout and eyes serious like a scolded child. It wasn't particularly becoming. 'I love you. Helen.'

She considered for a moment, then her eyes softened and she leaned back against me. If she'd but given me a moment I would have artfully worked it into the conversation.

Neither of us proposed to the other. Instead, our conversations turned to the kind of life we could lead if we remained together, and soon the idea that we would be married became a given. My twenty-first birthday was at hand, but Helen's was still two years distant – she celebrated it during my trial. If she married before then, we would require the consent of her parents.

After one such discussion, Helen said, 'You know, if we took the boat to Scotland, we could marry without their say-so.'

She spoke of it in a matter-of-fact fashion, not as some romantic notion to elope. Still, I was quick to discourage the idea. We would be much better off seeking the permission of her father, for then her dowry, annuities and legacies would be still forthcoming.

Helen thought for a moment, then nodded. 'You may be right.'

She reached across and pulled my watch from its fob pocket, checked the time and said she had to return home. 'Will you be able to come tomorrow?'

'I can't. There's somewhere I have to be.'

'What is it?'

I took the watch from her hands. 'Just something for college. I can be here the day after.'

I could see she wanted to enquire further, but instead she leaned over and kissed me. 'The day after tomorrow then.'

*

Barristers, litigants and idlers milled in the unwholesome air of the rotunda. The main hall of the Four Courts was a gathering place for every class and rank. Lawyers and their clients huddled in conference, and stole glances across the chamber towards their opponents. Senior fellows meandered from one cause to the next, beset by an array of applicants clamouring for particular notice. One QC exited Common Pleas, flushed from battle, and marched directly into Exchequer, a new client and set of assistants in his wake.

Pallid members of the junior bar stood in small circles, or trudged the hall in pairs, hoping for some manner of professional engagement. I could see in their countenance the melancholy of their unemployment. They were caped and bewigged, their faces sickly and jaded, their hands bereft of briefs, and I wondered at the superior air of legal students I had met in college.

Plaintiffs and defendants from every walk of life commingled. The most alien were the rural petitioners, in their coarse woollen coats and spurred boots. One scraped before his young counsel, and gently unfolded a tattered deed as if he opened a sacred text. The lawyer disdained to read it. He had probably copied out a thousand such leases while a novice, and could recite the clause that meant his client faced eviction.

And all the while there was the din of hurried steps on the marble floor, fervent conversation, tipstaffs bawling out notices from the doorway of each court, all echoing within the dome. The oppressive smell of the throng was made worse by the stink of the Liffey outside. The situation of the courts is so low and marshy, the river saps at its foundations. The great legal edifice is constantly undermined.

I stood apart in an alcove. The trial of Craddock's killers was imminent, but I wouldn't be called as a witness. Devereaux had sent word to say that my affidavit was to be considered during the trial; however, I would remain anonymous. His estimation of the defendants was correct. Under questioning, one admitted to the guilt of the whole party, including the third man who was subsequently identified. The Castle was loath to expose an informant if it could be avoided, and the courts tended to acquiesce. So I had come to Inns Quay just out of curiosity, to sit in the gallery and view the final turn of a wheel I had set in motion.

The case was announced and the jury called to the box. Twelve men detached from the crowd and assembled at the entrance to the court. A clerk led them inside. After a few minutes, the doors were opened to the public.

There was an aisle between rows of seats, like pews in a church, leading towards the elevated bench. The high-backed judges' chairs were still empty. Behind them, a royal insignia was fixed to the wall, beneath a draped half-circular canopy. Barristers and clerks surrounded tables near the front. Some bent and scribbled notes, others leafed through briefs, a few slouched, seemingly indifferent. Many of the benches in the public gallery were sparsely populated, though the first few were filled with the defendants' loved ones, just like at a wedding, or funeral.

I took a seat near the door and waited for the opening exchanges. Another man joined me. He appeared to be a reporter, judging from his lank hair and somnambulant expression. As he sat down he was breathing heavily, and he looked at me. 'I thought I was going to miss the start.'

I ignored him. The prisoners sat cuffed together in a box to the right. The two I had identified looked at their families, the one unknown to me regarded his twelve supposed peers who sat in the jury box, which was raised to the same level of the upper-tiered gallery on the left. By their dress it was clear the jurors would never have known the society of the accused, and it's likely none even professed to the same faith. One of the twelve leaned forward on the edge of the box to survey the court, size up the defendants and their manner, and the demeanour of the respective lawyers. I think I should have liked to have been on a jury once.

An official called for everyone to stand, then barked at those in the galleries to take off their hats. Three judges in wigs and ermine-lined robes emerged from behind a worn green curtain to take their seats on the bench.

The trial wasn't quite the spectacle I had hoped for. Much of the day was taken up with obsequious exchanges between the barristers and judges, mostly out of earshot. My interest was piqued when the defence counsel brought up the issue of my affidavit, and the legitimacy of an anonymous statement in these proceedings; indeed, the legitimacy of the system by which information was collected in Dublin Castle. A prosecutor pointed out that the statement had been used primarily to secure warrants for arrest, but since it agreed in so many particulars with the confession of one of the defendants, it was in fact a vindication of the methods employed by the authorities. The defence barristers didn't pursue the matter.

They produced one witness, a pockmarked young woman who lodged with one of the defendants, and stated that he had been home with her throughout the night of the attack on Captain Craddock. However, she was caught in several lies under the examination of the crown prosecutor. He bullied her with questions about her own life, and continually insinuated that she was a prostitute by referring to her as a 'gay woman'.

She left the witness box completely discredited, fixing her questioner with a hate-filled stare.

The journalist leaned towards me. 'If that is her profession, I'd say her clients get more than they bargain for.'

I didn't know what he meant.

'She's a wasp.'

When I frowned at him he said, 'You know, she's infected. She has a sting in her tail.' He looked up to note another exchange between the barristers.

During the session after lunch, a flash of colour made me notice a man who sat towards the front of the gallery. I could only see the back of his head, and partially the side of his face. But when he turned to whisper something to his neighbour, his yellow cravat peeked out above his collar.

I looked down at my knees. My presence in the courtroom now seemed perilous, and I berated myself for sitting amidst the loved ones of those I'd condemned. The journalist gave me a dark look as I tried to squeeze by. He moved his satchel from the floor and swung his legs up to make room for me to pass, causing the bench to creak. I pulled at the double doors of the courtroom, first one and then the other, but neither budged. A tipstaff standing nearby said, 'You have to push it.' The main hallway was less crowded, but I didn't stop. I made straight for the exit and stepped out on to the quays. A stiff breeze blew up from the bay, making the surface of the water shiver.

That evening, rain fell on Fitzwilliam Street in heavy showers. I sat with the parlour shutters drawn, sipping a bottle of wine from Meyler's, and reading over Hamilton's *Systems of Rays*. I thought back over the previous weeks. A few close shaves, but altogether I looked upon the experience with satisfaction. I had known few thrills in my life before then, and the reward money was enough to see me comfortably through the end of term. The most important thing now was to focus on college and attain my degree.

There was a soft rap on the front door. Miss Joyce had gone to bed. I put aside the volume and went into the hallway, repeating a law from Hamilton's book, which I can still remember: 'Rays which diverge from a luminous point compose one optical system, and after they reflect in a mirror, they compose another.' The last grey light of evening showed through the semi-circular fanlight.

I opened the front door wide. The man with the yellow cravat stood on my steps. Small beads of water had gathered on his shoulders. Tufts of tawny hair circled his pate, and he had no beard except for a few days' growth.

We regarded each other for a moment. I considered bluffing that I had three brothers upstairs, but he had probably observed the darkened house for hours.

'John Delahunt.' The soft tone of his voice surprised me.

'Yes.'

'Can I come in?'

The latch was cold against my fingers. I stepped backwards into the hall with my arm extended towards the parlour door. He walked into the room and shook rainwater from his coat. My book lay open beside a glass of wine, which glowed red in the candlelight. He took up the bottle to read the label, which was in French. 'Not drinking in Nowlan's this evening?'

'Clearly not.' I took the bottle from his hand, and brought it to the dresser. 'Would you like a glass?'

His face darkened. 'Do you think I came here for a drink?'

'No, but there's plenty of time to discuss what has to be done.'

I poured some wine and handed it to him, then pointed at

the armchair in which I'd been studying, and invited him to sit. I brought my own glass to stand beside the hearth, and propped one elbow against the mantelpiece.

The man looked up at me from my chair. 'If you sit down we can discuss your problem.'

'I'd prefer to stand.'

He shifted to get comfortable. 'It makes no difference.' The frayed ends of his trousers hitched up over his shins, revealing worn boots, one with the sole drooping down at the toe. He wasn't sure what to do with the wine. He placed his elbows on his knees, then changed his mind and sat upright.

I said, 'I'm sorry about your friends.'

'I never particularly liked them.' The scrolled handle of a candlestick teetered over the lip of the table beside him. He pushed it in safely with his thumb, causing the flame to drag sideways. 'They shouldn't have lost their heads with that old man.'

I agreed, and said it was a terrible business.

He set aside his wine, then withdrew a copy of the proclamation announcing the twenty-pound reward and showed it to me; just as I had done with Devereaux in the Castle.

He said, 'You'll have to give me the blood money.'

'What do you mean?'

'The reward you got for shopping Seanie and Fergie. Give it to me.'

'Why would I do that?'

'Because a word about this to my friends, and your life will become very uncomfortable.'

'I'm under the protection of the Castle.'

He raised an eyebrow and looked around the quiet, dimly lit room. 'You're not at the moment.'

I put my glass down on the mantel, and gripped it lightly

by the rim. 'Why don't we split it,' I said. 'Ten pounds each.'

'No. You're in no position to bargain.'

I was going to argue more, but he was right. It was my own fault for being spotted; a lesson to be learned.

'I've spent some of it. I can only give you fifteen.'

He frowned for a moment, but then nodded. 'Fair enough. I'll take it now.'

I went to a low bookcase in the corner and took an academic volume from the bottom shelf. I leafed through it, retrieving two hidden banknotes of five and ten pounds. When I turned, the man was already on his feet. He plucked the money from my outstretched hand and put it in his breast pocket.

'Thank you.'

Then he seized my left wrist, turned me around and pushed me against the wall by the fireplace. He deliberately twisted my arm, before dragging it across my back towards my shoulder. His fingers laced through my hair, and pulled my head back so his mouth was just over my eye.

'A month from today, I'll return, and you'll give me the same amount again.' He pushed my head sharply against the wall for emphasis. 'A month after that the same thing. I'll be paying visits here so regular, we'll soon be fast friends. If you breathe a word about this to anyone, I'll tell all the dockers on Arran Quay what you've done, and then pieces of you would show up in every canal in the city.'

He asked if I understood. I couldn't move my head but whispered a yes. The pressure on my arm increased. He seemed to feel his way towards its breaking point, and I was aware of the ease with which he held me pinioned, the potential force he hardly used. Then he kicked my ankles, and threw me down beside the hearth. He picked up the book from the floor, flicked through the pages to ensure no other money was hidden, and then tossed it down beside me. 'A month from today.'

The corner of the hearthstone dug into my hip. Before me, three fire-irons lay aslant in their bow-legged stand. The handle of the poker was made of thick brass, moulded into the shape of a lion's head. I reached across and gripped its blackened point.

He was almost at the door when I got to my feet. The noise made him turn, but I was upon him in a few steps. I swung the moulded end of the poker in a high downward arc, and it struck the top of his head, glancing down to crack into his right shoulder. His features briefly froze in an odd expression, like the aftermath of a sneeze, then his knees hit the floor, and he slumped forward without a sound.

I checked the handle of the poker to see if it was damaged; there wasn't a scuff. Then I pulled the parlour door ajar. Nothing stirred on the landing above; there wasn't a sound or glimmer of candlelight. I waited several seconds before closing the door again with a click.

The man lay face down. His stubbled cheek was squashed flat, and I could hear him breathe raggedly through clenched teeth. I could have roused the household and sent for help, but the police wouldn't have kept him for long. As soon as he was released, he would track me down again. Also, he could identify me as an informer to his coal-heaving friends at any time.

I took up the fire-iron again and considered its weight. Just how much force would be necessary? I rehearsed a couple of swings to judge their likely impact; the shaft flashed and hummed through the air. Best to err on the side of caution, I decided, reasoning no killing blow was ever faulted for being too hard.

I allowed the thick handle to caress the back of his head, and picked a spot just above and behind his ear, where a small amount of blood from the first strike had already matted his hair. I stood with my legs apart and knees bent, as if I was about to take a shot in croquet, raised the poker, and mustered every ounce of strength.

A thought occurred. Too hard a hit would spatter gore all over the furniture and rug. I lowered my arms. It wouldn't do for the man to bleed all over the place; removing the body was going to be tricky enough.

I grabbed his damp shoulder and rolled him on to his back, then fished in his breast pocket to reclaim my money. The cleanest kill would be to block his airways. My coat hung over the back of the armchair. Bundled up, it could do the job, but I didn't want to get it dirty. Looking about the room, my eyes fell upon the only cushion resting on the sofa. It had a simple pattern of flowers in a wicker basket, which Cecilia had sewn when she was little. I can remember my mother and sister sitting by the chimney breast at their needlework. Mother sat beneath a plaid blanket beside the fire, even in summer. She would smile and praise Cecilia upon the completion of each flower, every one in a different colour thread.

I picked up the cushion and examined it. The threads had begun to unravel, and the colours were faded.

I knelt beside the man, placed the pillow firmly over his mouth and nose, and pressed down. He was motionless so I couldn't tell if it had any effect. After a tense minute, I eased back and looked beneath. He was no longer breathing. His chest had stilled and his lips hung slack. I curled my index finger and placed it beneath his nose for several seconds. There wasn't the slightest draught.

When he snorted inwards, I pulled my hand back as if I'd

71

triggered a mousetrap. His breathing resumed with a gentle snore.

I inspected the cushion with a frown. Was it working at all? I held the clean side against my own face and attempted to breathe in. Air did come through at first; it was scant and thick with dust. When I pressed harder, it was indeed possible to prevent breathing. The method was sound. I just needed to be patient.

To apply more force I shifted my knee to straddle the man's chest, then bore down on the cushion with all my weight. I could feel his nose and chin through the down. One of his arms was by his side and pinioned beneath my heel. The other still lay outstretched, pointing at the hearth.

Outside, the wind blew harder and rain rattled against the window frame. Gusts made the panelled doors creak. I continued to listen for any movement in the rooms above.

Suddenly, the man's head pulled to the right, and his free hand swiped at my face. He tried to wrench his other arm from beneath my leg, so I clamped against it with my thigh. I squeezed down harder. I couldn't understand why he wasn't dying. The pillow slipped down from his brow, and his wide, frantic eyes looked into mine. One was bloodshot, to the extent that the whole white had turned a deep crimson. His other arm was coming loose; my leg seized with cramp as I tried to keep it restrained. At one point he managed to thrust his knee into my side, and I became furious. I dropped my weight on to his chest, and I could feel his strength begin to ebb. He gave up trying to pull his arm free, and after another moment his entire body shuddered.

I counted to ten, then slid on to the floor and lay panting. The cushion remained balanced on his face.

I crawled to the chair and poured some wine. But I couldn't recall if that was the glass which he had used, so I drank from the bottle instead. I slouched with my head in the seat, the bottle in my lap, and I considered the body on my carpet.

The mechanics of corpse disposal was not something I had ever pondered. Of course, it couldn't remain hidden in the house. May had been particularly warm, so if I stashed it in some forgotten room it would soon make its presence known.

I held the bottle against the candlelight to see how much wine was left.

The closest exit was the front door. Even in the dead of night one couldn't lug a corpse into the street and hope to remain unseen. The rear entrance was via the basement, and it would have to be dragged there. But then what?

The only way I could personally carry the body from the property was in pieces: packages underarm to be dropped in the canal, and reassembled by the coroner in a grisly jigsaw. But the thought of dismembering it: cleaving and sawing, wide-eyed and grunting; the old iron tub in the scullery slick with viscera – I took another drink.

There was an old cart in the stables, and it could stay covered and hidden in there for at least a day or two before it became offensive. I'd find a horse from somewhere and haul it to the city limits, wrapped in a few coal sacks – apt shroud for the coal-porter. The stables also seemed like an attainable goal. In the small hours, I could take the body through the long back yard unnoticed.

The plan was set. I brought the candle into the hall to light the way. When I went back into the darkened parlour, it looked like some drunken friend had fallen asleep after a party. I gathered up his legs, one knee under each arm, and dragged him through the ground floor. I would feel backwards with my heel before taking a step, ensuring no collisions with furniture or skirting boards.

Once the body was far enough down the basement steps, I clambered up to shut the stairwell door. Then I had to pause and massage my sore shoulder. It was tempting simply to tip the corpse down the steps; only the fear of the noise it would make stopped me. In almost total darkness, I took up his legs once more and carefully drew him down. As the head cleared each lip, it fell with a dull knock to the step below, and I did my best to keep a steady rhythm.

When only halfway down, there came a noise from above: a soft, creaking footfall in the passages upstairs, which could only mean that Miss Joyce had heard some of the commotion and come to investigate. From my perspective, the faintest light appeared in the crack beneath the door above me. She was in the hallway. The glow from her candle crept up the doorjamb on each side to mark her approach.

What a scene awaited her if that door opened. I considered scrambling over the body to go up and cut her off, but it was too late for that. The light was now right against the door, and there was no other sound of movement. I expected her at any moment to appear: nightgown, candelabrum and horrified scream. Instead, the light wavered and began to dim. Miss Joyce retreated upstairs and I was left again in blackness.

I was worn out by the time I reached the basement. It had become clear that I couldn't drag the body to the coach house without some assistance. I heaved it into the kitchen, then went to get a cup of water from the basin. The only source of aid I could think of was Devereaux. He had told me more than once that he drank most evenings in the Black Bull on Ship Street. But could I trust him enough to confess a killing? Might he refuse to help, or even use this information against me?

A set of house keys hung from a hook on the dresser. I was about to step over the body to retrieve them, then changed my mind and walked around it.

I could rehearse what to say on the way there: that it was self-defence; that the whole prosecution might have unravelled if I'd failed to act. And my work for the Castle had to count for something. This had all come about because of the report I provided on Craddock's killers, and surely the Department would wish to protect its informant. The clock over the mantel said it was a little past ten. I left the man with the yellow cravat in the basement and locked the door to the stairs as quietly as possible. Out on the street, I savoured the cool air, looked up at the darkened windows of the house, and then went in search of help.

The hanging sign of the Black Bull creaked in Great Ship Street. Inside, thick yellow candles sat at the end of spokes in a wagon-wheel chandelier, and also in nooks along the wall. The pub was within sight of the side entrance to the Castle, so it was a haunt of treasurers and civil servants, off-duty officers from the barracks and the police constabulary. I scanned the room for Devereaux, looking out for his dark curls and chin-strap beard, but he wasn't on the ground floor. There was another lounge upstairs with about a dozen tables. In the far corner, Devereaux sat in conversation with another man over pitchers of ale and a plate of chops.

When he saw me standing in the doorway, Devereaux leaned back in his chair and raised a hand in greeting. The other man, who was big and thickset, remained hunched, not curious enough to look backwards. I made my way to their table, and told Devereaux I needed to speak with him in private, but he insisted I join them.

When I was seated he indicated his companion. 'This is Ned Holt.'

The man put down a chop, wiped lamb grease on his shirt and extended his hand. I gripped it, then resisted an urge to deploy a handkerchief. Holt was a haggard man in his forties. He had a scar near the edge of his mouth which caused muscles on that side of his lips to sag. His tongue would often extrude to lick at that flaccid corner.

Devereaux said, 'Ned provides us with information in the Castle from time to time. Just like you.' He leaned over the table towards Holt. 'John here has been of great help to Sibthorpe over the past two months. One conviction under his belt already. Should be another three when the Craddock trial is finished.'

The man looked at me closely for the first time, then resumed chewing a stringy piece of meat held between both hands.

'That's why I needed to speak with you, Devereaux,' I said. 'Alone, if possible.'

Devereaux said that I could trust Ned. We were all working for the same department, after all.

'Very well.' I lowered my voice and told him it was about those men who killed Craddock. 'One of their friends tracked me down and tried to blackmail me for the reward money.'

Devereaux said, 'How did he find you?'

I couldn't think of a plausible lie. 'I went to look at the trial and he recognized me in the courtroom.'

Devereaux frowned. 'I made arrangements just so you wouldn't have to go to court, to protect your anonymity for this very reason. If you were going anyway, we might as well have put you on the stand.'

Holt spoke for the first time. 'I've done that a couple of

times.' He was looking down at the metal platter, and the clear red juice that ran around its rim. 'When you know your evidence is going to convict someone, it's hard to stay away.'

'That may be. But what do you want us to do about it now, John? Warn the man to keep away; rough him up? The Castle can't be seen to get involved.'

I shook my head and said that wasn't necessary. 'I just need some help getting rid of the body.'

Holt's noisy chewing slowed and came to a halt. Devereaux glanced at the tables close by to see if anyone could overhear. 'When?'

There was a clock on the wall behind him but it was stopped. 'About an hour ago.'

And where was he?

'In my kitchen.'

Holt made a noise as if he was tutting, and I looked to see if he disapproved. But he drew back his lips and picked out a piece of gristle that was stuck between his teeth. He examined the morsel for a moment, then scraped it against the edge of his plate.

I leaned my elbows on the table, but the surface was sticky, so I put them on my knees instead. 'I realize it's a great imposition, Devereaux—'

'Do you?'

'But I'm not sure where else I can turn.'

He sat up in his chair, folded his arms and hunched his shoulders, as if he'd been caught in a draught. He gazed out of the window for a few moments at the lights in the Ship Street barracks. 'What do you think, Ned?'

'I think I'm in the middle of supper.'

'Sibthorpe would probably want us to help the new recruit.'

'Sometimes it's hard to predict what Tom wants.'

'Even so.'

Devereaux had already finished his drink – white froth clung to the sides of his glass. But when a passing lounge-boy asked if he wanted another, he sent him away, which I took to be a good sign. Devereaux glanced again at Holt, who gave him a slight nod, and then leaned back towards me.

'We'll help of course, John,' he said. But first they needed to know more about the dead man – such as where he was from, and who else knew he had come to my house. Holt asked me what I had used to kill him.

'A cushion.' Their faces regarded me in the candlelight. 'Well, I hit him on the head with a poker first, but then I had to smother him.'

'So he's not cut at all.' He looked at Devereaux with a raised brow. 'York Street?'

Devereaux mulled this over. He asked Holt if he could find a horse and cart at this time of night.

I said there was a cart in my stable if needed. My notion was to bring the body into the countryside and tip it into a ditch.

Holt said he already had a cart. 'What about the form?'

Devereaux said, 'I might have a few spare copies in my desk.'

Holt's smile was crooked; I imagine it would have been even without his defect. 'All right. I'll have a cart in Lad Lane in two hours. Will you be ready then?'

'Undoubtedly,' Devereaux said. 'Are you right, John?'

We left the pub and Holt strode off towards Great Longford Street. Devereaux instructed me to wait in Ship Street while he entered the Castle to retrieve some items. He walked past two guards, who stood aside at his approach.

I lingered in the shadows beyond a street lamp. A spider web spanned its crook, with drops that hung suspended like glass beads. Devereaux soon emerged with a full shoulder bag, like those carried by sailors, and we took a cab back to Fitzwilliam Street.

It was past midnight. There were no lights in any window of the house, and only a few in the street as a whole. I asked Devereaux to go quietly lest we wake the housekeeper, turned the key with care and brought him into the pitch-dark hall. He fumbled in a pocket, withdrew a lucifer match and struck it against the doorframe. A bright spot hissed and engulfed the match-head, and I pointed towards a candlestick on the sideboard.

As I led the way down to the kitchen, I had a dreadful fear that the body would be missing; that the man had stirred and risen, and was hidden around each corner, seething and implacable. But he was as I left him: on his back in the centre of the flagstones, arms outstretched from how he was dragged.

Devereaux regarded him from over my shoulder. 'How long did you say he's been dead?'

It was about two hours.

'Then close over those arms before he starts to stiffen.'

I stood over the body and kicked the arms back in to their sides. Devereaux bent low and brought the candle over the man's face. He noted the lump on the top of his head, and the fluid smeared around his nose and mouth, sweeping the candle over the length of the body, like it was part of some ritual.

'Still,' he said, as if we had been in dialogue, 'we'll have to make some account for his injuries.'

He brought his bag to the kitchen table. First he pulled out a folded sack and length of rope, which he tossed beside the corpse. Then a pen, inkpot and a printed form.

'First things first. What would you like to call him?'

'Surely his real name will be easy enough to verify.'

Devereaux considered the man's face. 'He looks like a Kenny

to me.' He wrote on the sheet. 'And we'll say John in honour of he who wielded the pillow.'

I stepped behind him to observe the form on which he wrote. It was a death certificate from the South Dublin Union Workhouse.

Devereaux was busy inventing an age and place of origin for the man. He paused over the section marked, 'Cause of death'. In most cases there would be one word: 'Typhoid' or 'Scarlatina'.

He tapped the pen against his chin. 'We could say his head was bumped by a passing cart and he drowned in a deep puddle.' He spotted the large wooden basin of dishwater beside the hearth. 'We'll dunk his head in there for half an hour, make it a bit more realistic.'

I pictured the corpse on its knees, bent over the basin with its head submerged, as if afflicted by a terrible thirst.

But Devereaux was reconsidering. 'Though there'd have to be water in the lungs . . .'

'Maybe he was just smothered in the mud instead.'

Devereaux nodded, 'That'll do,' and began to write.

The man was relatively clean. I went into the yard and took a handful of sludge from beneath a drainpipe, brought it back and pressed it into his face. The cold wet muck went between his teeth and tongue and up his nostrils. I rubbed it through the coarse bristles on his chin. The flesh around his cheekbones had already become rigid.

Devereaux commended my good thinking. I asked should I smear some on the man's clothes, but he said that wasn't necessary as we were going to strip him.

Devereaux completed the form and added a signature at the bottom, completely illegible, but not lacking in flourish. He put it aside for the ink to dry.

'Let's get him in the sack.'

In the candlelight we began to remove the unwashed clothes, solemnly, as if we prepared the body of a fallen brother. As each item was taken off, Devereaux put it in his shoulder bag. Finally, I tried to untie the yellow cravat, but the knot was too tight. I took a knife from the counter, slipped the cold blade against his throat and sawed through the cloth.

When he lay there cold and naked, the man seemed so diminished; only hours before he had towered above me in the parlour upstairs. The hempen sack was unfurled. It slipped easily over his bent toes and legs, but we had to be more forceful to drag it over his torso as he lay, a dead weight. Devereaux tied the sack off with the rope and sat back. He took out a pocket watch. 'Holt will be another half-hour,' he said, looking around the kitchen. 'Open up a bottle of something.'

I poured two glasses of whiskey and we sat at the kitchen table, with the sack at our feet, as if we attended a wake. We spoke of small things. I recall Devereaux described the plot of some play he had recently seen, one of Sheridan's, though I'm not sure how the subject arose. We finished the drinks, and he checked his watch again. 'Ned must be here by now.'

We carried the body between us through the back garden. I removed the padlock on the gate and looked out into Lad Lane. A horse and cart was parked about ten houses up. Holt edged the cart forwards in a slow rattle, and the three of us lifted the body aboard.

Devereaux said, 'I'll ride in front with Ned. You get in the back.' He caught his breath. 'Make sure it doesn't fall out.'

There was no danger of it falling, for we rolled on to Baggot Street and along the north side of Stephen's Green sedately. Despite the hour, shadowy figures walked along the footpaths. We skirted the enclosed park, tall houses and grand public buildings, then turned right into York Street. Holt reined in the horse beside a high wooden gate.

Devereaux jumped down and rapped on a wicket door, then listened for the approach of a porter. From the bed of the cart, I could see the small doorway open and a man peering out. He looked at Devereaux, then over his shoulder at the cart and its load. Not a word was spoken. The porter moved out of sight in order to unlock the main gate, and held it open as Holt drove in.

We entered a small yard surrounded by outbuildings. A dim light glowed in the window of the porter's shed. The man fetched his lamp, then came up to Devereaux. 'Do you have the form at least?'

Devereaux reached into his coat and pulled out the death certificate with a grin. 'Of course. But be careful not to smudge the ink.'

He then called for me to help the man take the body inside. Devereaux led us into the building with the lamp, past a sign that said 'Service Entrance'. He seemed to know his way. We went down a staircase into a long corridor with a yellow-tiled floor. Moonlight slanted in from high barred windows set at ground level. There was a long trolley beside the stairwell, and we lugged the body aboard. One arm was cocked at an odd angle, which caused the sack to bulge. The porter beat the stiff limb down with a balled fist.

'Now,' he said, wheezing. 'Number three, I think.'

He pushed the trolley forward as if taking the corpse for a stroll. We entered a room already lit by an oil-lamp. Part of it was closed off by a full-length grey curtain. An odour of carbolic soap hung in the air. There was a large table of polished metal placed against one wall, and a naked body lay on its smooth, cold surface. I tried not to look as we lifted the sack on to the table to lie beside the dead woman. Her limbs were as thin as a child's, and gaunt joints protruded. She had light brown hair gathered over one shoulder. There was a crust on her lips, raw and peeling, and one eyelid was ajar, enough to reflect a glint of lamplight.

The porter said he had to change the ledger to account for the extra body, and he left Devereaux and me in the room. Devereaux picked up a small cardboard tag tied to the woman's toe with looped twine, and bent down to read.

After a second he said, 'Why do doctors always write in such a scrawl?'

He let the tag drop against her sole. It was cold in the room, colder than the night air above, and I asked could we leave. Devereaux had gone to the edge of the curtain and peeked inside. He puffed out his cheeks. 'Come and have a look.'

I said I didn't want to. So he pushed the curtain back. The rings moving over the metal rail sounded like a sword unsheathing.

There was another body left on the ground on a wide stretcher, a man who had died relatively young. His abdomen opened just above the pelvis, cleft all the way to the throat. Folds of skin and muscle were rolled back on either side to reveal a dark cavity. The man's ribs extruded above his chest, splayed and clipped, and one of the lungs had been removed. My eyes lingered. I would not have imagined a person could be so undone. I looked around the room, half expecting to see the missing lung on a shelf, squashed into a glass jar.

Outside in the hallway, there were hurried steps and raised voices. One was the porter, but the other spoke with educated tones and sounded displeased. Devereaux looked towards the door, then motioned for me to come and stand with him behind the curtain. He closed it over so we were hidden, and held his hand against the fabric to stop its sway.

The door opened and two men entered. The man in charge was speaking. 'There's a routine. We take in cadavers at seven in the morning. They can't just deposit them in the middle of the night.'

Devereaux held his finger to his lips. An odour wafted from the hollow of the dead man's chest, like the inside of a tannery.

The porter's voice sounded nervous. He said the form was correct, and he had been reluctant to turn the body away. 'You know yourself, sir, these days in the poorhouse, there's no room left in the morgue.'

'That's not our problem.' I could hear the sack jostle as the rope was untied, then a long moment of silence. The surgeon may have been impressed with the quality of the specimen for he said, 'I have a demonstration on Friday at midday. Bring this new one to me at the Benson Theatre.'

The porter readily agreed and said he would make the arrangements. As they left the room the dissectionist said he would be writing to the governor of St James's to make a complaint. Devereaux and I waited for their steps to recede before we slipped out.

When we emerged in the courtyard, I breathed in the night air despite the smell of refuse coming from an outbuilding. Holt stood by the cart. 'What kept you?'

Devereaux spat into the dirt. 'The smell in that room. I need a drink. We can leave the cart here.'

Holt nodded.

'What about you, Delahunt?'

I did want a drink but it was two hours past midnight. Devereaux said he knew a place.

He led the way through sloping cobbled streets, still slick from the evening showers, and regaled Holt with an account of our skulking behind the curtain. Digges Lane was dark except for a few street lamps, showing a butcher's shop with shuttered windows, the locked yard of a sign-maker and a terrace of ordinary two-storey houses. Devereaux opened the railing gate of one and took the steps down towards the basement. A hatch in the door slid open and a voice said, 'Let's see your face.'

Devereaux swept off his hat, then turned his head to show his profile in the dim street light.

There was muttering behind the hatch, but the door opened to allow us entry. We passed through a dingy hallway with broken mosaic in the floor. Beyond another door there was a large room – the basements of two houses knocked through. The whitewashed bricks turned yellow, then brown where they vaulted in the ceiling. Shelves containing empty glasses and various liquor bottles were mounted behind a plain counter.

There was a jumble of furniture, as if patrons had brought whatever seats they happened to own. In one corner, a round tabletop was nailed to a beer keg, and empty crates were the stools. But next to it lay a chaise longue, shabby and frayed. Some men sat with drinks around an oak writing desk with the drawers removed. Elsewhere a man sat in a leather armchair, like those seen in a club; his companion made do with the seat from a barber's shop. The clientele spoke under a pall of smoke, and I looked around at their colourless faces in the shadows, their lank hair, and pale, slender fingers resting on glass rims.

Devereaux pointed to some empty chairs. He went to the bar while Holt and I sat down. In the darkened corner behind us, a man lay awkwardly atop a woman. Her arms were around his neck, but she was otherwise motionless, and his hand disappeared beneath her petticoats. Devereaux arrived with a half-bottle of whiskey and three tumblers. He noticed the couple, went over and kicked the man on the sole of his boot.

'Take her to the back room.'

The man looked back, flushed and glaring. But perhaps he recognized Devereaux, for he rose without comment, and pulled the girl to her feet. She was pretty, with unfocused eyes and an unsteady step. Devereaux put the whiskey bottle down and stopped the couple as they passed. He took hold of the girl's face with a thumb and forefinger beneath her jaw, and tilted her head this way and that. When he let go, her chin sank into her chest, and a white thumbprint was left on her sallow skin. Devereaux smoothed a ruffled collar on the girl's blouse by rubbing along her collarbone three times.

He said, 'Let me know when you're done with her,' before pointing to the man in warning. 'And you better not leave any marks.'

The girl lifted her gaze, catching my eye for a second, before the man jerked on her arm to lead her away.

Holt poured three drinks as Devereaux took his seat, saying, 'You always did like to work on a blank canvas.'

A corner of Devereaux's mouth curled up, but he didn't reply. Instead, he raised his glass in a quiet toast, saying, 'To Delahunt's corpse. May he prove a great boon to medical research.'

I smiled as the glasses clinked. The amber liquid scorched my throat and I could already feel the twinge of a headache. Holt drained his glass in one gulp, then licked at his drooping lip.

After a few sips, I asked if the surgeon who had come in at the end might cause problems, but Devereaux shook his head. 'He'll forget about it in the morning. The dissectionists have few qualms about how they get their cadavers.' Holt had picked up the bottle to pour himself another.

'Anyway,' Devereaux said, 'if he does cause a fuss, Sibthorpe will have a word.' He leaned towards me. 'There's a fellow in here who could tell you all about the surgeons.' He indicated a man at the corner of the bar. 'That's Malachi Phelan. A resurrectionist.'

I looked to where he pointed. 'I don't understand.'

'He's a grave-robber. The surgeons are his best customers.'

The unassuming man had black receding hair and bulbous eyes, which gave the unsettling impression that he could see in the dark.

'Malachi can mine a grave in a couple of hours. Then leave it neat and pristine, looking for all the world as if it's untouched. Some people are still visiting gravesides today containing nothing but earth-filled coffins, thanks to Malachi.'

'Why doesn't the Castle stop him?'

He shrugged. 'The surgeons have to master their profession somehow. Better than practising on the living.'

It had been a year since I'd visited my mother's grave. I went with Cecilia just before she was married. To think the earth might have subsided as we put down the flowers – caved in on the void. I poured myself another drink. 'How does he get them?'

A simple shaft sunk to meet one end of the coffin. A hole cut in the lid and the body exhumed by hooks in the scalp or feet, depending on how it lay. The earth returned, and a fresh sod placed on top to conceal the disturbance.

Devereaux said it used to be a thriving trade. Every surgeon at work today had to deal with the body-snatchers when they were students, as the college would only allow them to work on cadavers they obtained themselves. He had heard of young educated men dressed in mourning clothes, walking into morgues, trying to dupe staff that they had come to retrieve a beloved family member. Or two students hailing a hansom cab to transport a cadaver from the house of a resurrectionist to the college, propped upright between them on the seat. On the way, the cabman halted outside a police station and said the fare had increased from two shillings to two guineas, and if they felt that was unfair, they could get out immediately. Or the student in the dissecting room who pulled back the sheet to reveal a favourite niece he had helped bury the previous week.

Helen's father had been a surgical student in Mercer's Hospital. I said, 'But now they get them from the poorhouses?'

'Well, that's the idea. But there's never enough to meet demand. And the college still has to shop around if it wants a body of a particular age or condition. They love pregnant women, for instance. They'll always pay extra.'

Holt was on his third glass. He recalled a woman died in Pill Lane a few years previous, who was six months gone with twins. Her funeral had been in St Michan's Church. 'Some of the mourners had brought their shovels.'

Devereaux chuckled in his glass, but then his smile faded. He said there was no doubt it was Malachi who took her in the end.

I looked again at the man by the counter. He held his glass on the bar in both hands, and looked over it into the middle distance. Perhaps he was forever haunted by images of his quarry. 'Were the twins dissected?'

Devereaux frowned. 'How would I know?'

I imagined the woman on the anatomist's table. The mother taken from the earth, and the innocents taken from the womb, their birth perfectly still. Maybe the tiny siblings still clung to each other, suspended in a jar of spirits, buried in a jumble of shelves. Surrounded in darkness on every side by the pickled organs of murderers and paupers.

'It's a bad business.'

'True, but it has its uses.'

'Like what?'

'Yours is not the first body we've deposited with the surgeons.' His glass was halfway to his mouth. 'And I doubt it'll be the last.'

The conversation entered a lull, and Devereaux looked over his shoulder at the doorway through which the girl had been taken. I felt drained. I had drunk a lot over the course of the night without eating, and I felt queasy. I thanked both men for their aid, and told them I wouldn't forget it. Holt said men in our profession had to look out for each other. His chin slumped forward to nod farewell. Devereaux offered his hand. As I shook it, he said he would be in touch. Then he rose as well and went towards the back room, leaving Holt with the last of the whiskey.

I left the establishment, wandered the narrow streets for a few minutes, lost, then emerged into South King Street and back on to the Green. I stretched my sore arm. It wouldn't lift above the height of my shoulder, and there was an unpleasant sensation that it didn't sit snug in its socket. But ultimately I felt relief. I was free of pursuit, and free of responsibility. Back home, I tidied up the parlour and the kitchen. I placed the poker back in its stand with a clink, and took the stained cushion up to my room. By the time I climbed into bed, the first light of a new day was filtering through, taking the edge off the darkness.

4

Sleep is wasteful, and its absence from the last few days pro-
vokes odd thoughts and waking dreams. Throughout the night
I lie quite still, and fix upon the semi-circle window high in the
cell. In the pre-dawn, its contour emerges from the black as
the barest light shows through the thick, scratched glass and
metal grille. At that hour I get up, keeping the thin blanket
around my shoulders, though the weather has mercifully
become warmer. Not quite the clemency I require. These are
the pangs I feel most keenly, the thought of walking in a walled
garden on a warm day, free of labour's demands and dark
thoughts, and with no risks to run. Actually, I struggle to think
of a time I experienced that.

Each morning, I retrieve the manuscript from beneath my
mattress and take it to the desk, then light a candle from
my dwindling supply. I'll have to inveigle more from the cleric,
on the pretence of nocturnal Bible study. I flipped through the
pages this morning, but I won't read over what's written, unless
I manage to complete it in time.

The routine continues when Turner brings me in a bowl of
oatmeal along with the post. I've received two or three letters a
day since my trial began. By the time they reach me the seals
are broken, the pages have been unfolded, and all metal clips

and pins are removed. My correspondents can be divided into three categories. The first implore me to turn with a contrite soul towards God and seek the extension of His grace; they counsel that salvation is still possible. The second assure me that God relishes the prospect of my punishment, and they pray for my perpetual torment. I find each category equally amusing as I read them flattened on the desk beneath my breakfast bowl.

The third class of letters are from people who wonder why I did it. Some are doctors who specialize in mental disorders, and they ask me to describe the symptoms of monomania that took hold of me. One such letter was among the latest batch, from a Dr Whitley, whose questions were not couched in flattering terms: 'Is your mental condition so wretchedly low, or so extensively muddled, as to render it totally unconscious that you were acting wrongfully in giving loose even to the wildest gratifications of your animal propensities?' I appreciated his letter though. It was particularly longwinded and he only used one side of the stationery. I'll be able to use the blank pages for my statement.

Another letter came from a Montfort Sweetman. I knew what that was about so I set it aside for later. The missive at the bottom of the pile was written by my sister Cecilia. She began as she did in every letter: 'My dearest John, I hope you're well.'

She was sorry to intrude on my unhappy state with more sad tidings, but she thought I would wish to know. Word had come from the office of the Secretary for War to say that Alex had been killed in a skirmish outside Kabul.

I paused and looked into the candle flame.

They had described the manner of his death. Alex's commanding officer had become stranded between enemy lines when he fell beneath a lame horse. My brother took it upon himself to lead his own mount into no-man's-land. He lifted the injured officer on to the saddle and began walking back to the British side, but was struck in the back of the head by a jezail bullet and died at once. His body was later retrieved and buried with full honours. The officer survived.

I wondered if Cecilia wrote to Alex about my conviction before his death. Even if she didn't, my trial was mentioned in *The Times of London,* and I knew editions were sent out to regiments in the field, though they took weeks to arrive. I pictured him in a dust-blown tent, being handed the paper by some companion, who'd point to the article and say, 'Don't you have a brother called John?'

On a happier note, Cecilia was with child. She had asked Captain Dickenson if she could name the baby Alexander if it was a boy, and he had said he would consider it.

She ended by saying she prayed for me every night. 'I shall always remember the kindness you showed me, and the gentle side of your nature. In your final hours I hope you find peace. I am, yours ever, Cecilia.'

Our old nursery in Fitzwilliam Street was up four sheer flights, and consisted of two small bedrooms with low ceilings and tall windows. When we were young, Cecilia and I would often lean on a sill and observe the street life below: carriages skittering on an icy road, or barefoot children chasing a dog, or a rag-and-bone man pushing his barrow. I remember once she nudged me and pointed at a figure walking from the direction of Fitzwilliam Square. He wore the clothes and grime of a tradesman, but he carried what looked like a bird-cage in the crook of his arm, and another slung on his back. Inside, several black, sleek forms scrambled and writhed. A short-legged terrier followed behind his master, the rat-catcher, though the dog probably had better claim to that title. Secure in our room, we watched the sinister figure pass below and out of sight, then resumed our idle vigil. Foreheads pressed against cold panes; foggy breaths obscuring the view.

I shared a room with Alex, our sparse belongings separated by an imagined boundary between his portion of the room and mine. His was larger to reflect his age; an arrangement I never thought unfair. Cecilia slept in the room next door with a parlourmaid named Ruth, who also acted as nanny. She was a Catholic girl from Wicklow, who seemed very grown up when I was little, but was probably still in her teens. Cecilia considered her a great friend, and Ruth was a playful, lively spirit in the house. She would often hide behind a curtain and pounce on Cecilia as she entered a room, resulting in shrieks and loud laughter.

Our bedroom was near the top of a deep stairwell, from which one could peer down vertically past each flight to the flagstones in the hallway below. Tall handrails meant there was no real danger, but Alex liked to slide down the top banister. I was anxious every time I watched him do so. He would grab the rail and haul himself up, so he sat as if riding side-saddle, his back to the void. It only took a moment for him to sweep down the railing, briefly become airborne and hit the landing with a few thumping steps. He never so much as stumbled. I always feared he would lean back too far while gliding down, and he mocked my unwillingness to try it myself.

Cecilia told Ruth what he was doing, and she in turn informed my father. Information, it seems, must always work up through a chain. Fearing that Alex would suffer a catastrophic fall, he had a stout net fixed in the gulf between the second and third floors. It was a blue cargo net, secured by hooks in the wood of the stairwell, and visitors to the house would often wonder at its presence.

Of course, I was the first to be enmeshed. Encouraged by the safety net, I attempted to copy my brother's trick one afternoon while alone. For the first few attempts I leaned too far forwards, wary of the chasm behind, and slithered off the banister after a few feet. On my third try I over-compensated.

The fall was so brief I can't recall the sensation. One of my fingers caught in a loop, and was pulled from its joint. The small knots in the rope scraped and burned my face, and the hooks in the stairwell bent. I came to rest face down, my view unimpeded to the stone floor another two flights below. I was scared to move lest the net gave way.

The noise of the impact alerted the household. My father rushed to the banister and gripped the rail with both hands, then bent over it, stretching as far as he could to reach me in the distended cords, as if he was a fisherman that had pulled a child from the deep.

About a month after that, in the weeks before Christmas, Cecilia and I became unwell. We were weak and feverish, and our mother put us to bed early. The following morning, an unpleasant sensation made me lift my bedclothes to reveal a rash of red spots arcing along my side and down the length of my arm. I ran to the room of my parents, woke my mother and showed her the hives.

As would be the case in any household, consternation ensued. I was carried back to bed. My parents examined Cecilia and Alex for similar symptoms. Spots were discovered on Cecilia's back; Alex escaped the contagion. They took his bed down to the parlour, and he remained there for the duration of the outbreak. My father was adamant that his children would not be sent to the infectious wards, and we were treated in our nursery.

Throughout the day our conditions worsened and we were truly wretched. What I recall most was the agony in my throat. It was so raw and sensitive, the slightest gulp was excruciating, as if I swallowed a thistle. Dr Moore arrived, and examined us both beneath the light of several candles, which hurt my sensitive vision. He noted that Cecilia's eyes were bloodshot, so he applied two leeches, one on each temple, to effect relief. He spoke in low tones to my parents while still in the room.

'They have both contracted scarlet fever,' he said, standing before my father. 'I must recommend that your wife be sent from the house in these circumstances.'

Dr Moore knew that my mother had suffered from respiratory problems throughout her life. But I was pleased when she told the doctor, there and then, that nothing would prevent her from caring for her children.

The doctor implored my father to exert his marital authority, and induce his wife to leave the house. My father looked into her resolute face, then curtly told Dr Moore that she would not be leaving, and that the doctor should instead concentrate on his ministrations. The astute physician bowed his head.

Our mother sat with us night and day and gave herself no rest. She bathed our inflamed skin in warm vinegar, an old remedy, and I can still recall the acrid smell. She administered various draughts, and spoon-fed us thin, tepid broth. It was always torture to swallow any liquid, and it rarely stayed down for long. Mostly she remained to provide comfort, stroking our feverish foreheads and softly singing.

One evening, she sat on the edge of my bed to hug me good-night. I put my hands around her neck, and could feel a patch of bumpy, roughened skin beside her ear.

I pulled my face back and said, 'Mama?'

She kept her eyes on mine as she felt beneath her hair, gently moving my hand aside.

She smiled and said, 'Don't worry, I'll be fine.' Then she kissed my forehead and leaned me back on the pillow. I watched her silhouette as she took the candle to the door. Before she disappeared from view, she brought her hand up to her neck once more.

Her death affected my father deeply. He hung over her body for hours, anguished at her loss, and full of remorse for ignoring the counsel of his physician. His spirit never fully recovered. In the community, at first, he was treated with much sympathy and condolence. But soon he began to neglect his professional duties. He had never been a teetotaller, but now, more often than not, he would finish a wine bottle after dinner. The interest he took in the lives of his children waned, and he became an irritable figure ensconced in his study or chamber, best unprovoked.

An unhappy year passed. Then one morning, Cecilia whispered to me that during the night our father had entered the room she shared with Ruth. He had climbed into Ruth's bed and remained for an hour. I looked at Cecilia to see if she understood what had occurred. The thought of him creeping through the house dismayed me. The situation only worsened when Ruth was given her own room downstairs. I lay awake at night and cringed at every creak on the floorboards, or click of a latch.

A few months later, all changed again. Ruth left the household. My father was absent on the day we saw her off. I recall her clinging to Cecilia in farewell, a kiss on the cheek for myself and Alex, her overcoat and hat, and her small brass-bound trunk sitting on the steps. At the time, I was relieved she was going. But from then on, the house was bereft of any kindly spirit. Our upbringing was placed in the hands of old, forbidding housekeepers.

The trial of Captain Craddock's killers concluded with a guilty verdict, and the three men were sent to Van Diemen's Land. In the days following my run-in with the man with the yellow cravat, I checked the newspapers, but there was no article dealing with a missing coal-porter. Either his absence had gone unreported, or it wasn't deemed newsworthy.

I kept to myself for the best part of a week, staying in the house as much as possible. One morning, I took the opportunity to speak with my father about Helen. While climbing the stairs to his room, I saw one of the hooks still bent in the wood of the stairwell, after all those years, the white paint surrounding it cracked and discoloured. The cargo net had long gone.

Miss Joyce had left the house on an errand. I knocked on my father's chamber, and he faintly called for me to enter. Only one shutter was open, but enough afternoon sunshine came through to make the room bright. A fire smouldered in the hearth despite the balmy day. Used bedclothes covered a writing desk in the corner, and beside that, a large terrestrial globe sat squat in its ornately carved stand.

My father lay in his marital bed, propped on several pillows, with folded sheets up to his chest. He suffered from a wasting in his bones, which meant the blood vessels in his skeletal frame were closing off, and he was tormented by arthritic pains throughout his body. Since he had been bedridden for more than a year, he was beset with other complaints: bed sores and rashes, inanition and muscular atrophy. He had never been a powerful man, but now he looked frail and wearied, with silver-yellow hair and an unkempt beard. He seemed to be much advanced in years, but he hadn't yet turned sixty.

It was rare enough for me to enter, and concern showed in his face.

'News of Alex?'

Alex had received his commission in the East Kent Regiment the year before. They had been deployed to Afghanistan, to bolster a British force intended to slow the advance of the Russians towards north India, and he'd already sent a couple of letters home describing the alien terrain and desert wastes. The boy who had been inspired by tales of Wellington and Napoleon couldn't possibly have imagined the geography or politics of that conflict.

I shook my head. 'There's been no word since his last letter.'

A bedside locker contained a row of carefully labelled phials. I picked one up, shook the clear liquid, and read the tag, which said, 'Tincture of Youthwort, one to one hundred thousand, ten drops twice a day'. I eyed my father over the watery tonic.

'Has the new treatment proved effective?'

'Please return that to the table. Miss Joyce has them arranged in a particular order.'

I replaced the bottle and pulled a chair to his bedside. He leaned over and ensured the phial was in line with the others.

We sat in silence for a while. Motes descended in the slanting sunlight, falling on the hearth and mantelpiece, and a framed watercolour on the wall above, which had been painted by my mother in her youth. It showed the steeple of a church and haystacks in an adjacent field – a scene from her native Antrim. The last I had seen of her was in that room eight years before: strands of dark hair on her wet face; an angry rash on her neck; a bloody handkerchief; the chamber pot beneath her side of the bed brimming with bile. She smiled at me weakly, and told me I must mind my sister. Then pain crossed her face and she lifted the rag to her mouth. She waved at Ruth to take me from the room, to the sound of her grating coughs.

The front door opened below, heralding the return of Miss Joyce. It was time to broach the subject that had brought me here.

'How much money do you have?'

He looked over at me, incredulous.

'You'll be glad to know that I've decided to take more interest in my prospects after college.' I said I planned to speak with Mr Stokes about the possibility of marrying his daughter, Helen. To do so, I would require a full understanding of our financial position.

He smoothed the bedclothes around his chest. 'Stokes of Merrion Square?'

'The very same.'

'Why would he allow his daughter to marry you?'

'Because she will tell him that she loves me.'

He laughed, and I was gratified that it resulted in a sharp wince.

'The consent of Mr Stokes isn't your concern. What I want to know is what will become of the house?'

He closed his eyes and leaned his head back. He said that when he was finally relieved of the burden of life, the contents of his will would be known.

'What does that mean?'

There was a knock on the door. Miss Joyce called in, 'Mr Delahunt, it's time to take your tincture of gypsum.'

'Who will get the house?'

The housekeeper bustled into the room carrying a tray, but stopped when she saw me at the bedside. She looked at my father. 'Should I come back in a little while?'

He waved for her to come forward. 'There's no need,' he said. 'John was just leaving.'

Helen went to her father and told him she had chosen a husband. At the same time, I wrote Mr Stokes a letter requesting to meet in order to ask for the hand of his daughter. A response arrived by return in Fitzwilliam Street, saying he, his wife and daughter would meet with me in my home the following evening to discuss the proposed marriage.

This encouraging missive was more than I expected, and I set about making the house more presentable for the prospective in-laws. Room by room I removed dust sheets, arranged furniture, scrubbed floors and straightened pictures. It began to look like the house I remembered as a child. Every shutter and window was opened to admit an airy light. I stood on chairs with a broom to remove cobwebs from the plasterwork in the ceilings. I dragged rugs into the yard and draped them over a beam in an outhouse. The trusty poker was used to beat out a decade's worth of grime, and I marvelled at the swirling clouds of dust that emanated.

I told Miss Joyce of the impending visit, and she helped in the spring-clean, perhaps in the mistaken belief that it would prolong her employment. She scoured the range in the kitchen, removing the build-up of brown grease to expose the original iron surrounding the stoves. I put sheets on all the beds, cleaned out the hearths and hid bric-a-brac away in chests and trunks. In the drawing room, I removed the empty wine bottles corked with knotted wax candles, and placed my college texts in the bookcase. Miss Joyce informed my father that the Stokes family were coming to visit, and for what purpose. A few hours before their arrival, I saw her ascend the stairs towards his chamber with his razor, brush and basin.

Helen's father was a lean man with a wide gait and slender fingers. His clean-shaven face was lengthened by receding hair at the temples, otherwise brushed forward in a youthful style, and only just beginning to grey. His wife had not aged so gracefully, and she appeared to be several years his senior. Mrs Stokes hailed from Edinburgh, and, despite her best efforts, could not conceal her accent.

When I opened the door, Mr Stokes immediately smiled and extended his hand, which put me at ease. Helen and her mother stood behind on the top step, and I was momentarily disconcerted by their resemblance. It was odd to grip Helen's fingertips to welcome her formally, and she seemed timid in the presence of her parents. Miss Joyce hovered to collect coats. I asked her to bring up some tea, then invited the guests up to the drawing room.

As we climbed the stairs, Mr Stokes asked after my father, and I said he was as well as could be expected.

'I'm glad. I'll call up to his room later, if he's able for visitors.'

We turned on the first-floor return and continued upwards.

He leaned towards me. 'You know, when you were young, Catherine and I visited here once or twice for dinner parties.' He looked around as if certain features would trigger memories. 'Before your mother died.'

'Yes, I remember.'

Before we entered the drawing room, he stopped and pointed further up into the stairwell. 'Unless I'm mistaken,' he said, 'there used to be a net spanning those banisters.'

The fire was already lit, adding to the soft light of oil-lamps and candles reflecting in the chandelier. Helen and her mother sat on a sofa facing the mantel. Mr Stokes and I took the arm-chairs on either side. Miss Joyce entered and placed a tray on a sideboard, and we all sat silently as she served the tea. She had only been able to muster three cups of the same design; I received the odd one out.

It struck me that I should be leading the conversation, so I asked after Arthur, directing the question towards Mrs Stokes. She offered some platitudes about his health and studies. Mr Stokes said that Arthur had taken it into his head to become a field-surgeon. He was planning to complete a course in York Street in the next term, and then attach himself to a regiment.

This allowed me to bring up Alexander's deployment, and they both showed concern for his well-being. Mrs Stokes seemed to recall my brother fondly. 'Now, he was a fine boy,' she said.

The conversation continued in a relaxed fashion. Even Helen began to join in – her observations would usually elicit a smile from her father. But the purpose of the meeting could not be put off, or at least Mr Stokes could no longer ignore the pointed looks from his wife. He placed his cup on the armrest and leaned forward.

'Perhaps we could speak in private, John.'

I glanced at Helen, whose eyes were downcast.

'Of course,' I said, and led him across the hall to the study.

We sat either side of the desk with the lamp between us. His face stood out against the looming shadows of the room behind, and for a moment he looked at me without speaking. He retrieved a pipe and small tin of tobacco from inside his jacket, then crumbled some leaves into the chamber.

'My wife expects me to refuse your proposal.' He packed in the tobacco with his thumb. 'And in reality, I probably should.'

He said mine was only one of three requests for Helen's hand, and the others promised far more financial security: the Reverend Blacker of Malahide, and Lieutenant May of Merrion Street.

Stokes struck a match, and after a few intakes his head was wreathed in smoke. I took a heavy glass ashtray from a drawer and slid it across the desktop, just as he shook the match out. He threw it in, then swept loose tobacco leaves from the table into a cupped hand, and disposed of them as well.

'But there are other things I have to consider.' It was obvious to anyone who knew her that Helen had been happier in the previous few months than she'd been for years. It was as if a weight had lifted from her, and he could see flashes of a spirit he had last seen when she was just a girl. 'It's not hard to deduce that you are the cause.'

He looked around the room. 'Helen told me you stand to inherit this house. It needs some work, but there's no reason it can't be made into a happy family home, as it was once before.' He returned his attention to me. 'If you attain your degree, you'll find employment to suit your talents. Your income will be modest enough, but Helen will never want for money.'

Then he laid aside his pipe. 'There is one consideration that sways my decision most of all.' Arthur had told him every particular of his brush with the law during the spring. Mr Stokes knew it had been in my power to identify his son as the assailant of the police officer during the scuffle with O'Neill. He said I had shown uncommon character, not to mention loyalty towards his son, by maintaining silence throughout the police investigation, and again in the witness box. 'You saved my family a great deal of humiliation and I have not forgotten. What's more, you have never since mentioned the affair.' The corners of his lips were downturned in solemn approval. 'Even now, when you have sought my favour.'

He nodded. His daughter would be well served by such integrity. But he warned his wife could not know of this. As far as she knew, Arthur was innocent, and he wished for that impression to remain. He gave a rueful smile. 'She will oppose this match, but I'm sure you'll win her over.' Details would have to be ironed out with some trips to the solicitors, but that would be a formality. He replaced the stem of the pipe in his mouth. 'Mr Delahunt, you may ask me for my consent.'

When we re-entered the drawing room, Helen looked up expectantly, and it occurred to me too late that I should have had a smile on my face. Her flicker of worry was banished by her father, who was on my heels. He beamed as he entered, and said we would soon have to prepare for a wedding. She clasped her hands, brushed past me in order to embrace him. I was about to go and shake hands with Mrs Stokes, but her false smile had set her face in a rictus that was not inviting. Helen turned from her father and hugged my neck. Conscious of her parents, I was unsure where to place my hands, so I patted her back as if consoling a distraught stranger.

Helen's father said a toast was in order. There was no champagne, but I had a bottle of claret that I was keeping by. I said I'd fetch it from upstairs, and take the opportunity to inform my father of the good news. I asked Miss Joyce to bring some wine glasses and the decanter from the scullery.

In my room, I retrieved the bottle from a press and swept dust from its label, then looked down at the forlorn iron bed in the corner. My father could sleep here from now on. Helen and I would move into the master bedroom. When I went to his chamber, he was sitting up, reading a document close to his face. He looked at me over the rim of half-moon spectacles and said, 'Well?'

'Mr Stokes and I have had a very cordial meeting. He gave his blessing for the marriage almost immediately.'

My father allowed his arms to drop down on to his lap, and he raised his brow. 'In truth?'

I've noticed that people only seem to believe me when I'm being dishonest. I held up the wine bottle. 'We're about to toast the engagement.'

He shook his head as if still sceptical, but then some of the lines around his eyes softened. 'I'm happy for you, John. It's a most advantageous match.'

I thanked him. 'I was also thinking that when Helen comes to reside here, we'll need some new living arrangements.'

He lifted an arthritic hand. 'I'd like to speak to Stokes in private though. Will you show him up before he leaves?'

He noted my misgiving and added, 'For a medical opinion.'

I said, 'Of course.'

He picked up a small paper-bound ledger, and began to leaf through the pages, as if he had no more to say.

'I'd better return to our guests.'

In the drawing room, Helen and her father were speaking to each other in bright voices. I showed them the bottle and said, 'Here we are.' The fire-side table was still bare. 'Has Miss Joyce not brought the glasses?'

Helen's mother said there had been no sign of her, with a note of disapproval.

'I'm sure she won't be long.'

I went over to the bureau, rummaged beneath my college notes and found an old corkscrew with a well-worn handle and tarnished worm. I held the bottle by the neck and twisted it in.

'My father is delighted with the news, of course.'

I wrapped my fingers around the handle and began to pull. 'Unfortunately, he told me to say he's not feeling well enough for visitors.'

Mr Stokes said that was a pity.

Bits of cork were coming loose, but the stopper wasn't

easing from the neck. 'It is, but there'll be many opportunities to meet over the coming weeks.'

I clamped the bottle between my thighs and tugged. The Stokes family watched my efforts keenly. The cork finally came loose with a loud pop. 'Now,' I said. The wine was rather musty so I put it on the desk. 'We'll leave it there to breathe.'

Helen was listing some of the people they would have to contact about the engagement: old friends of the family, and relatives in Scotland. Her gaze drifted over the mantelpiece while she thought of them, as if she imagined they were standing before the hearth.

She looked at me and smiled. 'Wait till Arthur hears.'

Indeed.

'And you'll have to visit Cecilia, and try to send word to Alex.'

Alex wouldn't be able to come, of course. I mulled over whom else I could invite. Some cousins on my mother's side of the family still resided in Antrim, but we had lost touch since her death. My mother would have been pleased.

Behind me, the door to the drawing room opened. Mr Stokes looked over my shoulder and frowned. Helen and her mother craned their heads to the left with puzzled expressions.

I shifted in my seat and glanced back. Ned Holt stood in the doorway, blinking in the lamplight. One hand was on the doorknob; the other held behind his back. There was a sheen of sweat on his forehead, and his coat had dark stains beneath the elbow.

He seemed relieved when he saw me. 'Delahunt,' he said. 'I thought I'd come to the wrong house.'

I couldn't pretend not to recognize him. 'Edward. I didn't hear you come in.' No one moved for a moment, and the silence grew uncomfortable. The loose cork rolled from the tabletop on to the floorboards with a soft patter. I said, 'Let's speak in the hall.'

Holt looked at the others and nodded, then stepped back out of the room.

Mrs Stokes said, 'You know him?'

'That's Ned, a local handyman.'

'He appears to be in some distress.'

'He always looks like that. A poor heart. I'll go and see what he wants.'

Mr Stokes stood up. I waved to him and said it was probably nothing, but Helen's father remained standing. I took the lamp and went into the hall, closing the door behind me.

Holt had gone further into the passage. When I got closer, I could see his other hand was covered in grimy streaks of blood.

I regarded him sternly. 'What did you do to Miss Joyce?'

He frowned at me for a second, then said, 'The woman downstairs? No, she's helping.' He took a breath. 'It's Sibthorpe, John. He's in your basement now, unconscious. He's been badly hurt.'

'Sibthorpe?'

'I was reporting to him in Hogan's pub and someone must have spotted us. We were set upon in Baggot Street. Tom's been stabbed.'

It was odd to think that Sibthorpe could be just as vulnerable as anyone else. 'But why did you come here? Just send word to the Castle.'

'This was the nearest safe-house.'

I watched his tongue lick at the flaccid corner of his mouth. 'This isn't a safe-house. It's my house.'

He took my arm. 'You have to go to the home of Mr Gorman, the surgeon in Mount Street. Tell him it's Castle business. Say it's an emergency, and bring him here.'

I declined to say one of Dublin's pre-eminent surgeons was in the next room. 'You're not thinking this through, Ned. Get a message to the Castle and they'll send all the help that's required.'

'Listen, Delahunt—'

'I can't, Holt. Not tonight. If you want, you can get Miss Joyce to fetch someone. But I'm going back to the others.'

The door opened and Mr Stokes came out. Helen and her mother had also risen, and they peered past him.

Holt let go of my arm and placed his hand on my shoulder, staining my good jacket.

'Sir, I must apologize for the alarm I've caused. A friend of mine' – he nodded to me – 'a friend of ours has been attacked. He's downstairs now in dire need of medical treatment. John has kindly agreed to fetch a surgeon.'

Stokes hesitated. He looked at us both in turn. 'But I am a surgeon.'

The hand on my shoulder tightened. 'How fortunate.' Ned wasted no more time. 'Please come with me.'

I thought Stokes would refuse, but his instincts as a doctor prevailed, for he followed Holt into the black stairwell. I went after them to provide some illumination.

In the kitchen, Miss Joyce knelt over the unconscious figure of Sibthorpe. His mutton-chop whiskers were neatly trimmed, but his face was pallid and lifeless. His jacket had been removed and his waistcoat unbuttoned. The white shirt he wore was sodden and red. Seeing him there in that state, he no longer seemed quite so intimidating.

A scuffed trail led to the back-yard door, where Holt had gained entry. Miss Joyce must have received quite a shock. Four wine glasses were placed on the hearthstone; one of them had tipped over and shattered. There wouldn't be enough for the toast.

Stokes only had to glance at Sibthorpe. 'That man will have to go to hospital.'

Holt said that was impossible, for Tom's assailants were still looking for him.

'You mean he wasn't just mugged? What did he do?'

'Not a thing, I assure you.'

'Of course not.' Mr Stokes regarded me as he began to roll up the sleeves of his shirt. He removed his wedding band, placed it in a fob pocket, and asked Miss Joyce to prepare some basins of water.

I tried to explain who these men were, and why they'd come to the house, but he told me to be silent.

He used a knife to cut away Sibthorpe's shirt, then bent down to examine the blood that seeped from a gash beneath his ribs. He told Holt that his friend wasn't in immediate danger of bleeding out, but he could not yet close the wound. The chest cavity had been pierced, and he would have to explore the length and angle of the stab to determine if any viscera had been punctured, or if any foreign bodies remained.

He asked Miss Joyce to fetch a needle – a bone needle if she had it – and some cotton or hemp thread. Then he instructed me to hold a candle above the patient while he carried out his examination.

First he soaked a cloth and cleaned away the filth on Sibthorpe's chest. Without the lumps of coagulated blood, the wound looked quite neat: just a three-inch-long slit, with fresh blood continually percolating. Without dithering, Stokes inserted two fingers very gradually to the depth of his knuckles. I couldn't help but wince, though Sibthorpe was completely senseless and didn't stir.

Stokes asked me to bring the light closer and I lowered the

candle. In the moment's silence I said to him, 'These men are actually with the police. I only know them—'

'Mind.' His other hand came across and caught three drops of molten wax before they touched the wound. I tilted the candle upright.

He withdrew his fingers, which clutched at their tip a small fragment of Sibthorpe's shirt that had entered the wound. He held the gory scrap to the light and examined it. 'That was the only thing I could feel, but I can't say for sure there aren't any other pieces.' He said the cut was relatively shallow, and by its angle the knife probably missed the vital organs. Miss Joyce returned with a needle and thread, and Stokes expertly created a suture to close over the wound.

After a final check of the patient's breathing and pulse, Stokes spoke to Holt. He said his friend would certainly die if he wasn't soon brought to a hospital. Ned said that would be arranged.

Stokes cleaned his hands in a basin; his clothes remained unstained. When he bent back up, his attention was drawn to the door. I turned and saw Helen standing on the threshold. I didn't know how long she'd been there, observing. Stokes came over and stood before me, folding out his white sleeves to button the cuffs.

I said, 'I can explain.'

But he had already turned his back. His boots clicked on the flagstones as he walked to the door. Then he took hold of Helen's wrist and led her away.

Holt said, 'John.'

Miss Joyce stood in front of me, her face in a scowl. 'How do you know these men?'

I heard Mr Stokes say something to his wife on the landing above, then the front door opened and banged shut.

'Delahunt, bring down some blankets. Tom is shivering.'

I said, 'All right.' But when I went upstairs, I retrieved the bottle of wine from the drawing room, brought it to my chamber and locked myself in. Miss Joyce rapped against the door for a while, but I refused to answer.

Holt must have made contact with the Castle during the night, for when I came down the following morning, both he and Sibthorpe were gone. The kitchen was spotless; there was no indication that anything out of the ordinary had occurred the night before. Two pennies had been left on the table with a note saying, 'To replace the broken glass.'

I wrote to Mr Stokes that afternoon, apologizing for the turn the evening had taken, and saying that Sibthorpe and Holt were police agents from Dublin Castle. I first came into contact with their department during the bother with Arthur and James O'Neill that spring, so I couldn't refuse them aid.

The mention of his son may have had an effect, for he wrote back saying he would look into the matter. A week later another letter arrived. Stokes said there was a problem. He had written to the constabulary in the Castle, but they had no record of a Ned Holt or Thomas Sibthorpe in their employ. Was there any way to explain this discrepancy?

I replied at once, that naturally there was no record since their department was a clandestine intelligence agency, but I had been in contact with them several times, and could assure him that they, and it, were genuine.

This time his answer was prompt. He wished to thank me for the aid I had rendered to his family in the past, but in the circumstances he could not grant permission for me to marry his daughter. He said the consequences of my association with the Castle could not be predicted, and he would not allow anything to imperil Helen. He wished me well, but this was the last I would hear from him on the matter.

The door to the Stokes house remained closed to me. Helen no longer walked in Merrion Park, even in the presence of her governess, and I wondered if she had been sent away.

I wrote her a long letter, setting out how I'd come to be involved with the Castle, first by helping her brother, and then by searching for the attackers of Captain Craddock, but I didn't mention anything about the man in the yellow cravat. I wrote that I was sorry not to have told her these things when we were together, but I had been afraid of what she might think.

I took the letter to our secluded meeting-place in the garden, and placed it on the bench beneath a thin piece of black shale. Over the following week I checked on it several times, until one day I noticed the stone had shifted to the other end of the bench. There was an envelope underneath addressed to me, its lettering smudged where rainwater had seeped beneath the stone.

Helen thanked me for my letter. She said she understood why I had chosen not to tell her those things, but from now on I should always confide in her – for she would take my side in any matter. She was still willing to marry me, and if I accompanied her to Scotland, we could exchange vows and return to live in Fitzwilliam Street. But she made clear that if we did so, she would be disinherited.

Elopement conjures ideas of romance and excitement, but for Helen and me it consisted of monotonous journeys by stagecoach and steam-packet to Portpatrick on the Scottish coast. During the crossing, we sat together on deck with a plaid blanket over our knees, and watched the dawn break over the approaching headland. Afterwards, Helen always kept that woollen coverlet in the bottom of her trunk as a memento. Maybe she has it still.

She came to live with us in Fitzwilliam Street, where an odd atmosphere pervaded the house for several days. Our marriage had caused a scandal, and Mr Stokes sent demands for Helen to return home to Merrion Square, even threatening legal action.

Miss Joyce did her best to ignore Helen and me. She counselled my father to expel us from the house, and at the start I thought it likely he would. But Helen went to speak with him privately soon after she arrived. When she came down to me, she smiled and said he would allow us to stay.

'How did you persuade him?'

'I simply said that I love you, and am willing to look after you.'

I pursed my lips and nodded. 'I'd have never thought of that.'

One morning Mr Stokes and Arthur came to the house, and we spoke to them in the front parlour. Her father said that this silliness had gone on long enough, and that if Helen returned home with him, they would put the unfortunate incident behind them. But Helen said our marriage was legitimate, and showed him the certificate from a church of the established faith in Portpatrick. Arthur asked did she realize what she was doing to their family. Helen said if only they would give our marriage their blessing, life could return to normal. But Mr Stokes got angry. He said he would never approve of this union, because she had so blatantly disobeyed his wishes. He gave her one last chance to return home with him, or face the consequences. In the silence that followed, Arthur pleaded with his sister to see sense, but she rose from her chair, and said if that was all, she wouldn't detain them. When her father and brother left the house, Helen wept for hours. The next day, a large trunk containing her clothes and belongings was left on our steps.

We were only married a few weeks when my father finally succumbed to his illness. Miss Joyce said it was the anxiety about my activities in the previous months that had finished him off. I was going to say that it was the useless tonics of her homeopaths that did the trick, but I didn't bother. I just sacked her.

We buried him in the graveyard of St Mark's on Brunswick Street, next to my mother in the family plot. Not many people attended the service, though Cecilia and Captain Dickenson were there. It was an awkward meeting. Cecilia and Helen did their best to make small talk, but it was clear my brother-in-law wished to have nothing to do with us. As soon as the ceremony was over, he whispered to Cecilia, and they soon departed. My sister hugged both Helen and me, and said that she would try to visit.

Before he got into his coach, Dickenson came up to me. 'Who's looking after the will?'

I said I'd get in touch with the solicitor.

'Because I'd be happy to look after the arrangements on behalf of the family.'

There was no need. I'd take care of it.

He smoothed his moustache with gloved fingers. 'Just make sure to contact me when the contents are known.'

I went to visit my father's solicitor in his office on Ely Place. Samuel Adair was a portly man in his fifties with a full grey beard. His desk was surrounded by shelves of leather-bound legal tomes with their spines unbroken. A dishevelled wolfhound lay curled up in a corner. He poured me a drink from a decanter of whiskey, then opened a drawer and withdrew a metal strong-box.

'I've been going through the items your father deposited here. It's all rather straightforward.'

Inside the box, there were bundles of letters, account rolls and ledgers. He took out a thin membrane of parchment folded on itself, opened it on his desk and cleared his throat.

'Let's see. This is the last will and testament of Maurice Delahunt, dated December 1839.'

I considered the date. Only six months ago; which was after Cecilia's marriage and Alex's first deployment.

'He appointed his eldest son Alexander Delahunt as his executor, to discharge all debts attaching to the estate and manage the bequests.' He looked at me. 'As we discussed in our letters, that duty has descended to you because your brother serves abroad.'

He continued reading. The only beneficiaries were the three children. My father noted that Alex had become an officer in the army, praised the gallant career path he had chosen, and left him the contents of a certain savings account in the Bank of Ireland. He wished Cecilia a long and happy marriage, and implored Captain Dickenson to care for his only daughter. After taking account of the value of her dowry, he left her some stocks and shares in the Ulster Railway Company.

Adair fixed his spectacles. 'The final paragraph deals with you.'

I sat up in my chair.

'He writes, "In recognition of the fact that my son John remained to provide companionship and care in my declining years, I bequeath him the house at Number Thirty-five Fitzwilliam Street."'

A warm feeling crept through me as I imagined the life I could have with Helen in our own family home. Though it might have been the Jameson's.

Adair retrieved another document from the box. 'There is,

however, a substantial charge attached to the estate. Do you know of a person named Ruth Meehan?'

I placed my glass on his desk. 'She was our governess several years ago. But she left soon after my mother died.'

'Ah.' Adair handed me the document: a statement of affairs with La Touche's Bank, detailing a loan extended to Ruth Meehan eight years ago for the sum of £2,000, guaranteed by Maurice Delahunt.

I leafed through the pages in the folio; they showed a long list of repayments in chronological order spanning a number of years. The amounts were small, and I realized they barely covered the interest. I reached the final page. A balance of £1,800 was still due to the bank, the amount underlined twice in red ink.

Adair folded my father's will. 'It often happens, John. The biggest beneficiary is some unknown half-brother or -sister, looked after when purse strings were a little looser.'

Beneath the amount, a note stated that the loan was secured against all that and those, the house, stables and yard at Number Thirty-five Fitzwilliam Street Upper. I tried to calculate what the property was worth, and resisted the urge to crumple the document. In essence, my house belonged to the bank.

5

I remember the day Helen and I arrived in Grenville Street. We carried her trunk between us up Gardiner Hill, past corroded railings and cracked paving-stones. Our new landlady, Mrs Travers, waited for us outside the front door of number six, just a stone's throw from the corner of Mountjoy Square. Most of the houses in the terrace had been split up and let out as rented rooms. They were advertised as 'furnished apartments for gentlemen', but in the main were taken by young tradesmen and their sprawling families.

Heaving the case up the stairs was a great hardship. Two young girls sat on one of the steps, shoeless and wearing ragged dresses. When I asked them to move, they stared back at me as if I'd spoken in another language. We had to squeeze between them. As I lifted the trunk over their heads, I made sure they had to duck.

On the first floor, the door to what was once the drawing room was open. A woman in a drabbet dress knelt beside an iron tub, in which two infants stood shivering. Other youngsters were scattered about, wearing sullen faces and grimy hand-me-downs, playing patty-cake or squabbling over toys. The hassled woman regarded the new tenants passing her doorway with unfriendly eyes. She remained silent even when Helen offered a cheery hello.

Helen and I lived on the second floor, in what was once the master bedroom. It was rather cramped, but it had two tall bay windows and a fireplace in the wall opposite the door. In the first few days, we swept the floors and polished the surfaces, then arranged the few pieces of furniture still in our possession. Helen would stand in the middle of the room and direct me to drag the bookcase a few feet to the left or right, and the kitchen table so it stood closer to the dresser. Then she'd consider the result with her head tilted, and say, 'Actually, they were better where they were before.'

Boxes of books lay jumbled in a corner for more than a fortnight, until I took it upon myself to put them away. I arranged them in the case first by subject, then changed my mind and put them in alphabetical order by author, then finally, for the sake of neatness, I grouped them together by the colour and height of their spines. It took most of the afternoon.

I watched Helen working at her writing desk, in the last light of a watery sun setting over the terrace opposite. There was a sheaf of letters received stacked in a small cubby to her left, and a couple of unopened envelopes with spidery lettering and London postmarks on her right.

She might have been the picture of a young married lady attending to her correspondence, except her hands wore finger-less gloves. Her dress wasn't of lawn muslin but coarse wool, and she had no headgear except a scarf around her shoulders that snagged on the pins in her hair. She still possessed some fine gowns, but they were folded up at the bottom of her trunk. She didn't want to wear them here, as they'd make her look out of place.

When I finished with the bookcase, I said, 'Would you like some tea, Helen?'

She smiled at me over her shoulder and said that I'd read her mind. I filled the kettle from the basin, then hung it from a hook over the coals.

We had done our best to make the room comfortable, but all refinement had been stripped away by the landlady and previous occupants. The windows had no drapes. There had once been a thick red carpet, judging by tufts that had caught on exposed nails in the skirting, but it had been removed. The oil paint on the architraves flaked off at the merest brush, and warps in the sash windows admitted cold draughts.

Steam began to whistle from the spout, so I picked up the kettle with a cloth over the handle.

There were some vestiges of former grandeur, such as the fine black marble fireplace. Also, the room retained its original plasterwork. A delicate central rosette and oval garland adorned the centre of the ceiling, but the chandelier they once surrounded was long gone. All that remained was a bare hole that allowed the ingress of various types of creeping fauna, with wriggling feelers and segmented bodies. Helen couldn't stand to have the bed directly beneath.

I took the teapot down from the shelf, and frowned at a small chip in its spout. The tealeaves were in a tin tray with a hinged lid, which had originally contained tobacco. I poured the tea without a strainer, added a pinch of sugar to Helen's mug, and placed it on the desk beside her. 'Who are you writing to now?'

'My father's cousin in Bristol.'

'Did you ever meet him?'

'Her. She visited once when I was little.'

Helen whiled away her hours by writing snatches of poetry

and stories in jotters; one tale in particular she hoped to turn into a novel. It was a hobby I had been unaware of; one that she had pursued for years at home in Merrion Square. Among her possessions when she moved into Fitzwilliam Street were a series of notebooks and a bundle of pages loosely bound into a manuscript.

Occasionally, while writing her book, she would lift her head to pose some obscure question, such as the term-length for a member of parliament, or the name of a certain type of carriage. Once she asked what was another word for 'profuse', and when I couldn't think of one, I said surely 'profuse' would suffice. I once requested to read some of her stories, but she became coy, gathered the pages to herself and said she couldn't possibly let anyone read them. I said, 'Of course, I understand.' I had only asked to be polite.

Otherwise she was at that desk writing letters to family members living in Britain. She would explain our situation, and enquire if there were any positions of employment in their households or localities. No matter the address to which she wrote, her parents had already sent word. All of the replies that Helen received expressed dismay at her decision to elope and abandon the Stokes name. Some of her particularly beloved aunts and uncles denounced her disloyalty with language most vitriolic. Helen carefully filed each response.

No one lived on the floor above us, but the miserable couple below were constantly arguing. The woman we had seen was married to a slow-witted handyman named Lynch. Helen and I would listen to their raised voices muffled through the floorboards while we huddled in the dark. It would start with an abrupt yell from one or the other, the wail of a child, and Helen would say, 'Here we go.' The strains of their voices would rise in intensity, and snatches of words became audible.

For amusement, we would take sides. I usually showed solidarity with the husband, and would concoct arguments to match the pitch and length of his complaints. When Mrs Lynch cut off her husband's lament to begin some shrieking rebuttal, it was up to Helen to take up the gauntlet. Mimicking her counterpart, she made up accusations of an increasingly base and depraved nature, and I was impressed by the breadth of her imagination. I had to wait for Lynch to lift his voice again before I could respond.

One night, their quarrelling became particularly ferocious, and was ended abruptly by the smash of a breakable and a heavy thud. Even the child stopped its crying. Beneath our covers, we listened to the heavy silence. Then Helen said, 'He was asking for that.'

Our first months in the apartment were relatively contented. The responsibilities of running a small household kept us occupied, and we were each sustained by the companionship of the other. By the end of September, Helen's only real dilemma was using the outhouse at the end of the yard, which consisted of a hole in a splintery wooden bench over a foul pit. The door of the shack wouldn't close securely, and Helen insisted I stand guard whenever she used it, lest one of the Lynches barge in.

We examined the latch together one morning. She said, 'Surely you can fashion something to lock it properly.'

I prodded at the bent piece of metal and said I wasn't a carpenter.

Her lips pressed together, and straightened in a way I'd come to recognize.

'But I'll do my best.'

I asked Lynch for a lend of a screwdriver, and set about my task. I had never been one for manual labour, but unfortunately by that time I was qualified for little else. My final examinations in Trinity at the start of the summer had not gone well. The result hinged on my passing an oral examination by my tutor, Professor Lloyd. On the morning itself, my fellows had gathered on the steps to the rear of Library Square, lounging about with notes on their laps. Most were committing phrases to memory, mumbling aloud as if preparing for some important oration. I sat poised and silent among them. It was not at all that I had confidence I would pass. But my experiences in the previous months had put this trial in some perspective.

Lloyd's office was on the top floor of the science building, up a grand Regency staircase. The panelled room was filled with shelves and glass cabinets, each containing rows of books, loose papers, or the most intricate optical devices used by Lloyd in the course of his experiments. The Professor barely acknowledged my arrival, waving for me to sit in the chair opposite. He referred to a sheet that contained a list of questions with my name printed on top. 'Mr Delahunt,' he said, 'explain to me the experimental procedure required to observe the conical refraction of light in a piece of biaxial crystal.'

I had never heard of such a phenomenon. I pursed my lips and looked to the right as if gathering my thoughts, but couldn't think of a single thing to say. The question had been too specific for me to start talking on some general theoretical point. Lloyd waited patiently with his pen poised over the sheet. When I said I didn't know, he simply made a note and moved on.

I fared little better with the other questions, even struggling with topics that I covered during my studies. I kept omitting important details and repeating others. When my final answer trailed off into silence, he looked up at me.

'Would you like to add anything?'

I said no.

'Very well.' He quickly totted the scores and signed his name at the bottom of the sheet. 'You failed.' He suggested that I retake my final year starting next September, or I would not achieve my degree.

'My father recently passed away.'

He placed my sheet atop a pile. 'On your way out you can send in Mr Delaney.'

As I withdrew each screw from the bolt in the outhouse, I methodically placed them in my pocket for safekeeping. The curved metal catch was surprisingly malleable, so I bent out its kink, then fastened it again slightly lower. The screws drove inward easily, their threads biting into the black, rotten wood. Despite my best efforts, one of the screws had gone missing, but the bolt was fast and secure.

Back in our room, a fire blazed in the hearth, and Helen was removing a kettle that had come to the boil. She had already set out two mugs on the table. I found the idea of her brewing a hot beverage for her handyman husband heart-warming. It was only as I advanced into the room that I noticed we had a visitor.

Sibthorpe sat in my chair beside the fireplace. It was hard to believe that it was the same man who had lain prostrate on my basement floor in Fitzwilliam Street a few months before. His mutton-chop whiskers had grown fuller, and his brown hair had been cropped short. He wore a black suit and grey cravat, which made him look like an undertaker. Helen seemed nervous as I approached, and she looked at me as Tom rose from my seat.

'John, it's good to see you again.'

I wiped my palm on my sleeve and shook his proffered hand.

Helen walked over and handed him a mug of tea, which he accepted with a nod. Then he sat down again without invitation.

She stood beside me and handed me the other mug. I looked at her. 'You don't want any?' She shook her head and went to sit by her writing desk.

There was no other seat in the room, unless I perched at the foot of the bed, so I leaned my elbow on the mantelpiece as if I posed for a portrait. Sibthorpe blew steam from his mug. 'I've already had a chance to thank your wife. I believe it was the ministrations of your father-in-law that saved my life.'

I said we hadn't heard from Mr Stokes for several weeks.

He took a sip of his tea and I noticed he held his right side in a stiff manner.

Helen leaned forward, her voice tinged with anger. 'Your intrusion that night had very serious consequences for us both.'

Sibthorpe appeared surprised that she had spoken. He met her eye, and then looked around the sparse room. 'So I see.'

She was about to speak again, but he raised his hand. 'I realize the events that night caused you much hardship and I truly regret that. But I wish to make some amends.'

From the fireplace I asked how so.

'By offering you some employment.' He placed his mug on the armrest.

I said my experience of working for the Castle had proved too costly already.

'Come now, John. Leaving aside my imposition that night, which I admit was bad timing, you had done rather well from your interaction with the Castle.' He turned to Helen. 'Didn't we keep your brother from gaol, and save your family's reputation – though you might not care about that now?'

Helen was stung, but before she could reply he addressed me

once again. 'And what about your bother with the coal-porter? Not to mention the twenty pounds we paid into your hand.'

Helen said, 'John earned that reward money.'

'And he could earn it again. Regularly.' He said my position as an agent within his department would be formalized. I would be under no obligation, but I could meet him in the Castle at any time with information regarding any issue, no matter how petty – a pub that opened after hours, a neighbour who beat his wife, the political affiliations of an acquaintance – and that information would be paid for, every time. 'Occasionally, you might be called upon to help with a certain case, a few hours' work here and there, often very lucrative.'

I looked over at Helen. The promise of a steady income appealed to me. But her voice was quiet.

'A paid informer?' She twisted the wedding band on her finger. 'It's hardly work suitable for a gentleman.'

Sibthorpe glanced at me. 'If I may, Mrs Delahunt, you seem too mindful of our society's double standards when it comes to honour. You yourself have suffered stigma, and for what? Marrying the man you love.' He paused as if trying to fathom the attraction. 'Where is the dishonour? Where is the dishonour in serving your city? In the Castle we maintain the common good. What matter if some of our activities are covert?'

Helen's eyes remained downcast. The mug of tea in my hand had begun to grow cold so I placed it on the mantelpiece. I told Sibthorpe we'd have to think about it.

'That's fine,' he said. 'In the meantime, how would you like to make five pounds assisting me this evening?'

Sibthorpe and I sat in a cab bound for the police station in Store Street, trundling down the slope of Gardiner Street towards the Customs House. He sat quiet and still beside me, and I was content to look out of the window at the evening traffic. We were delayed at the bottom of the street. Construction work continued on the new railway bridge that swept over the river, traversed Gardiner Street, and cast Frenchman's Lane completely in shadow. I looked up at the houses adjacent, and imagined their sash windows wobbling as great steam engines rumbled by.

'Our numbers in the Department have thinned recently.' Sibthorpe spoke without looking towards me.

I waited for him to continue. He said Ned Holt had been forced to lie low since the night they had come to my house. Holt had been working to infiltrate a gang of Rockites, members of the violent radical movement who spread mayhem at the behest of the fabled Captain Rock. But when Holt had been spotted meeting with Sibthorpe, suspicions arose, and they were both ambushed in Baggot Street. Holt fought off the attackers, but not before Sibthorpe had been knifed in the chest.

He lifted his hand to press against his ribs with a grimace. 'Holt is too big and ugly to mask his appearance so he had to go into hiding. Maybe he left the city.' He shrugged. 'Maybe he's dead.'

His indifference surprised me. 'You don't seem concerned either way.'

'All I know is that he's of no use to the Department. That's enough.' Sibthorpe cleaned a smudge on his window with the outside of his fist. The blockage in the road cleared and the carriage continued beneath the half-built bridge. He said, 'Now we have a problem with Devereaux.'

The younger agent had been arrested the previous night in a whorehouse in Montgomery Street. Sibthorpe pursed his lips.

'He left a girl in an awful state.' Devereaux's behaviour had been worsening for months; he had taken to drinking heavily and eating opium. 'The difficulty for us is that Devereaux believes he's impervious to prosecution. He knows far too much; he could compromise any number of agents and investigations.'

The cab pulled up beside the lamp-lit entrance of the police station. Sibthorpe shifted in his seat. 'We'll see what he has to say for himself.'

Tom spoke to a policeman at the front desk, who brought us to a holding cell in the basement. Devereaux sat at a stout wooden table, his manacled hands resting in front of him. He was much as I remembered, though his clothes were dishevelled and his eyes bloodshot. His carefully groomed chinstrap beard had become indistinct against several days of stubble. He gave a sardonic smile when he saw Sibthorpe enter, but looked rather more uncertain when I followed behind.

'What's he doing here?'

We ignored him. Sibthorpe asked the sergeant for the file, then told him that we would speak with the prisoner in private. I pulled across two chairs so we could sit opposite. For a moment, Sibthorpe perused the file, licking the tip of his index finger to turn the pages. Devereaux filled the time by fixing me with his familiar smirk. The manacles had enough give that he could fold his arms by gripping his elbows. He said, 'How's Miss Stokes?'

Sibthorpe spoke while still reading from the file. 'The name of the girl you hurt is Sarah Colgan from Kilkenny.'

Devereaux shrugged. 'She told me it was Honor Bright.'

Sibthorpe turned a leaf and shook his head. 'Such a list of injuries. Broken pelvis, wrist, shattered ear, gouged eye, contusions, cuts, trauma . . . elsewhere.' He closed the file, placed it on the table and looked up at Devereaux. 'What's the matter with you?'

'I don't remember doing any of that. The only thing I recall is them pulling me off her.' When Sibthorpe said nothing he continued, 'She was new, fresh from the country. Maybe she wouldn't do as told; maybe I was just breaking her in.'

He tried to look defiant, but eventually his eyes lowered as we regarded him in silence. He spoke in a small voice. 'Come on, Sibthorpe. Who'll kick up a fuss over some whore?' He closed his eyes, squeezing them slightly in an attempt to appear solemn. 'I promise it won't happen again.'

Sibthorpe placed his hand on the table, and drummed his fingers against the file in a rhythmic patter. He said they'd have to bring him back to the Castle and charge him with something. Devereaux's eyes opened. Even a public-order offence. 'Maybe we can arrange with the magistrate to let you off with a fine.' Sibthorpe leaned forward in his chair. 'But you'll pay every penny.'

I could see relief course through Devereaux. He gave an expansive nod. 'Absolutely. That's only fair.'

'You'd do well to bear in mind the nature of our work in future.' He rose and rapped on the door, then waited for the sergeant to re-enter. 'I'll be taking this prisoner back to the Castle and will process him there. Arrange for transport.'

The policeman flashed a glance at Devereaux, then nodded and withdrew.

Outside the rear entrance, a prison cart stood waiting. Two metal benches were embedded in the sides of the cart. There were hinged catches in the seats to which manacles could be tethered, but we didn't employ them. Sibthorpe handed me the key and told me to remove Devereaux's restraints. The metal was cold to the touch. As I released each clasp the chains slinked to the floor, and Devereaux rubbed his wrists theatrically.

Sibthorpe looked at him. 'You'll need to put them back on when we get to the Castle.'

We entered the Castle at Ship Street, continued to Lower Castle Yard and turned into the arched entrance of the police barracks. Sibthorpe ordered me to refasten the chains and Devereaux held out his wrists, as if in surrender.

The officer on duty in the cells didn't seem surprised by the approach of our party. Devereaux greeted him by name, but the young corporal would not meet his eye. He retrieved a key from beneath his desk. 'Number eight is free.' He took a lamp and led the way to the designated cell, which was beyond a corner in the old stone corridor.

Inside, Devereaux was told to sit. Next to the table, there was another of those hooked latches embedded in the wall in which manacles were secured. The young officer told Devereaux to slip his chain within. Devereaux drew back his wrists and frowned. 'Surely that's not necessary.'

Sibthorpe's voice was low. 'Devereaux, we have to do this by the book.'

The prisoner relented. The chain between his wrists was fastened to the hook in the wall, which was secured with a padlock. Sibthorpe took the key. Devereaux pulled at the chains to see how far he could move his arms.

Sibthorpe surveyed the cell. 'Right then. Someone will come in to take your statement, Devereaux, and make the charge. Hopefully we'll sort this out tonight.'

'Thanks, Tom.'

The rest of us withdrew from the cell. In the corridor, Sibthorpe turned to the corporal. 'You're dismissed. Return to your desk and remain there.' The young officer gave a curt nod and turned on his heel.

Sibthorpe looked at me, cocked his head at the cell door opposite, and beckoned for me to follow.

Two men sat at a table with a single candle between them. They wore the homespun clothes of country folk. One was older than the other, but they had the same build and hair colour, which marked them as kin. They each held a black wooden baton.

When I entered, the younger one rose from his seat. He regarded me with such hatred that I instinctively braced myself, but Sibthorpe held up his hand and spoke to the young man. 'This isn't him. This is my associate, Delahunt.' He turned to me. 'That's William and George Colgan, poor Sarah's brother and uncle.'

The older man got up from his chair. 'Where is he?'

Sibthorpe pointed across the hall. 'In there. Be quick about it.'

They pushed past and opened the door to the holding cell.

Devereaux's head came up. He was confused when he saw the two men enter, though only for a second. The younger man wanted to go for him at once, but his uncle said, 'Let's shift the table first.'

Devereaux's eyes fixed on the two men as they took hold of the underside of the table to drag it away. One of them had placed his baton on top. It slid off, clattered on the floor, and then rolled until it snagged in the join between two flagstones. Devereaux stood up, tipping his chair over, and pulled against his restraints until the chain was taut.

Sibthorpe and I remained in the hallway. Tom pushed the cell door closed with just his index finger, then kept his palm pressed against it for a moment, as if it might open again if he let go.

We could hear the beating commence: irregular thuds and Devereaux's unsettling cries. Above the lintel, a dark metal grille spanned the width of the door. Lamplight from inside the cell danced and flickered through the slits. Occasionally, the sweep of a shadow would match the sound of a baton strike. The Colgans had settled into a rhythm, like a pair of ship-builders working in tandem to hammer in a rivet.

Sibthorpe took his hand off the door. He stood with his arms folded and gazed around the passageway. 'You know...' He waited for me to look at him. '... When I started in the Castle this is where I worked.' He nodded towards the bend in the corridor. 'At the front desk where the corporal is.' His eyes lost some focus. 'We used to freeze during the winter. I'd sit hunched with my fingers cupped over the candle.' He drew in his elbows and lifted his hands to mimic the action. Then he straightened, and thought for a moment. 'They have it easy these days.'

It had been several seconds since Devereaux last yelled out, but the beating continued.

A cellar spider crept along the ground in the corridor. One of its delicate legs tapped against the wall, as if using it for support. It reached the cell door and slipped beneath the gap at the bottom. A moment later it came back out, traversed the sill and continued along the crook of the wall.

Sibthorpe fumbled in his coat pocket. 'Before I forget.' He took out a wallet, withdrew a five-pound note and handed it to me extended in his fingertips.

When the noises from inside had become sporadic, Sibthorpe slid back the peephole cover. He watched for a moment, then said, 'That's enough,' and opened the door.

The Colgans stood in the middle of the cell, breathing heavily with their shoulders stooped. Sibthorpe went up to the older man. 'Remember, we've allowed you to bypass the courts. Sarah won't have her name sullied in the papers.' He looked at them both in turn. 'So you owe us.'

The men nodded. Sibthorpe told them to go and they staggered out, the cudgels still clutched in their hands.

Devereaux slumped lifeless on the floor, his arms still held up by the manacles hooked in the wall, as if he was a joint on display in a butcher's window. One of his boots had come off. A strap from his braces had released, and coiled over his shoulder. His trousers were ripped where the men had stamped on his groin.

Sibthorpe only looked at the body for a moment. He called into the hallway for the corporal to come in, then he gave me the key for the padlock in the wall and told me to take the prisoner down. Close in, I could see the skin around his wrists had torn against the manacles. I fumbled with the padlock. When I turned the key, my knuckles brushed against his warm fingertips.

Two other men entered the cell, and they hauled Devereaux's corpse away. The corporal brought in two pails of water to douse against the wall and ground where Devereaux had been bleeding. The cell floor slanted towards a metal grille that covered a drain hole in the corner. The murky water sluiced away into Dublin's black pool.

I left the Castle by Dame Street and decided to walk home in order to clear my head, though the night was inclement. When the rain became particularly heavy, I stopped in a dingy pub for shelter, and stood propped against the bar with a glass of whiskey. Other men escaping the weather huddled beside the fireplace. Steam clung to a large gold-framed mirror behind the counter. After a few minutes, the barman offered to top up my glass, and I nodded.

I kept picturing Devereaux's face just before the beating, when Sibthorpe closed the door on him. Tom could have arranged for his wayward agent's throat to be cut in some side street. Instead, he had orchestrated an execution inside the halls of his own department. As I thought back, I realized there had been no need for me to accompany Sibthorpe that evening. He had intended for me to see it all.

Another man entered the pub, and I glanced past him to check on the weather. The rain still fell in slanting sheets.

What if I was to fall out of favour with Tom? Wouldn't the same thing happen to me? Perhaps I wouldn't even see it coming. One evening, walking home, I'd be bundled into the back of a carriage, a gag stuffed in my mouth, a hood pulled over my head, and all I could hope for would be a quick end. And there'd be no repercussions; no inquest or trial; barely a complaint. As far as Helen and my family would be concerned, I would have just disappeared.

A man at the end of the bar was muttering to himself. He grew agitated, and spoke into his chest with increasing venom until a word from the barman quelled him.

Surely Sibthorpe knew that his display might deter me from working with the Castle altogether? Or was it too late for that? If I refused to cooperate, he could reveal my false statement about O'Neill, which would forever bar me from re-entering normal society, or expose my involvement with the coal-porters, which would get me killed.

I called over the barman to pay for the drinks, rummaged in my coat pocket for some change, and felt the folded five-pound note. Tom had shown that he was willing to pay me. He must have thought I could be an effective agent or why would he have bothered? If I had little choice about working for the

Department, there was some solace in the knowledge that he considered me adept at it.

The barman frowned at me. 'Have you nothing smaller?' I checked another pocket and handed him half a crown. As he walked away I thought of Devereaux again, and the sounds of his cries coming through the metal-bound door. It must have been awful, to watch the Colgans enter, knowing you were restrained, and to be helpless as the blows rained down.

Though it wasn't as if Devereaux was an innocent party. What had he suffered except an eye for an eye? Sibthorpe had provided the Colgan family a type of reckoning that wouldn't have been available through the courts. And he'd rid the Department of an errant agent, while teaching his replacement a ruthless lesson. The more I thought about it, the more it seemed rather efficient. Perhaps I'd have done the same.

Before leaving the pub, I bought a bottle of wine to share with Helen, then stepped into the blustery night to return home.

She was at her desk beside the window. A blank page and inkpot lay untouched beneath a candle. She sat with her legs gathered up gracefully, and her head turned towards the door. It struck me that it must have been a worrying wait in the dark chamber; sitting alone while gusts made the candle flame shiver. I crossed the room, trailing small pools of water on the floorboards, and took the money from my pocket. She held the proffered banknote unfurled between her fingertips, then reached over to feel my wet coat. 'You'll catch cold,' she said. 'I'll relight the fire.'

I changed into dry clothes while she busied herself beneath the mantel. We sat before the fireplace upon an old blanket that acted as hearth-rug, and I opened the wine. She shifted on to her knees to unpin her hair. 'Where did he bring you?'

I told her about Devereaux being held in Store Street. They had never met, but I had spoken about him several times.

'Why had he been arrested?'

I said he beat up a girl.

'A girl?'

'She worked in one of those houses in Montgomery Street.'

'Oh.'

I recounted some of her long list of injuries.

Helen's eyes searched my face. 'Did you see her?'

I shook my head. She was in hospital.

I refilled the glasses and placed the bottle behind us, away from the heat. I told her how Devereaux was brought back to the Castle, how Sibthorpe tricked him, how two men from the girl's family were waiting to kill him.

Helen was staring into the firelight. I was going to explain that the Castle wanted rid of Devereaux because he knew too many agents, but there was no need. She looked back at me. 'If he hurt the girl that much then he deserved it.'

I leaned across to pick a piece of wood from a bundle of sticks, used it to stir the fire, then threw it on top. The edges began to char and smoke. I thought she might have expressed more concern for my safety. 'Working for the Castle will be dangerous, Helen. Though I'm not sure I have a choice.'

I kept looking at the fire, and she sat still beside me for a moment. A gust blew down the chimney, sending a thick wisp of smoke into the room.

She reached across to touch my cheek, then took my hand and held it in her lap. 'But you're good at it. And you're clever enough to keep out of trouble.'

I laced my fingers through hers.

She moved closer and leaned her head beneath my chin. 'If

we can keep making this kind of money, John, we could be comfortable. Even happy.'

We sat like that for several minutes. Raised voices drifted from below, signalling the start of another quarrel between Lynch and his wife.

Sibthorpe had described to me the type of information gathered by the Department. It was all-encompassing. Nothing was too trivial; no person was too lowly to warrant the Castle's attention. Also, reports didn't have to be of something criminal. They collected tittle-tattle and rumours like reporters in the scandal sheets. A man's predilections, proclivities and sympathies, anything that could be held against him, was collated, indexed and filed.

But not on Castle grounds. Having to traipse in and out of Little Ship Street was considered a threat to an informant's anonymity. I was told to go to an address in Fownes Street whenever I had anything to report. The building was entirely nondescript, unadorned by signs or nameplates, bordered on one side by a bookseller, and on the other by a commissioner for oaths. The door was always unlocked – no need for secret knocks or whispered entreaties to enter.

Inside the dim hallway, a bored sentry sat at a desk beneath the stairwell. It was a different guard every time, never wearing any kind of official garb. He would turn away any who wandered in by mistake. Those on official business, such as myself, were allowed to approach.

I was told by Sibthorpe to state my name and say I wished to speak with a man called Farrell. The sentry scanned a list of names on his desk, only ten or so. Mine must have been among them. He reached across and tugged on a bell cord that disappeared through a small hole in the ceiling. It rang in the floors above, just at the edge of hearing. After a few moments, another cord in the corner quivered, jerked up and sounded a small brass chime. The guard looked up from his seat.

'You can go up to the second floor.'

I ascended the crooked stairs and Farrell met me on the landing. He was a young man, wearing a waistcoat with white shirtsleeves rolled up. His fingers were ink-stained, and he had spectacles that sat perched atop short tawny hair. There were two entrances in the hallway. One was quite ordinary; the other, an imposing metal doorway with exposed bolts, like those in a bank vault.

I told Farrell that I was John Delahunt.

He nodded. 'I thought as much, since I didn't recognize you.' He invited me into his office, a small room with a desk cluttered by files, and boxes stacked on the windowsill obstructing the light. Once seated he asked, 'Any trouble finding us?'

'Sibthorpe's directions were quite clear.'

He smiled at me. 'Tom never leaves anything to chance.' He cleared a space on his desk. 'So, what have you got for us?'

It seemed to me a rather feeble story. Helen convinced me it was worth reporting. 'My neighbour beats his wife.'

Farrell held my eye for a second, and I feared I had wasted his time.

'Lovely.' He opened a drawer and pulled out a blank form and an index card. 'Let's get the particulars.'

I described Nicholas Lynch of No. 6 Grenville Street, his age and occupation, his wife and children. I told how he and his wife would argue almost nightly, their spats ended by the sound of blows and broken crockery. I said Mrs Lynch showed bruises on her face and neck. I'd never seen any, but Helen assured me they were there, artfully concealed.

Farrell finished taking down the details. There were spaces on the printed form to note the date and time and my initials. I asked if Lynch would be arrested.

He had set the sheet aside in order to fill in an index card.

'That's not quite how it works,' he said. The police couldn't follow up every tip-off. However, there was now a file on Nicholas Lynch in the Castle archive. If ever he came to the attention of the authorities again, say if he joined a criminal gang, or the radicals, the file could be retrieved, and the contents held against him.

'Everyone has their weak points, John. It's up to us to find out what they are.'

Lynch might live an otherwise blameless life and, if so, the file would simply gather dust. 'On the other hand, if he ever decided to do the wife in' – he frowned at a mistake he made, crossed out a letter and continued on – 'we could use your statement as additional evidence.'

He finished printing the details on the card in a neat hand and blew on the ink. 'Since this is your first visit, I'll show you the stacks.'

He led me back into the hall and unlocked the metal door, revealing a large chamber spanning the entire width of the house. Mahogany shelves lined each wall, stretching up towards the ceiling. Three double bays stood in the centre of the room. Each shelf bent under the weight of manuscript boxes and loose folders. An alphabetical order was evident as each box was labelled with surnames. It started high on the nearest shelf with the box 'Abbot – Adair', then 'Adam – Ahern', and continued in that fashion. There was no other furniture, except shuttered cabinets in one corner, which contained the card catalogue.

The room was cold, and the high bays cast deep shadows, so

Farrell lit an oil-lamp. Dust swirled in the light above the bevelled glass chimney. He gestured towards the shelves and said, 'The most extensive archive of Dublin's citizens.'

He went over to the catalogue, pulled up the shutter and opened a small drawer marked 'L'. Reams of index cards were stacked upright. His two fingers ran along the top, a single card pulled back with each stride. When he found the proper spot among the Lynches he slipped the new card into place.

Then he went to find the box among the shelves. He told me that other archives held collections of estate papers from the wealthiest families, or the documents produced in governance. 'But these are records of the most ordinary people. There's no other repository like it.'

I scanned the front of the boxes in their haphazard stacks, noting some of the names written. 'But they only record their misdeeds.'

'Precisely.'

He found the box marked 'Lydon – Lysaght'. I took the lamp as he dragged it down and removed the lid. He clamped the box between his chest and the shelves, freeing his hands to delve within and ensure the new file was put in the proper order.

We were standing in the narrow space between two bays. The opening at the end showed a section of shelving against the far wall which contained the Ds. One label said 'Delaney – Delmare'. I looked at the box above, but it was cast in shadow. Farrell ceased his rummaging and followed my gaze.

'Now, John,' he said. 'You don't think files on the likes of you are kept in here?'

'Where are they kept?'

He pushed the box back into its gap. 'Under Sibthorpe's bed.'

Back in his office, Farrell took a cloth-bound tombstone ledger from beneath his desk. It was a register of the inform- ation provided by each agent. Initials were written at the top of each page, and three columns on the right-hand side were headed: 'Information', 'Prosecution' and 'Other', with amounts of money recorded in each.

The book was arranged by alphabetical order, so many of the pages were left blank – to allow for the inclusion of new names. Still, I was surprised at the number of men employed. Some of the pages contained only two or three entries. Others were filled with text and figures, denoting a particularly prolific agent. One such page had the initials 'NH', which I guessed was Ned Holt. Though perhaps he would have been 'E' for Edward.

Farrell leafed through the ledger. 'Here you are.' The letters 'JD' were written at the top. Some items were already inscribed. Farrell lowered his spectacles and traced a finger over the page.

'Let's see. The case of James O'Neill. No payment – there must be a story there. The case of Captain Craddock.' The figure of £20 was written in the 'Prosecution' column. He looked at me over his glasses. 'That was you?'

I confirmed it was. He pursed his lips and nodded in approval.

He continued, 'I wrote in the latest entry just a few days ago. "Engaged to assist Sibthorpe for five pounds."' He looked around his desk for a pen. 'Don't worry, John. None of us mourned Devereaux's demise. An agent like that undermines the whole Department.'

Below that he wrote the date, then: 'Information on Nicholas Lynch', and '2 shillings' in the appropriate column. He said if the information was ever used in a prosecution, the payment would be increased to a pound, though he thought that unlikely. 'You won't get far on a few shillings, but you know yourself. Keep an ear out for any talk that might help convict a murderer, rapist or, worst of all, Repealer.'

A tally would be kept of all reports I provided, and work I carried out. 'You have to come here to collect your pay, on the last Friday of each month. It'll be with the guard down at the desk below.'

The spine of the ledger creaked as he closed it over. 'I think you'll be able to make a decent living at it. Do you have any family?'

I said I was recently married.

He screwed the lid on to his fountain pen, then looked at me closely. 'And your wife, is she very beautiful?'

I considered. 'Very beautiful' would overstate it. There were moments – when her head bent beside a candle and a lock of hair fell; or when she laughed over her shoulder . . .

Farrell was looking at me with an amused expression, and I realized I had mulled too long. 'She's handsome.'

He fixed his glasses back on top of his head. 'That's what I like,' he said. 'An honest informant.'

6

Helen swept the floorboards before the hearth. She took some of her manuscript pages and laid them on the ground, then sat with her back to the fire. One leg was folded beneath her dress; the other splayed out, bare below the knee, a blackened sole shown to the room. I poured two whiskeys and went to join her, sitting in a warm spot where the early afternoon sunshine fell upon the floor. Helen dipped her nib in ink, too far as usual, for a couple of black dots splashed upon the pale yellow sheet as the pen hovered.

'Let's start with mine,' she said as I placed the drink beside her.

She began to write out the names of Stokes family members residing in Dublin, the page headed by the name of her paternal grandmother, who was still living bent and incontinent in Ballsbridge. Helen tapped the pen on her chin as she recalled the names of cousins, their spouses, and even some of their children, to fill in the branches of her family tree. In short order, a full Stokes lineage was produced and left aside for the ink to dry.

My pedigree was more sparse. Since Alex was abroad, only Cecilia lived in the city, married to Captain Dickenson. To supplement my sheet I gave the names of fellows from college, classmates, as well as those I used to drink with in the Eagle. As such, Arthur made it on to both our lists.

We then set about noting the names of mere acquaintances: old lecturers and college staff; the ladies who attended the Stokes salon every Tuesday afternoon; Mr Stokes's wide circle of friends. I mentioned her coming-out ball, and she jokingly gasped. She said, 'Of course,' and began to list those who'd attended, who so far had escaped our recollection. After writing one name she prodded it with her pen. 'I've something good on him.'

'What is it?'

'I'll tell you when we're done.'

After an hour we could think of no others. I refilled the glasses, and we regarded the littered pages of smudged name-rolls and crooked bloodlines. Helen appeared wistful as she arranged the sheets more neatly.

'This could have been our wedding list.'

Farrell had taken me aside after my third or fourth visit to Fownes Street. He said it was all very well keeping an eye on our new neighbours in the tenements, and an ear on the loose talk in the pubs on Gardiner Street – which Helen and I had begun to frequent – but we should not forget the social circle to which we once belonged.

I told him the people we knew when growing up were loyal for the most part. He said that may be, but Sibthorpe liked to be able to call on influential people for favours. High-ranking surgeons, bankers and lawyers could provide any number of services to the Department. 'We've found that the more a man has to lose, the more he's willing to help.'

When I told Helen of the notion, she put down her pen and gazed out of the window. I thought she was considering the ethical dilemma of betraying the trust of former friends and relatives, but she turned back to me and said, 'A few names spring to mind immediately.'

I couldn't blame her. Another month had gone by without word from a family member or former friend. All we had was each other, and our only income came from my interaction with the Castle. Also, the small bit of money that had remained when we sold the house in Fitzwilliam Street, and paid off the bank, was almost gone. We were facing an uncertain winter.

So we made our lists. I pointed to a name of one of O'Neill's classmates, and told Helen how we had spoken once in the pub. He had drunkenly confided that he wrote articles for an underground newspaper, which operated from a basement in Temple Lane. Its title escaped me, some word in the Gaelic tongue. But he told me his pen-name was 'Penchant'. Helen giggled at its silliness. He was now studying in King's Inns, and was due to be called to the bar in a couple of years.

I asked Helen about the man she had noted earlier. She said he was a friend of her father, an accountant called Graves. He was Protestant, but he was married to a Catholic heiress, the only daughter of Paschal O'Brien, merchant of College Green. Mr O'Brien had insisted that any issue from the marriage would be raised in the Catholic faith, and inserted a stipulation to that effect in their marriage settlement.

They had a child named Christine, who was Helen's age, and a good friend when they were both young. Christine revealed to Helen that she was secretly being raised and tutored by Protestant governesses, all with the consent of her mother. If that was known, the marriage settlement would be void, and Graves would lose any claim he had to the O'Brien estate.

Helen took another sip of whiskey. 'Christine swore me to secrecy.' She began to write a note beside the man's name. 'But she hasn't answered a single letter I've written in the past three months.'

In the end we only came up with five or six stories that would be worth telling the Castle. The sun had dipped below the terrace opposite on Grenville Street. Helen stood up and stretched, then went to sit on the end of the bed. 'When you tell Farrell these things, does he just take your word for it?'

He did, as far as I knew.

'Then you could always make some things up.'

I looked to see if she was joking. She didn't seem to be. 'I'd get in trouble.'

She thought for a moment. 'But most of the information you bring isn't acted upon anyway. It sits in an archive gathering dust.'

'I'm sure agents who provide false information aren't employed for very long.'

'But they wouldn't know it's false.'

That was true. At least not until it was too late. The cheap whiskey was making my head ache, so I said I'd think about it.

On the last Friday of each month I went to Farrell's building to collect my earnings. I was given a specific time – three hours after midday – presumably so agents were spared awkward encounters at the pay desk. In my year and a half of bringing information to Fownes Street, I never bumped into a fellow agent in the hall, or passed one in the doorway.

Chance meetings between agents must happen from time to time. I wonder if they tip hats, exchange a brief conspiratorial grin or friendly word. Maybe they avoid eye-contact and shuffle past each other, as if they'd met in a shop that sells erotic prints – like the one on Earl Street that Helen and I once visited.

When I collected the money that November, the guard at the desk said Farrell wanted to see me.

I said, 'What about?'

He didn't reply, just reached across and pulled the cord.

I climbed the stairs to the archivist's office. Farrell looked up as I entered and gestured to an empty chair. When I pulled it from the desk, a hidden stack of files almost toppled off the seat.

He lifted his spectacles for a moment and squinted at them. 'Just throw those on the floor,' he said. 'Sibthorpe has a little job for you. Actually it's more of a demonstration.'

I grew uneasy, for I had seen one of Sibthorpe's demonstrations before.

Farrell began to search through folders strewn on his desk. 'He's interviewing someone in the Castle as we speak, and wants his file brought over.' He found the item he was looking for, a thin brown folder with 'Matthew Gibson' printed on the front. I recognized the name.

'The barrister?'

'The very same.'

Gibson QC had been making headlines for some time. He was a young Catholic lawyer who had gained a reputation by successfully defending several radicals in recent trials. He was about to take on the brief in another high-profile case, that of the head of the Rockites, who had been captured in Dublin over the summer. I knew about it because members of the oath-bound society had carried out reprisal attacks. They had smashed windows in government buildings, and a young police officer had been killed when the Brunswick Street station was set ablaze.

Farrell said, 'Don't dawdle.'

Sibthorpe interviewed Gibson on the third floor of the

barracks in Lower Castle Yard. The office was about as big as our room in Grenville Street, with a few filing cabinets in one corner, a bookshelf opposite the cold fireplace, and his desk beneath a large window. Gibson sat with his back to the door. He didn't turn at the sound of my approach, or when I held out the folder to Sibthorpe and said, 'I was told to bring you this.'

Tom took it and thanked me. 'Take a seat over there, John.'

Two chairs stood against the wall, from where I could see both men in profile. Gibson was a striking figure, tall and broad-shouldered. He was clean-shaven, with a straight nose and thick brown curls. He caught me looking at him, regarded me coolly for a second, then returned his attention to Sibthorpe.

I had interrupted a conversation. Gibson said he had come here because of an expectation that a proposal would be put to him regarding his client. So far nothing concrete had been discussed, and he had begun to suspect his time was wasted. 'I've a mind to quit this meeting and take my chances in the courtroom.'

Sibthorpe leafed through some documents in the folder. He said, 'But we're only getting started.'

The door opened without a knock and another man entered. He was of medium height, with a wiry frame and sunken cheeks. His most remarkable feature was his hair, for when shaving, he had brought the razor above his sideburns and ears, completely baring the sides of his head up to the level of his bald pate, so only a clump of dirty blond hair hung from the back of his head.

The man began to walk towards me, and I straightened in my seat, expecting an exchange. But he took hold of the other chair to drag to the desk. He positioned it at the narrow side of the table, facing towards Gibson. Before sitting, he extended his hand to the young lawyer and introduced himself.

'I'm Lyster.'

Gibson hesitated before gripping the hand.

Sibthorpe waited for Lyster to be seated. 'You said you expected to hear a proposal, Mr Gibson. Well, here's one. I want you to resign your position as advocate in the trial due to start next week, and further swear never to defend another radical in the course of your career.'

Everyone in the room was still. After a few seconds, a smile crept on to Gibson's face. He shook his head, took a pair of gloves from his coat pocket, and began to put them on. 'I don't have time for this. Gentlemen, meeting you has been quite instructive.' He shifted forward, causing his chair to scrape on the floor.

Sibthorpe looked down. 'I have before me two unsigned letters to a man called Simon Purcell of Holles Street, dated in the spring of this year.'

Gibson made a point of continuing to don his gloves, his fingers undulating as he pulled one tight. But a colour had come into his cheeks.

Sibthorpe held up one of the letters, its envelope attached to the top left corner by a metal pin. He read some of it aloud, his voice so drained of sentiment that it made the contents sound particularly ridiculous.

'"My dearest S. My beloved and beautiful friend. What words can I use to answer your charming lines received this morning? In the month we have been separated all has seemed lost."' Sibthorpe cleared his throat. '"I can't help but wonder: do you still sleep in your shirt-tails; do you still wake before dawn and stare at the ceiling; could you have found yourself another bedfellow?"'

He stopped reading and looked up. 'It's signed "MG". Did you write this, Matthew?'

Gibson remained silent.

Lyster said, 'I might be able to help.' He opened a folder on the desk. 'A few weeks ago, I wrote to Mr Gibson looking for a legal opinion.' He withdrew a document consisting of several pages. 'I must say his reply was very prompt.'

Sibthorpe said, 'Excellent. Let me quickly read from the second letter.' He scanned through the missive. 'Let's see, Matthew asks why Simon hasn't written back: "Could it be the letter was lost?" – not a bad guess. He wonders if Simon would be willing to move to London, as they had discussed several times, to embark upon a life together. "If you still wish it, meet me at our table in the Hibernian Hotel on the thirteenth at nine." And he finishes, "My one friend, I love you more than any living thing, and time nor chance nor age can ever lessen this love."'

Lyster said, 'Hold on.' His index finger traced over a page. 'Look what's written in this. "To do so would lessen your exposure to a fall in the stock price." Let's compare the word.'

They placed the love letter and legal opinion side by side and bent their heads to examine. Gibson took no notice of their charade. He turned his head to gaze out of the window.

Lyster said, 'Mr Gibson has very distinctive esses.'

Sibthorpe agreed. 'It's undoubtedly the same hand.'

'Very effeminate.'

Sibthorpe sat back in his chair. He regarded the young barrister. 'I hope you didn't wait too long in the hotel.'

I was impressed by Gibson's poise. He didn't seem humiliated, or angry at the intrusion. Perhaps he took solace in the knowledge that his friend had not rebuffed him as he must have believed. The letters had been intercepted, not ignored. I pictured Gibson at his table in the Hibernian, nursing a single drink, looking up expectantly whenever the door opened, his heart breaking a little each time.

Sibthorpe began to tidy the papers on his desk. 'I think you'll agree our original proposal was quite fair.' Gibson continued to look away, but he nodded once. It was unclear what Sibthorpe thought of the young man's vice. He spoke in a matter-of-fact tone. 'You'll find plenty of work to match your talent in Common Pleas, and Exchequer. Just stay clear of Queen's Bench.' He made a note on a sheet of paper, as if recording the minutes of a meeting. Then he said, 'You can go.'

When Gibson was halfway to the door, Sibthorpe hesitated, picked an envelope from the file and called the lawyer back. 'I'm afraid we also had to stop this letter from Simon addressed to you.' He motioned for him to take it. 'It's unopened.'

Gibson took the missive. His eyes lingered on the familiar handwriting, and the date of the postmark stamped in the top right corner. He turned the envelope over, gently brushing a gloved finger along the seal. Then he placed it in an inside pocket and left the room.

Lyster leaned back until the legs of his chair tilted, and said, 'That went well.' Then he turned in my direction and regarded me for some time, as if committing my features to memory. 'Who's this?'

Tom made the introduction. Since it was late in the afternoon, he suggested we go for a drink, but said, 'First I just have to check a few things.'

He led the way through a series of corridors, past the stairwell from which I'd entered, and into a large workroom. More than a dozen clerks were seated in two rows of desks with an aisle between them. A series of tall bay windows admitted wintry sunshine on the right, opposite a wall containing square filing cabinets and neat bookshelves. The desks were like those

I remembered from my schooldays: sparse wooden seats attached to their tables by wrought-iron slats. The clerks bent over their work, and didn't lift their heads as we passed. I noticed the more senior among them had seats close to the windows. The only noise was our shuffled footsteps, and the scratching of nibs over paper and parchment, lending the room the air of a scriptorium.

I had assumed that Farrell's archive was the extent of the Department's administration. But of course it required more: an inner circle of civil servants managing correspondence, writing memoranda, receiving petitions, preparing accounts. I looked at them trace their words, and wondered if they made a distinction between a request for funds from the Chief Secretary's office, or the warrant for someone's arrest and interrogation.

Sibthorpe's desk stood apart, beneath a slope in the ceiling caused by an external staircase, which meant he had to duck his head as he sat down. Five opened folders were set out. Sibthorpe took up a pen and scanned through the topmost document in each. When finished, he would sign his name at the bottom and close the folder over. However, for the last one he perused the letter for longer, wrote out a note instead of his signature, and left the file open.

An old clerk rose noiselessly, gathered the four closed files and placed them in a tray beside the cabinets. Then he picked up the opened one, glanced at its contents, and brought it to a worker in the far corner. The young man looked up anxiously, with eyebrows raised and lips parted. He appeared perplexed that his work had been found lacking, and made a show of reading Sibthorpe's note before it had been fully set in front of him. The older clerk turned on his heel and went back to his desk without remark. Lyster caught my eye and winced at the young man's discomfort.

Sibthorpe was writing in a diary, and as I watched him he appeared every bit the conscientious head of a department. I tried to match this version with the man who coerced witness statements from students, or the one who had Devereaux so ruthlessly killed.

Sibthorpe lifted his head to face me, as if he knew what I was thinking, but he was just glancing at a clock on the wall over my shoulder. He resumed writing.

Perhaps he'd ended up here more by accident, assigned by some harried under-secretary, who was unaware of Tom's peculiar aptitude. If he had been Head of Public Works, or Poor Relief, or Hospitals and Asylums, maybe he'd have shown the same zeal, the same single-mindedness.

Sibthorpe finished his entry and locked the diary in a drawer. He said, 'All right, gentlemen. Let's go.'

To leave the building, we had to descend a staircase and cut through the DMP station on the ground floor. Uniformed policemen walked through the corridors, or sat in offices or stood by counters. But none acknowledged our presence; none challenged or questioned our presence either. They lowered their eyes or stepped aside, and only a few returned a nod when Lyster greeted them by name. On the paths outside, I noticed a similar reaction. Court officials who walked together speaking loudly would become quiet as Sibthorpe neared, and then resume their conversation once we'd passed. A clerk carrying a large sheaf of documents stumbled over a step to the viceregal apartments, and his papers fell to the ground. Sibthorpe and Lyster bent down to help. The hassled worker continuously thanked them as he scrabbled about, but when he recognized the source of his aid, he became tight-lipped, and took the pages back with unseemly haste. He clamped them beneath his elbow and walked on.

Lyster said, 'There's gratitude.'

The three of us went to the upstairs lounge in the Black Bull on Ship Street – the room in which I'd met with Devereaux and Holt on the night we visited the dissectionists. Once seated, Sibthorpe told Lyster about the quality of information I was providing to the Department. Lyster listened with his head inclined, but he kept his eyes on me.

I said, 'Are you an agent yourself, Mr Lyster?'

He considered for a moment. 'I used to be.'

Sibthorpe said, 'Lyster's now our chief interrogator.'

Half an hour later we were joined by Farrell, who had come to retrieve Gibson's file. The Department was well represented by those at the table: the informer, archive-keeper, interrogator and overseer. It was an effective system; one I had now seen work first-hand.

As the afternoon wore on, Farrell began to speak privately with Sibthorpe, something about a shortage of space in Fownes Street. I had little option but to converse with Lyster. He drank from a glass of stout and tumbler of whiskey, taking sips from each in turn, judging the volume so both were finished at the same time. He told me the work I did was vital. It always made his job easier when Farrell had a file on a suspect he had to question. 'Did you provide that information on Gibson?'

'No,' I said. 'I just . . . delivered the file.'

'Well, even so, bill the Department for your time. Make sure that every piece of work you do or titbit you provide is paid for. I'm always suspicious when reports in a file have been given voluntarily. No man should ever provide information except for money.'

I was more interested in what happened when there was no file.

He shrugged. 'Then we explore other options.'

Presumably it required more finesse than a few hard clouts to the head.

He regarded me for a moment, as if flattered by my curiosity. 'Of course. They're no good to you unconscious. Also, it's not ideal to leave marks on the face, at least ones that can't heal after a few days.' He opened his hands before him. 'I like to focus on fingers. Especially for men whose work requires dexterity.' He brought both hands down on the table. 'A musician will tell you anything if you show him a set of pliers.'

Lyster caught the eye of a waiter and pointed to his empty glass, then leaned back towards me. 'But then again, every interrogator has his own favourite part of the body.'

He broke off to order another round for the table. He had noted the preferences as if for a style of literature. I remember Helen once asked me what was my favourite part of her body. She said, 'And you can't say my face.' I'm not sure why she assumed that would be my answer.

Lyster continued, 'We haven't had a good murderer in a while. They're usually the ones where you can be creative. No one admits to a murder if they're not guilty. When they finally crack you know you've done a good job.' He half closed his eyes and nodded. 'It's nice to get a feeling of satisfaction from your work.'

Farrell and Sibthorpe had finished their discussion, so talk at the table turned to more general matters. When Farrell said he had to go, I made my excuses and departed with him.

As for Helen, it was her neck.

Dublin went through a cold snap that December. Compact ice lay in the gaps between cobbles, local children ran around with rags tied about their feet, and wind whistled through the cracks of our north-facing windows.

But it had been a lucrative November. We both agreed that our chief comfort should be warmth, so we never skimped on fuel. A stack of firewood, a small bag of coal and a box of lucifer matches made one corner of the room untidy. Nor did we allow ourselves to run short of wine, supplemented with the occasional bottle of whiskey – north of the river they could be bought quite cheaply.

Helen would purchase provisions from the local markets; she said they always sold me produce on the brink of perishing. Since she had an uncanny ability to overcook meat, I assumed the cooking duties. For a student of the natural sciences, frying a chop was hardly a challenge. The warmth and smells seeped into the hallway, and the Lynch children would come up to play on our landing. Once in a while I liked to fling open the door and watch them scatter.

We had no incentive to rise early, and would often stay in bed till noon. That was when the room was at its coldest. We'd hunker beneath the weight of blankets, as well as overcoats and dresses used for extra bedclothes. As we lay awake, Helen liked to make plans and discuss them. We decided I should continue to earn money through the Castle for the time being, enough to retake my final year in Trinity the following September, and attain my degree. Then I could look for a more respectable job. She would complete her novel and post extracts to literary periodicals and publishing houses here and in London. Within a year or two, she said, we could have enough money to keep a house and re-enter proper society.

The cold weather meant there was much less activity on the streets. One morning, we heard a commotion coming from the corner of Mountjoy Square. A hansom cabbie had been killed when his horse skittered on the ice and he was thrown against the park railings. From our window we could just about see the edge of a crowd gather to watch the removal of the body. The horse stood to one side, its head bowed low.

Helen couldn't get used to the ice, and would cling to my hand whenever we ventured out. I kept telling her she had to lean forward while walking, but she didn't trust herself. I'd often have to hold her up after a slip. On one occasion, when she almost dragged us both down, I said, 'People will think you've been drinking.'

'Let them.'

The footpath opposite our window in Grenville Street dipped down at the entrance of a stable-lane. Children from the tenements would pour water on the small slope in the granite to create a hazard. Everyone on the street was aware of this and stepped over it. But strangers cutting through were often caught out.

One afternoon, I was bringing a mug of tea to Helen when I looked out to see an old woman approach the icy patch. I paused at the window. The woman was hunched as she walked, swaddled in a bundle of black shawls and scarves. I noticed some children in an upper-storey window across the street had gathered, and were looking down at the woman in eager anticipation.

The amusing thing was how she went down in stages. As her right foot began to slip, she planted her left foot to try and regain balance. For a fleeting moment it seemed she would remain upright, but then the left foot gave way completely, her legs kicked up, and she fell backwards with her arms out-stretched. I looked up to see the children explode in silent mirth: heads were thrown back, hands clapped over eyes; a few disappeared beneath the sill as if their legs had failed them. It was quite infectious and I chuckled in response. Helen looked up. 'What is it?'

'An old woman fell on the ice.'

She tutted and returned to her work.

I put the mug on her desk and went back to the window. The woman had rolled on to her side in an attempt to sit up. A moment later, the front door of a house opened and two figures descended the steps. I had seen them once or twice before. They were Italian migrants, both in their late teens. The taller one had a scraggy beard; the other was clean-shaven with straight black hair swept over his ears. They hurried to the prostrate woman and helped her back to her feet. One of them took her elbow to offer some support, but she shook it off and continued on doggedly.

The two boys watched after her for a moment. The shorter one began to feel the cold, for he pulled his coat tight and folded his hands beneath his arms. After another exchange they retreated back into the house. In the top-floor garret, a grubby flag of the Kingdom of Naples was displayed in the window. When I looked down again, the old woman had disappeared from view.

Warm pubs were popular during the cold nights. The closest establishment was Kavanagh's, which was just around the corner on Gardiner Street. It was relatively clean and well run, with a large hearth in the back wall. Three regulars always stood at the bar, though they never spoke to each other: a Catholic priest; a retired bookkeeper who was forever totting up rows of figures in the margins of his newspaper; and the tinker Cooney, who lived in an encampment beyond Dorset Street. He wore the same thing every night: a frayed tweed coat with the knot of a leather apron tied around his neck.

One evening the bar was full, so Helen and I took our drinks and leaned against a narrow ledge that ran along the wall. The two Italian boys were sitting at a small table nearby that had some extra seats. The taller one reached over and tentatively touched my elbow. When I turned, he gestured to the chairs and invited us to sit.

The table was cramped so we had to make conversation. The taller boy with the thin beard was named Angelo. His friend was Domenico. Both of them could speak English tolerably well. Though Domenico was mostly quiet, it seemed to me he had a better understanding of the language. Angelo told us they were old friends from the city of Bari. They had intended to travel to London, to try and make their fortunes, but they had only managed to find passage on a cargo ship to Dublin. They had been here for over a month, looking for work to pay for the remainder of their journey.

He patted his friend's shoulder. So far only Domenico had been able to make a few pennies, as an organ grinder on Carlisle Bridge. Helen smiled at the younger man and asked if he played any other instruments. He looked down shyly and shook his head. Angelo nudged his elbow and said something in Italian. He told Helen, 'He plays guitar. But he had to sell his back in Bari.'

Helen told them she had always dreamed of travelling the length of Italy as part of a grand tour. I glanced across; it was the first I'd heard of it. As she spoke of the cities she would visit and the sites she would see, the young men gazed at her. From their perspective she was a young, well-bred lady, bright and educated and only a few years their senior. She was relaxed and leaning forward, with ink-stained fingertips resting on her glass. The skin behind her collarbone dipped down into a shadowy hollow. She smelled of soap and unwashed clothes. They may even have found her dun hair and sea-green eyes exotic, lit from below by candlelight refracted through my glass of beer.

Angelo could not stay quiet for long. 'You' – then he glanced at me – 'both of you should avoid Florence and visit Bologna instead.' But Helen said she wished to see the streets where Dante met Beatrice.

Domenico asked her if she had read Dante.

She said only an English translation. 'If I ever get to Italy I will try to read it in the original.'

Domenico smiled and said he understood. After all, he had read Shakespeare in Italian.

Angelo couldn't hold his drink, and he became louder as the evening progressed. His stories were rambling and tedious, and he paid no heed to the quiet pleas from his friend to remain silent. When another table became available in the corner, we took our leave. Helen smiled at Domenico and said they would speak again. He extended a hand towards her, but Helen had looked around to gather her shawl from the seat, so he withdrew it.

Helen didn't stay much longer. She said speaking with the two Italians had given her an idea for a character, which she wanted to sketch out at home. I looked at the clock behind the bar. 'But it's early yet.'

She said I could stay for another if I wished. 'I'll be all right walking back on my own.'

'I'd better accompany you.'

'There's no need.' She smiled at me. 'I know my way around by now.'

'Have you got keys?'

She patted her hip and nodded, then leaned over to kiss my cheek.

After Helen left, I kept to myself. No more fuel was added to the fire and it dwindled to a red glow. The crowd began to disperse and, by midnight, fewer than a dozen patrons lingered in Kavanagh's. Angelo and Domenico still sat at their table. Once or twice I looked over to see them talking with their heads close together. The level of conversation had dropped to a murmur, and I could hear Kavanagh exchange the odd word with Cooney at the bar.

The Italian boys began to argue. Their discussion became louder and heads began to turn. Angelo, who was now very drunk, had half risen from his chair, and gestured towards his friend while he spoke in Italian. Domenico remained seated. His hand was on the table holding the bottom of his beer, and his head was bent forward. He only said one or two words in response to his friend's tirade. Angelo turned and walked unsteadily to the door; he passed my table without seeming to notice me. A swirl of cold air entered as he stumbled on to the street.

Domenico seemed aware that all eyes were upon him, but after a few moments the focus shifted away, and quiet conversations resumed.

When he stood up, his chair didn't scrape backwards, but rather it tilted up, and the legs fell with a clatter when he stepped away. He brought his glass to the bar and asked for another. While Kavanagh refilled it from a barrel, Domenico undid the bottom button of his waistcoat. A leather pouch had been sewn into his belt, and he opened the purse to fish out a coin. He was standing next to Cooney, who looked down with interest at the boy's fumbling.

About an hour after midnight, Kavanagh announced that he was locking up. I was the first of the stragglers to make my way to the door, which was wedged in its frame, warped by the heat of the fireplace and the cold outside. On Gardiner Street, a breeze whistled down the hill towards the river. I set off for home, stepping gingerly between frosty patches on the path. A hansom cab came towards me. The cabbie was wrapped in an oilskin coat, and the wide, soft brim of his hat was pulled down on both sides by strings that tied beneath his chin in a slip-knot. He slowed as he drew near, but when I made no motion to hail him, he carried on.

A few others had left the pub. Two of them stopped the cab and climbed aboard. Domenico had also emerged. He stepped out to cross the street towards a church further up the hill, but had to pause to allow the hansom cab to pass by.

He was being followed by Cooney, and I stopped in order to observe. By the time Domenico reached the opposite pavement he must have heard footsteps, for he turned to face his pursuer. They stood near the entrance of a stable-lane – one of those lanes that appears as an archway in the terrace with windows above, as if it had been tunnelled through someone's front parlour. Domenico lifted his hands with his palms held out, before Cooney grabbed his lapel, and forced him backwards and out of sight.

Faint sounds drifted on the cold street, but they may have been tricks of the wind, or the remote rumble of carriages.

In less than a minute, Cooney came back out alone. He stuffed something inside his coat as he turned north towards the junction with Dorset Street. Domenico should have emerged soon after, shaken and bloodied perhaps, but a couple of minutes passed, and there was still no sign of him.

The houses at that end of Gardiner Street were newly built and mostly unoccupied, though a few cracks of light could be seen in the shuttered windows. A street lamp close to the entrance of the stable-lane cast a diagonal shadow across its mouth, the edge of the darkness made jagged where it scaled pieces of rubbish, or dipped into the contour of a dry pothole.

Domenico was slumped against the wall near the back

entrance of the tunnel, as it emerged into the open stable-lane at the rear of the houses on Mountjoy Square. His head came up. Blood dripped from his upper lip into the mud. His left eye had already begun to close over and his face had become discoloured, though bruises hadn't yet formed. He slowly leaned his head to the side as if he was going to be sick, then spat on to the cold dirt beside him. With his head still bowed he said, 'The man at the bar.'

He refused to take my handkerchief, and flinched when I wiped the blood and grime from his chin.

Under his coat, Domenico's grey flannel shirt was darkened by blood, as if he'd been stabbed, but the cut was only to his hand. When held towards the street light, a neat slice could be seen on his bloody palm, bisecting the life-line. It had created a fold of skin that looked as if it could open and close like the lip of an envelope. His fingers were slender and grubby; the thumbnail was particularly long and cut square.

I used my handkerchief to clean the wound, then I tied it tightly over his knuckles. Domenico's whole body began to shiver. He was in danger of losing consciousness, and once or twice his head perked up, like a gentleman dozing over a book.

'Angelo is going to kill me,' he said. 'All our money was in the wallet, everything we saved for more than a month.' It also contained travel documents and letters of introduction to an Italian businessman in London. He took a deep breath and rubbed his uninjured hand over his forehead. 'We'll never get them back.'

'There are people in Dublin Castle who can help. As long as Cooney doesn't destroy the letters, the police will be able to retrieve them, and probably most of the money.'

He kept his head bowed. 'The police won't care.'

I said there was one department that cared about everything.

Once a report was made, it could be arranged for Cooney to be arrested and his home searched.

He rolled his head and squinted through his good eye. 'I thought you were just a . . .' and then a word in Italian.

'Tell me what happened.'

Domenico now sat with his back to the wall and his knees gathered up. His head bent forwards in the crook of his elbow. 'When I left the pub I wanted to see if the doors of the church were still open, but the man followed me.' He looked towards the mouth of the tunnel. 'There was a knife in his hand. He said he was going to take my wallet and pushed me into the alley.'

The information was probably worth a few shillings. It was no doubt a violent crime, but Domenico was correct – the authorities wouldn't care much about the mugging of a foreigner.

'I tried to tell him there was no money, only personal stuff, and he got angry.'

There wouldn't be much call for a file on the tinker Cooney either, a penniless drunk who lived beyond the city limits.

'He kept telling me to hand it over. He said other things but I couldn't understand his accent. I still said no, so he punched me.'

Domenico was still shivering. The blows he had taken to the face began to show as bruises. If he got sick and died, then maybe the information against Cooney would be worth more.

'He hit me three times, more while I was on the ground. I asked him to stop. He came at me with the knife. I thought he was going to kill me.'

If no one had come, then he would have lain here until he lost consciousness. It was already an hour past midnight. Another hour or two in the elements and he'd freeze to death.

The enclosed laneway was a lonely spot. Cold air funnelled past its cheap grey bricks, vaulted ceiling and uneven ground. Unless someone walked through directly, he wouldn't be spotted until morning. And if he died out here, then Cooney would be liable for murder.

'But he only began to hack at my belt. I tried to stop him. He said if I made a noise he would cut my throat.'

Information for a murderer would bring forty pounds. Enough money to last half a year.

At the bottom of the wall, the mortar around some of the bricks had become rotten. One brick in particular rocked back and forth like a loose tooth. It was damp to the touch, and pieces of it fell away as I took it out.

I tried to judge the brick's heft.

'He cut the belt, then took the wallet and walked away. He didn't say anything else. I just lay here.' He looked up at me. 'And then you came.'

When I brought the brick down on his head it broke apart like a clod of earth. It made a sound that I often hear in this place: the rhythmic crumbling impacts that drift from the stone-breakers' yard. Tiny pieces slipped down into the dark creases of his clothes, and the finest particles clung to his hair as if he wore a powdered wig. He slumped forward and to the side. For a moment he was still, lying face down. I allowed the last fragments of the brick to sift through my fingers.

The strike hadn't been hard enough. He stirred and began to crawl towards the lane's entrance to Gardiner Street. I knelt back down at the wall, but the other bricks were set fast, so I picked through the rubbish that was strewn about the laneway. My eyes fell upon a brown, empty whiskey bottle.

I glanced up. Domenico had managed to get close to the point where light from the street entered the lane. I closed on him and took up both of his legs by the ankles. With shuffling steps, I dragged him back into the middle of the alley as if he was a wheelbarrow. His hooked fingers could find no purchase in the ground.

I picked up the bottle by its neck, held my left arm across my eyes and swung it against the wall. A hollow peal rang out in the tunnel and my arm recoiled as the bottle bounced back, completely intact. If I had been launching a ship it would have been cursed. I swung again, with enough force that the glass shattered. Shards went everywhere. The broken neck was left in my hand but it had no sharp edge. I bent down and felt about for a large enough piece. Domenico had resumed his crawl towards the street and I had to keep glancing over my shoulder to check on his progress. Each flake of glass was too small, or the edge too dull. At one point I found two shards containing parts of the whiskey label, which fitted together like pieces of a jigsaw.

My hand fell upon the smooth round disc of the bottle's base. It had a slight concave bump which was easy to grip, and a long fragment of the bottle's side still attached. I touched its edge, which was sharp like a knapped piece of flint.

I've often wondered what went through Domenico's head that night. First, to be set upon in a strange city, beaten and robbed and left for dead. Perhaps he prayed for someone to find him, to somehow stumble across him in the small hours. And those prayers were answered. He was revived. His wounds were bound. Not only that, he was told that justice would be done; that his possessions would be returned and his robber punished. Then the brick came down. Was he trying to think what had he done as he crawled away? What had he said to make me turn against him? He died not knowing.

I re-entered the street and stopped beneath a gas-lamp to

examine the blood that covered my right hand. I rubbed the fluid between my thumb and forefingers, as if testing its thickness.

Domenico had been walking towards the Church of St Francis Xavier before Cooney stopped him. It was a little farther up the street and fronted right on to the pavement. Behind the railings, four large columns supported a triangular pediment, which covered a shadowy portico.

A marble font of holy water stood adjacent to the entrance, and a fragile pane of ice had formed on its surface. It broke apart as I pushed my hand through. Red tendrils expanded in the water like tea leaves in a cup. The cold was unbearable. I examined my hands, saw a scarlet tinge between my fingers, and beneath my nails, and plunged them back in to scrub again. The water rolled and fell from the rim of the font to splash upon the flagstones.

When all trace was gone, I dried my hands against my trousers, then dug them into my coat pockets, balling my fists to try and get the blood flowing. I set off towards Grenville Street. My hands began to cause me some concern. They had become painful; patches of skin had begun to itch and I wondered if I was suffering from frost-nip. I blew on them and rubbed them together. It was odd to see my fingers writhe over each other while numb to any feeling, as if they belonged to someone else.

A carriage approached from behind. As it bore down, the clatter of hooves grew louder and I considered ducking into an arched doorway. But I would attract far less attention by continuing to walk normally. Cooney was the killer. At this stage it didn't matter if I was spotted on the street, for how else could I have been a witness to his crime? Still, I had an uncomfortable sensation as the carriage drew near, like a drop of water rolling beneath my collar. The driver pushed the horses, and I feared the din would wake the entire street. I couldn't help but turn my head as the carriage trundled by, like an actor delivering an aside.

In Grenville Street, I glanced up at the garret where the Italians were living. The shutters were open and a faint light flickered in the window. Then a shadow moved across the glass and I looked away. Was Angelo surveying the street? He would have known that the pub had been closed for more than half an hour.

I hurried up the steps of number six, fumbling in my waistcoat for the front-door key. My fingers were so cold they could hardly function. I glanced over my shoulder, and saw a dark figure outlined in the top-floor window across the street. The key slipped from my hand and chimed on the granite step. I swept it up and stuck it in the keyhole. I looked back again. The figure hadn't moved, but then I realized it was only a shirt hanging against the window frame. I finally managed to grip the key properly, and turn it with a clunk. I pushed through the door and swung it shut, catching the handle just in time so it wouldn't slam, then leaned against the frame and listened to my own heavy breathing in the pitch-black hallway.

Helen had placed more coal on the fire before she went to sleep, so the room would be warm when I returned from the pub. The embers provided a scant light. I entered as quietly as I could. A few loose pages remained on her writing desk, together with an opened inkpot. The floorboards creaked as I passed the bed, but she didn't stir. I knelt at the hearth, removed the guard and held my hands close to the cinders. I could feel my fingers begin to thaw, and had to pull them back when the heat became too great. The glow from the fire made my hands look red, and I checked more closely to ensure they were clean.

How should a man react to witnessing a murder? He would go to the police, of course, but on a cold night such as this he could be forgiven for stopping off at home first. Would he shake his wife awake and tell her what happened? I looked over at Helen in the bed. Her sleeping face was visible over the covers, her mouth agape and crooked, snoring softly.

Perhaps he'd cross the street and bang on the door of the victim's only friend, rouse the household, move past candlelit figures in the hallway wearing nightclothes, seek out Angelo and tell him the terrible news?

I recalled my first payment from the Castle, and how I'd lost out on thirty pounds when I told on Captain Craddock's killers a day too early. What was it Devereaux said? *The information you collect is precious.* I'd let Domenico be found in the morning, and the police investigation begin. Let them flounder for a couple of days. Only then would I go to Fownes Street and make my report.

The problem was what to tell Helen. She would be upset at the young man's death and insist I tell Angelo what I knew straight away. I moved to the bedside and brushed a lock that had fallen over her eye. News of the killing was going to cause a sensation in these streets over the next few days, and I would have to pretend to her I knew nothing of it. I ran my hand down her cheek. Once the money arrived she would forgive me. I curled my finger and lifted her chin to close her mouth. In her sleep, she moved her head away from my cold touch.

What would be the best way to describe Cooney's attack to the authorities? The more detailed my account, the more I was leaving myself open to awkward questions. Such as why I didn't intervene; why did I not check on the boy when I saw Cooney leave the alleyway alone; and if I did, why not report the murder straight away? I fetched a tumbler and dipped it in the drinking cask. Somehow, I had to report the fact that Domenico's purse was stolen from his belt. If the wallet or any items within it were found on or about Cooney, then my report would be confirmed as the key piece of evidence, and the reward would follow. I knew about the contents of the purse – the money and letters of introduction – but I couldn't admit to it, since I gleaned that information by interviewing the victim.

I knelt beside the hearth once more. It occurred to me that the crime scene was rather a mess. But what could I say, Cooney was an amateur killer. I thought of the tinker waking to news that the victim of his robbery had been found murdered. Perhaps he would doubt himself, and think that he'd cut the boy's throat after all.

The heat from the embers made my nose run. I patted my coat pocket and a creeping awareness made my heart sink.

My handkerchief was still wrapped around Domenico's knuckles.

It was just an old rag so it couldn't incriminate me; but it undermined everything. Its presence made it clear that more than one person had been with the boy in the stable-lane. Nobody would believe that Cooney mugged someone, paused to dress his wounds and then killed him. Nor could Domenico have tied the cloth himself. It proved that the robbery and the murder happened at different times.

If Cooney was going to be cleared then the information I had was worthless. I went to stand by the window. The street was empty. The light in Angelo's room had gone out.

As I retraced my steps to the laneway, I scolded myself for being so foolhardy. The Church of St Francis Xavier loomed in the distance. Surely it was better to forget the whole scheme – let Angelo move away and life return to normal. At that hour, all the windows on Gardiner Street were darkened. I heard a carriage on the other side of Mountjoy Square, but no one else walked on the street. Once or twice I slowed and considered turning back, but I had become fixated. If I could just take back the rag, then everything might still work out.

I stepped beneath the archway at the entrance of the lane, and saw a coach parked in the middle of the tunnel. Two horses faced towards the rear of the passage, standing patiently. In the gloom, I could make out the coachman kneeling over the body in the gutter. He must have heard my step, for his chin came up sharply and he looked towards me. Before he could speak I called out, 'What's going on here?'

A head poked out from the window of the carriage and looked back. It was an old woman, her gloved fingers clasped on top of the carriage door. The coachman spoke calmly. 'There's a dead boy here. He's been murdered.' He stood up, went to his seat at the front of the coach, and returned with a lantern.

It was too late to turn on my heels so I came forward. The coachman waited for me with the light held aloft. He wore a dark blue cape and a stovepipe hat. He had a thick black beard and glowered as I came near. I made a point of not looking directly at him, but rather down at the prostrate figure of Domenico, still hidden in the shadows.

'How do you know it's murder?'

The coachman lowered the lantern. Domenico lay face down with his head bent slightly towards the light. His hair had fallen across his brow, and dust from the brick was still visible. The light showed the results of Cooney's punches: patches of deep violet and red against his pallid grey skin. His lids were open, but the eyes didn't reflect the light. Only a small part of his neck was visible above his collar, where the corner of a ragged gash peeked out.

Domenico's head rested in a pool of blood, the nose bent and slightly submerged. His tongue extruded between parted lips into the blood puddle, as if he was about to lap. His arms extended out before him, the injured hand nearest the wall. I glanced at the soiled bandage.

I brought my palm up to my mouth and shook my head. There was a faint metallic smell on my fingers. 'Who would do such a thing?'

The frail, wrinkled woman in the carriage wore a heavy lappet over her grey hair, and fox fur over her shoulders. She gave the impression of being slightly drunk. She said, 'It's just ghastly. Charles, I'm beginning to get cold.'

It was easy to see why the reports subsequently referred to Domenico as the Italian boy. He was as tall as me, and only a few years my junior. But lying there, he seemed so slight.

The coachman bent back up. 'I'll have to bring Lady Findlater home. I'll wake the stable-boy and send him to Store Street.'

'Don't bother. I'll go and fetch the police. Which house number are you?'

He pointed out into the stable-lane and said number nine, the one with the red gate. He would come back out once the lady was safely inside.

I nodded, and immediately set off on my supposed errand. The coachman climbed back into his seat, but then paused and called back to me. 'What's your name?'

I said, 'Devereaux,' and continued on.

He flicked the reins and they moved away with a rattle. When the carriage had gone about twenty yards, I doubled back, bent over Domenico and took hold of his cold hand. I pulled the tied handkerchief away like I was peeling off a glove. The blood and grime had frozen into the cloth and it was stiff, as if it had been over-starched. I stuffed it into my pocket. When I was back on the street, I considered tossing it into the gutter, or over the railing into Mountjoy Park. But having risked so much to retrieve it, I wanted to leave no trace.

Once more I had to creep through my own chamber. The fire had ebbed further. Only a few red lines glowed through the dark ashes. I threw the cloth in and used a poker to stir the embers. It seemed as if it wasn't going to take. I was about to fetch the matches, but then a bloody edge blackened and smoked. A small flame appeared in one corner, licked along a crease, and the fabric curled up as it was engulfed. I felt an odd sense of relief and held my hands against the brief flare.

'What are you doing?'

I looked over my shoulder towards Helen. Her head was raised from the pillow and she squinted at me through sleep-filled eyes. The flame cast odd shadows into the room.

'It's just a used rag.' I shifted over to block her view of the hearth. 'Go back to sleep.'

7

The inside of the police carriage was cramped and poorly lit. A gaslight burned at the head of the cabin, casting a blue glow over the occupants, and the pre-dawn sky showed as dark violet against the barred windows. Iron bands girded the timber slats, with two metal benches attached on either side. Five of us sat in silence as we trundled through the early morning streets.

An Irish Constabulary sergeant with streaks of grey in his tawny moustache sat on my right. Three of his colleagues faced us on the bench opposite. They were younger and clean-shaven and our shoulders moved in unison to the gentle rocking. There was hardly any space between our legs. At one point the carriage made a sharp turn left, and I slipped forward in my seat, causing my knee to brush against one of the constables. The young man instinctively pulled his leg away, as if the contact was unseemly.

Like the others, he was dressed in a black uniform, his jacket closed over by a brown leather belt about the waist, and a row of shiny buttons, about the size of sovereigns, fastened up to and beneath his chin. His spiked helmet had a short peak over the brow. The constabulary insignia showed on the front: a harp on a red background beneath a crown.

The policemen sat upright, with their fists resting on their knees and a truncheon held in one hand. None of them spoke. I had attempted a few pleasantries with the sergeant, but he only gave gruff, one-word answers. The man closest to the rear of the carriage faced forward like the others, but he would occasionally turn his head quickly to look at me, as if he thought I was whispering his name.

It was cold again, and the chill made me fidget and squirm, continually gather my coat under my chin, or fold my hands beneath my arms. I was suffering a bout of flu, though Helen said it was just a cold. My raking coughs elicited disapproving looks from the others. The constable in the middle kept his face turned away from me, as if that could prevent contagion in the tight enclosure.

I felt an unmistakable tickling build up behind my nose. 'Could any of you gentlemen lend me—'

My request was cut short by a series of sneezes, which I directed against the front wall of the carriage on my left. As soon as one finished I felt the approach of the next. Afterwards my nose and mouth were covered in mucus, which I did my best to snuffle and siphon away. I was loath to use the cuff of my coat, so I sat there making unpleasant snorts and throaty gurgles.

The sergeant's fist closed tight over his truncheon until his knuckles turned white. After another minute of my spluttering he reached into a side pocket.

'Perhaps you'd care to use my handkerchief.'

I took the proffered cloth. 'Thank you.' I unfolded it. 'I appear to have mislaid my own.'

The handkerchief was quite clean, with the initials 'F.X.' embroidered in one corner.

'What does the X stand for?'

He remained silent.

I draped it over my nose and blew, folded the cloth once and blew again. I dabbed at my nostrils, then handed it back to the sergeant.

'Keep it.'

Houses had become sparse, replaced by trees and tall hedgerows. After several minutes, the driver rapped on the roof of the carriage while we were still in motion.

The sergeant straightened. 'Right, lads. We're close.'

Subtle changes came over the faces of the three constables. Jawlines became more prominent; lips pursed; eyes focused. The man on the far side looked at me again.

We came to a halt. Another knock on the roof and the sergeant removed the latch on the door in the rear of the car. He gave it a nudge and it swung outwards silently. The three constables rose from the bench, their heads bent beneath the carriage ceiling, and filed out of the back. He then turned to me. 'Remain close and keep quiet.'

I followed him out. In the gloaming, I could see the extent of the convoy. Three other police carriages had pulled up beside a ditch, and a dozen men had assembled on the road. Their commander, the head constable, had a full grey beard and a helmet with a flat top. He walked along the line, a lantern in one hand and a bundle of unlit torches in the crook of his elbow. Every second man took a torch. When he got to the end of the line he lit a firebrand, and a young constable rotated the head of his torch in the small flame until the pitch-soaked rag caught and blazed with a steady light. He held the flame out to the next man in line, and each torch was lit in a relay, until the company stood in brightness. A word from the head constable and they formed a column, two abreast. Those in front carried a thick iron battering ram. The sergeant that had accompanied me took me to stand at the rear.

Hushed orders were spoken and the company set off at a fast march. They took care to tread softly, and their boots sounded a muffled rhythm on the uneven surface. We walked for a few hundred yards along the rural road, the fields on both sides bounded by ditches. After a bend we came to a gap in the hedgerow spanned by a crudely built gate about eight feet tall, made from an assortment of planks and beams constructed against poles wedged into the earth on either side. The makeshift barrier was rickety and leaned out over the road. A padlocked chain looped through the slats to hold it shut. Beyond that lay the tinkers' camp.

The head constable held up his hand and we stopped. He motioned to the men carrying the battering ram to come forward. When they reached the gate they paused and awaited his order. Their commander looked back over the troop. He held his truncheon up and said, 'Ready.'

The constable just in front of me rotated his neck. The spike on his helmet described a circle.

The commander nodded once and said, 'Now.'

The two men took the battering ram back and swung it forward, as though they were throwing a drunk on to the street. It connected with the padlock, and burst through with little resistance. The chain broke with a snap, and pieces of wood split and fell away. That was the signal for the men to rush ahead; the sides of the gates were trampled underfoot rather than thrust apart. One of the men roared an indistinct cry, and the others – as if waiting for his prompt – let forth bellows of their own.

It struck me that it must take a certain confidence to be the first to let out such a bawl. I'd be reluctant to cry out first, lest I was the only one to do so. They continued their shouting as they swarmed into the clearing.

The itinerants had set up camp in a field about a hundred yards wide. It was bounded by the roadside ditch, a smaller scrub-lined gully that ran along a stream and, at the far end, a brick wall. There were five dwellings in the camp. Two of them were unhitched gypsy wagons, with their distinctive vaulted roofs. The other three were tumbledown hovels constructed from loose timbers and thatch, arranged in a rough circle. The space in between was littered with debris, rusting pike heads and plough blades. Cold campfires were dotted about: some had raked ashes and half-burnt timber; others were just rings of stones around scorched patches of earth. Four lean horses, tethered at the rear of the site, shied at the noise and blazing torches of the raiders.

Pairs of policemen split off and went towards each dwelling. I stayed back with the sergeant beside the demolished gate. The head constable stood alone in the clearing and surveyed the operation. By the time the first of the constabulary began to kick in doors, yells were coming from inside the houses.

The back window of a wagon opened and a couple of children, only about eight or nine years of age, tumbled out. One of the constables kicked in the door at the front, and both he and his comrade pressed into the cabin with loud shouts. The light from their torch emerged from the opened window as a flicker of darting shadows. A woman's scream was cut short. A man attempted to follow his children out of the window. He emerged up to his waist, before arms with black sleeves closed over his neck and shoulders and dragged him back in. His sons were looking up as he disappeared. The older one took his brother by the sleeve and they ran barefoot to the side of the camp, where they disappeared through a gap in the frost-covered hedge.

The occupants in some of the other homes were more

subdued. Two constables were already hauling a man from the door of one of the hovels. He stumbled as they pulled him along, and couldn't regain his footing, so his knees dragged along the ground, ripping holes in his nightclothes. His wife stood in the doorway, holding a small child who buried its head in her neck. Another peeked out from behind her legs. She screeched at the policemen as they took her husband towards the centre of the clearing.

Cooney emerged from the door of one of the other makeshift houses. He walked without a struggle between two constables, one of whom still held a blazing torch. Cooney either slept in his normal clothes or he had taken the time to don his coat and shoes. His wife also appeared in the door, but she wasn't distraught to see him taken away.

They brought him to stand in the centre of the clearing with the others: five grizzled men in various states of undress, corralled together with their heads bowed.

Some of the policemen turned to force the wailing women and children back into their dwellings. The constables roared into their faces, using most foul language, with their truncheons raised. One of the women refused to move and a policeman shoved her so she fell backwards on to the dirt. Her husband moved from the clearing to go to her aid, but he was set upon by the constabulary. They dragged him aside and beat him with their sticks about the head and legs. After a few moments the head constable ordered them to stop, and the subdued man was brought back to the others. He could no longer stand, so he sat on the ground amidst his fellows. Cooney bent down to help him, but the commander barked at him to stay where he was.

A quiet settled over the camp. The field was on high ground and faced east. In the distance, the sun crested the hill of

Howth, and the first rays filtered through wispy clouds to show trees in silhouette on the horizon. Long shadows cast by undulating hills and crooked hedgerows stretched over the landscape. The hoar frost in the camp was shown as a dusty white, except for a multitude of dark spots and a criss-cross of tracks from footsteps and dragged bodies.

The tinkers shivered in the middle, surrounded by the constabulary in their black uniforms standing in a broad circle. The head constable looked back at the sergeant who stood beside me by the gate. He swung his arm and called out, 'Bring forward Delahunt.'

Two weeks before the raid, on the morning following Domenico's death, I had awoken in Grenville Street feeling ill. I raised my head to check the room. There was no sign of Helen. The clock on our mantel hadn't worked for several weeks, but judging by the light streaming past the shutters, it was mid-morning. If she had gone to the markets, then she probably already knew the boy was dead. She hadn't set the fire before leaving, but no trace of the handkerchief remained.

My whole head felt congested. There was a burning in my throat and I shivered despite the weight of the covers. I was still in my clothes, and lifted my arms to check if there were stains on my cuffs. My shoes lay some distance apart at the side of the bed. I couldn't help the situation by getting up, so I remained covered up and tried to stay warm.

My heart quickened when I heard Helen's key scrape in the door. I turned away, dug my head into the pillows and pulled the blankets higher. She bustled inside and placed a basket on the table. Then she called out, 'John.'

She knew.

I heard the soft sounds of her hat and scarf being hung on the hook. She called my name again.

Rather than pretend to be asleep, I spoke into the pillow. 'What is it?'

Her knee came on to my side of the bed and she pulled at my shoulder with both hands.

I squinted my eyes as if caught in a glare, then turned over to face her. 'What?' I lifted my head from the pillow. 'Have you heard back from a publisher?'

She shook her head, and blurted out that one of the Italian boys had been murdered in a laneway.

I frowned and looked towards the window for a few seconds. 'One of the lads across the street?'

She nodded. Everyone in the area was speaking of it. They found him in a stable-lane early that morning. Her eyes had widened and her breathing became shallow. 'Someone cut his throat with a razor blade.'

I couldn't help but glance at her. Then I shook my head and raised myself on to my elbows. 'I can't believe it.' Platitudes can be useful in moments of drama. 'Which one was it? Angelo?'

She shook her head. It was the smaller one. 'Angelo has been arrested.'

I tried to keep my head still as I digested this news. Helen continued, 'John, we were speaking to them both just last night.'

I pulled back the covers, pushed past Helen to go and stand by the window, and looked across to the Italians' garret. I'm not sure what I expected to see. It looked no different.

Helen said, 'There's a rumour that they were arguing in the pub not long before it closed.'

This wasn't part of the plan. 'I was still there when they were quarrelling.' I was silent for a moment as if trying to recall. 'But it didn't seem to be about anything serious. Angelo left early and Domenico stayed in the pub on his own.'

Helen asked what were they arguing about and I said it was all in Italian. She said, 'Maybe Angelo waited for him to come out.'

I couldn't let Angelo take the blame. Cooney was the one who attacked the boy and left him for dead.

Helen asked what time did I leave Kavanagh's? I wanted to check her face to see if there was a hint of suspicion, but I kept looking out of the window.

'A while before closing time. Domenico was still there.' I snuffled for effect. 'I could feel myself getting a chill so came home.' I turned towards her. 'I woke you when I threw my handkerchief in the fire.'

She nodded, her eyes focused in the middle distance. 'Yes, I remember.'

We stayed in the room and discussed our interaction with the two boys from the previous night. We agreed Domenico was a charming character and it was a great shame. We also agreed that we weren't so impressed by Angelo, but he gave no hint that he could be a killer. I said perhaps if we had stayed talking to them for longer the whole thing might have been avoided.

As it happened, the police released Angelo from custody the same day. His landlady provided him with an alibi. Soon enough he was seen walking again in Grenville Street, with shoulders hunched and his thin beard unkempt. His neighbours stopped and looked at him as he passed. Old women pointed. Children taunted him; in sing-song rhymes they told him his friend was dead.

Reports in the newspapers began to appear. *The Freeman's Journal* had only a paragraph in the middle pages, but the

Evening Post splashed the word 'Murder' on its front page. We bought all the editions over the coming week. The journalists made Domenico out to be some kind of stray orphan, an Italian waif who wandered the streets of Dublin. The descriptions of his injuries at the inquest were recounted word for word, and the papers revelled in their gory, clinical detail. Helen read them out to me one morning over breakfast.

They speculated about the boy's origins and the whereabouts of the killer. Most reports mentioned that Domenico's wallet had been stolen – I assumed Angelo had reported that fact to the police – but they indulged in more fanciful conjecture as to the real motive for the attack. One paper bragged of a covert 'source' who recounted a fantastic tale of a hired killer, sent from Italy to hunt down the young man because of an illicit love affair in his native Sicily.

Then the tone of the coverage shifted. Editorials began to criticize the authorities for their incompetence in finding the culprit. Sub-headlines would declare that the police were 'Baffled', 'Stumped' or 'Confounded'. A cartoon appeared in one edition that showed a policeman wearing a blindfold and groping in a dark alley. A body was hunched over in the gutter behind him in a pool of blood. A figure in silhouette stood in the entrance of the lane. He wore a stovepipe hat cocked to one side. His cloak was drawn across his face and he gripped a blade in the same hand, pointing downwards. The caption beneath said, 'Blind man's buff'. I studied the figure for several seconds. It didn't look anything like me.

Printed bills began to appear on lamp-posts and street corners offering a reward of forty pounds for information that led to the capture of the killer of Domenico Garlibardo. It was the first time I saw his surname. Denizens of Grenville Street stopped and examined every particular of the notice. Word had spread that the boy was still in the pub at closing time on the night he was killed. People began to wonder who else had been present. Kavanagh knew, of course, but like all good barmen he remained silent. What use was forty pounds to him, the takings of a month or two, if he lost the trust of his customers?

All the while, I dithered about coming forward. My illness was an excuse to remain in bed for the first week. Part of me hoped that Cooney would be arrested anyway. I was even willing to miss out on the reward money, if the incident could just be forgotten. But as soon as I thought such things I berated myself. Why else had I done it except for the money?

No, I'd have to make a report eventually. I could keep it vague, just that I saw the boy being followed by Cooney after they left the pub, and let the authorities figure it out from there. But still I was cautious. To march into the Castle and report a crime I had committed myself: that could surely have unintended and unfortunate consequences.

Ten days after the killing, I felt well enough to venture outside, and began to go on errands for Helen. Life in our part of the city had returned to normal. Perhaps I only imagined the lingering glances that passers-by seemed to throw in my direction. The grubby flag in Angelo's window had disappeared.

One afternoon, someone left a sealed note for me beneath the door. My initials were printed on the front, and by the stationery I knew it came from the Castle. Sibthorpe wrote that the Department was coming under pressure because of the Italian's murder. It had happened in my area so I should listen out for any rumours, and report anything I heard. I balled up the letter and threw it on the fire.

Helen looked up from her desk. 'What was it?'

'Nothing. Just Sibthorpe asking me to keep an ear out.'

I sat by the window and observed the garret across the street. The landlord had rented it out to new tenants, a middle-aged couple, who moved about, arranging their belongings. Below, a man with a bag slung over his shoulder approached a lamp-post and pasted on a notice, covering an old bill with one freshly printed.

I donned my coat and went down to have a look. The new poster declared that the reward for information regarding the murder of the Italian Boy – even the official notice began to use the name – had been increased from forty to sixty pounds. I studied each word. My fingers worried the corner of the still wet poster until it came away, and I peeled the entire sheet from the street lamp. I waved it in the air for a moment, to allow the excess paste to dry, then folded it once, placed it in my coat pocket, and set off towards Fownes Street.

Farrell's office was lit by an oil-lamp which sat upon a filing cabinet; his desk its usual clutter of folders and loose sheets. I had to wait while the archivist was busy in the stacks. He soon entered, with his shirtsleeves rolled up despite the cold weather, and his glasses perched on his head.

He said, 'Delahunt,' in greeting as he walked towards his chair. Once seated he regarded me. 'You look terrible. What have you got for us?'

I reached into my pocket and withdrew the poster. Its folded sides had stuck together, but the notice was still clear. I laid it on Farrell's desk.

He only had to glance at it. 'You've heard something?'

I had seen something. On the night of the murder itself.

Farrell frowned. 'You mean you're a witness?'

I nodded.

'Why the hell haven't you come forward?'

'I've been waiting for the reward money to increase.' I smiled at him as if to say I knew he'd understand.

He wasn't amused. 'Delahunt, the Department has been frantic about this one. The press has been awful. I'll have to tell Sibthorpe straight away.' He picked up a pen. 'Just tell me what you saw.'

I narrated the statement I'd practised in my head on the way over. Farrell quickly took down the details. He placed the document into a folder, then said, 'Come with me.'

On the ground floor, the sentry lifted his head at the sound of our footsteps. Farrell told him that I was to remain in the building until word came from the Castle. The guard nodded and pointed to a chair beneath the stairs, while Farrell left by the front door.

The statement had caused more of a stir than I'd expected. I sat in the chair and looked at the sentry. He read from a news-paper laid flat on the desktop, and I wondered what he would do if I attempted to make off. Surely he was forbidden to abandon the premises and leave the archive unguarded? The desk was about twenty feet away; the front door another fifteen feet beyond that. I counted how many strides it would require. But there was no way I could get past the desk before he'd have time to react. And even if I did get away, what then? The Castle knew where I lived.

As the time dragged, my uneasiness turned into irritation. Once again, I was waiting on another's pleasure, sitting beneath the steps like a scolded child. I began to tap my heel against the wooden floor; the guard glanced up at the noise. I remember Helen once asked me to fetch a fresh nib from a shop while she worked at her desk. When I returned, shaking snow from my coat, she smiled at me and said I was very biddable, then bent her head again to her work. She meant it kindly, but I was stung.

After half an hour the door opened and the head of a boy poked through. He wore a plaid coat and a red flat cap. He looked down the hall and said, 'Delahunt is to come with me.'

The guard must have known the lad, for he gestured for me to go without glancing from his newspaper. The boy led me into Dame Street and towards the Castle, but instead of turning left into the grounds we continued on. I followed him into a narrow alley called Crane Lane, where litter was scattered about on the cobbles. The boy had a key, which he used to unlock a side door. We climbed an unlit staircase which emerged on to a small landing with a single door. He knocked on it, and a voice inside called out to enter. The boy turned without a word and disappeared back down the stairs.

I pushed the door open to reveal a small office. A fire burned in a hearth on the left. The wood-panelled walls had no decoration except for a small crucifix. The desk stood between two tall sash windows which looked out over Dame Street, and more particularly across at the grubby façade of City Hall with its green copper dome. A ladder went over the curved roof in short, segmented pieces, and a worker perched on one of the rungs. He was scouring a section of the corroded metal surface with a yard-brush.

Sibthorpe was alone in the room, sitting at his desk and reading the statement that I had just furnished to Farrell. He pointed to a seat.

I shifted in the chair until I was comfortable. I had become weary of people regarding me sternly during pregnant pauses. While Sibthorpe did so, I looked over his shoulder and out of the window.

'It's not up to agents to decide how much a piece of information is worth.'

The fire had made the small room disagreeably warm. I unbuttoned my coat and looked at the cross affixed to the wall above his head. Perhaps Sibthorpe was Catholic.

He didn't seem bothered that my eye wandered. 'When you know something that might be of use to the Department you report it straight away.'

His chair didn't sit directly beneath the cross. From my point of view he was half a foot to the right of centre. I looked up at it, and then down at him again. His disregard for the alignment made him seem less daunting.

I said the last time I did just that, and lost out.

'The situation with Craddock was different.' He set aside my statement. 'For the most part, we don't stint or quibble. You should know, Delahunt, that we look after our agents well.'

I said I didn't know that.

'Excuse me?'

'I don't know that. The only other agents I've met were Holt and Devereaux.'

He held up a hand. Did I mean the ones who carted a dead body from my house?

I ignored him. 'One of whom is missing; and the other, I'm quite sure, is dead.' I met his eye directly. 'I didn't report that murder either.'

Across the street, the worker on the roof finished his task. He held out the brush by its handle and let it drop. It skittered down the face of the dome and landed in a rain-gutter. Sibthorpe had taken up a pen and began writing a note at the end of my statement.

'Have it your own way, Delahunt.' He said because of my actions, my anonymity could not be protected in this case. I would have to accompany the police and identify Cooney myself. If the tinker lived beyond the city limits, as I claimed, then the Irish Constabulary force would make the arrest. He glanced at me. 'And they don't suffer fools gladly.' When it went to trial, I would be confined in the Castle for the duration of the proceedings as the Crown's chief witness. I would testify and be cross-examined. He finished writing and fixed the lid on his fountain pen. It was going to lessen my effectiveness as an agent. 'Newspapers will give your name and address and describe your appearance.'

I nearly said that it was about time I received some recognition, but stopped myself.

He said the constabulary would be in touch. With that he rose from his seat, walked to the door and held it open. 'You may go.'

His eyes fixed on me as I passed him by.

The head constable stood in the centre of the itinerants' clearing and waved for me to approach.

He shouldn't have called out my name.

I stood beside the sergeant near the encampment gate and said to him, 'I could just identify Cooney from here.'

He put his hand on my elbow and led me forward. I walked towards the tinkers, who stood in a line, except for the beaten man who sat in the middle. Cooney, second from last, was the only one not to eye my approach. I walked beyond the cordon of policemen and their circle of torches to stand beside the head constable.

'Well,' he said. 'Which one is it?'

I hesitated. Cooney stood with his head bowed and his hands in his pockets. What if I pointed him out and he wasn't convicted?

My gaze swept over the others. As it passed over each man they looked away, and I realized they were more afraid of me than I was of them. I went to the first man and stopped within arm's length. There was no peril. It was like stepping to a point just beyond the reach of a tethered dog. I then walked along the line and studied each man in turn. The first two had pinched faces and days-old growth of beards. They wore long underclothes and looked at me with bloodshot eyes. I stared at them both for several seconds, and was gratified to see anxiety creep into their faces.

None of these men was honest. They were each guilty of something, and they had no idea which one of them was to be picked out, or for what reason. The third man was the one who'd been beaten. He sat on the cold ground with his head slumped forward. He didn't even resemble Cooney in stature. Still, I told the head constable I needed to see his features. One of the policemen stepped forward, grabbed the tinker by the hair and yanked his head back so his face was pointed at mine. The man's eyes rolled backwards and his jaw hung slack. I looked at him for a moment, then shook my head. As the policeman released his grip he pushed his hand forward, causing the tinker's chin to hit his own chest.

I stepped in front of Cooney. He was half a head taller than me. His red sideburns had grown out and his nose bent to the left from an old injury. He knew why I was here; perhaps he recognized me from the pub. I made a motion as if I was going to continue on and look at the last man in line, but then I stopped. I lifted my hand, with index finger extended and thumb held up, like a child mimicking a duelling pistol, and pointed it into Cooney's face.

'That's the man.'

The head constable said, 'Search his house,' and three

officers broke off to go towards Cooney's hovel. The commander followed them, and motioned for me to come along.

The shack was a simple lean-to. A tree trunk spanned two supports to form the apex of a roof. A wattle of timber and sheet metal was stacked against the frame to create a rough triangular structure, and the gaps were plugged by muddy thatch. A door that had come from some other building was pushed open and the policemen entered.

The interior was dark, smoky and smelled like an animal pen. Two of the policemen had torches, which provided ample light. Fern fronds and hay covered the ground, kicked aside in places to reveal the dark earth below. Flimsy pieces of furniture were dotted about. Cooney's wife stood at the far end of the enclosure, now with an infant in her arms. She was expecting another. A filthy mattress on the floor lay beneath a tangle of blankets. The child's cot sat next to their bedding, an elegant piece of furniture made of delicately turned wood. Each of the white spindles had moulded features of tiny seahorses painted in gold.

The police began their search. They pulled open drawers and turned over chairs. Pieces of crockery lined a shelf on one of the walls. A policeman picked up each cup to peer within. Once he saw a cup was empty he simply let it drop from his hand, and several broke on the ground. In one of the drawers there were old pieces of cutlery. All the knives were examined against the light of a torch. A knife handle with a concealed blade was discovered and set aside to be taken as evidence. They also found his work-apron among a bundle of clothes. Dark stains were visible on its surface so they kept that as well.

Cooney's wife watched without apparent emotion as their meagre possessions were ransacked. The blankets on the bed were pulled up and shaken out. The mattress was turned over and the ground beneath examined. I pointed out that no one had yet searched inside the cot. I looked at the woman's face to see if my observation would elicit a reaction, but she remained impassive.

The head constable went to the baby's crib and took out the covers. He let each one unfurl, then folded them neatly on the side-rail. A cushion was wedged between the bars at the bottom. He lifted that up and felt underneath.

'Bring the torch closer.'

He took the cushion out and set it aside. A leather pouch was sitting in the cradle. I could already see it was not the one worn by Domenico, but the policemen could not know that. The head constable lifted it, hefted it for a moment, then called for a man to cup his hands.

He loosened the string at the top of the pouch and carefully tipped out the contents. The torch was lowered. The commander sifted through the coins with a long index finger. They were mostly coppers, a few shillings and one guinea. I had hoped that some of the documents that Domenico said he'd kept in his purse would appear. But why would Cooney keep hold of such items in the midst of a murder hunt?

The head constable said, 'Wait.' With his thumb and forefinger he rummaged in the loose change and extracted a small coin. He held it up to the light and we all gathered around to look. The unfamiliar images struck in the brown metal were not of this kingdom. In tiny letters around the edge it said, '1 soldo'. Cooney must not have noticed it, or else could not bring himself to throw money away, even if it was Italian.

The head constable examined the coin close to one eye as if he was an avid collector. He then looked at me. 'It seems, Mr Delahunt, that you were right after all.'

I tried to look solemn. 'I'm just glad the culprit has been caught.'

Notice arrived for Cooney's trial in late January. The crown prosecutor, Mr Monahan QC, sent me a summons in Grenville Street saying I would have to attend Dublin Castle the day before the trial commenced, and be confined there for the duration of the proceedings – the letter made clear that every comfort would be provided for. I looked upon it as a pleasant retreat from the tenements.

Things had returned to normal in the weeks following Domenico's death. Some diplomacy was required with Helen to atone for my dishonesty in the days following the murder. She asked why I didn't trust her enough to tell her what I knew about Cooney. I said that sometimes it was best not to know things, especially when dealing with Sibthorpe's department.

As anticipated, she was mollified by the knowledge that sixty pounds would be earned if Cooney were prosecuted. We returned to our routine within the household, and otherwise it was an entirely uneventful start to the year – except that Helen gave up on her notion to become a writer.

During Christmas week she began to hear back from publishing houses to which she'd sent samples of her work. Each response was negative. At first, Helen accepted the rejection letters philosophically. After all, she had sent away to more than a dozen publishers and periodicals, and these were just the first to respond. She carefully read the comments made by the editors for hints on how she might improve. For the most part the advice was generic: to keep trying, to concentrate on character, to use more concise language.

During the first weeks of the year she began to feel more slighted by the rebuffs. She would agonize about opening letters, but would still refuse to allow me to do so. I would watch as she eventually plucked up the courage to break the seal and unfold the envelope. When there was no reaction after she read the first few lines, I knew the news was bad once again. One time she tossed a letter aside. 'They didn't even read it.'

She spent less time at her writing desk, rose later in the day and invariably opened a bottle of wine before the sun went down. Money became scarce again, and I began to take more care with how much fuel I put on the fire. If Cooney escaped conviction, we would have a problem.

I recall one of the rejection letters was particularly unforgiving. Helen opened it on a cold morning in mid-January while she sat at her desk. I busied myself setting the fire. She spent longer poring over the contents than usual. When the fire finally took, I looked back to see her head bowed. I went to stand beside her and put my hand on her shoulder, which felt gaunt beneath the woollen shawl. She didn't move. I picked up the missive from where it lay beside her elbow.

In quite kindly terms the publisher methodically set out why Helen's writing was not close to the required standard: muddled verb tenses, unclear pronoun references, mixed metaphors and clichés, sweeping generalizations, banal characters, wooden dialogue. He completely dissected her entire writing style. It took me a few minutes to read through the whole thing. It was a particularly well-written critique.

As I read the rejection letter, Helen rummaged beneath the desk. When I finished, I looked up to see her kneeling beside the fire. She held all the pages of the manuscript that she'd been writing for more than six months, a great wad of ruffled yellow pages with spidery lettering, inkblots and strike-throughs. Without ceremony, she dumped the entire sheaf on to the flames, which threatened to smother, rather than feed the fire. The sheets at the bottom caught light and the whole manuscript started to smoulder. Helen picked up a poker and began to stoke the pages as if she was about to prepare dinner.

'What are you doing?'

I hurried to her side and pulled the poker from her hand. The sheaf had blackened at the edges but was mostly intact. I put my hand into the billowing grey smoke and dragged it out on to the hearthstone. About a dozen pages were already ablaze and I had to leave those on the coals. Some of the rescued pages continued to smoke and burn. I picked them up and blew at them. Their charred edges flared briefly in the gust, but soon extinguished. Dark fragments detached from the sheaf in flurries.

Helen stared at me. She seemed so small, kneeling and hunched over with her hands held in her lap. She had seen her husband refuse to allow her dream to go up in smoke, and a hint of a smile appeared on her face.

I just didn't want her to burn it all at once. There was enough tinder in the pages to last until spring. But I noted her reaction. 'You've worked too hard at this.'

She took the sheaf from my hands, her fingers caressing mine, and straightened the pages against the floor. She brought them back to the desk and placed them in the bottom drawer. Then she swept the charred scraps of paper from the fireplace. Finally, she knelt back down at my side and kissed me.

Throughout Cooney's trial I stayed in a room on the top floor of the Ship Street army barracks just inside the Castle grounds. It was slightly smaller than our room in Grenville Street but with a much higher ceiling. Whitewashed stone surrounded a large, ancient-looking fireplace that sat beneath an oak mantel.

A four-poster bed without a canopy took up one corner. A table and chairs stood between two sash windows that looked out into a narrow courtyard. Directly opposite was a non-descript building, identified to me as the army ordnance office. Just visible beyond that and to the left was one side of the viceregal state apartments. I had ample time to consider the view during the four days in which I was confined.

Crown witnesses were detained by the authorities mostly for their own protection. Prosecutions were too often imperilled by threats made against the life of a vital witness, particularly in cases against members of radical societies. Even in murder cases, like this one, where there was no such danger, the Castle preferred to know exactly where their witnesses were at all times throughout the proceedings.

I found the system to be quite agreeable at first. On the morning I presented myself at the barracks, I was shown to the room by an amiable corporal from the country. He explained to me the times I would receive meals and when I would be allowed outside to take some air. Cooney's trial began on a Friday morning, so he warned it was likely I would have to stay over the weekend. I looked at the cosy fire, the basket of fruit on the table and the clean soft linen on the bed, and welcomed the prospect. I asked if I could have a bottle of wine. It was an hour before midday and he looked at me sideways. He said I couldn't in case I was called to testify early. But I could have a glass of claret with my evening meal. I said that was more than satisfactory. I dropped a bag containing my clothes and a number of books next to the bed.

It was disconcerting when he left and locked the metal-bound door after him. The sound of the key turning in the lock echoed in the empty room, and for a fleeting moment I thought this was what it was like to be a prisoner. But few prisoners had such comfort. I took to the bed immediately for a mid-morning nap, to be woken by the arrival of lunch. It was rather plain fare, but hot and wholesome. I spent the afternoon in an armchair at the window, dividing my time between reading and gazing out at the rain-swept courtyards.

Late in the afternoon, as the day grew dark, I watched from above as clerks left their office jobs. They held newspapers over their heads as they scurried through the puddles. The corporal re-entered the room in order to light some lanterns, and told me that I had some visitors. Without enquiring who they were, I asked him to send them in. Any kind of diversion would be welcome.

It was Sibthorpe and Lyster. They poked their heads around the door as if they were calling on a relative in a nursing home. Sibthorpe said they knew I had been confined for Cooney's trial, so they'd come to help pass the time. Lyster walked straight to the table, took an apple from the fruit bowl and crunched into it as if he was breaking his fast.

I became strangely house-proud, and began to clear my dinner plates; then I invited them to sit. Sibthorpe made himself comfortable, but Lyster remained standing as the corporal brought us in mugs of tea. I enquired about the trial and Sibthorpe said it was proceeding as expected.

He asked had I ever taken the stand before and I told him that I had, during the case of James O'Neill.

'That's right.' He leaned his elbows on the table. 'Remember not to come across as too confident. Juries don't like it. They'll think your testimony is made up, or too rehearsed.'

Lyster threw his apple core across the room into the fire, where it sizzled and spat. He reached into the bowl for another.

Sibthorpe continued, 'Just keep your answers short, don't embellish what you said in your statement.' He leaned back in his chair. 'It should be fine. The case is pretty solid. Everyone in the Department thinks Cooney will be convicted.'

Lyster rotated the fruit in his hand until he twisted the stalk away. He said, 'Even though we all know he didn't do it.'

He dropped the stalk, which glanced off the edge of the table and fell twirling on to the floor.

Sibthorpe kept his eyes on me as he nodded thoughtfully. 'Absolutely. Nothing could be clearer.'

I said I didn't understand. They had just admitted the case against Cooney was a strong one.

Lyster frowned at a bruise on the underside of the apple. 'You can make a strong case for anything. I asked Cooney myself and he said he didn't do it.' He put the damaged fruit down and picked out another. 'He says he robbed the boy all right, but he didn't cut his throat.'

That was preposterous. How could they possibly believe him?

'Because I didn't ask him nicely.'

Sibthorpe folded his arms and stretched his legs out in front of the chair, crossed above the ankle. 'There's more than that. Cooney had a pocket-knife that he used for the robbery, but supposedly used a broken bottle to slice the neck.' He pursed his lips and shook his head. 'That's difficult to believe.'

Maybe he dropped the knife and couldn't find it.

Lyster grimaced. 'The boy's hand was cut with the knife. No, someone else came across him and finished the job. Someone else who was walking the streets at the same time.' Apple juice ran down his chin.

I reached across to the table for my mug of tea. I blew at the steam, then took a sip.

Sibthorpe said, 'Then there's that mysterious chap seen by Lady Findlater's coachman.'

Lyster chuckled. 'Oh yes. Him.'

'The concerned citizen who promised to fetch the police and was never heard of again. Do you know what the coachman said his name was?'

Lyster said, 'What?' He threw another core towards the fire, but it bounced off the fireplace on to the wooden floor.

'Devereaux.' Sibthorpe looked at me. 'That's a bit of a coincidence, wouldn't you say?'

Lyster pulled out a chair. 'The dead arose and appeared to Lady Findlater.'

They were now both sitting across the table looking at me. The heat from the mug had begun to sting my fingers. A crooked smile crept on to Sibthorpe's face.

'For God's sake, Delahunt. When you're asked to give your name in a tight spot just say Smith.'

'It wasn't me.'

'Of course.' He began to twist a wedding band on his finger, which I hadn't noticed before. 'How will your young wife be coping in your absence? You know she's allowed to visit you here.'

I said I knew. She might come on Monday.

He nodded. 'It's nice to have a break now and then. And writers, I'm told, like the peace and quiet.'

Lyster had begun to use my fork to clean the grime from beneath his fingernails.

I stood up and went over to the hearth. One side of the apple core had become warm where it faced the grate. Lyster's bites had gone right to the centre, and pips were visible through small dark holes. I picked it up and tossed it in the flames. 'Thank you both for coming to see me. But now I'm rather tired.'

Sibthorpe touched Lyster's arm and motioned with his head

towards the door. As they filed past he stopped and put his hand on my shoulder. 'Best of luck on the stand, Delahunt.'

The corporal was waiting with the key. Without asking if I wanted anything else, he closed the door and turned the lock. From inside the room I could hear his key-chain rattle.

Not long after that I went to bed. I lay awake, listening to the ticking of the clock and watching the embers in the fireplace dwindle and die. I decided the two of them were just trying to catch me out. They might have been suspicious but they couldn't know anything for certain. Devereaux wasn't all that unusual a name. The more I considered it, the more I thought I'd handled the situation rather well.

When I woke the next morning it was close to nine o'clock. The corporal had said I would get breakfast at eight. Maybe he had been and gone. I lifted my head and looked across at the table. The empty dinner plate and stained, half-filled mugs remained from the previous night. The hearth was full of cold cinders.

When there was no sign of anyone by eleven o'clock, I got up and went towards the door. I tried the handle, knowing full well it wouldn't budge. I rapped on the door and called out. There was no answer. I knocked a few more times and then gave up. The cold floorboards were making me shiver so I went to get dressed.

I was going to clear out the hearth and start a fire, but realized there was nothing to light it with. I sat in the armchair with a blanket pulled from the bed wrapped around my shoulders. Perhaps they operated to a different schedule on Saturdays.

Lunchtime came and went and still no sign of life. I shuffled towards the door with the blanket held around me and thumped on the thick oak slats. I called out, 'Hello,' put my ear against the door and listened without breathing. There was silence, but then I thought there were footsteps just at the edge of hearing. I banged on the door and shouted again. The noise had gone.

They could hardly have forgotten about me. I went to the window and looked down on the grey, empty courtyard. Some lights flickered in the windows of the building opposite. A young man with a black winter coat pulled beneath his chin dashed across the wet cobbles. I was five or six storeys up, but still knocked on the latticed glass with my knuckles. Even if I'd been on the ground floor, I doubt he would have heard.

I turned to survey the room. The only food was a pair of apples still in the fruit bowl. Plenty of fuel was stacked by the fireplace, but I had no matches. The chamber pot was already half-full. The clock showed it was three in the afternoon.

Outside, the clouds cleared as dusk fell and the temperature dropped. The lanterns and candles remained unlit. I stood with my head pressed against the window as the darkness gathered, and watched the lights in the building across the courtyard go out one by one. A few more people traversed the yard beneath me. One of them heard my frantic tapping. He stopped and looked up; his eyes swept the front of the building. I waved my arms but by then it was almost completely dark. I yelled out and hit the window again. Whatever he heard, the poor man must have been quite unnerved. After a moment he turned and continued on his way, his step slightly quicker.

I felt for an apple and took a bite, more to quench my thirst. It was the one with the bruise that Lyster had disdained to eat. I sucked the juice from the core. By six o'clock it was completely dark and bitterly cold. I went to the door once more and made a racket but I knew there was nobody there to hear. There was nothing else for it but to climb back into the bed, try to stay warm and wait for dawn to break.

This was Sibthorpe's work. I shivered and pulled the blankets tighter. What if they just left me here to die of thirst? The summons from Monahan could have been a ruse. Maybe they had no intention of using my testimony, and I had willingly packed a suitcase and presented myself for my own execution.

The clock ticked out its incessant rhythm.

If they wanted me dead then there were easier ways than this. Cooney's trial was real – I had seen the notices in the paper. They were willing to let the tinker take the blame to assuage public opinion, and if they wanted a conviction, they would need the testimony of their chief witness. This was all just to scare me, let me know that I might be able to get away with murder, but I couldn't lie to the Department. The corporal would bustle in come the morning, or perhaps on Monday, and apologize profusely for the terrible mix-up. With that thought in mind I finally managed to fall asleep.

I remained locked up and undisturbed on Sunday, but by then it came as no surprise. I stayed in the bed as much as possible, just rising to relieve myself in the hearth and listen at the door. There was no point in knocking again. I ate the last apple and gazed out of the window for a time.

Throughout that day I didn't see another soul. I was very thirsty. The half-drunk tea in the mugs remained on the table from Friday evening. I took a spoon and skimmed the thin layer of scum that had collected on the surface in each cup. Then I poured all the dregs into the mug I had used. I sniffed at the beverage. The milk in it had started to turn, though the room had been cold enough so it wasn't completely sour. I held my breath and downed the brown liquid in a few gulps. The pleasure of the slaking was enough for me to ignore the taste. I would have happily drunk another.

Since I stayed mostly in bed, I dozed fitfully throughout the second night. In the dawn light I watched the small hand of the clock creep past seven. A few minutes before eight I heard footsteps and muffled voices in the hallway outside. I didn't stir. Maybe they expected me to hammer on the door in distress. I watched the minute hand creep towards the hour. When it finally clicked vertical there came a scraping in the keyhole. The door pushed open and a moment later the corporal walked in bearing a tray, which held a porcelain basin, a bowl of porridge and a glass of water. He placed the items on the table, then cleared the soiled dishes on to the tray. I watched him from my pillow. He turned towards me. 'You'll be called to the courthouse some time before midday. Make yourself presentable.'

I sat up. 'I want to see Sibthorpe.'

He said he didn't know any Sibthorpe.

'He was here two days ago. Thomas Sibthorpe, the head of the Department.'

'What department?' Before I could speak again he said, 'Just be ready when I come to fetch you.'

With that he walked out and locked the door again.

8

That room in the Ship Street barracks was in effect my first cell, even though it was spacious and fairly comfortable. My final abode in Kilmainham, by comparison, is dingy, damp and narrow. I'm not sure the bunk would fit if I dragged it sideways. But I've grown fond of it. For the most part, I'm left alone and feel oddly secure. No one can get at me here. There's a comfort in the routine that the officers stick to. And the room itself has a symmetry, in that the barred arched window aligns with the stone barrel ceiling and curve of the doorframe.

My warder, turnkey Turner, appeared late in the afternoon and said, 'Come along, John. We have to make you presentable for the big day.' He led me to a cell outside of which three other inmates were waiting. One by one we were called within, and judging by those ahead of me, who emerged clipped and shaven, this was the prison barber. I was surprised when I entered to find that the barber was himself a convict. His cell was just like mine, except a chair had been placed in the centre beside a small table and a basin that brimmed with murky water. The light from his window separated on its oily surface. The floor was covered with assorted hair, as if some mottled beast had crawled into its den to moult.

When I sat down, the barber spoke to me with the affected

cheeriness common to his profession. 'So,' he said, 'are you in here long?'

'Less than a month.'

He took some hand-held clippers I'd have thought more suited for livestock, and began to roughly bare my head. 'That's no time at all.' Tufts of dark hair tumbled over my shoulders and into my lap.

Then he dipped a shaving brush in the basin, swept it twice over a yellow soap and dabbed at my face.

'What did you do for work on the outside?'

'I was a student.'

The razor he used was dull and abrasive. Its wooden haft was worn smooth so the handle had more gleam than the blade. He pulled the skin taut over my jaw, and scraped the edge along the underside of my chin.

'How did you end up in here?'

'I killed someone.'

The blade paused, and he asked my name.

'Delahunt.'

'Oh.'

The blade resumed.

He didn't speak after that. When finished he merely grunted, wiped my face with a foul cloth, and told me to send in the next in line.

As Turner escorted me back, he told me employing a prisoner in this fashion had been his idea. 'I thought, rather than putting this delinquent barber to work breaking stones, why not have him shave his fellow prisoners and even some of the guards?' He was clearly proud of the scheme, as if the idea put him at the forefront of enlightened prison-keeping. 'But Shankly's term elapses in a few weeks, so that'll be the end of it.'

I suggested the prison should hire a barber to continue the

initiative, but Turner was confident another of that profession would be committed here soon enough. I feared the next Dublin barber who found himself before the assizes would be in for an unpleasant surprise come sentencing.

Turner looked at me sideways. 'Anyway. It'll hardly concern you.'

True enough.

We walked for a while in silence. As we neared the condemned cell Turner said, 'I sent out that message today, as you asked.'

'Will that be enough time?'

He pulled open the door. 'If he wants to respond, he will.'

Cooney's trial concluded in the first days of February with a conviction. The evidence had been too strong: my witness statement; the Italian coin found in his purse; the bloodstains on his leather apron. He claimed, truthfully I'd imagine, that the splashes came from a type of cement mixed from heifer's blood and lime. The jury wasn't convinced.

He was sentenced to hang, but not too many people went to see it, for the weather was particularly foul on the morning of his execution. In Dublin, one can never depend on the weather for anything. Helen and I weren't going anyway. In the days leading up to it, I asked her if she wanted to go along for old times' sake.

She frowned at me. 'We can't go to the hanging of a man you helped convict.'

My smile faded. 'Why not?'

On the morning itself we remained in bed as rain drummed against our window. We'd recently bought a mahogany clock shaped like Napoleon's hat, and I watched as the hour ticked past ten. A gust made the door creak.

'That's Cooney gone,' I said.

Helen was only half-awake. She raised her head to look at the time, then rolled over and went back to sleep.

I thought of the hangman, his hand slippery on the lever. The tinker at the end of the rope, buffeted by the wind, his black hood drenched. In the ceiling above me, water seeped along a crack, collected in the corner, and dripped down on to the floorboards in a slow rhythm. Perhaps Cooney pitched about, so that his bound legs bumped against the edges of the platform. I pictured the cleric, head bent against the slanting rain, shouting his prayers over the bluster. The windows shook again. I pulled the blankets higher and sank down beneath their warmth.

I went to collect my money from Fownes Street that month as usual. There was only one item in the ledger: 'For information that led to the conviction of Richard Cooney – £60'. We spent half the money straight away, when I applied to retake my final year in college. I wasn't sure it was necessary, but Helen insisted. She said once I attained my degree I could find proper work, and we could move back into more respectable society. It should have been pleasant to have something to work towards. But I found I was unmoved by the prospect of returning to the cobbled paths of Trinity, and its dark wooden lecture halls. I rummaged in the bottom of the trunk for my old college notes. Helen cleared some space in the drawers of her writing desk, and said I could evict her whenever I needed it. I preferred to read by the window.

Those few months were among our most contented. We had enough money to live comfortably, and our year ahead planned out. The harsh winter gave way to a mild spring, and Helen and I would take strolls in Mountjoy Square, just as we did when we first courted in Merrion Park. Leaves had begun to sprout, and children from the surrounding streets played on the lawns. Grenville Street was near the northern outskirts of the city, so if we walked a mile we could reach the countryside. Our favourite route was to go by the widows' retreat on Drumcondra Hill, then turn left at the infants' school, and continue along the canal as far as Whitworth Hospital. On the way, Helen picked snowdrops and crocus flowers from the roadside hedges.

Hidden behind the hospital was a long narrow graveyard surrounded by sycamore trees, with gravel paths and listing granite headstones. Helen liked to wander among them, read the epitaphs, and speculate about the lives of those interred. Many graves contained married couples. In one, the husband had died young while the wife had lived on for another half-century, and Helen imagined the woman's long widowhood: sitting alone in a draughty parlour, her grey hair pinned and black dress pressed, dry arthritic hands gripping wooden arm-rests. In another grave the couple had lived to ripe old ages, but the husband had been born in Sligo and the wife in Wexford, and Helen wondered what accident of fate had brought them together: a chance meeting at a family gathering, or on a channel crossing, or at a debutante's ball. Another headstone recorded the death of a newborn boy only a few days old, and his mother who died a fortnight after. Helen read the inscription with her head tilted and said, 'Perhaps if the baby had lived, she would have as well.'

At the end of the cemetery, one lonely grave was marked by a plain wooden cross and a rectangle of untidy earth. There Helen would place the flowers she had picked along the way.

I thought the humble grave probably meant that the person had died in penury or disgrace, and one day I said to her, 'For all we know, he could have been a scoundrel.'

Helen removed a marigold weed, looked at the matted roots for a moment as if considering the source of its nutrition, and then tossed it away. 'It doesn't matter.'

Back in the tenement, we began to notice small twigs and pieces of bark falling into the hearth, which could only mean that birds were building a nest in the flue. Helen was loath to light the fire, but I said the smoke would force them away. The next day, as we returned from the park, we saw two jackdaws flapping and dancing around the chimney stack, their attempts to reach their clutch repelled by billowing smoke. Later, when I went to the market, there was no sign of them.

Helen and I began married life cut adrift from our families and her friends, so we had nowhere to turn for advice in certain matters. When we moved into Grenville Street the previous summer, Helen had approached Mrs Lynch downstairs, who was happy to direct her to certain apothecary shops, and also lend some of her own folk remedies to stay clear of the 'family way'. I pointed out that the Lynches had six children; Helen said they were determined not to have any more.

Our first port of call had been Simeon Boileau, the Huguenot druggist on Talbot Street. His shop had bright moulded window frames and a glass front door. Rows of shelves contained coloured bottles neatly stacked, a pestle and mortar, and weighing scales of various sizes. Boileau wore a full-length coat and a monocle at the end of a chain, which he used to read labels. When we first spoke to him, I wasn't sure how to broach the subject, but Helen told him what we needed. Boileau nodded and disappeared into a back room. He brought back a small jar of pills labelled, 'Plumbum'.

Ignoring me, he leaned forward and spoke to Helen in a low voice. 'Take two each month, a week before you expect your period.' He gave the container a slight shake. 'It will ensure that event is realized.' I hooked my little finger and swept some lint from the counter-top. She reached out to take the jar, but Boileau maintained his grip for a moment. 'Don't take more than two at a time. It can lead to . . . complications.'

She thanked the chemist and slipped the bottle into her purse.

While walking home she considered the name of the tablets. 'I wonder if it's a play on words, referring to internal plumbing.'

I glanced down at her. 'Is that really what you think?'

'Well, what is it then?'

'*Plumbum* is the Latin name for lead.'

Helen looked again at the label and said, 'Oh.'

The tablets had proved effective for the best part of a year, until the middle of April. She gave me the news one morning while we were still in bed. I studied her face to gauge her feelings, and stopped myself from asking if she was sure. After a moment, I pushed a strand of hair away from her eye.

She took my hand and held it on the pillow. 'I don't think it's the right time to have one, John.'

I pursed my lips as if considering.

She squeezed my fingers. 'It would arrive in the middle of winter. We'll be scraping by because you'll be in college.' She rolled backwards, enough that she could look up towards the ceiling. 'I don't want our first child to be born in this place.'

A long dark smudge stretched from the corner of her mouth to just beneath her earlobe. She must have rubbed her face with an inky finger.

Helen turned back to look at me. 'If we wait another year or two, you'll be working. My book will be complete. We'll be living somewhere decent and safe.'

I realized I hadn't said anything yet. I pressed her hand against my lips.

She was right, of course. I was only concerned with her well-being. We had years in which to start a family.

A crease between her eyebrows disappeared. She moved closer to me and spoke into the collar of my nightshirt. 'I thought you'd be upset.'

I didn't answer, just draped my arm over her shoulder.

We began to peruse advertisements at the back of the cheaper evening papers. One caught our eye: 'Ellis's pills for ladies: acknowledged remedy for anaemia, bloodlessness and all ailments of the female system. Extra strong.' We sent off the sixpence and received the tablets within a week. They came in a packet which contained the warning: 'On no account to be taken by persons desirous of becoming mothers.' Helen took the tablets with a tumbler of water. She looked at them in her opened palm for a few seconds, swallowed them, then cleaned the glass in the washbasin. Another week passed by and there was no noticeable effect.

She went downstairs to speak with Mrs Lynch, who said the remedies advertised in the papers weren't worth a curse. They couldn't be too strong, for if the mother became sick, the peddlers would be prosecuted. Helen asked if she should return to Boileau, but Mrs Lynch said she was too far gone for him to risk helping her now. In any case, the lead pills were still the best thing to try. Helen was wary of using them. She always felt ill for a day or two afterwards, and she feared to take them in a larger dose.

One evening, she sat beside the cold hearth with her hands pressed over her stomach. She hadn't yet begun to show. 'Mrs Lynch knows of a woman who provides a proper service.'

I looked up from my book and considered the word 'proper'.

But it was an unpleasant operation and cost five pounds. The woman who did it was a retired midwife who lived in Old Dominick Street. I thought of poor Domenico.

We still had twenty-five pounds of the Cooney money. 'If you want to go, you need only say.'

She smoothed the folds at the top of her skirt. 'I'll try the other remedies first.'

The other remedies turned out to be a series of folk medicines made from various herbs and compounds. We spent hours over the fire brewing acrid tonics of nutmeg and caraway seeds, gin and salt, tansy and washing soda. Helen would sniff at each glass, then gulp down the liquids as fast as possible, squeeze her eyes and try not to gag. Once or twice she felt ill, and our hopes were raised, but the queasiness soon passed. The final attempt consisted of boiling a fistful of copper coins in water for an hour, and then drinking the liquor that resulted. I remember straining the pot, and tipping the shiny coins back into the money tin. Each separate tonic was given a few days to work, and the weeks passed.

One day I returned from the market to find Helen doubled up on top of the bed. She had wrapped her arms about her stomach and buried her head beneath a blanket. The shutters were drawn over, but even that dim light was hurting her eyes. When I put my hand on her back, I could feel she was rigid. She gave low moans with each wave of pain in her abdomen, and she leaned over the chamber pot, heaving drily.

I built a fire in the hearth – my hands trembled as I struck the match – dragged the basin of water next to it, then gathered clean blankets and towels, and brought them to the bed.

Helen said she had a piercing pain in her head above her temple, so I placed a damp cloth over her brow. Her breathing had became short and sounded as if it squeezed through a narrow gap in her throat. At one point, she lifted her right hand and showed it to me. Her fingers were stiff and bent into a claw. She said, 'I can't move them.'

I took her hand and massaged it. Her fingers were malleable, and they remained set in whatever position I put them, like soft metal.

'I'm sure it'll be all right,' I said.

I put her hand beneath the covers next to her body, where it would be warm. She tensed up with another wave of nausea.

'What was the last tonic you drank?'

Her head hung over the edge of the bed. 'I took four of the lead tablets this morning while you were out.' When she lay back her mouth was slack, and I could see a blue tinge around her gums.

'I'll have to fetch a doctor.'

She gripped my arm. 'You can't leave me.'

'Well, I'll go and get Mrs Lynch. She at least can help.'

Helen took a deep breath and tried to compose herself, but another spasm made her wince. 'No. It'll be out soon.'

But nothing came. She didn't bleed, and the cramps sub-sided during the night. When she concentrated, she could move the fingers of her right hand by tiny fractions, but it remained paralysed. Just before dawn, Helen said the pain had almost gone. She looked up at the ceiling. A tear ran from the corner of her eye down her temple and into her hair. She rubbed her stomach. 'What are we doing to it?'

I said this had gone on for too long. 'We'll have to go to the woman in Dominick Street.'

She rolled her head to look at me, and nodded once.

Helen thought she was approaching the end of her third month. Occasionally I would ask her if she could feel anything inside, and she said no. Any illness came from the remedies she took, rather than the pregnancy itself. There had yet to be a quickening, and she was glad of it. She wanted the procedure to be complete before the baby stirred.

Ten years ago in Limerick, a woman was convicted of murdering her husband and 'pled the belly' for leniency. The judge, Baron Pennefather, ruled that pregnancy alone without quickening was not enough to stay execution, so he dispatched both the mother and her unborn child to the gibbet. I know about that case because Pennefather presided at my own trial. It was my counsel's way of letting me know I should fear the worst.

Helen made an initial visit to Mrs Redmond in Dominick Street on her own. When she came home she told me about it over a glass of wine. The retired midwife had taken one look at her stiffened fingers and recognized the effects of the lead tablets. She gave Helen tea and described the procedure she would employ. Helen asked if I would be allowed to accompany her on the day itself. Mrs Redmond was surprised I would be willing to do so, but said I could come to the house if I wished, but not into the delivery room.

I looked at Helen over the rim of my glass. 'Is that what she called it?'

She shrugged. What else could she call it?

The appointment was made for Thursday morning in the first week of June. Helen couldn't sleep the night before the operation. When I woke up, she was already dressed and sitting by the window, with her knees gathered up and her head resting against the jamb. The sash frame cast one side of her face in shadow.

I spoke to her from the pillow. 'You know you don't have to go if you don't wish to.'

A pigeon landed on the sill outside. Helen tapped on

the pane so it started and flew away. She said, 'I know.'

While I was getting ready, someone knocked on the door and Helen went to answer. One of the Lynch children, the second-eldest girl, stood in the hallway. She craned her head past Helen's hip.

'A man downstairs gave me a note for John.'

Helen said, 'You mean Mr Delahunt.'

I walked to the window and looked out. 'Is he still there?'

A hansom cab passed in the street, and a woman in a light cotton dress crossed the dusty road in its wake.

The girl said he was long gone. There was a lilt in her small voice. 'He told me to say that he knows you're here.' She handed the note to Helen, then turned from the door and went back towards the stairwell.

I crossed the room, the ends of my black cravat hanging loose from my collar, and took the note. Helen looked at me as I read, her hand resting on the doorknob.

It was a short message from Lyster. There was something he had to take care of in Eden Quay. I was to meet him at noon in Bracken's Tavern.

'What is it?'

'It's nothing.' I was going to crumple the sheet, but Helen held out her good hand. As I passed it to her, I said there was no need to worry. I was going to ignore it.

She read the note, then twisted the page to check the blank side overleaf. 'You can't go with him.'

'I just said that.'

She shook her head and walked towards the fireplace. 'They can't expect you to drop everything at a moment's notice.'

'I have no intention of going, Helen.'

She struggled to ball the sheet, then threw it into the cold hearth and placed her hands over her stomach. There was a small bulge, just where her white starched blouse met the waistline of her skirt. No one would notice unless they were looking for it.

I went to stand beside her. Taking her hands, I said we wouldn't worry about the Castle, or Sibthorpe, or Lyster today. I pushed her hair over her shoulder; it was still damp from being washed. She would get the procedure over and done with, I would take care of her for a few weeks, and things would soon return to normal.

Her chin lifted. She noticed my cravat was still loose and she tried to tie it, but her right hand couldn't grip. After a moment, I took the ends from her to finish the task.

The houses in Dominick Street were three storeys over basement, and, like those in Grenville Street, had been split up into tenements and furnished lodging-houses. Mrs Redmond lived and worked in the basement of number fourteen. When we knocked, the door was answered by a woman in her late thirties, with grey streaks in long red hair. She introduced herself as Mary, Mrs Redmond's daughter, and invited us both into a large, warm room. It had once been the kitchen for the entire house, and it reminded me of my home in Fitzwilliam Street. A large fireplace took over most of the back wall, where a fire was lit despite the summer day. A black kettle and small cauldron hung suspended over the coals. The wall adjacent contained a cooking range, with polished metal stoves and a ceramic butler's sink.

Mrs Redmond stood at the kitchen table, peeling potatoes taken from a muddy sack with a short blade that was slick with starchy water. The sleeves of her floral housedress were pulled up over wiry arms. Her hair was pinned, but silver strands hung down over her lined face. Three children played on the ground on the other side of the table, two girls and a boy between the ages of about four and seven. They were engaged in a loud conversation, but they quietened when their grandmother shushed them. Mary called over, 'Mammy, Helen is here.'

The heads of the children all turned to look at us. Mrs Redmond squinted at the doorway and smiled. She dropped her knife into a large pouch at the front of her apron, then wiped her hands on a cloth. As she came closer she said, 'Show me your hand.'

Helen did so, and Mrs Redmond examined the fingers. 'Try to close your fist, as hard as you can.'

The sinews of Helen's wrist stood out. Her fingers only curled in by half an inch, but Mrs Redmond was satisfied. 'It will heal eventually, but it might take a few months.' She looked at me for the first time and seemed to size me up while speaking. 'Boileau is quick to sell the lead tablets but he never fully explains the hazards.' She offered her hand. 'You must be John.'

I said yes and gripped her clammy fingers.

Mrs Redmond led us both to the kitchen table. Her daughter had been preparing tea, and she brought over a tray with a pot and four mugs, a tumbler of water and a bottle of laudanum with a yellow, creased label. The old midwife smiled at Helen and said there was no need to worry; it would be over soon. She pulled the stopper from the laudanum and allowed three drops to fall into the glass of water. Faint tendrils expanded and disappeared. 'Drink this,' she said. 'It'll help you relax.'

Helen sipped at the water. One of the little girls came over to inform her grandmother of a transgression committed by her brother. Mrs Redmond turned the girl around with a hand on her shoulder, and said she would deal with him later. The little girl toddled off, satisfied that justice would be done.

Mrs Redmond asked if we had the money. I was going to suggest we wait until after the procedure, but now wasn't the time to cause a fuss. Mrs Redmond slipped the banknote into her apron, where she had put the knife, and looked at Helen. 'Are you ready, dear?'

Mary said she would get the room ready, and went out into the hallway. Helen handed me her bag. The midwife told me there was a couch in the corridor where I could sit and wait. She patted my shoulder. 'It won't take long.'

The corridor was dimly lit with three rooms leading off it. Mrs Redmond pointed to a ragged yellow couch, then she opened one of the doors and brought Helen inside.

For a moment, I could see into the delivery room. A fire burned low in a wrought-iron fireplace. Mary was already in the room, unfolding a large white sheet and placing it over a long table, as if setting it for dinner. An uncovered worktop contained white porcelain basins, several folded rags, and a number of metal instruments, such as a long scissors with tongs instead of points, a set of pliers with spiked teeth in the jaws, and a tarnished pair of forceps with a corkscrew handle.

The door closed. I tried to make out the muffled voices within, but all I could hear was the chatter of the children back in the kitchen. I threw Helen's bag on to the sofa and sat down beside it.

The bottom half of the hallway was covered in panelled wood painted white; the top half had a green wallpaper. The walls were bare except for a crucifix and a framed print of Pope Gregory. The open doorway to the kitchen allowed a rectangular glare of sunlight to intrude. I had nothing with which to tell the time apart from the light, and I watched it creep up the jamb to the lower hinge.

Out in the street, a church bell tolled for midday. Lyster was

217

waiting for me in Bracken's. Perhaps I should have sent him a message, to let him know I wouldn't be able to meet him.

A cough in the hall made me turn my head. The youngest girl stood at the edge of the kitchen looking at me. Her bare feet made no noise on the brown tiles as she came forward, with a ragdoll held in the crook of her elbow. She clasped it awkwardly, so one of the doll's arms was forced up and over its face. She stood before me, only a head taller than the front of my knees. Like her mother, she had thick red hair and a square chin, and she regarded me with serious eyes.

'Would you like to know my doll's name?'

I said I wouldn't.

She nodded, as if she didn't seem to mind. She looked over her shoulder at the closed door, and then back at me. 'Granny is helping that lady feel better.'

It had been a while since I had heard Helen referred to as a lady.

The child pricked her ear, then turned and ran back towards the kitchen. A moment later I heard what caused her alarm: footsteps coming towards the door. I sat up in the couch.

Mrs Redmond's daughter came out. She only opened the door wide enough so she could squeeze through. Red streaks covered a white apron that she had donned. She swept a broad lock of hair from her eye with the back of her thumb, keeping her bloody fingers extended and away from her face.

Mary composed herself, then turned to me. 'It worked.'

From inside the room I could hear Helen emit a moan – for long enough that she ran out of breath.

'All we have to do is stop the bleeding. I need to fetch some more water.' She disappeared into the kitchen.

The door hadn't been closed properly. It slipped from its latch and creaked slightly ajar so I could see a sliver of the room, including the lower half of the table. Helen's knees were raised up and draped with a blanket. Her lower legs were bare and her toes gripped the edge of the bench. The white cloth covering the table was doused in blood. Helen cried quietly with quick uneven sobs. I had heard her cry like that once or twice in Grenville Street; late at night, when she thought I was asleep.

I didn't know if this was normal. There was always going to be a degree of trauma. When Mary came back from the kitchen I looked away from the door. She carried a bundle of cloths beneath her arm and a basin of clean water. She had taken the time to wash her hands.

I stood up so she couldn't pass, and spoke in a low voice in case Helen could hear me. 'Please tell me, is she in danger?'

One of the cloths slipped from the bundle on to the floor, and Mary looked down as if glad of the diversion. I picked it up and draped it on her arm.

She thanked me. 'She's bleeding more than she should. The womb has been scraped and it may have been cut. We just have to wait for the blood to clot.' She inclined her head towards the room. 'I have to go back in.'

That didn't answer my question, but I stepped aside. She went through the door and closed it over with her heel, pushing against it from the inside to ensure it shut tight.

I listened at the door with my ear pressed against the wood. I could hear the muffled voices of Mrs Redmond and her daughter. Occasionally Helen would let out quite a loud cry and I was tempted to walk in. But I'd be of no help, and might have caused further distress. I thought I should pace up and down the hall, but I couldn't see the purpose of that either, so I retook my seat on the sofa.

The little girl and her sister peeked at me from the door to the kitchen. They were standing there as Helen's cries became louder. The final one was particularly long, with an inflection almost of disappointment. The girls' eyes widened. The smaller one put her hands over her ears.

Afterwards there was silence, except for the faint clatter of a horse passing on the street outside. The doorknob turned and Mrs Redmond stepped out. Her shoulders were stooped and there was no colour in her face. She looked to her right and slowly shook her head.

'Wait till I get my hands on you two.' The girls in the door-way scurried off.

She turned to me. 'Helen will be well. She's lost quite a bit of blood, but the haemorrhage has stopped.' She bent her head to the side to stretch her neck. 'Mary is just cleaning her up, then you can go in and see her.' She walked towards the kitchen with a weary step, her arms behind her back to untie the apron strings.

When I was allowed in, Helen still lay on the table, though the bloody sheets had been removed and were balled up in the corner. There was a metallic smell in the room. Her legs were resting flat and a blanket covered her lower half.

Mary cleared away basins of murky water. Another table was covered in used rags and the metal instruments lying askew. On a sideboard, a smaller basin stood alone. It was of white porcelain, with hairline cracks and a blue rim, covered with a folded yellow cloth.

I bent over Helen and kissed her pale forehead. She lifted her arm and laid it over the back of my head. Mary brought in a chair and placed it beside me. I sat, leaned over the table so my face was close to Helen's, and stroked her hair. The basin across the room was in my eye-line. At a point along the rim the yellow cloth ruffled up, but the gap into the bowl was too shadowy to see.

I wondered what they were going to do with it. The fire burned in the hearth behind me. Were they just waiting for us to leave before they put it in there?

Helen's eyes were closed and her breathing had become steady, as if she was drifting to sleep.

There would be a long back garden attached to this house. Plenty of room for a stillborn graveyard. Helen's eyelids fluttered open.

Maybe they were going to hand it over to us as we left, concealed in a small box, and tell us to take care of it ourselves.

A tear gathered, and trickled over the bridge of her nose. 'I'm sorry, John.'

I told her she had nothing to be sorry about.

Helen continued to suffer over the next several days in Grenville Street, and, for the most part, she was confined to bed. Mrs Redmond had given her a bottle of laudanum to bring home, telling her to take three drops with each meal. She also gave her a thick glass syringe with a leather plunger. Twice a day, Helen had to inject herself with tepid water while squatting over the chamber pot – to remove blood clots and other fragments that might have remained. I waited on the landing while she did so. She dreaded it, for the sting was excruciating, and she began to take a dose of laudanum an hour before each rinse.

She abstained from food and even water as much as possible, and would lie in bed for hours in a stupor. The more alert she was, the greater the pain. At night she suffered insomnia as a result of being bedbound during the day. Once more, laudanum was the solution. The sedative allowed her moments of feverish sleep. She would squirm in the bed and speak nonsense. Sometimes she would push the tangled bedclothes off when it became too hot, or open her eyes suddenly and look at me as if I was a complete stranger.

One night she began to speak about her family. She said we would have to tidy the room because her mother was coming to visit tomorrow. They were going to make plans to celebrate her brother Arthur's commencement.

I reached over to shake her shoulder. She sat up and sought out my face in the gloom. 'Arthur never liked you,' she said. Then she lay back down again.

It fell to me to look after the household, though that only meant bringing in supplies and keeping the place relatively tidy. With my college fees, the rent, and the trip to the midwife, only fifteen pounds remained of the Cooney reward money. I became frugal with my purchases, selecting cheaper bottles of wine and secondary cuts of meat.

I began to wonder how much the Castle might give for information on a back-street abortionist.

One afternoon in late June, I was reading a textbook by the windowsill. The sash frame was open a few inches, and sounds from the street drifted from below: children at play, carts trundling by, housewives in conversation.

Lyster stood on the pavement across the road looking up at our room. He wore a light flat cap and a waistcoat over a white shirt, unbuttoned at the neck. His hands hung down by his waist. I paused at the window and regarded him. How long had he been standing there? He continued to stare at me for several more seconds, then put his hands in his pockets and walked away. Still standing over my chair, I watched until he reached the corner and disappeared.

Helen was in bed, lying on her side, sore and lucid. She asked what had caught my attention.

'Lyster was outside looking up at our window.'

She raised her head from the pillow, then reached across for the laudanum on her bed-stand. 'Him again.'

That night, her sleep was feverish once more. She pushed herself up on her elbows and looked around the darkened room with glazed eyes. 'John, where's that bloody rag?'

I told her she hadn't been bleeding for more than a week. 'Go back to sleep.'

She swung her head towards the hearth. 'No, the one in the fire.' Her eyes seemed to gain focus. 'I saw you burning a bloody rag in the fire.'

I reached out and brushed her cheek. Her eyes didn't waver. I said it was gone; all burnt up.

She nodded, laid her head down and drifted back to sleep.

Helen got through the first bottle of laudanum in less than two weeks. I bought her another, which only lasted ten days. When the liquid was nearly gone she reduced the dose, taking only a couple of drops at a time, and she complained that she could hardly feel any effect. When there was less than a teaspoon left, it had to be sloshed about so enough could collect on the dropper. Once or twice I saw her lick the glass wand, like a child licking jam from a knife. She asked me to go to Boileau and buy some more.

'Why don't we wait to see how you're feeling in a few days?'

Helen was hunched over her desk, scraping the nib of her pen in a spiral over a sheet. The ink had long since run dry. She shifted in her seat. I thought she was going to argue, but instead she nodded. 'I'll try.'

When the bottle was empty, I gathered it up with some other rubbish to throw on a tip in the back yard. Helen stopped me. 'There might be a dose in it yet.' She filled it with water and left it on the table to soak for half an hour, then drank directly from the bottle.

The sediment and residue inside the glass was more potent than she realized. After a few minutes, I noticed her breathing had become quick as she sat at the kitchen table. She said she didn't feel well and leaned forward on her elbows. One of them slipped from the edge and her head dipped, as if she'd dozed off for a moment.

She giggled and stood up, tipping the chair over, and walked towards the bed with an unsteady step. I put my arm around her waist in case she fell.

Helen tried to pull away. 'Mrs Redmond said you're not to touch me for a month.'

She laughed again, but there was no mirth in her eyes, and she struck the top of my hand with her balled fist.

'Helen, please.'

She broke free of my grasp, crossed the room and fell face first on the bed. She lay perfectly still, with her face between a pillow and the covers, and her feet still on the ground. I picked up her ankles and placed them on the mattress, then put my hand on her back. Her breathing was shallow, as if she struggled to fill her lungs, but there was no distress on her face. I pulled tangled hair away from her mouth and nose and turned her so she lay on her side. She weighed very little.

Two days later, I lounged on the bed, sitting against the headboard with my shirtsleeves rolled up. Helen shivered beneath the blankets beside me, wrapped in a shawl, a cold sweat on her forehead. 'It's no use,' she said. 'I need more of the medicine.'

I put my book down on my stomach. 'Are you not feeling better at all?'

She said she was feeling worse. 'I ache all over.'

'That's because of the laudanum.'

She began breathing heavily through her nose, signalling

another wave of nausea. She scrunched her eyes, then abruptly pushed back the covers and pulled the shawl from around her shoulders, allowing it to slip on to the floor.

I put my hand on her forehead. During these flushes she liked it as she said my fingers were always cold. I spoke to her softly. 'Try to give it another day.'

She kept me awake during the night with her incessant scratching. The skin beneath her knees and on the inside of her thigh had become red and inflamed as if infected with scabies. The itching drove her to distraction and she couldn't help herself.

The rhythmic rasping set my teeth on edge. Mostly I was disturbed by the way she held her breath while doing it, then finished with a long sigh and heavy panting.

'You're just making it worse.'

'I know.'

'Does it not hurt?'

She said it stung like anything. But after a few minutes she started again. I reached over beneath the covers and took hold of her wrist.

The following morning she felt wretched again. Her teeth chattered while she spoke. 'You'll have to get me some more.'

I asked what of her original ailment, had that not healed?

She didn't reply. Beneath the covers she continued to shiver. I lay down beside her and draped my arm over her shoulders, but she twisted them and turned away. 'I can't breathe when you do that.'

I rolled over and sat up at the edge of the bed.

Her voice came over my shoulder. 'Why won't you get it for me?'

I said it was for her own good.

She began to kick off the covers, and I thought she was

having another hot flush, but instead she got up. 'I'll go to Boileau myself.' In her nightgown she walked to the shelf behind the table and pulled down a round tin tucked back in the corner. She lifted the lid, saw that it was empty and looked at me.

'Where's the money?'

It was in my pocket.

'What are you doing with all of it?'

I said it wasn't very much. We only had two pounds left. She looked back into the empty tin. That brief physical exertion had left her drained, so she went to sit at the desk. 'What happened to it?'

'College fees, the midwife, I had to bring the rent to Mrs Travers a week ago.' I said the truth was we couldn't afford bottles of laudanum; soon we wouldn't be able to afford much of anything.

She folded her arms in her lap, and rocked slightly with her weight on the balls of her feet. She thought for a moment. 'You don't have anything to take to the Castle?'

'No. Well . . .' I waited for her to glance up at me. 'Apart from Mrs Redmond.'

She looked down at the floor. Her eyes had become glassy; her shoulders continued to move back and forth. 'And how much would that bring?'

I brought the information to Fownes Street in late July. When I asked how much it was worth, Farrell had to check the handbook. He pulled a ledger from his desk: an alphabetical register of crimes with a payment schedule attached to each. This particular crime was first on the list. It was five pounds for the initial report, ten if there was a conviction. But he doubted they'd arrest Mrs Redmond straight away. In cases like this the police would bide their time, wait for some troubled girl to go down the steps in Dominick Street, then swoop in and catch the midwife red-handed.

It meant our coffers were full for the rest of the summer. Helen no longer felt any pain from her operation, but she continued to take laudanum. It got to the stage that she was lucid only for a few hours each day. After a dose she would lie in bed, or wander around the room in her nightgown. She'd stand by the window and I'd pull her away, saying people on the street below could see her. She'd look at me quizzically, as if wondering why that would matter.

One evening she brought me the bottle while I sat at the dinner table. She said, 'Why don't you try it?'

The taste was so bitter I had to resist spitting it out. I remained in my armchair for an hour looking into a candle flame. I didn't notice any effect.

The new college term began in the middle of September. On the day before classes started, I brought my armchair to the window to catch the afternoon light, and placed an opened book on my lap. My eyes scanned the pages for a few moments, before drifting to the passers-by on Grenville Street. As they crossed the road, their forms expanded and bent because of warps in the windowpane.

Helen sat at the desk, working on her manuscript, some of the pages charred and blackened at the edges. She made notes and annotations; occasionally she would strike out a whole section, write a new paragraph on a fresh page, and insert it into the sheaf.

She wore her fingerless gloves and held the pen awkwardly between stiff fingers. As she bent her head over the desk, a distinct line of scalp could be seen in the parting of her hair. Helen put aside the pen and reached for the small bottle at the side of the table. She leaned her head backwards, then held the tip of the glass over her protruding tongue. Two drops fell almost immediately, but she waited, as if parched with thirst, for a third.

'That's enough for today,' I said. I brought the bottle to the shelf above the dining table. As I pushed it between the salt cellar and money tin, the canister scraped over the wood and the coins inside rattled. Helen finished the page she was working on before getting up. When she was halfway to the shelf I said, 'Leave it, Helen, or I won't buy you any more.'

She paused, but only for a second. 'This isn't where it goes.'

She carried the bottle to the cold fireplace. 'It's kept here,' she said, placing it among some other items on the mantelpiece – her hairbrush, and a small music box with no key.

It had been well over a year since I had set foot in the cobbled quadrangle of Parliament Square. The college was much as I remembered, though construction of a new building had commenced next to the Fellows' Garden. The paths were busy on the first day of term. Youthful first-years with full satchels walked about, unsure of themselves. Older students were more comfortable, catching up with friends after the summer break, walking and laughing in groups. The route I took was a familiar one, to a demonstration room in the science building. A work-table and lectern stood at the front, and six concentric benches rose in tiers, split by a staircase going up a central aisle. I went to sit in the back row.

At ten minutes to the hour, other students began to drift in while chatting together. A few cast glances in my direction, but I ignored them. They all took their seats close to the front. In my day, we scattered about the benches at random, but in this class about twenty were bunched together in the first three rows. I considered gathering my books and going to join them, but what did it matter?

Professor Lloyd entered and the murmur of conversation quietened. He welcomed the class back, trusted we had an enjoyable summer. He noticed me sitting alone in the rear, but made no comment before starting his lecture.

While Lloyd spoke, he kept his arms tightly folded in front of his chest. But he'd disengage his left arm to make expansive gestures, or turn the page of his notes, or stroke at his clean-shaven chin. When he did so, he always kept his right arm pressed against his ribs, as if nursing an injury. Once the left hand had completed its motion, it would burrow back into the crook of his elbow.

I realized that a student in the second row on the far left was looking at me over his shoulder. He had wavy brown hair oddly parted just off-centre, and straight eyebrows that met at the bridge of his nose. I didn't recognize him, but when I held his gaze he dipped his head once, then returned his attention to Lloyd.

The Professor was casually referring to physical laws and mathematical equations I had never heard of, but my class-mates weren't perplexed; one fellow was nodding his head along to the lecture, as if his own findings were being confirmed.

I shifted in my bench and leaned forward. I wasn't paying close enough attention. It would take a while to regain the con-centration necessary to follow such advanced teaching. Lloyd spoke of optical axes and the propagation of light along crystal lattices; he spoke of rays incidental and rays tangential. He unfolded his left arm again and held up one finger. 'And then, of course, we shall encounter conical refraction.' He smiled and said, 'The radiant stranger.'

Several in the class laughed, apparently familiar with the reference. I was at a loss. I looked to see if the man who had peered back at me was amused, but he was busy writing in his notebook.

Over the next several minutes my interest wavered. I scraped my dry nib over the tabletop. It was quite easy to leave a mark, so I inscribed a J into the wood. The curve of the D was more difficult, so I left my initials unfinished as 'JI', placed the pen in my satchel and got up to leave. The aisle descended through the middle of the lecture hall, and all the students turned at the sound of my footsteps. Professor Lloyd's voice trailed off for a moment. When he saw me move towards the door he said, 'Usually, gentlemen manage to make it to lunch hour.'

Rain fell in a fine mist as I picked my way over slippery cobbles in Library Square. The grey buildings provided scant protection from a crosswind that caused the Union flag above Regent House to snap. I waited beneath the arched portico at the front entrance of the college for the rain to ease, looking out at the traffic on College Green, and down the length of Dame Street towards the Castle, which was hidden from view.

'John Delahunt.'

The student who had been observing me in class stood by my side. One of his straight eyebrows lifted at an angle. 'Do you remember me?'

I searched his face. His features weren't familiar.

'Because I remember you. You were a friend of James O'Neill.'

He smiled at my reaction to the name.

'And you refused to testify against him when he was tried for assaulting that policeman. He thought highly of you.'

'That was a year and a half ago.'

'I know, I was just a junior freshman, but I saw you once or twice in the Eagle with James and Arthur Stokes. I'm Michael Corcoran.'

'Is O'Neill still in Trinity?'

Corcoran shook his head. 'He was expelled when convicted, which meant he couldn't go to King's Inns either. But his father has connections in America, and he's going to complete his degree in Philadelphia. He'll be leaving Ireland soon.'

'That's a shame.'

'I was surprised to see you this morning. I'd no idea you were to repeat your final year. The rumour was you had married the Stokes daughter.'

'I did marry Helen.'

'Oh.' He apologized and enquired after her health.

'She's convalescing at present.' I could have left it at that. 'A miscarriage.'

He frowned, looked down at the ground and said he was sorry for my loss.

'It couldn't be helped.'

He hadn't meant to pry.

I allowed the silence between us to grow uncomfortable as he fixed a button on the cuff of his coat.

How did he know what O'Neill thought of me?

'Well, James was a founder member of the Repeal Society in the college. I attended its early meetings.'

'There's a Repeal Society in Trinity?' I was surprised to learn this. It had been my belief that the university didn't allow the expression of radical opinion in the debating clubs.

Corcoran said there was, and that he was now the secretary. 'We have a room overlooking Botany Bay. Perhaps you'd like to come up?'

I allowed my gaze to drift down Dame Street once more. Corcoran seemed to think I needed more convincing.

'The fire will be lit, and there may be some wine.'

I pretended that settled it. 'In that case,' I said, 'lead on.'

Helen didn't lift her head from the pillow when I came in. I threw my satchel in the corner and placed my jacket on the bare hook. She was wearing her coat beneath the covers again. I leaned over the bed and looked into her face. She was awake, and I waited for her eye to meet mine. Her pupils suddenly narrowed as if a flaring match was held against them. After another moment her eyelids widened, and I wondered if she was aware of me at all.

I spoke her name.

She gave two languid blinks, and the ghost of a smile appeared. 'How did it go?'

I continued to look at her in silence to see if she would drift away again, but she remained focused, and her brow creased.

'The classes were difficult to follow, I'll need to do some more reading. But I met someone who used to know your brother.' Her lips tightened. 'He invited me to join a society for the radicals, which I did. I'm sure the Department will want to know about them. It could be a nice source of money.'

'That's good.' She reached out and brushed my cheek.

What had she done during the day?

'Not much. A bit of writing.'

How much laudanum did she take?

She took her hand away from my face. 'I didn't take any.'

I looked over at the cold hearth. 'I'll start a fire to make dinner.'

She pulled the blankets up to her chin and said she wasn't hungry.

The bottle of laudanum remained on the mantelpiece, its label turned against the wall, just as it was the day before. Had she carefully positioned it so it would appear untouched? It was about a third full. With my thumbnail, I made a small mark in the label, just at the level of the liquid.

The first few weeks of the term drifted by. Helen was at her most coherent in the morning, though more often than not she remained in bed while I got ready for college. I would pause at the threshold and wish her a good day, closing the door over in the ensuing silence. I stopped attending lectures so spent most of my day in the common room of the Repeal Society. By all appearances, I was its most ardent member, though I never took part in the few conversations relating to politics, or volunteered for any of their weekly debates.

There were always books and newspapers strewn about the neglected billiard table, and I would take one and read in the corner, with a bearing that indicated I didn't wish to be disturbed. The other members seemed to tolerate my brooding, dishevelled presence. They would nod to me or greet me by name as I entered, and enquire if I wished for coffee whenever it was brewed. They believed that I had been a close confidant of the club's founder, James O'Neill, and that I had sought to protect his liberty by remaining stony-faced during his trial. Furthermore, there was a certain cachet to the fact that I'd eloped with a sought-after debutante, and that we lived together shamelessly in a one-roomed garret near the city's northern limit.

But Helen remained in a state of lethargy throughout October. One afternoon, I decided to sort out the mess on her writing desk, which was cluttered with strewn papers, stained pens and one dried inkpot with its lid removed. I had never been curious about Helen's novel before, but that day I picked it up to have a look. Her handwriting had become very spidery and smudged. The paragraphs were numbered, but not sequentially, and some of them were struck through with a line from the bottom left corner to the top right.

It had been my belief that Helen was writing a novel set during the Congress of Vienna, which took place after the Napoleonic Wars, a tale full of intrigue and romance.

From what I could piece together from stray paragraphs and fragments of chapters, her newest text was about a character named Gideon, who had been committed to an asylum on a desolate island off the Scottish coast. His main interaction was with the institution's governor, a man called Dr Lucian. Helen seemed to make no delineation between Gideon's speech and the jumble of thoughts spoken only in his own fervid mind. The asylum was populated with a cast of grotesques, and Helen described each of them and their low habits in disturbing detail. Other long passages seemed to recount bizarre nightmares and hallucinations witnessed by Gideon: bedclothes that became swarms of insects; faces of children ageing and decaying in a matter of seconds; buboes in his armpits and groin with gaping, grinning mouths. Was this what she saw when she stared about with vacant eyes, or when she whimpered in her sleep? She shifted under the covers, and I hurriedly replaced the sheaf on the table, as if I had been caught reading her diary.

I was convinced she was taking extra doses of laudanum, so I checked the amount against the mark I had scratched in the bottle's label a few weeks before. The level of liquid was still as high as the notch.

I was perplexed. If she wasn't misusing the tonic then she had to be suffering from some other illness. I went to sit on the bed and pulled the blanket down from her face. My knuckles rested against her chin, and her uneven breath tickled the top of my hand.

She hadn't been eating properly for weeks; her sleep was erratic. For several hours a day she was left on her own in the tenement, and she hardly ever took fresh air. She began to shiver so I took off my coat and laid it on top of the bedclothes. I brushed a lock of hair over her ear. A strand caught in my fingernail and came away.

I recalled how she had looked at her coming-out ball: the gown she wore, pearl-white in the warm drawing-room light, the topaz crystals in her hair, the flash in her eye. When I sat beside her that night, our knees had touched, and we both pretended not to notice. When she spoke into my ear, I had felt her breath brush against my cheek.

She stirred in the bed, slowly blinked and studied me for a moment. Then she rose into a sitting position, placed a hand on her forehead and spoke in a mumble. 'I must write to Arthur.' She began to push the bedclothes down. 'I promised him I'd write.'

I hushed her and said she was only dreaming. With a small amount of pressure, I eased her back on to the pillow.

Throughout our time in Grenville Street, no matter our circumstances, Helen always maintained certain standards. She never allowed unwashed dishes to build up on the sideboard. She swept the room and cleared the cinders from the hearth each morning. Though washing clothes was a nuisance – for once immersed they tended to remain damp for days – she always insisted we change our attire each week.

Fetching and heating enough water for the bath-tub was laborious and we only made the effort once a month. But each Saturday, Helen washed her hair over the basin, dragging it in front of the fire during cold weather. She would kneel and gather her hair forward, soak and lather the tresses with a bar of soap, and squeeze suds through her fingers. Then she'd rinse, by pouring water over her head from a bowl that she dipped in the larger basin. Her neck bent forward so the knoll at the top of her spine protruded. Slim, bare arms emerged from her white sleeveless shift. She was all elbows throughout, but in a way strangely graceful. The water would cascade down and burble into the washbasin, the ends of her hair floating on the frothy surface.

She was no longer able to do that, so I took it upon myself to clean her clothes. A small amount of washing soda remained in a burlap pouch on the shelf. I wasn't sure how much was needed so I tipped in all of it. I swirled my hand in the basin to distribute the salts, then went to open Helen's trunk. An array of soiled clothes were bundled beneath the lid. I held my breath, gathered two armfuls and brought them to the basin. I washed the garments in batches, vigorously scrubbing folds of stockings, petticoats and dresses against each other, as if rubbing sticks to start a fire. I wrung them out as best I could, and draped them from the clothes line that spanned the room. Helen remained asleep throughout.

The water in the basin had become cloudy. I frowned at red blotches that appeared on my palms and admired the gleaming whites of my fingernails. Helen's trunk was almost empty. The dresses that remained were of high-quality velvet and muslin, which she hadn't worn in over a year. There was also another nightdress folded up which smelled clean, so I took it over to Helen and gently shook her awake. She squinted up at me.

I said, 'Change into this, and I'll wash the one you're wearing.'

She regarded the lace gown in my hand for a moment, then looked over at the basin beside the fireplace, and the laundry suspended from the line.

I dragged back the covers. 'Come along. This one's cleaner.'

I helped her out of bed, but she just stood there, bare feet on the floorboards, with her head bowed.

'Will you hurry up?'

When she made no movement I reached over and undid a string on her nightdress. She drew away from my touch, and crossed her hands over her shoulders. I thought she intended to remain like that, but then she tugged at the short sleeves of the nightdress and allowed it to slip on to the floor.

I held out the clean gown. Already she had begun to shiver, and her gaunt shoulders stooped. She kept her arms folded in front.

'Take it,' I said.

Helen's skin had a yellow tinge, her rib-cage was visible, and two hollows dipped behind jutting collarbones.

'You'll catch cold.'

She remained still. I was about to pull the gown over her head myself, but then she turned her face towards mine and stared at me between the parting of her hair. She held my eye as she reached across to take the dress, and I looked away as she put it on. Then I bent down to her feet.

'Mind,' I said.

She stepped out of the crumple of linen on the floor and I picked it up. The stained nightgown was still warm. When I threw it into the basin it floated on top for a moment, until the water saturated the cloth and it sank into the murk.

9

Coppinger Row is a narrow lane that runs aslant and cobbled in the warren of houses between Trinity and the Castle. One side is taken up in its entirety by a wing of the Powerscourt townhouse, a gaudy Palladian mansion that sits incongruous amid the mazy streets. The other side has a terrace of old dwellings squeezed together, some with Dutch-billy gables, others with shopfronts on the ground floor.

I knocked at the door of one of the houses. After a moment, a bright voice approached inside the hallway, and then my sister Cecilia opened the door wide. She still spoke to someone over her shoulder, so didn't notice me at once. Her hair was loosely pinned beneath a maid's cap with a lace trim.

When she turned, she searched my face for a couple of seconds, and her right hand came across to rest on the door's edge. 'John, I hardly recognized you.'

I stroked my chin. 'I'm letting my beard grow out.'

'No,' she said. 'That's not it.'

Then, as if it only just occurred to her, she stepped forward and embraced me precisely. I was about to hug back, but she straightened and held me at arm's length.

I said, 'I like your hat.'

She smiled at that, and it may as well have been the face that peered at me across the dining table, trying not to giggle while our father said grace. She reached up and unpinned the maid's cap. 'We're doing some spring-, well, autumn-cleaning.' Footsteps in the hall caused her smile to fade, and she glanced backwards.

A stocky housekeeper holding a rag and jar of brass polish descended the stairs. She openly craned her head past Cecilia to look at me.

'My brother has arrived unexpectedly, Sally. Could you bring us some tea upstairs?'

The woman looked down at her cloth, as if a break from her chore was an inconvenience, nodded brusquely and disappeared.

Cecilia led the way up a cramped staircase to the drawing room and sat in an armchair beside the fireplace, which was set in a diagonal chimney breast in the corner. I pulled at the lid of a piano just inside the door, expecting it to be locked, but it swung upwards on its hinges. A booklet of sheet music drooped open on the stand.

'Are you learning to play?'

'No. The piano came with the house, though Charles plays it occasionally.'

I opened my fingers in a V and played two ivory notes at random. They didn't harmonize.

'Not so loud. He was at a ball last night and didn't get home till late.'

'You didn't go?'

She hadn't been feeling up to it.

I replaced the lid. On top of the piano, a few framed pictures sat in a row unaligned. One of them was the mounted silhouette of my mother. I reached towards it, but its support was faulty, and the heavy frame slipped on to its back with a clatter, causing the piano strings to hum.

'Sorry.'

'Will you not come and sit down?'

I nodded and picked my way to an empty armchair. 'It's a lovely house, Cecilia.'

'Thank you.'

'Very cosy.'

She looked at me more closely to see if I made sport. 'Charles's parents are coming to visit in a few days. That's why we're sprucing it up.'

'Ah yes,' I said. 'The dreaded in-laws.'

She smiled, but then seemed to recall the relationship I had with my own, and looked away. A package wrapped in brown paper rested on a side table. I ran my finger over its hard, lumpy edge, then picked it up to examine closer. It turned out to be a stock of lead bullets.

Cecilia watched me handle the parcel. 'How is Helen?'

'She's fine. In good health. She continues to write her novels.' I put the bullets down. 'They're coming along very well.'

It was disconcerting to see items from my childhood: cushions on the sofa that Cecilia had sewn when she was a girl; the painted terrestrial globe that once sat in my father's chamber; the garish oriental rug that lay in our front parlour.

A young maid entered, and we both sat silently while she laid out the tea. When she left, I said to Cecilia, 'I've gone back to Trinity to get my degree.'

'Oh good.'

'Yes, though the fees are very high.'

Cecilia staked her wet spoon in the bowl. 'What have you been doing for money?'

For a fleeting moment, I considered telling her. 'I've found some work here and there to match my talents. But you know how it is.'

She nodded and another silence developed. Then she turned her head towards the writing desk. 'I meant to say, I received a letter from Alex.'

She went to the desk, opened a drawer and withdrew an envelope. The letter consisted of two sheets, but only one had writing on both sides. Several of the lines had been expunged with neat black strokes. Before I could comment Cecilia said, 'That's how it arrived. The war office must have seen it first. I can't imagine what he wrote that would have to be concealed.'

My eyes flitted over some of the uncensored passages. Alex wrote the usual account of life at the front: the long days of inaction followed by bursts of excitement; the constant wariness of infection; the incessant search for wood in order to make fires and brew tea – anything was used, the stocks from old rifles, the sides of broken stretchers. And interspersed were expurgated sentences hidden under ribbons of black ink. I held the letter up against the light in case a hint of the writing could be seen beneath. But the clerk in the war office had been commendably thorough.

'What do you think?'

'It's a mystery.' I put the pages aside. 'Cecilia, I came here because I need a loan.'

She stayed still for a moment, then retrieved the letter from the table and folded it back into its envelope.

I said we both knew the inheritance I'd received was practically worthless. I had done my best to find employment to support myself, Helen and our household, but now that I was back in college, that was more difficult. 'Helen and I live very frugally. Ten pounds would see us through to the new year.'

A door opened and closed in the floors above, and there were heavy footsteps on the landing. I expected to hear them descend the staircase, but after a few moments all was quiet once more.

I said, 'I'd prefer it if Charles didn't know about this.'

She went to replace the letter in her writing desk, and I followed her into the middle of the room. As she brought the shutter down on the bureau, her back was turned for a few seconds.

She said, 'Charles isn't on active service so he's only receiving half-pay. I'm afraid I couldn't lend you ten shillings, John, let alone ten pounds.'

'And yet you've enough to employ two servants.'

Her face darkened. 'How we spend our money is not your concern.'

There were more footsteps in the floor above. This time they sounded in the stairwell.

'I'm sorry, Cecilia. I shouldn't have asked.' I stood for a moment with my hands in my pockets. 'I'd better be getting back.'

'I could speak with Charles. Arrange for you both to meet. Perhaps—'

'No, I don't want that.' I forced a smile. 'I'm being silly. Helen and I will manage just fine.'

Before she could speak again, the door opened and Captain Dickenson entered. His shirt-tails hung loose from his waistband, and the ends of his moustache had been waxed into points. He paused when he saw us standing in the middle of the room. 'John,' he said. 'What a pleasant surprise.'

'Charles. I'm sorry for calling in unannounced. I happened to be passing by.'

'Not at all. You're always welcome.' He smiled at Cecilia.

My sister hesitated, then said, 'Actually, John wished—'

'No, it's fine.' The mantel clock's chime for midday came

as a relief. 'I was just leaving. I must get back to Helen.'

Cecilia took a step forward. 'But, John . . .'

I was already walking towards the hall door. 'I'll see myself out.' I stopped at the entrance and looked back. 'I'll write soon, Cecilia.'

With that, I slipped down the stairs, past the housekeeper, who was polishing the brass letter box, and out of the front door. I walked up Coppinger Row, turned the corner, and only then withdrew the item concealed in my jacket pocket: the silhouette of my mother in its solid silver frame.

I immediately went to a shop in Exchequer Street. Three metal balls painted gold hung suspended beside a sign that read, 'Money advanced on plate and jewellery, items of apparel, and every type of property', beneath the name 'Clifford & Son'.

The shop-room was low and gloomy. A counter spanned the back wall, divided into three booths by wooden partitions. Mr Clifford and his son each dealt with a customer. Clifford senior examined a gold necklace with a magnifying glass, the chain drooping between his fingers. The younger broker spoke with a woman who clutched a bundle of ball gowns. He held each one up by its hanger to judge the design and quality of the cloth, as if choosing a gift for his wife.

I stood near the counter to wait my turn. The shop was cluttered with heirlooms and keepsakes brought in by their owners as collateral for loans, and now abandoned. One table contained assorted chinaware with chipped rims and faded patterns, and a wooden box filled with pocket watches jumbled together. Above that, several heart-shaped lockets hung suspended by different lengths of chain. Each of them was clasped shut and I wondered if any still hid miniature portraits of young lovers.

When my turn came, I handed Clifford the picture for appraisal. I knew the frame was of good quality. The moulding was solid and weighty, made of hallmarked silver decorated with delicate scrolling by the silversmith Thomas Meade. My father once pointed out his initials stamped on the back.

Clifford's eyes swept over the frame for a second, and then he looked at me closely. 'I don't want this,' he said, returning it to the counter. 'You're trying to fence it.'

He wrote a note in his ledger, as if our business was concluded.

'I can assure you this picture has been in my family's possession for decades.'

The broker's pen stilled, and he seemed to reconsider. Perhaps he was swayed by my accent, though that was easily mimicked. More likely his job made him adept at spotting liars. And what I said was strictly true.

But then he shook his head. 'No, you'll have to take it elsewhere. If you really owned that you'd have hocked it months ago.'

I picked up the frame and regarded it. There had to be a way to prove ownership.

Once when I was a child in Fitzwilliam Street, I played a simple game of tag with my brother in our father's study. Alex chased me round and round the desk; occasionally he would stop abruptly and reverse course, and I had to prevent myself from running into his simple trap. During the game, I brushed the picture and it tumbled to the floorboards. The thin glass pane covering the silhouette shattered.

Our mother happened to be on the landing and she came in. She strode over to pick up the damaged frame, visibly upset. I stood to one side, knowing I would surely be punished once my father found out. She regarded us both in turn, then daintily picked out a shard that had stuck in the surround, and said perhaps our father wouldn't notice. It was only a piece of glass after all. She told Alex to fetch the dustpan.

While he was gone, she undid the small clasps at the rear of the picture, removed the stiff brown backing, and then tipped the card into her hand. She turned the leaf over and showed me the reverse, which was bare with mottled specks of grime. In one corner there was a small inscription in pencil.

My mother said she'd written it for my father just after they were married, and before Alex was born. She hadn't seen it in ten years.

The handwriting was neat and precise, but I couldn't decipher the joined-up letters. She traced her finger lightly over the message as she read. When she finished, I looked up at her. A strange expression had come over her face, though I couldn't describe it then, and memory is too fickle to judge it now. She was reflective at least, wistful, perhaps melancholic. She smiled when she noticed me gazing at her, and her face returned to normal.

I said to the pawnbroker, 'There's an inscription on the reverse of the portrait.'

'You could have seen that any time.'

'Just look.'

He frowned at me, but then unfastened the backing and took out the card. He took his magnifying glass and examined the bottom corner.

I recited from memory. 'It says, "Henceforward, I am forever yours, Clara, May 1817."'

One of his eyes scrunched shut; the pores on his cheek were made large by the looking glass. He nodded. 'That's indeed what it says.'

'She was my mother, Clarissa Delahunt.'

'If only she could see you now.'

Before I could reply he said, 'Do you want to sell it to me, or pawn it?'

His slender fingers were leaving streaks on the familiar silver surround. I changed my mind. 'Pawn.'

'Very well.' We discussed the value of the loan. I was never good at haggling, and besides, now that I intended to buy the frame back, it seemed wise to keep the price low. Clifford charged a rate of 20 per cent. If I returned in a month's time with the principal plus interest, I could have it back, otherwise he would sell it in the shop. He wrote a docket in duplicate, and we signed each other's copy.

Clifford counted out the money, then handed me the silhouette, which was still out of the frame. 'Better take this now,' he said. 'Just in case.'

Usually at this time I'd still be in the Repeal Society rooms in college, but I decided to make my way home via Moore Street. I meandered through the market stalls buying in-gredients for a beef stew, then stopped at Meyler's on Great Britain Street for two bottles of wine: a cheap one to braise the beef, a less cheap one for Helen and me. A slow-cooked stew would do her good. Even if she couldn't eat the meat, the broth would be warm and wholesome.

But when I arrived home Helen was gone. Her chair had been neatly pushed in beneath the writing desk, and the coat-hook was bare. The clothes still hung from the washing line in the middle of the room, except one dress was missing. I felt one of the other petticoats. It was still slightly damp.

If she had gone out dressed in wet clothes then she could get pneumonia. I thought for a moment. Or was it rheumatism? I pictured her wandering Dublin's streets like Ophelia, with uncombed hair and mismatched clothes, making peculiar enquiries of passers-by, becoming transfixed by the shimmer of sunlight in a puddle, or stumbling unaware beneath clattering hooves. There was nothing for it. I fastened my coat and went to look for her.

From the steps of number six, I surveyed Grenville Street, hoping she had just stepped out to take some air. The mid-afternoon sunshine had disappeared, and a breeze caused pieces of litter to scurry over the roadway. I cast my eye over the women and taller girls on the street. Helen usually wore a knee-length, navy-blue coat with a plaid pelerine about the shoulders. My eye was drawn to garments of a similar colour, but I was disappointed every time.

I checked the enclosed garden of Mountjoy Square, the inside of Kavanagh's pub, and our local food market in Gloucester Diamond. Some of the stallholders would have recognized me, and known Helen by name, so I considered asking if she had passed this way. But I didn't want anyone to know our business.

The light had faded by the time I turned left into Montgomery Street. Small grimy houses closed in on either side in the soft drizzle. Pairs of young women walked with arms linked. Others stood together in doorways, or leaned against dark lamp-posts. In the dwindling light all their coats took on a navy hue, and with their bird's-nest hair and blank expressions, any one could have passed for my wife. I walked between them, looking from face to face. Not one of them lowered her eyes.

One woman stood alone near the end of the street, beneath the head of a lamp that curled above her like a bishop's crosier. Her coat was like Helen's, as was the colour of her hair. She leaned against the post with her left leg crossed before her right shin, the toe of her shoe resting in a puddle. Her face was hidden, and she stood with her shoulders hunched and arms folded.

I thought she would lift her head at the sound of my approach, but she remained still until I stood beside her. This close I could see the design of her coat was slightly different, and her shoes had a prominent heel, the type that Helen never wore. The girl looked up. She had dark eyes, set a little far apart. Circular smudges of rouge on her cheeks only drew attention to her pallid skin. She smiled at me. One of her incisors was missing. The other was made of a yellow metal.

She said, 'I was miles away.'

I remained silent as her eyes searched my face. She tilted her head to the house behind. 'I've a room upstairs.'

I told her I was sorry. I thought she was someone else.

The toe of her shoe scraped a few inches in the puddle. 'You're looking for someone in particular?'

'Yes.'

'Do you know her name?'

'Yes.'

At the other end of the street, a lamplighter was going from post to post with a small flame at the end of a long pole carried over his shoulder. The women teased him as he went about his nightly chore.

'Well, maybe I know her.'

Before the lamplighter could get any closer, I left the prostitute and turned the corner into Amiens Street, doubling back towards the pepper-canister dome of the Customs House.

I was never going to find Helen like this. She could have been anywhere – across the river, in the next street, or even back in the house. I made my way home, still looking into the faces of women as I passed, still glancing down stable-lanes and alleyways. In the dim hallway outside our room, I listened at the door for movement, then turned the key and went in.

The room was cold and empty. I lit two candles and placed them on both windowsills. I also lit the fire, hung my wet coat over the back of Helen's chair and left it before the hearth, then began to prepare dinner as I had originally planned.

I set out the ingredients on the dining table, took the sharpest knife from the drawer and began boning the joint and peeling vegetables. Butter sizzled in the bottom of the pot. I browned the meat, then poured in water and wine, added the sprig of herbs and watched it come to a simmer. I didn't want it to over-boil, so I used the poker to shift some of the embers to one side, and placed the lid on top.

There were noises in the stairwell. I crossed the room and pulled open the door, but I only startled two of the Lynch boys who were looking at a picture book. By their efforts to conceal it I'm sure it wasn't suitable for their tender years.

I shut the door and poured another glass of wine. It was now almost completely dark outside. Any figure walking in the shadows might have been her. I took Helen's clean clothes from the washing line and folded them on the bed. I lifted the lid of her trunk with the toe of my boot, and carefully laid the bundle inside.

A clink of glass made me pause. Something was concealed beneath her old muslin gowns. I lifted the dresses away to reveal several small, empty phials. Some stood upright, others had tipped over on their sides. One tucked in the corner was still half-full. I picked up the laudanum, swirled it about, and then looked up at the fireplace. Helen's decoy bottle still remained on the mantelpiece, a sham symbol of temperance.

The phials in the trunk rested upon a stack of opened letters written on creased yellow paper. They all began the same: 'My dearest Helen'. And they were each signed off by her brother, Arthur.

I went through them in chronological order. Arthur had begun writing that February. He had seen my name appear in the *Evening Post*, identified as the chief prosecution witness in the Cooney trial. Though their father, Mr Stokes, had forbidden all communication with Helen after our elopement, Arthur felt compelled to write and enquire after her health and happiness. Her reply must have been positive, for in the second letter Arthur declared himself glad that I had found lucrative work and that we lived comfortably, albeit in Grenville Street. He wondered why Helen had to be circumspect about the nature of my employment. As for her request to arrange a meeting with their father, he said he would try his best.

I heard footsteps on the landing below. But they were heavy and sounded like those of Mr Lynch. The door to the room downstairs creaked open and clicked shut.

Next, Arthur wrote to say he was sorry, but it was clear that their father had no intention of forgiving Helen for the dishonour brought upon their family name. However, he would allow the correspondence between brother and sister to continue. One of the subsequent letters was dated early June, which was during Helen's brief pregnancy. She must have told Arthur that she was ill, as he expressed concern for her wellbeing. With terse language, he noted her news that I had applied to retake my final year in Trinity. He did not wish to belittle me, he wrote, but it was his belief that I did not possess the aptitude or dedication required to complete my final exams, and he feared the money spent on college fees had been wasted.

I glanced over the letter's edge to the steam escaping the black lid of the bastible pot. It was difficult to feel slighted by so shrewd an assessment. I got up, added the chopped vegetables to the stew and checked the clock. They'd require twenty minutes to cook.

There were only two letters left. The first made mention of a loan of one pound sent by Arthur to Helen, which piqued my interest. This was during the difficult weeks following her operation. I picked up some of the empty phials. She probably spent a day going from one apothecary shop to the next.

The most recent letter was only a fortnight old. Arthur was dismayed at Helen's latest missive, the crooked handwriting and peculiar passages. He seemed to be under the impression that I had taken the pound previously advanced and spent it on drink. He said that he enclosed another, and pleaded with Helen to keep the money concealed from me.

I shook my head. It seemed I had given her too little credit.

Arthur said if he did not soon hear that our situation had improved, he might have to take matters into his own hands. I rummaged in the trunk to see if there were any letters received since that date, but it was otherwise empty. I put everything back as I found it, laid Helen's clean clothes on top, and closed the lid.

I went to check on dinner, and then set the table with two white bowls, each flanked by a tarnished fork and spoon. I laid out the bottle of wine and a pair of mismatched glasses, a tallow candle in its squat holder and the heel of a stale loaf.

When Helen came back in I was sitting beside the fire. She immediately lifted her head at the smell of the cooking and the sight of the table settings. I remained with my legs folded, an opened book resting on my lap.

She took off her hat and shook water from the brim, then put her coat on the hook so it covered mine. She came towards the candlelight.

I said to her, 'I was worried.'

'What's all this?'

I marked my page. 'I even went out looking for you.'

She went to the desk and dragged her chair over to the fireplace. She seemed stronger and more alert than before. Perhaps the fresh air had done her good. She sat down opposite me and pulled off her shoes, then extended her feet towards the flames. Her dark grey stockings had become black where they were sodden at the toes.

'I'm sorry if you were worried,' she said, as if the fault was mine, 'but I lost track of time. You kept telling me I should rouse myself, so I went for a walk.'

'In the rain?'

'It was fine when I left.'

That much was true. I leaned across, took the lid off the pot with my sleeve and stirred the stew. 'This will be ready now.'

'Where did you get the money?'

I said the Castle had been in touch. Some obscure bit of information handed in months ago had resulted in a conviction, so I'd collected two pounds. I berated myself as soon as I said it. I should have told her the reward was only a guinea. Holding a towel, I lifted the pot from its hook and brought it to the table. 'We've been scraping by for the past few weeks, so I thought you should be indulged.'

'What have you done with my dresses?'

They were back in her trunk. She went over and lifted the lid, then changed out of her wet clothes. I ladled some stew into my bowl and said, 'You must be hungry.'

I waited for her to join me, pouring her a glass of wine. Helen sat down with her arms by her sides, looked at the dish and swallowed, as if a wave of nausea had come over her. But then she lifted her spoon, dipped it in the broth and took a sip.

I expected some kind of reaction, or thanks, but she just took her fork and skewered a piece of beef.

'Where did you walk?'

She said around Rutland Square and through Sackville Street, down the quays as far as the Four Courts and across the river to Christ Church, then around Stephen's Green.

'Did you meet anyone?'

'No.'

Helen slurped whenever she ate soup or broth. But she seemed unaware of it, for she'd often berate me for the same failing. It was so long since I'd seen her eat like this, I noticed the sound again. She would raise the spoon to her lips, pause and blow at the slight wisps of steam; then came the quick intake of breath and the wet ripple.

A small amount of broth ran from the corner of her mouth down her chin. She used the sleeve of her dress to wipe it away – the one I had cleaned a few days before.

When finished she pushed the plate towards the middle of the table and leaned back in her chair. A slight colour had returned to her cheeks. She even offered to tidy up.

I used the last bit of bread to mop up the gravy in my bowl. Then I fished in my pocket and placed two of the empty laudanum phials on the tabletop between us. Helen looked at them for a moment before she realized what they were.

The colour in her face deepened. She took a slow breath and her shoulders rose. She hadn't looked so striking in some time.

'I saw your letters. Why would you lie about me to Arthur?'

'How dare you go through my belongings?'

I put my cutlery on the plate, with the edge of the knife inserted between the tines of the fork. 'You sound like one of your characters.'

She studied my face, and it was difficult to imagine how

those eyes ever looked upon me with affection. She said, 'You've learned your trade too well.'

With that, she rose and brought her glass to the mantelpiece. She took the stopper from the old bottle of laudanum, poured some into her wine, then began to drink the concoction with small gulps. I crossed the room in a few strides and knocked the glass from her lips. It hit the marble top and shattered, causing some of the wine to splash and hiss in the fire.

Helen covered her mouth with her palm, as if she had just let slip a secret. She pushed past me towards the door, but I held her by the crook of her elbow. She twisted around and struck my shoulder, so I grabbed that arm as well and shook her.

'You'd fall asleep in the gutter after taking that much, and then what?'

She shrank back away from me, with her head bowed and eyes scrunched. Her teeth were bared as she sobbed, and I could see a cut inside her lower lip.

Her strength began to ebb, though I knew it was just the opium taking effect. She stopped crying. Her face relaxed, and she began to breathe heavily, as if she was already asleep while standing up. When I let go she tottered, so I scooped her up and dropped her on the bed. She lay face down in the covers for several seconds. Then her head jerked to the side. She took a gasping breath, and settled into an uneasy slumber.

I went to the door-hook and rifled through her coat. One pocket was weighed down by two new phials. I looked further, found her purse, and emptied the coins on the table. Then I gathered all the laudanum, including the bottle on the mantelpiece and the half-phial from her trunk. A gust made the papers on Helen's desk stir when I raised the sash window.

Raindrops fell on the sill. I took the stopper from each bottle and upended them outside. The liquid was whipped into droplets by the wind and mingled with the rain. As the bottles emptied I placed them in a row on Helen's desk. I went back to the table and ladled out another bowl of stew.

The leafy enclosure of Botany Bay could be seen a hundred times in raindrops that clung to the window of the common room. Occasionally, a strong gust made the branch of a nearby birch tree lash against the panes. The bad weather meant that the room of the Repeal Society was busier than usual, so more than a dozen students lounged about. I sat in the corner reading a book, forever losing my place because of the loud conversation of three members who occupied a couch before the hearth. One was a law student called Crawley. I didn't know the others. They spoke of a gathering they would attend that evening, and some of the eligible daughters who would be present. Crawley was the most offensive of the three, cajoling one of the others to ask a Miss Jameson to dance during the ball, wagering five pounds that she would say no. His friend demurred, saying he could not begin a courtship with a young lady if there was money involved.

Crawley leaned forward and looked at the floor. 'What size boot do you take?'

His friend gave a sidelong glance and said, 'What? Why?'

'If you're not willing to bet money, I'll stake a brand-new pair of riding boots I bought in Cadiz.'

The other two chuckled. But for the next few minutes Crawley kept repeating, 'What size boot do you take?' as if his wager was in earnest.

Corcoran, the club secretary, entered the room with a sheaf of papers tucked under his arm. He placed the printed leaflets on the billiard table and spoke with the three men before the fire. Then he noticed me in the corner and came over.

'Morning, John,' he said. 'Nose in a book again?' He pulled a chair from the wall and sat down. 'How is Mrs Delahunt?'

I folded the corner of the page. 'She still lives.'

He smiled, but then said there was a slight matter that had to be dealt with. The mid-point of Michaelmas had just passed, and so my subscription for the second half of term was owing. 'As you know, it's just another shilling.'

I had not heard Corcoran make a personal demand for payment from any other student. Perhaps he suspected I was evading my dues.

'Thank you for reminding me. I'll bring the money in a few days.'

'It's just that—'

His attention was caught by a hubbub near the door, where a few members had congregated and spoke in raised voices. Others had risen from seats and craned their necks to look towards the entrance. The cluster of students moved into the room and then parted to reveal James O'Neill, smiling and shaking hands with club members. He was much thinner than I remembered, his brown hair was brushed back and he wore a green ribbon in the lapel of his jacket, which clashed with the blue of his cravat. Corcoran immediately got up and went to greet him.

I hadn't seen O'Neill since the day I gave evidence at his trial. Although the Castle had used the statement that Sibthorpe took from me in order to convict him, I had been allowed to feign ignorance on the stand, and say that I hadn't observed what transpired that night. But could O'Neill have remembered something else in the meantime?

I remained seated in the corner, unfolded the dog-eared page in my book and pretended to resume reading. But that seemed an unnatural thing to do when an old acquaintance had just entered, so I placed the book on the seat beside me. Corcoran shook O'Neill's hand and they exchanged friendly words. I considered slipping out, but to reach the door I'd have to walk past everybody. Even if O'Neill's back was turned, someone was bound to mention my passing.

As I pondered these things, O'Neill spoke with Corcoran in a voice loud enough so the group could hear. He said he would be departing for America in a few days to begin his new life, but felt he had to call in once more to bid farewell to the society and its members. The others mumbled a mixture of thanks and good wishes.

Then he noticed me over Corcoran's shoulder. The good humour ebbed from his face and his brow furrowed. Corcoran followed his gaze, seemed to sense the significance of our reunion, and stood aside without comment. The others watched as O'Neill picked his way towards me.

He had to take a meandering route past sofas and strewn satchels, pausing at one point to push a chair beneath a desktop. I waited for him to get near, then placed both hands on my thighs and lifted myself up, timing it so I reached my full height just as he stood before me. He narrowed his eyes and stayed still, as if waiting for my features to swim into focus. After a moment I said, 'Hello, James.'

At the sound of my voice he turned towards the others. 'How long has he been a member?'

Corcoran hesitated, glanced between the two of us, and said, 'Just a few weeks.'

'Why didn't anyone tell me?'

This time the club secretary made no reply.

O'Neill looked at me again and took a breath. 'Delahunt.'

'Yes?'

He extended his hand. 'I never had a chance to thank you.'

I let his hand hover in the space between us for a moment, until a flash of uncertainty crossed his features, then I reached across and gripped it firmly. O'Neill placed his other hand on my shoulder and shifted to the side so he could address the room. 'If any of you are ever called upon to stand by a companion, you would do well to heed Delahunt's example.'

The other members regarded me keenly, and I felt uncomfortable beneath their scrutiny. Crawley looked sceptical, as if he couldn't believe I warranted such praise from the club's founder. After an appropriate pause, Corcoran said there were some new members for O'Neill to meet. Before he broke away, James leaned close and spoke in my ear. 'I want to talk with you alone before I leave.' With that he turned away. He spent the next half-hour chatting to students individually and in small groups. Other members of the society had heard of his presence and came to the common room to pay their respects. Eventually, someone suggested they go for a final drink, and O'Neill said he would catch up with them.

As most of the members filed out, O'Neill came back to my corner and sat beside me. He was silent for a moment, and he smoothed a crease in his trousers, displaying a self-consciousness I had never seen before his trial.

He said, 'Would you like to come for a drink with us?'

'I can't.'

He nodded. 'You're right. I've hardly touched the stuff myself. Not since . . .' He absentmindedly rubbed the ribbon that looped through his buttonhole. 'I never had you marked as a Repealer, John.'

Perhaps this was a moment to be candid. 'The truth is . . .' I waited for him to glance at me. 'I just like having a warm room to escape the weather.'

Another gust shook the window and O'Neill smiled at me. The ribbon came loose in his hand. He regarded it for a moment, then checked to ensure those in the room were out of earshot. 'I'll be glad when I don't have to wear this thing any more.' He slipped the emblem into his pocket. 'My time in prison rather . . . altered my perceptions of my countrymen.'

'What was it like?'

His eyes lost some focus. It was more difficult than he had imagined. That summer had been particularly hot. The inmates baked in the stone cells, and there was an outbreak of typhoid. The sound of the retching kept him awake at night; he could still recall the smells of the sickness, and the images of sunburnt men being carried from their bunks, not to return. In the overcrowding and degradation, fighting between prisoners was a daily occurrence, and he couldn't believe their treachery and heartlessness.

I'd spent that time with Helen in Merrion Park. It had been quite warm, now that he mentioned it.

'But the worst thing', he said, 'was being punished for something I couldn't remember doing.'

I kept my eyes lowered, and scraped my fingers over the cushioned armrest leaving raised furrows in the nap of the cloth, which I then brushed down again. 'You don't remember any of it?'

'Just a few things. Us leaving the pub. I can still picture the policeman arriving with the whistle in his mouth. Then him lying face down in the puddle.' He pinched the bridge of his nose. 'I remember casting about to see where his helmet had rolled.'

He remained still for a moment, leaning forward with his

elbows on his knees. The few students in the room paid more attention to our conversation, probably wondering why it had become so hushed, so solemn.

O'Neill said, 'You were never much of a drinker, Delahunt.' When I didn't say anything he leaned closer to me. 'You must have seen something that night.'

I continued to worry the fabric of the cushion. 'As I said at the time, I'd already walked away—'

'No,' he said, and I detected a note of anger in his voice. But when I looked up at him, his eyes were not accusing, but rather anxious, almost pleading. 'You don't understand.' The way they described the incident in court had kept him awake at night. He couldn't accept the claims that he had been so brutal, and yet the witnesses, the Castle, the prosecutors, they all seemed so sure. He furtively checked the room, as if embarrassed to admit such things aloud, then reached over and held my sleeve. 'What if it was to happen again, John? Could I stop myself? Would I even know I was doing it?' His voice trailed off and he bowed his head.

Another student entered the common room. When he saw O'Neill in the corner he began walking towards him, but seeing the club founder apparently so dejected, the young man paused and joined some others by the hearth.

I pulled my arm away. 'I did see what happened that night.'

O'Neill's head tilted up.

'And I'm afraid you did hit that policeman.' He allowed his eyes to close briefly. 'But it wasn't as they described in court. You just swung your arms in the melee, and struck him . . . more by accident.' Something occurred to me. 'I couldn't say that at the time, though. If I'd said you punched the policeman, even by mishap, you wouldn't have stood a chance.'

He nodded his head. 'Yes, yes. I understand.'

'But you asked if you could have acted as brutally as the prosecutors alleged. Well, I can tell you, James, in all sincerity, that you were not capable of such a thing. Not that night.'

O'Neill's eyes squeezed shut and he exhaled through his nose. 'Thank you, John.' He noted the clock above the mantel. 'I'd better go and join the others. Are you sure you won't come?'

'I'm sure,' I said and wished him well. We shook hands again.

'If you ever find yourself in America . . .' he said, and I nodded. With that, he turned and left the common room, pausing only to bid farewell to the few students who remained.

I stayed in my seat and looked out of the window. Rain still fell outside, with the occasional squall rattling against the panes. I felt a sudden pang of jealousy for O'Neill and his departure. I imagined sailing across the slate-grey ocean, standing at the prow of a barque, all my knotted entanglements and problems and pressures left behind, dissipating with each passing league. I wondered if it rained as much in America.

By midday the weather improved, and most of the students left to attend lectures or go home for the afternoon. Only Crawley remained, dozing with his head bent back over the top of the couch. His heavy breathing was the only noise in the room except for an odd spark that burst from the coals.

I got up and stood behind him. His mouth was slack and the bottom of his teeth visible. He hadn't shaved, so a distinct line went across his throat and over a prominent Adam's apple. I stood closer. My impulse was to trace a delicate finger along the neckline of his beard. I considered what would happen if he was found here in the radicals' common room with a cut neck. The papers would love the mystery, the setting, and the politics, but there could only be one suspect. Still, the thought of the consternation made me smile.

The coals in the fire shifted and Crawley opened his eyes. He remained still, staring up at me for a second. Then he closed his mouth, leaned forward and cleared his throat.

'I was just leaving,' I said. 'And thought I should wake you lest you sleep the entire afternoon.'

He fumbled at a chain in his waistcoat and removed a pocket watch, but didn't open it. He said that was very kind of me.

I said, 'Good day, Crawley,' and left the room.

While climbing the stairs in Grenville Street, I passed Mrs Lynch and two of her children. She looked at me as I squeezed by and said, 'So you're leaving us?'

I paused on the landing. 'Pardon me?'

But then one child struck the other, and their mother began to yell at them.

The door to our room was unlocked. When I entered, I saw Arthur sitting in my armchair. He watched me as I came in. Helen's writing desk was bare. Her trunk was also missing, leaving a large dirt-free rectangle on the floorboards. The dishes from the meal last evening had been washed and cleared on to the dresser.

I closed the door behind me. 'Where is she?'

He didn't answer. I went towards him and stood in the middle of the room, suddenly conscious of the shabby appearance of my clothes. There was a seat at the writing desk, but that was Helen's chair, so I perched on the end of the bed. I saw Arthur's gaze sweep over the dishevelled covers.

'I've taken her home,' he said, and then withdrew Helen's key from an inside coat pocket. It had a lilac ribbon tied to the bow so we could tell them apart – she said mine always jammed. He placed it on a side table. 'She'll no longer have any need for this.'

Since his youth, Arthur had been soft-spoken despite his background and education. Now his speech seemed to have an additional assurance. It was clipped and without inflection.

'Why are you here now?'

'Helen was only going to leave you a note. I said the least you deserved was to be told of her decision in person.'

I unbuttoned my coat, but kept it on for there was a nip in the air. 'The decision wasn't hers to make, Arthur. You'll have to bring her back.'

An irritated look briefly came over his face, as if he'd hoped the conversation wouldn't take this turn. He pinched his fingers beneath his nose and smoothed his moustache by expanding his thumb and forefinger.

Before he could speak again I said, 'I thought you'd disowned her anyway.'

'Our family will put all that behind us. Mother and Father have gone to Edinburgh for the winter, so Helen can remain in Merrion Square at least until she's recovered. We'll arrange a reconciliation in the meantime.'

'You've no idea how that abandonment affected her. The amount of times I had to comfort her during the night while she wept.' I looked down at the bed and shook my head. 'Now you come here and claim her, as if your own family wasn't the root of her unhappiness.'

Arthur remained silent so I pressed on. 'All I have to do is report this to the authorities and Helen will be delivered back here in the morning.'

'The authorities won't care.'

'Helen may have told you that I have friends in the Castle.'

'She told me you live in fear of running into them.'

I forgot that Arthur had had his own dealings with Sibthorpe's department. He knew what they were like. I was about to say that I'd just run into O'Neill, but Arthur cut me off. 'Besides,' he said, 'Helen has no obligation to stay when you treat her with such cruelty.'

'I've done everything possible to look after her.'

Something caught his attention. He went over to the mantelpiece and stood with his back towards me. 'You forget that I've seen her, John.' He picked up the music box that rested on the corner, and held it up over his shoulder. 'This is hers.' It went into the pocket of his greatcoat with small tinny chimes. 'We met in Morrison's yesterday. She looked half-starved, wearing a ragged dress, like some . . .' He shook his head, unwilling to say it. 'But for the fact she had come to see me, the manager wouldn't have let her in.'

I said that was just the effects of the laudanum.

He twisted around, his left sole scraping on the hearthstone. 'That's just the point. How could you let her become so addicted?'

'She was almost weaned a month ago. Then you started sending her money. After that she could get as much as she wanted and use it in secret.'

'I sent that money so she could buy food. Money that you stole.'

I allowed a pause. 'Then how did Helen buy the drug?'

There was no answer. He returned to my seat and leaned forward on his knees. 'You must have—'

'Helen is in this condition because of her own nature, Arthur. She's manipulated you. She's become so adept at lying.'

'Don't speak of her like that.'

I asked why not? If anyone had the right to speak the truth about Helen, it was I. This situation was entirely of her own making. She was the one who had pursued me in Merrion Square and convinced me to elope. When our circumstances changed and we moved to Grenville Street, I had gone out to earn a living, while she remained here scratching out a novel that every publishing house told her was unprintable. There wasn't a member of the Stokes family who hadn't spurned us. It was only when I returned to college to improve our prospects that she was free to indulge her habits, all funded by her foolish brother.

I may have misjudged my tone. Arthur left his seat, crossed the room and lifted me up from the bed by my lapels. His knuckles dug into the bottom of my chin. I had to cock my head backwards and cling to his forearms for balance.

'Don't blame me for your own—'

'Did she tell you she became ill because she insisted on having an abortion?'

His grip didn't loosen, but he paused and searched my face. The pomade on his moustache smelled of lavender.

'No,' I said. 'I didn't think so.'

Arthur looked down at his fists holding my jacket askew. He let go and walked towards the window.

'The laudanum was prescribed by the midwife.' I straightened a collar that had been left upturned. 'I did my best to keep it from her. But it didn't take her long to find other sources.'

'Stop.' Arthur looked down at the traffic on Grenville Street for several seconds. The sound of carriages trundling on the rutted roadway drifted up. He felt along the outside of his coat pocket, where the music box was hidden. I thought for a moment that he would take it out and replace it on the mantel.

Finally he said, 'No,' and moved his hand away. His voice had become monotone. 'It doesn't matter what Helen has said or done. I remember what she was like before you came into her life.'

One of the shutters was slightly folded out. He pushed it flush into the shutter box. 'I'll tell you what brought me here in the first place. I'm willing to pay the legal expenses required to petition the Court of Conscience to have your marriage annulled.' He turned around to face me. 'I'll also give you two hundred pounds if you agree to cooperate.'

Watery sunlight slanted through the window, casting his frame in silhouette. Two hundred pounds was enough to live comfortably for a few years. I could move to a nicer room, closer to the college. There would still be time to focus on my studies and attain my degree. I couldn't deny that Helen and I had struggled in the tenement over the last few months. If a stranger had knocked on the door and offered to dissolve the marriage, return Helen to her family and give me such a large sum, I'd have agreed without hesitation. It was like wiping the slate clean. We could both start again.

Well, I could at least.

'You don't have to answer now.' He opened the door and paused at the threshold. 'But the offer stands. If you see sense, send me word.'

When the door clicked shut I was left alone.

10

I've had a cellmate for the past two nights. He only comes in after dark, usually when I'm in my bunk and the candle is extinguished. I hear movement in the corners and scratching beneath my bed. Once I saw him dash across the floor, his slight black form flitting beneath the desk. Some prisoners trap and keep them as pets; I don't have the time to form an attachment. I searched the cell for where he was gaining entrance in order to close it off, but I couldn't find anything. The bottom of the door is snug against the ground; there are no gaps between the masonry or holes in the window. I was going to ask Turner if the gaol had a good mouser. But after consideration, sharing the cell with a cat would be even worse.

So yesterday I fashioned a snare of my own design. I put the water basin on the floor, pulled a thin strip of veneer from the flimsy writing desk and leaned that against the rim like a ramp. I had a deck of playing cards, given to me by Turner when I first arrived. I wedged a card – the knave of spades – between the strip of wood and the lip, just enough that it caught and remained horizontal, extending out over the water. Then I laid some bait: a few crumbs of bread sprinkled along the sloping length of wood; and a morsel of hard yellow cheese on the edge of the playing card.

Late that evening, I was disturbed in my writing by soft sounds on the cell floor behind my chair. The mouse was near the bottom of the ramp, sitting on his hindquarters testing the air. After a moment, he began to ascend towards the rim, stopping a few times to eat the crumbs. He got to the top, placed one foot on the delicate platform, and then the other. It didn't budge. He stepped out fully on to the card and went to the edge, picked up the cheese with his front paws, and remained hunched while he ate, looking out over the pool of water.

The card dropped, and he disappeared beneath the rim of the basin, causing the water on the far side to ripple. I placed my pen flat on the table and went to observe. The mouse scrabbled at the edge of the bowl, his front paws finding no grip on the slippery surface. When I stood above him he went still, as if playing dead, and drifted for a moment. But when he began to sink, his legs kicked again. The playing card still floated in the centre of the basin like a raft, and the mouse went towards it, though as he tried to clamber aboard, it was pushed below. He continued to swim in a circle; the water swelled gently in his wake; his long tail slid wetly along the ceramic like a dark strand of hair.

It would be more humane to push him under, so I picked up the strip of wood that still lay against the basin and placed one end above the mouse, following his slow progress, letting its edge caress the top of his head. I dunked him by an inch, but he floated back up and continued swimming.

His hopeless persistence touched something in me and I changed my mind, dipped the wood beneath the surface and scooped him out. A filament of water splashed upon the stones; the mouse landed, rolled and lay in a drenched heap, completely still. I went back to my desk to resume my work.

When I looked over my shoulder a few minutes later, he was gone.

I spent the day following Arthur's visit cleaning the room. I brushed dust from every surface on to the floor, swept up small peaks of lint and grime and long hair, then used the dustpan to shake it all out of the window. I bought a carbolic soap and scrubbed the tabletop, dresser and mantelpiece, throwing blackened cloths into a wet mound in the corner. There was no mop, so I dragged a soaked towel over the floorboards beneath my foot, scraping it behind me with each stride as if I'd been struck lame.

The remnants of the stew remained in the bastible pot. Helen had usually been the arbiter of a food's freshness, but to my nose the meat hadn't begun to turn. I kept it aside for later. I cleared the cold cinders and began to wash the hearthstone, bringing out the colours of the inlaid ceramic. There was a large black smudge near the front of the grate where I'd pulled Helen's manuscript out of the fire. I removed the stain with a few swipes of the cloth. Kind deeds rarely leave a lasting mark.

I went out to buy a bottle of wine and reheated the stew. It tasted better for its few days in the pot; the meat was even more tender. I sat at the table facing towards the fire. After each mouthful I'd put the fork down, take a sip of wine and stare into the embers. The evening passed pleasantly.

In bed, I lay awake for an hour, looking up at the filigrees of plasterwork in the fire's last glimmer. I pondered Arthur's offer. It occurred to me that the figure of two hundred pounds was in effect an opening gambit. What was to stop me demanding four or five hundred? The more I thought of it, the more it seemed an ideal solution for everyone. I did want Helen to regain her health, and she'd have a much better chance of that in Merrion Square.

But what then were her prospects? No suitor would seek the hand of a divorced twenty-year-old. And how would she spend her time? Would she re-enter salons hosted by her neighbours, accompanied by her mother, to become the subject of whispered slights and knowing glances? I pictured her sitting demurely in a splendid drawing room, wearing a fine silk dress, a cup and saucer held in her lap, surrounded by strident dames and their fashionable daughters, but with her head bowed.

The judder of a chair-leg and muffled shouts between Mr and Mrs Lynch drifted from the floor below. I looked over at Helen's empty pillow for several seconds, and recalled how we used to make fun of their arguments when we first moved in. Then I reached over to the pillow, plumped it up, and placed it beneath my own. There was no sense in it going idle.

I didn't attend college at all that week – with Helen absent there was no need to escape Grenville Street for part of the day. I rose late and read by the window, or took long walks through the city and meticulously planned my meals. During the evenings, I would go to the pubs around Gardiner Street and drink alone. The hours were beginning to drag. Whenever I stumbled back into the cold empty room, I would picture Helen as she was before her operation: sitting at her writing desk with one knee drawn up, smiling at me over her shoulder. I'd stand on the threshold for a moment, think about lighting the fire, then climb beneath the covers without removing my clothes.

On the fourth day, I spent most of the afternoon looking down at the passers-by on Grenville Street. I began to check the face of every young woman, wondering if Helen might return of her own volition. I even rehearsed what I might say to her if she did appear. I'd hurry to my chair and pick up a book, only deigning to mark the page and set it aside a full minute after she'd entered the room. I'd listen to what she had to say, remain calm but stern throughout, and say that she was forgiven. We all make mistakes.

I only thought such things because I wanted her back. More accurately, I wanted her as she was before she visited Mrs Redmond in Dominick Street. A few scenarios played out in my head. I could delay agreeing to an annulment until Helen was fully recovered, and then insist she be returned to me. Or perhaps it would be possible to conspire with her to go through with the divorce, so I could collect the money from Arthur. Then we could abscond to London, or even America, and start again. I had to say I liked this idea, though I thought it unlikely Helen would agree to betray her family for a second time.

But even if Helen came back, I'd still need money in the meantime. The following morning, I shaved, changed into my cleanest shirt and brushed my jacket. Fownes Street lay just beyond College Green, so it was only a few minutes' extra walk to get to Farrell's office. The archivist was among the stacks, carrying out a survey of all the boxes, weeding out files of the dead. Farrell said he hated the stocktaking. It had to be done once a year and always took the best part of a week.

I told him I had some information that he might like.

'Oh? What's that?' He rummaged in an open box, checked an old folder against an index card, then placed it on a pile marked for destruction.

'There's a Repeal Association Society in Trinity College. They recently accepted me as a member.'

Farrell didn't seem to listen. He wrote a note on a sheet of paper with a neat hand.

I said, 'I'll be able to give you the name of its secretary.'

'You mean Corcoran?' He brought the box back to its space on the shelf and pulled out the next. 'Give us some credit,

Delahunt. The only reason Trinity allows that club to meet is so the Castle can get the names of its members. I'm afraid that's not worth anything.'

'What about its newest members?'

'Like you?'

'I can get you the society's roll book. It has all the names.'

A crooked stack of files on the ground tipped over and spread across the floorboards. Farrell cursed and began to pick them up. 'The last thing I need is more names.'

I went to help gather some of the files but he stopped me. 'You're not allowed to touch those.' I dropped the few folders I had already lifted. 'Delahunt, I'm too busy for this. Just make sure what you give us is worth our while.' He started to assemble a new stack. 'Like the stuff you used to bring.'

I stood by the railing in Fitzwilliam Street and looked up at my old home, number thirty-five. The current owners had painted the front door a deep blue. The letter box and knocker were polished and gleaming, and a cracked pane in the stained-glass fanlight had been replaced. The window to the parlour was directly in front of me. Its drapes were open, and I could just about see the top of a yellow sofa. A scruffy Yorkshire terrier with fox-like ears jumped up. When he saw me standing so close, his head tilted to the side and he began to bark. He was joined on the couch by a young girl, who clambered on to the cushions. She put her hand on the dog's head to quieten him, and we regarded each other for a few seconds.

I took my hand from my pocket and waved at her. Her eyes followed the gesture, and she waved back without smiling. Then she turned into the room, causing her hair to swish about. She pointed at me through the glass while speaking to someone out of sight. I pulled down the brim of my hat and walked a little further up the street.

The boy I'd been waiting for turned a corner and came running towards me. He was about nine or ten, wearing a dark jacket buttoned up to his chin. His trousers were tucked into the top of tightly laced boots, and his schoolboy cap had a soft peak. I'd only met him on the street ten minutes before, when I engaged him on an errand.

I said, 'Well?'

'He's not there, sir.'

'You went to the right house, number sixty-eight?'

'Yes, sir. The maid said Mr Stokes had gone to his club and wasn't due back till the afternoon.'

I pondered this for a second. It was plenty of time. 'Very good. You did well.'

When I tried to walk on, he stepped in front of me. 'You said you'd give me sixpence.'

I pushed past him and walked towards Merrion Square. I'd forgotten how genteel these buildings were. The houses in Grenville Street were of the same design – though on a smaller scale – but here, the pavements were level and no weeds grew between the flagstones, the railings bore no sign of rust, and the lawns in the park were neat and well kept.

I walked up the steps of the Stokes house, banged the knocker twice and looked at the storeys above. Helen's chamber faced out over the back yard, but she might have been in the front drawing room. Footsteps approached in the hall so I smoothed down my hair. A young maid opened the door. She half smiled and said, 'Yes?'

'I'd like to speak with Helen.'

The smile disappeared, and her eyes dipped down to regard my clothes. Perhaps she'd been told to watch out for my arrival.

'I'm afraid Miss Stokes isn't well enough for visitors. But if you give me your card I can pass it on.'

She had moved the door slightly, enough that her left shoulder was now behind it.

I said, 'Tell Miss Stokes that her husband wishes to discuss certain matters. I'll remain here until I receive her reply.'

Her cheeks became flushed, but she nodded once and hurriedly closed the door.

I scolded myself. I should have barged in and waited in the hallway. Too late now. I took a few steps back to see if I could spot movement in any of the windows. A drape stirred on the third floor, but the window was open so it may have been a gust of wind. I went back to the top step, cocked each knee to regard the soles of my shoes, then cleaned them on the boot-scraper. I put my fingertips against the door and gave a push in case it wasn't secure on its latch.

Several minutes passed. Perhaps they were willing to wait for me to become exasperated and leave of my own accord. I considered lifting the letter-box flap and calling Helen's name. That didn't seem becoming, or a good strategy when I was hoping to convince her to return. I could bang on the door. But that would also have to be judged correctly. Too many thuds with excessive force might come across as menacing and brutish. Surely, though, I was within my rights to knock again and seek a response to my enquiry.

The door opened to reveal Nathan, the Stokes family's coach driver. He was a burly man in his late forties, and his hair was tousled, as if he'd just been roused from his sleep. This was the first time he had spoken to me directly, so I was surprised by his forward tone. 'You shouldn't be here, John.'

'I've just come to see my wife.'

He shook his head. 'But Miss Stokes doesn't wish to see you.'

'She said that?'

He didn't answer immediately. 'Anything you have to discuss should go through Mr Stokes.'

I looked past him into the hall. 'This is ridiculous.' Nathan's frame took up most of the opening, but still I said, 'I must see her,' and tried to push my way in. He placed a thick hand on my shoulder. When I tried to twist away, he took hold of my collar, with a grip more used to restraining the bridles of stallions. I struggled in vain for a moment, then shouted Helen's name over his shoulder.

He pulled down his hand, causing me to lean forward. 'Don't make a fool of yourself.' Then he pushed me away. I stumbled over the top step, tottered down three more, and banged my hip against the side railing. Nathan looked concerned for a moment, as if he hadn't meant to be so rough, but then his face darkened and he shut the door.

Two middle-aged ladies were walking by, with feathered hats and clasped parasols. They regarded me slumped against the rails. One of them tutted. I straightened and moved directly towards them so they had to part to allow me to pass. I brushed shoulders with one and could hear their horrified gasps. Once across the road, I looked back at the house.

A face appeared behind the curtain in a second-floor window. But it was only the maid.

Burke's pub stood on the corner of Amiens Street and Buckingham Street, a three-storey building with a narrow triangular front because of the acute angle of the crossroads. There was very little to recommend it. Its walls were bare except for a few stuffed terriers mounted on shelves, their coats as tattered as the peeling wallpaper. The chairs were uncomfortable, the clientele hardly spoke, and it was a ten-minute walk from Grenville Street. But that night, as I passed, I saw a chalkboard announcing that Burke's was hosting a night of rat-killing. I knew gin was sold for next to nothing on such evenings in order to draw in the gamblers, so I stopped in.

The second floor contained a low, wide room with four pillars in the centre supporting the ceiling. The pillars were about eight feet apart, and joined by vertical, chest-high boards, creating a large square pit. Inside the pit, the timbers and floorboards were painted a startling white, with a dark green trim along the top. A shelf went around the edge against which customers could crowd and lean their elbows. The only light came from a hanging gas-lamp, which made the pit very bright, but the corners of the room were cast in shadow.

A mesh-pen in the corner contained the rats, a swarming black throng that smelled like the Liffey at low tide. As I took my seat I saw the arrival of a rat-catcher with a new batch in his own bird-house cage. He had a word with the owner, holding up the cage for inspection. Then the lid in the pen was opened and the new rats were tipped in. Mr Burke put a coin into the rat-catcher's bandaged hand. The grimy fellow had to pass me on the way to the door. He gave me an appraising look as I sat with my glass of hot gin, and I nodded back to him.

Some of the customers had dogs present, with their leashes tied to the table legs. The animals tended to be small and bow-legged – bulldogs and English terriers. Some sat calmly at their owners' feet. Others strained at their leads with frantic excitement, their noses pointed at the rats in the corner.

Just before the sport began, a teenaged boy donned a thick leather glove up to his elbow, reached into the cage and began tossing live rats into the pit. Most of the rats congregated in the corners; though some sat unconcerned in the middle on their haunches, rubbing their faces or nibbling at their tails.

I took a seat by the window, and divided my time gazing over the rooftops and railway bridge towards the thicket of ships' masts on the quays, and back in at the men leaning against the pit, waiting for the first match. They were mostly of the humbler classes: dockworkers and costermongers. A few were marked by finer clothes as professional men, and two soldiers stood at one corner with their red jackets opened at the neck.

From the window I could also look down the extent of Montgomery Street. Young women stood beneath lamp-posts, their breath visible in the cold air. Others lounged in the door-ways of the low terraced houses.

The first dog was brought to the pen, a black bulldog with a white diamond on her face. Her master vaulted the enclosure with the dog held tight against his chest. He let her on to the floor, but kept a hold of the leash. This close to the rats, the dog growled and whined and strained to be set free. But her owner kept a firm grip as the odds were called and the bets made. Some thought she'd kill a dozen in the allotted two minutes. Others gambled on twenty. Burke and his underlings collected the stakes.

I ignored them and watched the men outside who strolled through Montgomery Street. Some walked in groups of twos and threes, egging each other on with friendly shoves and expansive gestures. The girls became animated as they drew near, calling out to them and inviting them indoors. Others went through Montgomery Street alone, their hands deep in their pockets and their heads bowed.

A man with a briefcase perused the women. As he approached one, his stride shortened and the brim of his hat tilted up. The girl stood straighter, placing a hand on her hip. When his head dipped down again, she relaxed, and slouched back against the lamp-post. He passed each girl like this, all the way to the end of the street without stopping. Perhaps he lost his nerve.

Several shouts from the centre of the room meant the dog had been unleashed. Mr Burke stood at one corner of the pit, looking at his pocket watch in an exaggerated pose. The floor was already strewn with five or six dead rats. Most of the living had fled to one corner, and scrambled over each other to create a writhing hillock that reached halfway up the sides. It was easy for the dog to insert her snout and come away with a rat between her teeth. She then shook her head with a fierce growl until the rat went limp, and her owner called from the centre of the pen to drop it. The dead rat fell from the dog's jaws, and she sought her next victim.

Burke didn't like that the rats had clumped together in the corner, so he directed one of his workers to pour hot water on them. This had the desired effect. The rats scattered across the white floorboards and the dog had to hunt them down in earnest. But she proved adept; snapping up any who strayed too close, gnawing on them until her owner yelled at her to stop. And the spectators cheered with every new kill.

Near the end of her allotted time, the dog chased one rat into the corner. It scrabbled against the boards for half a second, then turned and sprang into the face of its pursuer, covering the dog's face like a mask and biting her muzzle. She recoiled at first, then chomped on the rat's hindquarters and whipped her head about. The men hooted at the spectacle.

Burke held his watch in front of his face and called out, 'Time! Time!'

The dog's owner tried to take hold of his pet, but she wouldn't settle until the last rat perished, and its teeth were loosened from her face. When that was done, the owner held her up by the scruff in the middle of the pen, and the spectators gave a round of applause.

It would take a few minutes for the dead rats to be counted and the final score tallied. I resumed my watch over Montgomery Street. A new girl had appeared at the lamp-post nearest the corner with Amiens Street. Even from a distance, I could tell it was the girl I had spoken with on the night I searched for Helen. I checked my watch. It had just gone eight o'clock.

A man with a flat cap and wide moustache turned on to Montgomery Street and walked towards her. He spat into a puddle. Either he knew her, or he was willing to engage the first prostitute he met. They spoke for a few seconds, and the man looked up at a window in the house behind her. He nodded, and she turned to lead him through the front door.

One of Burke's employees stood by my table. 'Sir, would you like to place a bet for the next match? We're offering evens on ten rats or more.'

'No. Just bring me another gin.'

He dipped his head and moved on to the next table, where a man was eating some mutton chops, with a napkin tucked in his collar.

I kept an eye on the house as squeals, growls and cheers came from the rat pit. The latest dog didn't perform so well, and the spectators became restless, whistling and jeering its owner. There were only eight clean kills; two other rats were still alive, but badly injured. Since many wagers had been placed on ten kills, the test was performed. Burke withdrew a piece of chalk tied to a length of string. He put the end of the string beneath his thumb and drew a white circle on the floorboards. The two injured creatures were taken from the pit and placed in the middle. Then a candle was brought close to their hindquarters, and the rats tried to crawl away from the singeing flame.

The customers seemed to enjoy this new spectacle just as much. One rat made it out of the circle with relative ease. Burke stepped on it, producing a sound like cracking knuckles. The other stopped moving forwards after a few inches, though its eyes remained open and its nose twitched. The flame was brought closer. Wisps of smoke came up from its fur, but it wouldn't budge.

Burke called out, 'Enough. The count stands at nine.'

A wave of muttered curses went through the crowd.

It didn't take long for the man to come back out of the prostitute's house. He held his coat shut with both hands in his pockets, and then walked towards the pub. I thought he might come in, but he passed beneath my window and disappeared up Buckingham Street.

I checked my watch again. Five minutes later, the girl re-emerged. She looked no different than before. I thought she might smooth her dress, or fix her hair, but she just took up her position beneath the gas-lamp.

As the night wore on, she was engaged twice more. When the second man came out, the crowd around the pit happened to let out a loud cheer, as if we'd been waiting for him. He heard the muffled noise and looked up at the window. Though he couldn't possibly have seen me in the gloom, I turned my face away.

The girl's third client that night was a large, broad-shouldered fellow. I noted every particular about him. He wore a long frock coat and carried a wide leather satchel, like a doctor's case. His black beard was thick and untidy, but his moustache was waxed into points. Curly hair emerged in tufts from the sides of a squat stovepipe hat. She looked very small standing beside him. When she brought him inside, he insisted on holding the door open like a gentleman.

I'd have found going where two men had gone so soon before slightly off-putting. But I suppose he wasn't to know.

My head began to hurt because of the cheap gin, raucous shouts and rank smells. But I waited until the big fellow came out of the house. It didn't seem to take too long. Burke shouted out that there was only one dog left, so we should get our bets in. I regarded the last mouthful of gin in my glass and swirled it about. The man sitting near my table finished eating his supper, and made his way over to the pit to view the last match. I went to his table to pick the knife from his plate, which had a wooden haft and grey serrated blade. I slipped it in my coat pocket. Then I walked past the crowd and went up to the barman.

'Where's the jakes?' I said, exaggerating a slur in my speech.

He glanced up. 'Downstairs. Door on the right leads to the yard. Just follow your nose.'

I thanked him. But once downstairs, I slipped through the lounge and out of the front entrance.

Compared to the room upstairs, the night air was cold and silent. It didn't take long for the girl to come out of her house. She closed the door, and ensured it was locked by pulling and pushing against the handle. She didn't take up her station beneath the gaslight. Instead, she walked towards the corner with Beaver Street. She must have lived elsewhere. Either three men was her limit for a night, or she had worked her allotted hours. I followed after her.

Beaver Street leads to Mecklenburgh Street, but it's a dark, narrow road, bounded by the perimeter walls of long back yards. When I turned on to it she was only ten yards ahead of me. I concentrated to match my step with hers, so the sound of her hard heels clicking on the wet cobbles masked my footfall.

I grasped the handle in my pocket, used my thumb to test which side the blade was facing, then rotated it to the correct angle. At this distance I could make out the colour of her hair and detect a trace of perfume. I'd have to close the last few paces at a run. What then? Grab a fistful of hair; pull back; draw the knife across. There were only five yards between us now. I pulled at the knife, but it caught on a loop of thread in the seam of my pocket. I tugged until the thread snapped and the knife came free.

When I looked again the path was empty. I examined the buildings – still just side walls and yard fences, no doors she could have slipped through. But after a few steps I saw it: the entrance to an uncovered stable-lane on the left. The lamplight didn't reach this far; nor were there any windows to provide a flicker of candlelight. I could just about discern the black, over-cast sky against the uneven height of the surrounding walls.

I entered the lane, keeping my fingers against the bricks for bearing, with the knife held out in front like a blind man's cane. It occurred to me that I hadn't heard her footsteps for several seconds. I stopped and listened. The only sound was a rhythmic wooden banging much further up the lane, as if a wicket gate was loose on its hinge.

I felt something cold against my neck, and then the point of a knife dig against the side of my throat. The girl grabbed my coat from behind. Her breath brushed the back of my earlobe as she said, 'Drop it.'

When I didn't immediately comply, she pushed the point in further. There was a sharp sting, and then a warm trickle ran down my neck. My knife clattered on the ground, and she swept her foot to kick it away.

The front of her bodice pressed into my side. I could smell

the perfume quite clearly now; it was familiar. Perhaps Helen once wore something similar. Then I realized it was water of Cologne, a type I'd used myself. It must have rubbed off her last client. I snuffled through my nose to exhale the scent.

I tried to keep my voice steady. 'I'm sorry if I startled you, but I only wished to talk.'

She let go of my jacket and felt downwards to fumble in a side pocket, the point of her knife kept steady at my throat. She tried one, then the other, but they were both empty.

'Rest assured, I had no intention to rob you. Or . . . force myself upon you.' Which was true at least.

She moved tight against me, reached around and began to pat my chest. She felt my key in the breast pocket and her palm lingered, her left arm wrapped around me in an odd embrace. It was as if she'd found a lover staring pensively out of a window, and had stepped forward to comfort him. Next, she'd rest her head between his shoulder blades. He'd reach up to take her fingers, and hold them against his lips.

But her hand moved on and searched elsewhere, down into my trouser pocket. She rummaged and felt the change at the bottom.

I couldn't bow my head because of the knife. 'You know, I've had a very trying day.'

She dipped into the other pocket. In all I had about a pound and four shillings. She took every penny.

'I'm not even allowed to see my own wife.'

'Turn around and put your hands on the wall.'

As I did so, the tip of her blade traced a line around my neck until it pointed at the base of my skull. I leaned forward as if feeling nauseous. The surface of the brickwork was damp and crumbly.

Her voice was soft with a country lilt, possibly from the

north-west. 'If you turn before I'm gone, I'll stab the knife to its hilt.'

All was silent then. After a few seconds I thought I heard the swish of a skirt and a quiet tread, but I didn't raise my head to check. The crook of the wall was strewn with rubbish. Some weeds grew in clumps of soil, as well as one daisy flower with its petals closed over. I wondered how it had survived this long into early winter.

Footsteps approached so I kept my head down. But it was only an old man who sidled up beside me. He swayed as he undid the front of his breeches and relieved himself against the wall. In mid-flow, he said, 'You all right, son?' He spoke with paternal concern. 'A bit worse for wear?'

I looked at him over my outstretched arm. 'A whore has taken all my money.'

He half closed his eyes and nodded in understanding. I moved away before he could splash my shoes.

For the next few days, it was difficult to think of a reason to get up. The room had become untidy, despite my efforts to clean it in the previous week. Items of clothing hung from the backs of chairs or were draped over the windowsills. The cold ashes in the hearth remained untouched, mainly because there was no fuel to start another fire. Empty wine bottles and stained glasses covered the tabletop.

There was very little to eat. An old potato sat forlornly in the back of the cupboard. It was soft and sprouted several gnarled roots, but I knew I'd have to scrape them off to see if it was edible. I couldn't afford to go to the market. Perhaps there'd be some food in the Repeal Society rooms at college. Though if I went there, Corcoran would be looking for the subscription money.

Early one afternoon, I heard scuffled noises on the landing, and some tentative knocks on the door. For a moment I thought it might be Helen, but then came quiet titters and mutterings between some of the Lynch children. There were a few shushes, and a louder knock. I reached over to the bedside table and picked up a squat metal candle-holder, which I flung across the room so it thumped against the door. The rails shook, and a splintered scuff remained in the white paint. The children shrieked and rushed down the stairs with loud laughter.

I got up and shuffled about the room in search of loose change. The money tin on the shelf had long been empty, but still I picked it up and gave it a silent shake. I jammed my hand down the back of the armchair and felt along the seam. It was sticky with grease and crumbs, and my fingers scraped over exposed staples, but there were no coins. Happily, I did discover a dust-covered shilling lying under the bed beside one of Helen's old petticoats.

I went to my trunk and began rummaging through clothes, curling my finger into the tight fob-pockets of waistcoats, and turning my trousers inside out. In one pair I felt the thick waxy paper of a folded banknote, and I tried to recall what money, if any, I could have overlooked.

But it was only the docket from Clifford's pawnshop, describing the silver frame that had held the silhouette of my mother. Only a week left to repay the loan: two pounds and eight shillings. Otherwise the frame would be kept by the pawnbroker. I looked around the room at the mess made from my searching, then down again at the note. I tensed my fingers to crumple it up, but changed my mind. I laid the docket on the writing desk and smoothed it flat.

Perhaps it was time to speak with Arthur.

By the time I had traversed the city, clouds had gathered and a heavy rain began to fall on Merrion Square. I lingered at the south-west corner beneath the branches of an old sycamore tree that overhung the black iron railing. The exterior of the Stokes home was about halfway up the terrace. It wouldn't do to show up at the door like a drowned rat, so I remained sheltered and looked at the clouds to judge how long the shower would last.

The rain had sent the few pedestrians on Merrion Square scurrying indoors. A passing carriage sprayed water from the gutter, which I managed to avoid. Then a gate to the enclosed garden almost opposite the Stokes home opened, and two women stepped out. Both wore long dresses, bonnets and shawls, and sheltered beneath an opened umbrella. Helen stood erect, with her shoulders back. She held her shawl tight beneath her chin with one hand and the umbrella with the other. Her old governess Mrs Bruce had turned and bent to lock the gate.

I didn't know whether to hide my face or call out. Once I got to the house, it was probable Arthur wouldn't let me see Helen, even if he and I did come to some arrangement.

Mrs Bruce withdrew the key and reached up to take the umbrella from her charge. They walked to the edge of the path and looked both ways for passing carriages.

Just as they were about to step out, Helen disengaged her arm and dashed out from under the umbrella to cross the street in the rain. Her governess squawked in protest, but Helen reached the other side, twisted about with her arms outstretched and smiled at the old woman's worry. I was astonished to see her move like that. She'd only been out of Grenville Street for half a month. Helen went up the steps two at a time and banged at the brass knocker on her front door.

Then she undid her bonnet and tilted her face up into the rain. Her hair was pinned and didn't move. She stood in profile, with her eyes closed and her neck arched back.

Mrs Bruce crossed the road as fast as she could, holding her skirts up out of the puddles. She reached the top step just as the front door opened, and ushered Helen inside. I let my eyes linger on the closed door.

Helen had twirled just like that, with her arms spread out, on the day we found that disused grove in the garden. I looked into the park, but my view was blocked by the bushes.

A thrush joined me under the branches. It alighted on the railing between two spikes, shook droplets from its head, then rummaged beneath a wing to smooth down its feathers. It didn't seem to notice me.

Two hundred pounds just didn't seem worth it. If spent carefully, it would grant me a few years in respectable digs. But what then? I'd not yet be twenty-five, with no possible access to her social circle. I'd never meet another like her. At first I thought that a separation might have been best for us both. But now it was clear to me. All I wanted was her return.

I held out an index finger to offer the thrush a perch. It leaped off the railing towards the pavement, opened its wings and swooped about ten feet away on to the dwarf wall. The bird hopped through the bars and disappeared into the undergrowth. I withdrew my hand, gathered my coat and turned away. There had to be some way to speak with Helen alone.

11

I opened the barrel lid of my trunk and rummaged beneath a jumble of clothes and college papers. A small pile of documents lay in the bottom corner – items once considered important, like the certificate from Trinity informing me that I'd failed my final exams, or the correspondence from the solicitor Adair outlining the contents of my father's will. Several sheets of the same stationery were letters from Cecilia, received during the first year of her marriage. They told of inconsequential domestic news, but it seemed the custom was to keep hold of such things, so I'd yet to discard them.

There was also a letter I sent to my mother while still a child. One summer, Alex, Cecilia and I stayed with our spinster aunt in rural Antrim. Each of us wrote home to Fitzwilliam Street, but mine was the only letter to be preserved. As a postscript to the short missive describing a day spent fishing, and complaining of the weather, I had written, 'Mother, here is some grass from your old garden.' I picked up the envelope and peeked inside. The withered yellow blades remained, tangled up like a lock of hair.

A faint scratching noise and small titter came from the hallway. The Lynch children were misbehaving on the landing again.

At the very bottom was an envelope with my name in Helen's handwriting, the brief note she penned to me nearly two years before still inside. It read: 'So you don't have to sneak into the garden.' Her handwriting was smooth, with small flourishes at the end of each stroke. She had obviously taken care while writing it; I'm not sure why I didn't notice at the time. I smelled the paper, but it had no trace of perfume. The thick iron key to Merrion Park tipped on to the desktop with a thud.

Another scurry of footsteps sounded in the hall, followed by a loud knock on the door. I'd had enough of the young Lynches and their constant nuisance. I took a black leather belt from the trunk, wrapped one end around my closed fist so the metal clasp hung loose, and crossed the room. When I yanked the door open, Lyster stood alone in the threshold. His arms were crossed at the wrists; the jacket he wore was too big, and the cuffs came almost to his knuckles. He regarded the belt-buckle dangling from my hand with a raised eyebrow, then walked past me into the room. I poked my head out of the door. The landing was empty.

Lyster stood over my opened trunk, where I'd left the letters on the floor. He scraped one aside with the toe of his boot to observe another underneath.

'What do you want, Lyster?'

'Tea would be nice.'

'There isn't any.'

He dragged Helen's chair to the kitchen table and sat down, pushing aside some dirty crockery. Then he rubbed his palms together, raised his coat collar and folded his arms. 'Jesus, Delahunt, it's colder in here than it is outside.'

I stacked some of the plates on the table and brought them to the washbasin, allowing them to slip into the murky water with a clatter. Lyster took hold of the tabletop between his thumb and forefingers and wobbled it.

'Sibthorpe has become concerned about you.'

'You can tell him I'm fine.'

'When I say concerned, I mean bothered and vexed. I came here a few months ago and left word for you to meet me in Bracken's. Do you remember?'

I let my gaze drift to the side, as if trying to recall. 'Helen wasn't feeling well that day.'

'So I heard.' He fished a sheet of paper from his coat pocket, folded it on itself three times, and wedged it beneath the nearest leg. When he shook the table again it didn't budge. 'I'd say your baby felt even worse.'

I had wondered that myself: if it could feel anything.

'Where's your wife now?'

I didn't answer, just sat in the seat opposite, shifting the chair to the side so I could cross my legs.

Lyster said, 'Do you want me to bring her back?'

'No.'

He smiled, although his eyes didn't change shape.

'Why did you need me that day anyway?'

'It doesn't matter,' he said. 'Maybe I just wanted the company. But when you didn't show up, it made Tom think that you're unreliable.'

'I'm still trying to bring information to Fownes Street.'

'Like the names in your college club. A waste of everyone's time.'

Lyster picked up an empty wine bottle to read the label, wrinkled his nose and put it aside. Then he puffed out his cheeks, and began a long continuous tutting with the rhythm of a horse-trot. Finally he said, 'Delahunt, I know it can be difficult. I was much like you once.'

That wasn't a comforting thought.

'You start off and everything you report seems to pay off, then things begin to dry up. But you have to keep working at it.'

He rubbed his unshaven chin with an open palm, which caused a rasping sound. Then he scrunched his eyes and yawned, baring the blackened tops of his lower teeth. He apologized, and said he hadn't had much sleep the night before.

'Because of something in the Castle?'

'No. My youngest is teething.'

'Oh.'

'You showed with Cooney that you know what to do when the opportunity arises. Tom may have given you a hard time because of it, but I was impressed.' He looked at the mantel clock. 'I don't live far from here, just at the top of Capel Street. We should meet for a drink now and then, and discuss work.'

'I've been thinking of finishing with the Castle, Lyster.' I looked at him frankly, as if I treated him as a confidant. 'Once I get my degree, I'm going to seek more stable employment.'

He drummed his fingers; the nail on his middle finger was long and clicked against the wood. Then he bent down, took the paper from under the table leg and replaced it in his pocket. 'Suit yourself.' He buttoned the top of his coat, and pushed both hands behind his neck to flick his hair over the collar. 'But did you ever wonder, Delahunt, how someone who has had such a dire effect on so many lives is still able to walk the streets unharmed?' He thought for a moment, as if he was troubled by my naivety. 'I'll just say that you don't want Sibthorpe to decide you're no longer useful.' He extended his hand across the table, and I shook it. When I tried to let go he maintained his grip. 'That's the last thing you want.'

*

It rained for a week after Lyster's visit. During long spells of wet weather, water dripped from the ceiling through the hole in the central rosette and a crack in the plaster above the fireplace. A deep pan collected the water in the middle of the room; a glass tumbler did the job beside the hearth. At first the drops were slow and sounded several seconds apart. They fell at different rhythms, which over the course of a few minutes would converge with and then diverge from each other. Every time they got close I listened out, but the drops never hit their vessels at exactly the same moment. When the tumbler filled, I'd pick it up, examine the cloudy water in the light of the window, then drink it down. It had a metallic taste, like the nib of a pencil.

The heavy skies made the room cold and dark even in the early afternoon. Our kitchen dresser was an old piece of furniture that belonged to the landlady, Mrs Travers. It had three drawers, but only one was being used to hold the cutlery. I broke the other two apart and used the kindling to build a fire. I also pulled off some of the cabinet doors, leaned them in the crook of the wall, and stamped on them till they fractured into rough planks. Mr Lynch called up that he was trying to sleep, but I ignored him.

Once the fire was lit, I rummaged through the cutlery drawer. There were several types of knife. One was a carver with a wooden haft and six-inch blade. The butter knife had a rounded point, with handle and blade made from a single piece of pewter. The metal had no gleam, which I thought lacked elegance. A few dinner knives remained from a set that had come from my home in Fitzwilliam Street. They had serrated blades of Sheffield steel and mother-of-pearl handles. I remembered the hardboard box in which the set was kept in our old dining room. A sheet of felt paper lay beneath the lid, and a dozen knives and forks sat snugly in their own grooves in a crimson baize mount. We only used them on special occasions: dinner parties and religious holidays. Over the years, pieces were lost or broken, so now only a few remained.

I hefted one knife in my hand. It was a good size, fitting easily into my coat pocket. I tested its edge against the corner of the table. It sawed through the wood cleanly, leaving nice deep nicks. The blade also tapered to a sharp point, which I pressed against my fingertip. The slightest pressure would break the skin. I closed the drawer, and sat at the table with the knife placed horizontally in front of me. The scratches in the wood looked like a letter carved on an ogham stone.

As the day wore on, I remained bundled up in a wool blanket sitting directly on the deep windowsill, back propped against the jamb and legs gathered up. From there I could watch the passers-by hurrying through the rain, skipping puddles and holding their hats against strong gusts. It was pleasant to be so close to the window, dry and relatively warm, while drops lashed against the panes. When the street was empty, I'd breathe on the glass and draw pictures in the condensation. My fingertips made thick lines, but I could use my unclipped nails for finer details. One of my first attempts was to trace Helen's face in profile. But the features I drew were rather manly, so I changed tack and added a beard. It turned out quite well. Over the course of half an hour, his unfamiliar countenance evaporated.

The drips from the ceiling grew more rapid, creating an unnerving tempo when combined with ticks from the mantel clock. I got up, snapped a length of wood over my knee and put the pieces on the fire.

Despite the weather, I left the house for short walks each

afternoon. On some days I brought the knife with me, and on others I left it at home. Rainwater swirled through gutters in rivulets, and turned the road surface into a mire. Nobody lingered on the footpaths. Men and women walked quickly with their faces bowed, hidden by slanted umbrellas, or with coats draped over their heads like wedding veils.

One day I passed the North Dublin Workhouse on Constitution Hill, a large austere building with a grey façade, small windows and a high perimeter wall. The central buildings enclosed stone-breaking and exercise yards. I wondered how it worked in practice. Did one just walk up to the porter and request a bed for the night, or month, or year? Surely there'd be some sort of appraisal of condition before admission – of health, strength and mental faculties. If so, I'd be sure to impress the assessor.

I imagined the interior passages: whitewashed walls tinged by damp and soot; each airless room crowded with bunks, filled with unknown men perspiring, exhaling, shedding scabbed skin into their blankets. The sounds in the dead of night: heavy breathing, demented muttering, scratching, coughing, rats shuffling on the flagstones. Then during the day, lined up with fellow inmates in our striped blue shirts and cloth caps, breaking stones, crushing bones or picking oakum.

I'm sure one soon got used to it.

The weather finally broke on a Wednesday morning. Clouds thinned and sunlight appeared, making the wet pavements glisten. Water continued to gurgle through drainpipes and gutters, though the roads began to dry in the weak December sunshine.

I picked up the pan from the middle of the floor, almost full to the brim, and brought it to the mirror. With my horsehair brush and the last sliver of soap, I lathered my chin, and shaved away a week's worth of growth with diligence. In the mid-morning glare my complexion appeared pale, with shadows beneath my cheekbones like smears of ash. A crack in the looking glass divided my face, so one eyebrow appeared higher than the other, as if I regarded myself with an arch expression.

Helen and her governess usually walked in Merrion Park between the hours of two and three. My old key to the gate in the western railing still worked, so I let myself in and scouted around the serpentine paths. It didn't take long to spot them. The two women emerged from a copse of ash and turned on to a path that led to the garden's central bandstand. I followed after them, keeping my distance at first. Mrs Bruce held a furled umbrella, though the threat of rain had passed. The governess did most of the talking, some meandering anecdote involving her sister. Helen only made the occasional comment, but her voice was soft and clear, and had regained some of its former brightness.

Compacted earth and dead leaves made the ground soft. The white wooden bandstand loomed ahead, where another pair of women stood beneath its slated, conical roof.

Before they could get much closer, I adopted a mild tone and said, 'Helen.'

She glanced over her shoulder and stopped walking. Mrs Bruce may not have heard me, for she continued a few steps. When she turned, her face set in a scowl and she said, 'What are you doing here?'

'I just wish to speak with my wife for a few minutes in private. You can remain nearby if you wish.'

'You won't say anything to her. We're going home.' Mrs Bruce tried to move while keeping a grip of Helen's arm, but she wouldn't budge.

'Come this instant or I'll fetch Arthur,' she said, as if Helen was still her young pupil.

I said, 'Go ahead. I only require a few minutes.'

The old woman narrowed her eyes. 'I will not leave her alone.'

A cold, gentle wind pushed Helen's skirt against her leg. Then she spoke for the first time. 'I'm sure John doesn't mean to carry me away.'

It was pleasant to hear my name so spoken. Mrs Bruce said, 'But, Helen . . .'

'Perhaps it would be best if you did bring Arthur.' She placed a hand on her governess's arm. 'We can settle all this here and now.'

The old woman wasn't convinced. Helen looked over her shoulder and pointed towards a bench, saying, 'We'll remain there until you return.'

Mrs Bruce glanced between the two of us, considered for a few more seconds, then started back towards the gate, giving me a wide berth. I tipped my hat as she passed.

Helen and I were left facing each other. She brought her fingertips together, but then changed her mind and let her arms hang. One side of her bonnet fluttered quietly against her cheek.

'You look . . .' I was going to say 'much improved', but that didn't seem complimentary. 'You look very well.'

She searched my face. Perhaps the same couldn't be said of me. Helen walked towards the bench and sat down, arranged her dress over her knees, then stared at the path.

I went to sit beside her, leaving a hand's width between us, and paused to see if she'd shift further away.

'Your health has improved?'

'Yes, thank you.'

'I'm glad.' A scent of rosewater hung around her. The smell coming from my unwashed coat must have been somewhat less appealing.

'Have you reconciled with your parents?'

'They'll be in Edinburgh until the spring. But Arthur has written to them.'

'I see. Did they write back?'

Helen rubbed her hands together. She appeared to have regained all movement in her fingers, and the whites of her fingernails were perfectly clean. She took a balled pair of gloves from a coat pocket and put them on. For a moment I thought it was a precursor to getting up, but she remained with her hands in her lap.

'Why did you come, John?'

'To see you.'

'Arthur has been anxious to hear your response.'

'You know what he's offered me?'

She nodded.

'Was it your idea?'

This time she made no reply. On the lawn before us a red squirrel searched for food among the dead leaves at the base of a willow tree. The bole twisted above its roots like a wrung cloth.

I said, 'The less time I spend in Arthur's company the better, especially after our last meeting.'

Helen thought it was sad, since he and I had once been good friends.

I shrugged. 'You said yourself he never liked me.'

'I said no such thing.'

'You did.' I let the moment linger so I could hold her gaze at close quarters. Her eyes were dark and full of mistrust. 'Though you may not remember.'

She frowned and looked away, perhaps ashamed to be reminded of her former condition, and the change it had wrought in her behaviour. The two women in the bandstand descended the steps and walked past us. Helen waited for them to pass beyond earshot.

'Yes, it was my idea. Arthur suggested the annulment, but he worried you would dispute it. So I told him to make the offer.' She picked a twig from between the slats and dropped it on the ground. 'But not as some bribe or pay-off. I wanted to be sure you could start your life again. What we did, John, our marriage . . . it was a mistake.'

This meeting wasn't going as I'd intended. I shifted in my seat, resting an elbow on the back of the bench. When I spoke, my voice was low. 'Helen, I came here because I want you to come back with me to Grenville Street.'

Her head was already shaking.

'Listen, I want the two of us to start again. And perhaps even—'

'No.'

Embarrassed then by the thick sentiment of my tone, I bowed my head. A shirt-cuff had disappeared beneath my sleeve. I pulled it out, up to the heel of my hand. Helen's cream skirt was stark against the green of the bench. Hundreds of tiny fleurs-de-lis had been sewn into the fabric, visible only when their soft thread caught the watery sunshine.

When I lifted my head, Helen regarded me with the corners of her mouth downturned. I didn't want her to say any more, so I spoke before she could.

'Have you resumed writing?'

She sensed the reason behind my change of subject and nodded. 'Yes. On my . . . original book. The one you rescued.'

'That's good.'

She said she worked in her father's empty study because it had the best light. His bureau was of thick, dark oak. 'It doesn't wobble beneath my pen. I miss my rickety writing desk.'

I said I had little use for it in Grenville Street.

'I've thought of you a few times sitting alone in the tenement.' She almost sounded wistful. 'How is the old room?'

'Leaky.'

She smiled then, and a constriction in my chest eased, which only served to make me aware of it. Helen remembered herself, and straightened her mouth.

'And cold. I'm being tormented by the Lynch children.'

'Then take the money, John. Move out of that terrible place.'

'It wasn't so bad to begin with.'

'It was always bad.'

My expression must have darkened. Helen turned away, enough for her profile to become hidden once more by her bonnet.

I said, 'I'm sorry you thought so.'

She remained still.

I checked the path for any sign of Arthur and Mrs Bruce. The walkway was clear.

'An annulment won't do you any good, Helen.' I gestured towards the tops of the houses on Merrion Square that peeked over the treetops. 'These people won't accept you back into their fold. Everyone will know you were once married, and no other man will ask for your hand.'

'Perhaps I have no wish to marry again.'

'So you'll be happy to die alone . . .'

'I'm sure I won't be happy.'

'And childless?'

She was stung more than I intended. During the months

that Helen was unwell, we never discussed the procedure she had undergone, or its consequences.

We sat for a while in silence. The squirrel crept from the shrubbery on to the path, paused and sat motionless on its haunches, as if hoping not to be spotted. I scraped my foot in the dirt, which caused it to dart into the opposite verge.

Helen said, 'He would have been due around now.' I looked over, but her eyes remained downcast. 'Our son. He would have been born this month.'

I didn't know it was a boy. I had never thought to ask. Had the midwife in Dominick Street told her? That didn't seem likely, especially since the procedure had been so distressful. Helen must have seen it, seen him, briefly in Mrs Redmond's delivery room. The sight must have haunted her.

I hesitated, reached over and placed my fingers on hers, and was relieved when she didn't withdraw her hand. 'I'm sorry, Helen.'

We sat like that for several seconds, and I was reminded of when we first began courting, in a nearby grove in the same garden. Sometimes, between conversations, we would just sit with our fingers entwined amid the gentle sounds of the park and the dappled spring sunlight. Back then, Helen said the fact we could do so for so long and not get bored meant we were supposed to be together. Perhaps she was recalling it as well.

'Come back with me to Grenville Street.'

She disengaged her hand. 'I can't.' Before I could speak again she continued, 'It's more than that, John. I don't want to. We were so miserable in that house.'

'Not always.' I didn't know if she was ignoring the times we supported each other, laughed together, made plans, made love, or if she genuinely couldn't remember. 'I know how difficult it was towards the end.'

'You don't really. You don't know the number of times . . .' Her lips pursed. 'The number of times I lay alone and held the laudanum bottle against my mouth, daring myself to drink it all.'

This was a moment when exactly the right thing had to be said. But I knew I hadn't the ability to think of it, so it was best to remain silent. I wanted to take her hand again, but suspected she'd shake it off.

Helen reached up and undid the string beneath her chin. The prospect of seeing her head uncovered pleased me, but she just tied the string tighter.

'I don't know why you won't accept Arthur's offer.'

I said I didn't want to lose her.

'It would be best for everyone. You'll have the means to start again.'

The money didn't matter to me.

'All our marriage did was ensnare us. If you don't contest the annulment, then . . .'

'Then it'll be as if it never happened.'

'Exactly.'

'Just like our son.'

Helen took a sharp breath, and her mouth tightened.

I was abashed enough to look down. 'I shouldn't have said that.'

'No. You shouldn't.'

She looked over my shoulder, and I turned to see Arthur approaching, accompanied by Nathan. Mrs Bruce followed a distance behind, unable to keep pace. Helen got up and went to meet her brother, leaving me sitting alone on the bench. He took both her wrists and listened while she spoke close to his ear. Mrs Bruce caught up, and Arthur left Helen in her care before advancing on me with only his coachman in tow.

301

When they stood above me, Arthur said, 'I'm out of patience, John. If you ever come here again . . .' He took a moment to compose himself. Nathan, who stood by his shoulder, looked down and smiled at me. Arthur continued, 'I'll give you one more chance. Agree to the annulment right now or we'll proceed without you.'

Further down the path, my wife and her former governess watched our exchange.

I stood up and straightened my coat. Both Arthur and Nathan were taller than me, so I had to raise my chin. 'My marriage is legitimate, and I refuse to renounce it.'

Arthur took a step back. 'Nathan, Mr Delahunt is trespassing. Please escort him from the garden.'

The coachman's grip was hard and unyielding. He pulled me in the direction of the furthest gate, and I stumbled as I tried to keep balance.

Then Helen called out, 'Nathan,' and everyone stopped to regard her. 'He has a key to the gate. Make sure you take it from him.'

That was the last thing I heard my wife say. Nathan nodded brusquely, and dragged me away.

I didn't want to walk home, for what was there to go home to? I wandered through the city, favouring streets I'd never gone down before. A slight swelling made the skin on my cheekbone smooth and taut where Nathan had punched me before evicting me from the park. I kept brushing it with my fingertips, intrigued that so light a touch could cause such a sharp sting. Beyond the Royal Exchange and Christ Church, the streets became narrow and winding as I neared the Liberties. One of my teeth had come a little loose, and I wiggled it with my tongue. On Francis Street, I stopped to view the newly constructed Catholic church of St Nicholas, one of the first built after the relief acts. It was tucked away from the main thoroughfare behind a neat railed courtyard, hemmed in by tall houses on both sides. I stood and considered its Roman design for a minute, then went towards its entrance, thinking perhaps I could rest for a while out of the cold. But the large, iron-bound doors were locked.

I was about to turn away, but then noticed a narrow alley that skirted the side of the church. At points it wasn't wide enough to walk two abreast. It emerged into Plunket Street, which had a peculiar meandering route, dimly lit by the odd street lamp in the early evening light. The cold air rang with the shouts of children. Broken cobblestones littered the roadway and bed sheets hung suspended between upper-storey windows. In the cold weather they'd take days to dry, though Helen and I had discovered that leaving wet sheets indoors just made a room humid, and every surface clammy – not what young families desired when consumption was rife.

A group of boys played some distance up the street, kicking a football made from the head of a ragdoll. But my attention was drawn to the house opposite, where a pregnant woman stood in a doorway with her son. He was slightly younger than the others, but he tugged on his mother's skirt and asked for permission to join them. She looked so tired; one forearm leaned against the doorjamb, the other rested on her swollen stomach. Strands of dark hair fell beneath a cap and clung to her forehead.

Her son continued to plead until she finally relented. Before letting him away she removed a green scarf and placed it around the boy's neck, tucking it beneath his collar. He scampered off immediately, and his mother watched after him. Something about her reminded me of Mrs Blackwood, the woman we saw hanged. Probably her black hair, drawn face and grey clothes. She distractedly rubbed her belly with both hands, as if satisfied after a large meal, then turned into the house and closed the door.

A coalman in a horse and cart rattled slowly through the street, and one of the boys shouted that they should jump on to the empty bed. They scrambled and jockeyed as the cart passed. The bigger ones moved to the front and with agile leaps made it safely aboard. The remainder were not so graceful, making frantic grabs at wooden slats and using their friends for leverage. Those aboard were helping their favourites and in short order most had clambered up.

Only the smallest boy remained. He grimly chased the vehicle and caught tight hold of the bed. When he jumped on, his legs were left dangling from the back. Then one of the older boys moved towards him, placed a muddied foot on his shoulder and pushed him back off.

The boy landed face first in the road and lay motionless as the catcalls from his friends receded. Once the cart turned the corner with Patrick Street, all was quiet.

'Lad,' I said from the pavement.

He was surprised at the noise, as if unaware that I had been standing so close.

'Come here and let me see if you're hurt.'

Obediently, he got up and came over. He was dressed in nankeen trousers and a chequered coat, beneath which his mother's green scarf was visible. A round blue cap covered dark curls, though his eyebrows were a few shades lighter.

'You seem unharmed,' I said, and he nodded.

'Any cuts on your hand?'

He looked into his palms, then held them up to me with his fingers outstretched, as if I'd asked how many were the commandments.

'I'd say you've suffered worse before.'

He brought his arms to his side and lowered his head.

'Is your father at home?'

'No.'

'When do you expect him back?'

'He's been gone over a year.'

I glanced again at his small house. 'But your mother is with child.'

He didn't answer, just put both hands in his pockets. 'I have to be getting back.'

'Wait.' His coat had been ripped and sewn back together at the shoulder – its check pattern misaligned along a five-inch seam. I pictured his mother darning it by candlelight, the coat draped over her knees. 'How would you like to make sixpence helping me with an errand?'

Another horse and cart clattered through the street and I took the boy's arm. 'Mind,' I said. 'Step up off the road.' The cartwheels bumped over the cobbles and we waited for the din to fade.

He said, 'I should ask Mam.'

'No,' I said, slightly louder than intended. 'No, I don't have time for that.' I rummaged in my coat and withdrew a thruppenny bit. 'You can have this if we leave now, and the rest when we're done.'

The coin looked big in his small hand. He regarded it for a moment, and then closed his fist. 'All right.'

I checked the street. A few old women spoke together in a doorway, and a labourer passed on the pavement opposite.

'Follow me,' I said.

Vendors on Francis Street went about their business, arranging stalls outside shopfronts, sweeping doorsteps and speaking with customers. The boy had to quicken his pace to fall into step beside me. His feet were bare, covered in grime, and I wondered how they must feel against the cold pavement. He altered his gait instinctively to avoid broken paving stones, sharp pieces of refuse and the more offensive spillages.

'What's your name, boy?'

'Maguire.'

'I meant your Christian name.'

He skipped around the paths of two men wearing top hats and greatcoats. When he returned to my side he said, 'Thomas.'

A butcher's shop stood at the end of Francis Street. Four pig carcasses hung from metal hooks outside its window, preserved in the cold air. The trotters and heads had been cut off and their underbellies slit length-wise. Inside the shop, a butcher was at work beside his gory block. He cleaved a piece of meat with a downward hack, left the blade embedded in the wood, and wiped his hand on a smeared apron.

At the crossroads I paused to decide which direction to take. Thomas waited beside me with his arms folded. I knew there were large areas of half-built streets on the outskirts of the city – bare fields with high-walled orchards, and even fenced-off pasture with animals grazing. There'd be no people; no witnesses. To our left, Thomas Street ran past St Catherine's Church towards Kilmainham village. But I was unfamiliar with the roads in that direction.

Something occurred to me and I looked down at the boy. 'We're on Thomas Street,' I said. 'Like your name.'

He nodded. 'I know. Mam says that every time we come down here.'

I didn't want to turn back into Francis Street to go south towards the canal. And the road to our right only led to the city centre, past Christ Church, the Castle and on towards Trinity

College. No, it was best to keep going forward, north over the river to more familiar ground.

I said, 'All right, let's go.' But Thomas had wandered a few yards to the entrance of a stable-lane, where he stood with his head bowed.

'What is it?'

He pointed. 'There's a rainbow in the puddle.'

I stood behind him. It was just a dribble of oil on the surface, and I told him so. 'Come along, we have to cross the river.'

He leaned down to look closer. 'I didn't know oil had so many colours.'

It was rare enough that I could demonstrate my trifling knowledge of optics. I told him the colours of the rainbow were already inside the light. We could see them in the puddle because some of the rays had reflected from the surface of the oil, and some from the surface of the water beneath. Since we were looking at light from two different points simultaneously, the wavelengths of their various colours merged to produce a spectrum.

He remained quiet, and I realized he couldn't have understood a word of my explanation.

'It's very pretty though,' he said.

I looked at the puddle again. A scrap of paper floated across its surface; tiny eddies of yellow, green and indigo swirled in its wake.

'Yes,' I said. 'I suppose it is.'

We resumed our journey towards Cornmarket Square, before turning left down Bridge Street. The road there descends steeply to the river and has an odd curve that traces the outline of Dublin's medieval wall. We walked in silence for a while. Then he asked, 'How did you know all that stuff? About the colours.'

'I studied it in college.'

He nodded with pursed lips, as if the answer was what he expected.

'Have you ever gone to school?'

'No. Mam taught me some letters and numbers. I'll learn more when I'm an apprentice.'

'Your mother can read and write?'

'Yes,' he said proudly. 'She used to run her own shop.'

I checked to see if he was in earnest. 'But she doesn't any more?'

He said his father used to steal the takings and spend it all on drink. They had to move from the shop, a cake shop, into the Liberties several years ago, and the father had abandoned them to go to England. 'I can't remember much about it, only that I was never allowed to eat the cakes.'

His face appeared glum at the memory and I smiled. 'You look much like your mother,' I said. 'You must take after her.'

We emerged on to Merchant's Quay, and had to wait while a man drove six head of cattle along the dockside, grunting and whistling and touching their flanks with a long stick to keep them in line. When the way was clear, Thomas and I went on to Whitworth Bridge. The Four Courts loomed across the river, with its Palladian façade and high copper dome. Out here, beyond the shelter of the narrow streets, a cold wind blew down the Liffey towards the sea, conveying a faint odour of carrion from the slaughterhouse on Usher Island. The boy went quickly to the middle of the bridge, and the crest of its hump, untroubled by the cold. His head just about reached the coping, so he stooped down and looked between the balustrades.

I felt inside my pocket, to make sure the knife was

unconstrained. I rubbed my thumb over the mother-of-pearl handle.

A barge approached with the current, laden with goods lashed down by a cargo net. The bargeman stood at the stern, his feet planted a yard apart for balance, holding a long oar steady in the water. Thomas put his head further through the granite pillars to see the bow slip under the arch. As the barge-man got close, the boy called out, 'Hey, mister!'

'Thomas,' I said with a hiss, grabbing his collar to pull him back. His head scraped against the stone, and his cap fell on the path. He put his hand against his ear and shrank from my grip.

'You're not to draw attention.'

I scooped up his cap before it could blow away, brushed off some grit and fixed it over his dark curls. The fear in his eyes unsettled me. 'I'm sorry. I didn't mean to be rough.'

A passing dockworker turned sideways to get by on the narrow path. Thomas remained still with his eyes downcast.

'Let's get off the bridge,' I said, turning him about, 'or you'll catch cold.'

I nudged his shoulder to propel him forward and, together, we completed the crossing to the north side.

12

The clouds had grown darker and the breeze picked up. Yellow lamplight emerged from the opened door of the Four Courts, where three barristers stood in huddled conversation. One removed his wig to scratch his head, leaving grey wispy hair standing on end. He looked over his shoulder at Thomas and me as we passed. When we reached Essex Bridge, I pointed north up Capel Street and said, 'This way.'

It began to rain, just a drizzle at first, but then more heavily. Conscious of Thomas's bare feet, I took him into Drake's pub, where we stood beside the fire. The old barman said we'd have to order something or get out. I asked for two mugs of coffee and some soda bread, and we took a seat by the hearth.

I tried to move a thick candle to one side, but the wax had melted over the holder, making it stick to the wood. I wondered if I'd draw more attention by blowing it out.

Thomas said, 'What happened to your face?'

The candlelight caught in his eyes as he regarded me. I touched the bruise on my cheek. 'I was in a fight.'

'With who?'

'A coachman.'

'Did you win?'

'No.'

Drake arrived with the coffee and bread. While putting the items down he looked at me and nodded at the boy. 'Don't let him make a mess.'

Thomas sniffed at his mug suspiciously, and said he didn't drink coffee.

'Fine, I'll have it.' But when I reached over he drew the mug away, drank some down and tried to hide a grimace.

'Do you like it?'

He nodded. I took a sip of my own. Admittedly it was pretty bad.

But he did enjoy the bread, holding each slice with a crust in both hands and taking large bites from its centre. Jam stuck to the corners of his mouth, which he wiped away with a coat sleeve across his face, leaving vivid red streaks running to his jaw.

He said, 'I never win at fights either.'

'Do you get into many?'

He placed an uneaten crust on the plate. 'The big lads pick on me. Especially since my dad left.' He said one of his friends once punched him in the face over a game of conkers. Thomas's father had seen it from his window, marched out of the house and kicked the other boy squarely in the stomach, leaving him slumped in the gutter in Plunket Street. 'After that they didn't come near me.' He took up another slice of soda bread. 'But not any more.'

So was he sorry his father left?

He thought for a moment. 'No. Mam was very sad when he was here.'

I swirled the dregs in my mug, leaving dark silt against the sides.

'Did you ever . . .' Thomas said. 'When you were young, I mean. Did the other boys bother you?'

'Not really.'

'They never spoke behind your back, or yelled names, or left you out of games?'

'Well, yes, but it never troubled me.'

'They say things about Mam because she's having another baby. I see them pointing and laughing at her when she's outside the house.'

I told him they did that because they knew it upset him. Let them whisper and smirk as they pleased, because he knew the truth about his mother, and what she was really like. What else mattered?

The door to the pub opened, admitting cold air and a brighter light. Thomas looked out and said, 'It's stopped raining.'

'I know.'

The last warmth had left my mug. I placed it down and used my thumb to clean the coffee stains around its rim. After a moment, Thomas began to pick at the solid folds of candle wax stuck to the table.

'This is what I'll be doing soon.'

I looked across at him.

'As apprentice to Mr Pierce, the chandler on Francis Street. Do you know him?'

I shook my head.

'It's all arranged. I'll have to live above his shop when the new baby comes. If I don't Mam says we'll end up in the work-house.' A nugget of wax broke away in his hand. He held it over the candle flame until drops fell and hissed against the wick. 'I don't want to go though.'

'Sometimes we have to do things we don't want to, Thomas. It can't be helped.'

He singed his fingers and pulled them away, placing their tips in his mouth.

I tidied the dishes on the table, placing the two mugs and jam pot on the empty plate. They only just fitted. Thomas watched me for a while, and then said, 'Wasn't there something we had to do?'

The jam pot was in danger of toppling, so I rotated the handles of both mugs and used them as a buttress. 'Yes,' I said. 'You're right. It's time we were off.'

We left Drake's and continued up Capel Street. From the top of the street it was only a short walk to the parkland around King's Inns – though it could well have been locked so late in the day. We could turn right, past Rutland Square towards Grenville Street. But was there a danger in getting too close to home?

At the next corner, a couple of men stood in conversation outside a house. At first I could only see the broad shoulders of the man nearest, but he shifted his weight, giving me a glimpse of the other man's lean, leering face. It was Lyster.

I turned on my heel. Thomas was walking directly behind and bumped into me. He looked up in surprise.

'We can't go this way.'

'What?'

I pushed past him. 'Come.'

We crossed the road diagonally towards Strand Street. At the corner I risked a glance back from behind a parked hansom cab. The two men still spoke to each other. Lyster was smiling and held his palms spread apart, as if boasting of a caught fish.

If Thomas wondered about retracing our steps he didn't say. The refreshments seemed to invigorate him and he skipped ahead. A sweet smoky smell of sawdust drifted over the footpath from Fottrell's mill. He stopped to look through the fence at the great circular band-saw.

I stood beside him but kept my eye on the road behind.

'What makes it turn?'

A man came around the corner but it wasn't Lyster. I said there was an underground river that powered a mill.

'Look, they're bringing another tree.'

I peered through the fence. The saw was the height of a man, housed beneath a roof that rested on exposed iron pillars, like a bandstand. Four men fed a limbless bole towards the spinning teeth. Two others stood to the side. One held a hose at the ready, the other leaned against the handle of its pump, to spray the blade with water if it overheated. The trunk inched closer and closer till finally it met the saw, which emitted a noise like the cry of a newborn.

Thomas let out an excited whoop as the trunk was carved. After a moment he said, 'What would happen if a man fell on it?'

The path behind was still clear. 'What do you think?'

'I bet it would cut right through him.' He seemed to relish the prospect.

It had been a mistake to come so close to home, where any number of people might have recognized me. Back on the quays, I paid the penny toll and we went through the turnstiles to cross the metal footbridge. As we climbed the hill on Fownes Street, I glanced at the nondescript door of Farrell's office, and the flicker of candlelight in the upper windows. The traffic was heavy on Dame Street, so I held Thomas's hand as we dodged between carriages. We cut through stalls in the south city markets and emerged on to William Street beside the Powerscourt mansion. Thomas couldn't believe that the townhouse was home to just one family. His gaze swept across its nine bay windows and he said, 'They must keep getting lost in it.'

A grey mongrel with long skinny legs approached him

warily. It began to sniff at his pockets. The boy laughed and stooped to pat its head.

We stood at the corner of Coppinger Row. I looked along its extent to the exterior of my sister's house. The shutters in the parlour were closed and the only light came from the servants' quarters in the top floor. I hadn't seen Cecilia since taking the silver frame. Would she even allow me in if I called? She always had a forgiving nature. But I couldn't knock now for she'd only ask questions about the boy.

'Let's keep moving,' I said, looking down.

Thomas no longer stood at my side. I surveyed the street and considered calling his name, but that would be too conspicuous. I hurried towards Mercer's Hospital, my eye drawn into every gloomy shopfront. Any flash of blue made me start. At the crossroads before the hospital I looked about, bobbing to see past pedestrians and standing on tiptoes. A middle-aged woman stopped to ask if everything was all right.

Without thinking I said, 'I've lost a child.'

She brought her hand to her mouth. 'What's he dressed like?'

I described his blue cap and nankeen trousers, then stopped myself. 'It's all right. I'll search for him alone.'

'Look,' she said. 'There's a policeman over there.'

'Really, it's fine. I think I know where he's gone,' and without saying anything more I hurried around the corner into King Street.

I saw the dog rummaging in the refuse from an upturned bin. But there was still no sign of Thomas. The dog wagged its tail at my approach, and I scratched behind its ear. Up ahead the paths were thick with people crossing between Grafton Street and the corner of St Stephen's Green. They crowded both sides of the pavement while waiting for a carriage to pass, then advanced on each other as if to join battle. I kept petting the dog, rhythmically tapping the top of its skull, which made its eyelids bat. An anxiety in my throat had eased, and a tension in my shoulders had disappeared. I said, 'Maybe it's just as well.'

Then a deep voice called, 'Delahunt.' I turned to see Lyster walk towards me, leading Thomas gently by the hand. He smiled and pointed down at the boy. 'Is this yours?'

Thomas's face lit up when he saw the dog. 'You found him.'

'I happened to see this chap wander from your side.' Lyster let go and rubbed Thomas's head, leaving his cap askew. His eyes lingered on my bruised cheek, as if gauging the force of the blow that had made it, and the time elapsed since the strike.

I said, 'I was just bringing him home.'

'You're taking a very scenic route.'

'Thomas, I'm finished with you now. You can make your own way from here.'

'But you still owe me thruppence.'

'Just go.'

'No,' Lyster said quietly, placing his hand on the boy's shoulder. 'Don't worry, Thomas. We're not done with you yet. Wait here.'

He took my elbow and walked a few yards up the street, then stopped in the doorway of a barber's. When he looked into my face the corners of his eyes crinkled in amusement, then became serious.

'What's the plan?'

I said there wasn't one.

'Where were you thinking of doing it?'

Water dripped from the end of a red and white pole in a steady rhythm. The drops kept missing Lyster's shoulder by inches.

'Do you really think me capable of that?'

'Who were you going to blame it on?'

Thomas tapped his chest with both hands to get the dog to stand on its hind legs. The poor creature stared up at him with its head cocked.

'His mother.'

Lyster's mouth dipped down at both sides. 'His mother? Jesus, Delahunt.' He thought for a second. 'But she'll do. You know what she looks like?'

I nodded. It was an odd relief to say it out. 'She lives alone in Plunket Street, no husband. And she's pregnant.'

'Even better. She can plead the belly.'

'It doesn't matter though, Lyster. I'm not going through with it.'

Before he could speak again, I turned and walked towards the corner of the Green. But Thomas saw me depart and ran to my side with the dog at his heel.

'Go home, Thomas.'

Lyster caught up and grabbed my arm. 'It'll get Sibthorpe off your back.'

I pulled my hand free, and continued at the vanguard of our odd company.

'Shop the mother and I'll have a confession from her by noon tomorrow.'

I frowned at Lyster for his loose talk. But Thomas paid no heed to what we said. The dog trotted up to a horse-trough, placed its front paws on the rim and tried to lower its head to drink, but couldn't reach. Thomas sat on the lip, cupped his fingers and drew water from the fount, wincing because of the cold. He let the dog lap from his hands.

Lyster looked along the extent of the Green. 'There's a spot beyond the canal. You know Pembroke Lane?'

It wasn't far from where I grew up. Alex and I used to play in it. 'Yes.'

'An empty field skirts the coach houses.'

Thomas could no longer stand the touch of the freezing water. He shook his hands in the air, much to the dog's confusion, then stuffed them under his arms.

'People will see me bring him there.'

Lyster ran his hand over his shaved head, then called out, 'Thomas, come over.'

The boy was blowing into his fingers as he approached. Lyster pulled a small notebook and pencil from a breast pocket. He opened it and began to write something, his features cast in a half-smile. When he was done he pocketed the pencil and tore out the page, folding it twice. 'John and I need this message delivered to a friend of ours. Do you know of the canal beyond Baggot Street?'

Thomas nodded.

'Of course you do.' But he gave the directions all the same. 'Just keep to this side of the Green and go straight, straight, straight.' He sliced the air three times. 'Then go over the bridge and take the first road on your right. You'll see a field, and that's where our friend will be.' He held up a finger. 'If you arrive and he's not there, wait for him. Speak to no one until you see him.'

The boy's face was solemn as he listened to these instructions.

'Show me your right.' Thomas held up the correct hand and Lyster placed the note within it. 'We'll give you the rest of the money when you return here with his reply. Do you understand?'

Thomas looked at me, as if wondering why I wasn't speaking. 'Yes.'

'Well, off you go.'

Without another word, Thomas turned his back and was away. The dog tried to follow, but Lyster grabbed it by the scruff until it lost interest.

'I'll wait for you in the Winter Palace and we'll get the story straight.' He offered his hand for me to shake. I ignored it so he slapped my shoulder. 'He'll be as well out of this world as in it, Delahunt. Don't keep him waiting.'

Lyster clucked his tongue and the dog ambled to his side. He raised the collar of his coat, and after a few steps he looked like any other passer-by.

The tall houses in Stephen's Green had become indistinct in the gloaming. Lamplight illuminated windows in the terrace in a random pattern, like dots in a row of dominoes. A governess stuck her head from a top-floor window and called for her charges to leave the garden and come home for tea. She said they knew they weren't allowed out after dark.

There were no street lights beyond the canal, where a small terrace of newly built houses ran to the first corner. The laneway on the right bounded a marshy field with stagnant pools that shivered in the breeze. Several posts were staked in the ground to mark plot outlines, and a few low outhouses and rubbish heaps were dotted about.

Thomas sat on a kerb with his arms wrapped around his chest, rocking back and forth in the cold. He turned his head at the sound of my footfall, and began to run towards me, calling out, 'Mister, I have a message for you.' He recognized my features and stopped.

'There was a change in plan,' I said. 'Our friend found us on the Green so there was no need to deliver the note. But I couldn't let you stay out here when I knew that no one was going to come.'

'You can't have your money back.'

'Keep it. You've earned every penny.'

He began to turn away so I held up a hand. 'I'm going to be collected in a jaunting car in a few minutes. I can give you a lift back to your home.'

He shook his head and said it was all right. He would run back.

I tried to keep my voice from shaking. 'It's too dark for you to return alone. I shouldn't have made you come all this way. Really, the car will be here any minute.'

I rummaged in my pocket and took hold of the knife.

'Maybe.' He looked towards Baggot Street, then back at me. My hand had stilled. 'Maybe I will ride in the car. Thank you.' With that he walked a little into the field and sat down on a heap of broken terracotta tiles.

'Good.' I rotated the knife so the blade faced down. 'It won't be a moment.' I stood awkwardly with my elbow protruding, lifted my chin and pursed my lips as if there was some faint sound on the breeze.

The boy began to pick up small pebbles from the heap and toss them towards a muddy puddle. I could hear the water splash as each stone submerged.

I paced up and down on the verge, my palm slick against the mother-of-pearl handle. Thomas had drawn his knees up to his chest, his calloused soles resting on the broken masonry. He looked up sharply at the junction, and I twisted my head expecting to see someone approach, but the road was empty.

I tutted. 'My friend seems to have been delayed.'

'If I'm not coming home soon my mother will beat me.'

'I'm sure it won't be long.'

When I looked at him again, he held a long twig horizontally in front of his face. Even in the dusk I could see a spider crawl along its crooked length towards the tip. At one point it moved down to walk along the underside. The boy kept his head and hand still, and followed the creature's progress with his eyes.

When the spider got to the end of the stick it fell off, but saved itself with a gossamer thread. It hung there, suspended from the tip, and swayed in the breeze. Thomas laughed briefly. He brought the stick to the side, with the spider still tethered like the bait on a fishing rod, and laid it gently on a broken block. He rotated the stick to snap the thread, then lifted it away like a conductor's baton, leaving the creature undisturbed on the ground.

I withdrew my hand, leaving the blade where it was, and turned to sit on the pavement with my boots in the gutter. I put my head in my hands. The brim of my hat pushed back from my brow.

The boy got up. His bare feet made no sound on the grass, and when he came on to the pavement I could hear soft scuffs on the uneven stone. Then he sat down beside me. I turned my head towards him. His feet were crossed beneath the frayed ends of his yellow trousers. He said, 'Maybe he's forgotten about you.'

He brought both hands up to his mouth and coughed into them for a few seconds, then wiped his palms against his bib.

'That sounds bad,' I said, and he shrugged.

'Stand up, Thomas.'

We both got to our feet.

'Do you have any lumps in your throat?'

He placed his hand against his neck and frowned.

'Let me feel.'

I pressed my fingers against the smooth skin around his

gullet and felt along his small jawbone. I had to move aside his mother's green scarf.

I stepped behind him. He raised his head, at first I thought to look back towards me, but he did so for me to examine him more easily. I felt his throat with my left hand, then pressed my palm against his brow and pushed his head back against my stomach. He didn't resist. My right hand dipped into my pocket and came out with the knife.

I held it down by my side so Thomas couldn't see. He tried to shift his head, probably from discomfort, but I kept him steady and took a breath. Just draw it across, as straight as possible. Don't let blood get on your sleeve. I could feel his eyebrows twitch beneath my fingers. The handle was slick. Quick and smooth like the bow of a cello. Still lowered, the haft began to slip between my fingers. It was thicker and rounded at its base, and I felt the bump ease past my little finger, then the ring, then the middle. Thomas reached up and took hold of my wrist. The knife hung suspended between my thumb and knuckle. I sensed it slide further, like the fingertip of someone falling from a precipice. Then the blade clicked against the ground.

Thomas was squirming now beneath my grip. I said, 'I'm sorry,' and shoved him away.

He staggered a few yards and twisted around to look at me, his eyes wide with fright. 'What were you . . .'

'Nothing.' I straightened my jacket, picked a blue thread from my cuff, then extended my hand as if we could shake on it and put the incident behind us.

He backed away again and looked to be on the verge of tears.

'No, don't cry, Thomas.' I lowered my arm. 'Just go back home. Go back to your mother.'

But I was blocking the path to the main street so he

hesitated. He seemed very small, with his arms folded in front and head bowed. He began to sob quietly. Sometimes when I wept as a child, I'd stand in front of a mirror just to see what it looked like. I said sorry once more, and then walked away, back on to the main road, over the canal and through the gas-lit streets. I didn't stop until I reached Grenville Street. I shuffled up the stairs of number six, crawled into bed and buried my face in the pillow, pulling the blanket over my head, so no part of me touched the air.

It was still early in the evening. I could hear the clatter of traffic on the street and the ticking of the mantel clock. A coldness seeped through the cover, but I didn't rise to light a fire.

When I woke a few hours later the room was silent except for a breeze that whispered through cracks in the glass. It could have been any time. I pulled the blanket to my chin and could just make out the looming corners of the chimney piece and the outlines of the windows.

The folds of the bedding formed a strange shadowy landscape of knolls and furrows. I could only see a couple of feet across the coarse woollen cover. But in the stillness, I pretended my perspective was different: that I stood on a lonely summit, and a path before me wound between black slanting hills. I studied each feature; imagined what might lie between the peaks; what was over the crest on each side; where the path went when it curved out of sight. Every time I rolled over, the landscape looked different.

When I next woke, the window frames were visible against a grey, pre-dawn light. The wind outside had picked up, making the sashes shake and the door creak. I heard a chain from a horse's bridle rattle on the street below. The temperature had dropped further, and no matter how I lay I couldn't get warm.

A crack of light appeared along the doorsill. I raised my head to look at it. Something shuffled on the landing, then the light crept up the jambs on both sides and a glowing spot appeared at the keyhole.

A loud thump broke the stillness, and the door shook against its hinges. I had barely time to get to my elbow when there came another. This time the door broke open, and collided with the side of the dresser. Two DMP men stood illuminated on the threshold, a battering ram held between them at the top of its swing. They dropped the ram and stood aside, allowing four others to rush in with cudgels raised. The light behind them cast long shifting shadows against the ceiling.

The first brought his baton down on my shoulder, and only then did I think to protect my head. Arms covered in thick navy cloth dragged me from the bed. Another baton fell on my side and someone kicked me in the thigh, which was by far the most painful blow. A fat policeman stepped in front of me and told the others to hold me up. The strap of his round helmet dug into the flesh on his chin. He carefully gripped the end of his baton, his fingers closing over the handle in a wave, and brought his arm back.

'Enough.' An officer stood between the two door-breakers, who now held lanterns aloft. The officer was a slighter man, wearing a flat cap and neat moustache. His arms disappeared beneath an oilskin cape. I heard an infant cry below, and Mrs Lynch called to her husband to shut their door.

The officer surveyed the room, then told the one who was going to beat me to search the dresser.

The thwarted policeman held my eye as he slipped his baton into a loop on his belt. He went to the sideboard, which was in a bad state since I'd gutted it for firewood, and pulled out the only remaining drawer. He tilted the box and looked in, as if panning for gold, then brought it to the table. With a sweep of his arm he sent a mug and a few plates crashing to the floor, then upended the cutlery on to the tabletop.

The officer approached and asked for a lantern to be brought near. He sifted through the knives and forks for a second, then reached into his coat and took out a white napkin parcel. He unfolded the cloth at each corner to reveal a knife.

The point at the end of the blade had broken off. The steel was covered in translucent streaks of red, thicker and deeper along the serrated edge. The swirled bloodstains on the handle matched the mother-of-pearl so well it could have been part of its design.

I wanted to touch it, to confirm it was real. I even reached across, but one of the policemen grabbed my wrist and pulled it behind my back.

The officer picked up one of the knives from the same dinner-set among the jumble on the table and placed it beside its stained counterpart.

He said, 'A match.'

My family had used those knives for meals during feast days. Perhaps all of us had held that particular one at various times. It would have felt no different.

The officer turned to me, his lower lip hidden beneath the bristles of his moustache. 'John Delahunt.'

He wasn't asking for confirmation, but still I answered yes.

'I'm arresting you for the murder of Thomas Maguire.'

I looked again at the smudged face of the blade. Little islands of steel remained untouched and gleaming. In places, Thomas's blood had dried to a rusty brown. I stared at it, then met the officer's eye.

'Yes,' I said. 'I understand.'

*

I was brought to a holding cell in Store Street and placed in manacles and shackles. They only allowed for a half-stride, so I shuffled around the cell like a hobbled horse. The irons were heavy and cold to the touch. When I was first escorted in, the fetters were in a heap in one corner. The guard picked them up and cursed. He struggled for a while to untangle the chains, but only managed to pull one leg-iron and one handcuff free. I offered to hold them while he unravelled the rest. After considering a moment he placed them in my hands. With a bit more unpicking he managed to get the chains loose, and he thanked me while slipping them on.

After that I was left alone. I sat at the table, placed my hands beside an oil-lamp and waited. After the initial shock of my arrest, I realized it was vital that I be allowed to make a statement, to tell the police what Lyster had done. But one thought began to weigh on me. These were the cells to which Devereaux had been brought when he fell foul of the Castle. And he didn't survive a day.

Throughout the afternoon, footsteps sounded in the corridor outside, but each time they'd pass my door and begin to fade. As the light declined outside it began to sleet. Small grey flecks swirled against the glass, melting as soon as they struck. I turned down the lamplight so I could see better. It was the first hint of snow in a mild December. The Christmas before had been particularly cold. Helen and I pushed our seats beside the window, huddled beneath a blanket and watched a blizzard fall on Grenville Street. Cartwheel tracks that criss-crossed the empty roadway slowly disappeared, and several inches built up on the windowsill. The next morning she woke me by dropping a handful of snow down my nightshirt. I sat up to see the sash window ajar. She smiled at me while kneeling on the bed. That was before she became unwell. Her cheeks were pink, tousled hair fell across her face and over her shoulders, and her nightdress hitched up so one knee was uncovered. And I was annoyed with her.

The warder came in before nightfall with a mug of water and a chamber pot.

I said, 'I need to make a statement.'

He said people would come from the Castle in the morning to deal with me.

'Can I not give an account to someone here?'

But he took the oil-lamp and locked the door without another word.

In the dark, I folded my arms on the table and rested my head. During the night it became so cold that I had to fetch the blanket. It was difficult to draw over my shoulders because of the manacles. A few times I heard a metal door closing and conversations in the hallway, and I was convinced that they had come for me. But dawn broke and I was undisturbed.

Later that morning, the peephole slid aside and a key scraped in the door. A young man entered. He had dark hair parted at one side and swept behind both ears. His thin eyebrows were set in a furrow, as if someone had said something to vex him. Without looking at me, he brought the other chair to the table, opened a satchel and laid out a sheaf of blank paper stamped with the Castle seal. Then he went to the wall, placed his satchel by his feet, and stood with arms folded.

I'd never seen him before. Maybe he didn't belong to the Department. I said, 'Are you here to take my statement?'

He remained silent. Did he mean for me to write it out? The sheaf faced towards the empty chair. I was going to speak again, but then the door opened and Lyster walked in.

He stood in the threshold and regarded me for a moment. Any lingering hope that I had ebbed away.

He strode to the table, placed a thick file on top and looked at the manacles on my wrists, as if judging the reach of the chain. Then he took his seat.

I said, 'I've nothing to say to you.'

There was a thin gash along the top of his little finger. He twisted open the lid of an inkpot, turning it twice more than needed, then placed it ink side down on the table. 'We'll see.'

He turned his face in profile. 'William, I'm going to speak to Delahunt alone. Wait for me upstairs.'

The young man leaned forward and hesitated. 'But . . . Mr Sibthorpe told me to stay and observe.'

Lyster stared at his assistant with a face devoid of expression, as if he examined the mortar between the bricks. William only withstood the gaze for a few seconds. He picked up his bag and left the cell.

Lyster turned back to me. 'One of Tom's new recruits. I don't think he'll last.'

We were left alone and sat in silence for a few moments. I gathered up the slack of my chains and let them spill on the table so they wouldn't weigh on my wrists.

'There's a problem.' Lyster dipped the nib of his pen in the inkpot, then laid it flat on its rim. 'It seems the DMP don't know the meaning of discretion. I told them exactly where you'd be, and that you were on your own. But still they went with six men and a battering ram.' He squeezed the bridge of his nose. 'Your name was out before noon yesterday, and printed in the evening papers.'

I thought of Helen reading the reports, or Cecilia. I couldn't think of anyone else. Really, a man my age should hope to disappoint more than two people.

'Then some journalist recalled that you were Crown witness in the Cooney trial and awkward questions were asked.' He spoke in a wheedling voice. 'How could one man be involved in two murder cases? How much had the Castle paid him during the trial of the Italian boy?' He pulled a watch from a fob pocket and checked the time. 'Journalists can be very trying. Otherwise we'd have arranged an accident for you last night. But if we did that now, it would just confirm suspicions.'

Some hope was rekindled. If I could make it to trial, I'd have the opportunity to speak about any number of things the Castle wished to remain secret. They could deny whatever I said, of course, but once the truth is revealed, it's always hard to cover up again.

My musing may have played on my face, for Lyster regarded me with a half-smile.

I said, 'Can the Department get me off?'

'No. Most of the city saw you with the boy. Then there's the knife. I'm afraid you're going to be convicted.' He pulled the folder closer to the edge of the table but didn't open it.

If my guilt was already assumed then the best I could hope for was a lenient sentence. I wasn't sure I could survive breaking stones in Van Diemen's Land for twenty years, but what was the alternative?

'You'll have to arrange that I get transportation and not the gibbet.'

'We have no sway over the judges. Besides, there'd be a riot if you escaped the noose.'

'You've got to do something, Lyster, unless you want your name to be widely known.'

He opened the folder, picked up a few pages fastened at the top by a metal pin, and placed the document on the table before me.

'I took the liberty of writing you out a confession last night. You just need to sign it.'

I looked down at the front page. The first words were *I, John Delahunt, state positively*, written in Lyster's angular, non-cursive hand.

He said it simply set out my original plan: that of killing the boy and blaming it on his mother, solely for the purpose of receiving a reward. I read over a passage: *I do now confess that the hope of getting again into the pay of the Castle was my strong motive for committing the deed. If I had succeeded I don't know but I might have done a similar deed again had my conscience yielded to a similar temptation.*

I looked across at him. 'I don't even speak like that.'

He shrugged. 'It was late when I wrote it.'

'Lyster, why would I sign this? What difference to me if I'm killed in a holding cell this week, or hanged in a few months?'

He began to rummage in the file again, then stopped. 'You know, our original plan wouldn't have worked.'

'Why not?'

'We couldn't have blamed Thomas's mother. She had an alibi beyond reproach.'

He waited for me to ask, but I began to read again from the confession.

'She went into labour the same afternoon. A month early.' He laughed. 'It's hard to credit. You must be cursed, Delahunt.'

I recalled the woman standing in her doorway in Plunket Street, the way she held her stomach, and the strands of hair that clung to her pallid face.

Lyster said, 'I had to break the news to her in the Coombe.'

'You told her?'

'Someone had to.'

An image of Lyster at her bedside came to my mind: lightly gripping her fingers above the covers, his face solemn.

'Did the baby survive?'

'I didn't ask.'

He took a single dog-eared sheet from the file. It contained a list in spidery, uneven writing – a roll of about ten women's names. One of them in the middle had been struck through. The bottom one was 'Helen Delahunt'.

'What's this?'

'Do you remember giving us some information a few months ago on Mrs Redmond, the abortionist?'

Four of the women had Mary as a first name.

'She was picked up at the end of November. And just like you, she was eager to avoid the drop. We told her we'd go easy if she gave the names of her most recent clients.'

I scanned through the names. To work as an abortionist was a capital offence, but the police hardly ever went after the mothers.

'But why? You're not going to arrest these women.'

He seemed genuinely bemused by the question. 'Because it's what we do.' He noticed a spot of ink on his thumb, licked his forefinger and began to rub it off. 'Mrs Redmond is being tried next month. And that list can be made public or not. It's up to you.'

Helen was already dogged with scandal. If she was cast out again she wouldn't survive. It would be hard enough for her in the next few months with reports of my trial. I looked again at the sheet. My surname was affixed to her like a millstone.

I pointed to the name on the list that had been crossed out. 'What happened to this one?'

'She died.'

I glanced up at him.

'Nothing to do with us.'

He took the sheet from my hands. 'But this would just be the start, John. We know you spoke to Helen about the

331

Department while you were cooped up in the tenement. We can't have it.'

'She wouldn't say anything.'

'There's only one way we can be sure. And if she's abandoned by her family, well, she'll be that much easier to get to.' He scratched his chin. 'We could find out where she lives and supply her with cheap laudanum.'

If it was anyone else, I might have deemed that an empty threat. I turned the confession over and read from the other side. *I kept him nearly half an hour in the lane. He twice asked me was I coming home soon, as his mother would be beating him. I said that I was waiting for a jaunting car.*

'What's to stop you going after her whether I agree to this or not?'

'I suppose you'll just have to trust us.' Once again he let his face became devoid of expression: no curl of the lip or furrowed brow, no flicker of sentiment in his eye. 'But you can be assured, John, that if you mention any aspect of the Department on the stand, I'll deal with Helen personally.'

There was space for a signature beneath the last block of text.

His back was then to me, and at that moment, while he was in that position with his head drawn back, I cut his throat and threw him from me. He fell on his face; he uttered no cry, nor did he make any noise whatsoever. On getting about three yards from him I looked back, and saw him on his feet again, going in the direction of a cottage in the field. I was about to follow, but then he fell and ceased moving.

It would be painful to put my signature to a statement with such poor style. I reached for the pen, and held it for a moment. It felt unnatural to write with a weight on my wrist. I placed the nib down, and a tiny circular blot began to expand on the page. I began to write. As soon as I crossed the 't', Lyster took the statement back, blew on the ink and placed it in his file.

He folded a crease in Mrs Redmond's list just above Helen's name, then tore it along the corner of the table and handed the scrap to me.

I watched him as he tidied the sheaf and made ready to leave.

'Why didn't you just let Thomas go, Lyster?'

He tucked the folder beneath his arm and stood up. 'You've done the right thing, John.'

'How much did you get for turning me in?'

'You know,' he said. He stepped behind his chair and pushed its legs beneath the table, before he paused and held my eye. 'The usual.'

When he left the room, I regarded the scrap of paper in my hand. Then I tore it in the middle and tossed the second half away. The piece that remained simply said, 'Helen'.

13

There is a silence that falls over Kilmainham in the hours before dawn. Shouted conversations between the cells quieten. The noises of warders on their rounds become less frequent. Even the sobs and moans of the most distraught inmates fade in the smallest hours. I've heard the hush descend for three nights while working by candlelight, filling every page with handwriting as small as I could make it, with no margins, or space between lines, or paragraph breaks. If a sentence at the top drooped at the end, then all subsequent lines did the same, as if they followed the contour of a bound page.

As the nights wore on my hand would become stained and cramped, and at times I'd stop to flex my fingers, the way my sister used to when she pretended to cast a spell. I'd look out of the window for the first sign of dawn, always surprised at how suddenly it would arrive. One moment the window is black, unseen against the wall. Then I write a paragraph, look again, and a pale sheen has infused the night sky, as if someone parted a curtain. This morning, I held my sheet against the candle in order to better see the daybreak, and realized the next time I saw the sun rise, I wouldn't see it set again. The page glowed like a paper lantern, with the flame flickering behind, the writing shown up like a votive offering.

A plate of stringy mutton and suet pudding lay untouched by my feet. I've stopped taking food these last two days. I dislike the idea of lying forever with my last meal half-digested.

I remember reading once of an ancient body found in the Bog of Allen, so well preserved that at first the police had been called to investigate a possible murder. Those that witnessed the bog body were amazed to see stubble on the chin, pores in the tanned skin, and cracks in the fingernails. They say his face was calm and solemn, as if he had just fallen asleep, and he lay with his legs drawn up and his hands clasped before his chest. But when he was brought to Dublin, some antiquarian removed his stomach and rummaged within to catalogue details of his Iron Age diet. They won't find anything in me.

Turner came in as usual with my bowl of oatmeal a little after nine o'clock, and placed it on my desk. I didn't glance up from my work. 'I told you I don't want any.'

'I still have to give it to you.'

He picked up the untouched supper from the previous evening, and the nubs of two used candles. On his way out, he stopped in the door and said, 'I should tell you, they've just arrived. The governor is speaking to them now.'

I shifted in my seat. 'How long?'

'They'll be here in fifteen minutes.'

After he left, I gathered the pages of my statement and hid them beneath my bedding. I washed my face in the water bowl and frowned at my reflection in the shifting surface: the shaved head and gaunt face. I scrubbed my fingers, but could only remove some of the ink stains in the cold water. Then I tidied my bunk, flattening the blanket and tucking it beneath the mattress.

I was sitting at my desk when they entered. Turner came in first, followed by a man in a suit carrying a leather satchel.

335

Finally, Helen stepped in behind them. She wore a burgundy travelling cloak with the hood down. Her head was otherwise uncovered, and her thick hair was loosely pinned. As she entered, she kept her eyes on the floor, as if mindful of where she trod. Her gaze swept over me briefly, and I saw she made an effort to keep her face expressionless.

I stood up and said to her, 'Would you like to sit, Helen?'

But the other man stepped forward. 'Mr Delahunt, I'm Montfort Sweetman, solicitor for the Stokes family. We've been in correspondence.'

Helen's hands disappeared into the deep, wide pockets of her cape. A healthy colour had returned to her cheeks, and her lower lip had regained its former fullness.

Sweetman continued, 'As you know, a petition was lodged with the Court of Conscience for a decree of nullity to be made against your marriage. On behalf of the Stokes family, may I say you were most gracious not to contest the issue.'

He paused, as if he expected me to acknowledge his kind words. Helen glanced up at the moment's silence.

'As I indicated in my last letter, the court granted an annulment last Friday. All that remains is that you and Mrs Delahunt sign the document together, witnessed by a third party, in which capacity Mr Turner has agreed to act.'

The warder nodded soberly.

Sweetman placed his satchel on the desk, and took out a folded parchment. He said, 'Would you like to read the decree?'

Helen shivered all of a sudden, and pulled her cloak tighter.

I said to her, 'It does get cold in here. I've grown used to it by now.'

She didn't lift her head.

'Mr Delahunt, would you like to read what you're about to sign?'

'No, thank you. Though . . . I'm curious as to the grounds for annulment.'

'Well, Helen was not of the legal age required in this part of the kingdom to grant consent when you were wed.' He withdrew a pen from his breast pocket. 'And you were cognizant of that fact.'

Helen's voice was quiet but clear. 'We both were.'

Sweetman cleared his throat, unfolded the document and took an inkpot from his case, even though mine was open on the table. He handed the pen to Helen, pointed to a space on the sheet and said, 'If you just sign here.'

She stood near me, close enough to touch her arm if I reached across. Her head bent over the document, and a lock of hair fell loose. She swept it behind her ear with her middle finger. When it fell again she left it be. Helen seemed to hesitate, and I wondered if she was having second thoughts.

Then she turned to her solicitor. 'Which name should I use?'

'Your married name.'

She nodded, and immediately began to write. The rest of us stood in silence as the nib scraped over the parchment.

When she finished, I held out my hand for the pen, but she handed it to me through her solicitor. I signed my name directly beneath Helen's, starting a little to the right so the Delahunts would align.

Sweetman then called Turner over. The warder examined the document. 'Where do you want me to sign?'

'Just there, sir.'

I noticed that Helen was studying me. Her eyes drifted across my face and over my prison garb, and I became self-conscious enough to rub a hand over my clipped head.

'Where exactly do you mean?' said Turner.

'Beside the space that says, "Witnessed by".'

Turner began to write his name slowly, forming each letter with care.

'Would I be permitted to speak with my wife . . . I mean with Helen in private?'

Sweetman said, 'I don't think that's appropriate.'

'I'd prefer to hear her reply.'

She stood still for a moment, and then lifted the hood of her riding cloak to cover her head. 'No.'

'But there's something I need to tell you.'

'I don't want to speak to you.'

'It's important.'

Turner finished his signature. Sweetman sprinkled the wet ink with pounce, and immediately folded the document into his satchel. He said, 'Miss Stokes,' and she looked at him. 'You are under no obligation to remain here.'

'Then I wish to go.'

I said, 'Helen, wait.'

Sweetman pushed the cell door open, and Helen began to walk towards it.

I wanted the last thing I told her to be truthful, so what could I say? That I was innocent; that I didn't deserve my fate? But I wasn't innocent, and I did deserve it.

'I'm . . . not as bad as people think.'

She had already left the room without glancing back. Sweetman followed after, and I heard another guard outside escort them away.

I went over to the bunk and slouched down. Turner stood awkwardly in the middle of the room. I was about to ask him to go as well, but then he said, 'Your message was received.'

'What did he say?'

'That he'll think about it. There's still time. If he does come here I'll show him in.'

I retrieved my statement from beneath the mattress and brought it back to the table. Turner looked at me as I leafed through to the final page and took up my pen.

'The yard will be empty if you want to get some air.'

'No, I can't.'

'You won't get another chance.'

'I'm not finished yet.'

It was dark when I finally put down my pen and flipped through the pages, dissatisfied with the scrawled writing, the strikes and interpolations. I decided not to read through it, lest I be tempted to purge certain passages or embellish others. I numbered the sheets, tidied the bundle and left it on my desk.

At around midnight, the cell door opened and Turner came in. He nodded to me once, and then beckoned towards someone in the hall. Farrell came in wearing a dark coat. His shirt collars stood up against his jaw, and he wore his small round spectacles.

Turner said, 'He can only stay for a few minutes. No longer.' He left his oil-lamp on the floor and withdrew.

Farrell looked around the gloomy cell, and squinted at me through his glasses. He said, 'Short hair doesn't suit you.'

'You got Turner's message?'

He nodded.

'What did he say?'

'He said that you have some information for me.'

I invited Farrell to sit on the bunk, but he preferred to stand.

I picked up the ruffled pages of my statement and handed it to him. 'It's already written out.'

'Usually we like agents to be a bit more succinct.'

'I want you to keep this, Farrell. But you can't let Sibthorpe see it. Or Lyster.'

'Why not?'

'You'll know when you read it.'

He scanned the first few lines. 'If this undermines Sibthorpe in some way, then I'll have to show it to him.'

'But why?'

He looked at me over the rim of his glasses.

'Please, just read it first. All I want is for it to be kept some-where. Maybe no one else will ever read it. Maybe it'll be read and not believed. I just want it to be preserved.'

Farrell decided to take a seat after all, and he perched at the end of the bunk. 'Where do you expect me to put it?'

'In the archive.'

'You want me to keep a statement that lays bare the work-ings of the Department within the Department itself?'

'Yes.'

He considered this for a moment as he flicked through a few of the pages. Turner pulled open the door. He looked in and said, 'It's time to go.'

Farrell got up and came to stand over me, the statement held by his side in his right hand. I thought he was about to hand it back, but then he pursed his lips, undid the top button of his coat, and stuffed the manuscript inside. With that he turned on his heel and left the cell.

Turner said that they would come to fetch me at dawn, and began to close over the door.

'Thanks for your help, Turner.'

He cocked his head. It was the least he could do.

I remained sitting on the bunk, cross-legged with my back against the wall, and stared at the candle flame as it trembled and swayed in the cold draughts. It appeared as a brilliant white against the surrounding gloom. I pulled the blanket around my shoulders and let the hours drift by.

I wasn't fearful. I only experienced a numb unease, much as I felt before my first day at college, or when homesick while staying in Antrim. Thoughts of what might happen in the hereafter didn't bother me. If I believed anything, it was that God would grant oblivion to those who wished it. But my mind couldn't help turning to the mechanics of my execution, and I found the prospect troubling. I pinched the front of my throat and become alarmed at how little force was required to cause pain. Maybe there was a way to hold one's neck that increased the likelihood of a break? Something to ask the hangman. But then I feared that in the commotion of the morning's preparations, I might forget to seek his advice, so I rose from my bunk, took up my pen for the final time, and wrote 'ATH' in capital letters on the back of my hand. As the ink dried, I smiled at the thought of people trying to decipher this final message.

An hour after dawn, the prison began to stir. I rose and changed into the clothes that Turner had left for me the night before: a dark grey jacket of coarse wool, corduroy trousers and a crimson waistcoat, all in a nearly worn-out state. They fitted quite well and I wondered where they came from. Then I lay on the bunk and looked down the length of my body, imagining what I'd look like confined in a pine box. The morning light continued to gather in the portion of sky visible through my arched window, inexorable and indifferent.

I heard footsteps. Three or four people approached, the clicks of their hard heels against the stone marking them as dignitaries. The steps grew louder, and torchlight began to flicker in the metal grille above my door. Someone spoke in a muffled voice, his tone quite conversational, and he was answered by another, in a pitch equally carefree. Then came the rattle of Turner's chain. Metal knocked against the keyhole, then scraped and grated in the lock as he turned the key. The bolt released with an echoing thud. Turner pulled open the door, sending a draught through the room, which caused the candle to gutter and blow out.

When that young turf-cutter found the Iron Age man in a bog in County Meath, the most remarkable thing wasn't the dignity of his preserved face; nor was it the leather-bound psalter they found buried next to him; nor the tattoo on his forearm of a rearing horse in vivid blue ink. What every witness first noticed was the rope tied around his neck, the loose end frayed where it had been roughly cut. It was as if those who buried him intended for us to know.

AN AFTERWORD

I remember when I first came across John Delahunt's story: it was while researching my first book, a social history based on the inhabitants of Fitzwilliam Square, Dublin, called *Lives Less Ordinary*. One of the square's residents was Edward Pennefather, Lord Chief Justice of the Queen's Bench, who presided over the trial of Daniel O'Connell in 1844 for conspiracy to repeal the Act of Union. In that book I found it was possible to retell much of Irish history through the perspectives of Fitzwilliam Square residents, by following them to political gatherings, or on to the battlefield, or, in the case of Mr Pennefather, into the courtroom. So I set about searching for descriptions of the trial. The following, for instance, was written by Anthony Trollope: 'Look at that big-headed, pig-faced fellow on the right – that's Pennefather! He's the blackest sheep of the lot – and the head of them! He's a thoroughbred Tory, and as fit to be a judge as I am to be a general.'

The outcome of O'Connell's trial was never in doubt, mainly because the jury was packed with twelve Protestants. Trollope again: 'Fancy a jury chosen out of all Dublin, and not one Catholic!'

Charles Gavan Duffy described the Repeal leader's reaction

to the guilty verdict: 'O'Connell himself at that time whispered to one of the traversers that the Attorney General was moderate in only charging them with conspiracy, as those twelve gentlemen would have made no difficulty in convicting them of the murder of the Italian boy.'

I paused when I came upon that passage, intrigued by the title given to the crime, the clues about the unnamed victim, and the fact that O'Connell could allude to its notoriety. Duffy added his own footnote: 'The murder of the Italian boy was a mysterious crime which had recently caused a sensation in Dublin and baffled the skill of the police.'

When I sought out articles relating to the murder, I first came across the names Domenico Garlibardo, Richard Cooney, and the crown witness, John Delahunt.

Lives Less Ordinary stemmed from my fascination with the people who lived in Dublin's Georgian houses, and the fragments of history they left behind: a coat of arms hidden in a stained-glass fanlight; a letter from a young lady to her mother describing her first dinner party; a simple childhood drawing of infant brothers playing in a nursery, while knowing one of their lives would end on a battlefield. The research carried out for that book provided a setting for Delahunt's story, as well as a cast of characters. Bit-part players such as Professor Lloyd, Dr Moore, Captain Dickenson, were all, in reality, Fitzwilliam Square inhabitants. Some of Delahunt's memories of childhood – his fear of coalmen, and the cargo net that spanned the bannisters in the stairwell – were based on the autobiography of A. P. Graves, Robert Graves's father, who grew up in the square in the 1840s.

As for Delahunt's exploits, there were any number of sources to consult: medical, court and newspaper reports, editorials and satirical pamphlets, memoirs and reminiscences. *The*

Convictions of John Delahunt is primarily a work of fiction, especially with regards to Delahunt's character, background and family, but the set-piece events were based on real episodes: the attack on Captain Craddock, the murder of Garlibardo, and the murder of Thomas Maguire. There were two sources that I used directly. One was the report of the phrenologist, Dr Armstrong, upon which the first scene is based. The second was the convict's final statement. Though presented as Lyster's creation, the quoted passages were taken directly from Delahunt's real confession.

Printed in the newspapers on the morning of his execution, the confession exposed the inner-workings of Dublin Castle to public scrutiny and comment. Soon after, a pamphlet appeared in the stalls of booksellers and stationers in the city, written under the alias *An Informer* (the author was James Henry, a classical scholar and medical doctor, who also happened to live in Fitzwilliam Square – in fact, he was Edward Pennefather's neighbour). The pamphlet began:

> Although the public had been previously, to a certain extent, aware of the nefarious system by which informations against criminals were obtained in Dublin, they were by no means prepared for the startling disclosure of Delahunt, that the nature of the system was such as to actually tempt the informer to commit the crime, for the sole purpose of prosecuting and convicting an innocent person of it, and thus entitling himself to the blood-money.

The existence of a spy system in the Castle would have come as no surprise to Dubliners. Informers had thwarted the United Irishmen in the capital in 1798, and police infiltration would scupper the Fenians in 1867. But the revelations gave nationalist newspapers and politicians the opportunity to deride the regime as a whole, and Delahunt's role was brought up in the House of Commons. Less than a fortnight after his hanging, an editorial appeared in *The Freeman's Journal* under the heading 'The Spy Establishment':

> We asked some days ago if it was intended by the present administration to retain the colleagues of the late Mr Delahunt in office . . . In his place in parliament, the Secretary for Ireland stated in reply to Mr John O'Connell, that the system of administering criminal justice through the agency of stipendiary witnesses and professional informers was not at present to be changed. Lord Elliot did not dare to blink the shameful question. He said that he knew 'some crimes must be attributed to the temptations held out by the system to depraved persons.' *Some* crimes! A trifle of blood!

Lord Eliot was the Chief Secretary; John O'Connell a Repealer MP for Kilkenny, and the son of Daniel O'Connell. The editorial continued:

> [Lord Eliot said] that 'witnesses must be PROCURED,' to convict persons charged with capital crimes.' Procured;—fie— Lord Eliot,—fie! It is an infamous and filthy word, but we do confess most fit and applicable to its purpose.

In reality, Delahunt's evidence against Richard Cooney wasn't believed, and the murder of the Italian boy remained unsolved. Frank Thorpe, a police magistrate writing his memoirs in 1875, said: 'I strongly suspect that if Delahunt really knew anything about the crime, it was owing to himself being the perpetrator.'

But Thorpe also wished to dispel the notion that Delahunt was in the pay of the Castle:

For a considerable time after his execution, he was reputed, especially amongst the humbler classes, to have been a police spy, and to have been in receipt of frequent subsidies from the detective office ... I feel perfectly satisfied that, instead of deriving the wages of an informer or spy from the metropolitan police or from the constabulary, he never cost the public one penny beyond what sufficed for his maintenance in gaol whilst under committal for his diabolical offence, and to provide the halter which he most thoroughly deserved.

The Freeman's Journal reported that a crowd of 10,000 people assembled to see Delahunt hanged on Saturday, 5 February 1842:

Fortunately for society there has rarely occurred amongst our population a crime of so sanguinary a character, or marked with features of such peculiar atrocity, and perpetrated for such an object, as present. The feeling or curiosity in the public mind to witness the murderer expiate his offence in this world by the forfeiture of his life was consequently excited to an almost unparalleled extent ... The beam from which the rope was suspended had been put out at an early hour in the morning, and that done, almost all was in readiness to terminate the existence of the culprit.

When Delahunt was brought up to the scaffold, his nerve failed him. He fainted on the platform more than once, and when the fatal moment came he was lying motionless on the grated trapdoor.

In this position the bolt was withdrawn—the drop fell—the death struggle was brief—a very few minutes elapsed, and John Delahunt ceased to live.

Delahunt's body was left suspended for forty minutes while the crowd drifted away. He was then lowered and brought to an apartment in the rear of the prison, where a plaster cast of his head was taken under the supervision of Dr Armstrong:

It was remarkable that the countenance presented scarcely any of those marks which the features of persons who have suffered death in a similar way so generally exhibit. The face was by no means of a livid colour; there was no protrusion of the tongue, nor were the eyes at all distorted; the only symptom of violent death visible was a slight distortion of the mouth, which appeared somewhat drawn to the left side.

In the evening, Delahunt was placed in a simple coffin provided by the Governor of Kilmainham, Mr Allison. He was still dressed in the clothes he wore when executed: a dark grey frock coat of coarse cloth, corduroy trousers and crimson waistcoat.

At six o'clock the body was consigned to its last abode, in a remote extremity within the bounds of the gaol, called 'the gravel yard,' and about which no prisoners are located.

Andrew Hughes
Dublin, July 2013

ACKNOWLEDGEMENTS

I wrote this book while attending a writers' workshop led by the brilliant author John Givens, and it wouldn't have been possible without his expertise, careful reading and guidance. I can't thank him enough. I'm also grateful to all the other writers who attended the workshop for their opinions and ideas, particularly Caroline Madden, for her encouragement, friendship and for some very crucial suggestions, and Oliver Murphy, for his good sense and great humour. Many thanks to my agent Sam Copeland for taking on the project and for his terrific enthusiasm and support. Also, thanks to everyone at Transworld and Doubleday Ireland, particularly my editor Simon Taylor for his excellent work. Thanks to Naomi Mott for her well-timed tweet, and Jenny Dunne for tracking down references to Delahunt in the National Archives. I'm very grateful to the Arts Council for the grant they gave me in early 2012, which proved to be a timely boost, and to the Irish Writers' Centre for initially hosting the workshops. As always, thanks to my siblings for reading drafts, giving their thoughts, and many other reasons. And most of all thanks to my parents, Margaret and Kevin, for all their support.

ABOUT THE AUTHOR

Andrew Hughes was born in Co. Wexford in 1979 and was educated at Trinity College, Dublin. A professional archivist, he worked for RTE before going freelance. It was while researching the histories of the Georgian houses in Fitzwilliam Square in Dublin (a social history published as *Lives Less Ordinary: Dublin's Fitzwilliam Square 1798–1922* by The Liffey Press) that he stumbled upon the story of John Delahunt. *The Convictions of John Delahunt* is his first novel. Andrew Hughes lives in Dublin.